THE FREEZE

VOLUME 1

PUBLISHED BY
TOP COW PRODUCTIONS, INC.
LOS ANGELES

IMAGE COMICS, INC.

Robert Kirkman — Chief Operating Officer
Erik Larsen — Chief Financial Officer
Todd McFarlane — President
Marc Silvestri — Chief Executive Officer
Jim Valentino — Vice President
Eric Stephenson — Publisher / Chief Creative Officer
Corey Hart — Director of Sales
Jeff Boison — Director of Publishing Planning & Book Trade Sales
Chris Ross — Director of Digital Sales
Jeff Stang — Director of Specialty Sales

For Top Cow Producti
For Top Cow Productions, Inc.
Marc Silvestri - CEO
Matt Hawkins - President & COO
Elena Salcedo - Vice President of
Vincent Valentine - Lead Producti
Henry Barajas - Director of Opera
Dylan Gray - Marketing Director

THE FREEZE, VOL. 1. First printing. May 2019. Published by Image Comics
2701 NW Vaughn St., Suite 780, Portland, OR 97210. Copyright © 2019
Productions INC. All rights reserved. Contains material originally pub
form as THE FREEZE #1–4. "THE FREEZE," its logos, and the likenesses o
trademarks of Dan Wickline and Top Cow Productions

THE FREEZE

VOLUME

WRITTEN BY **DAN WICKLINE**
ART BY **PHILLIP SEVY**
LETTERS BY **TROY PETERI**
EDITED BY **ELENA SALCEDO**
EDITOR IN CHIEF **MATT HAWKINS**

COVER BY **PHILLIP SEVY**

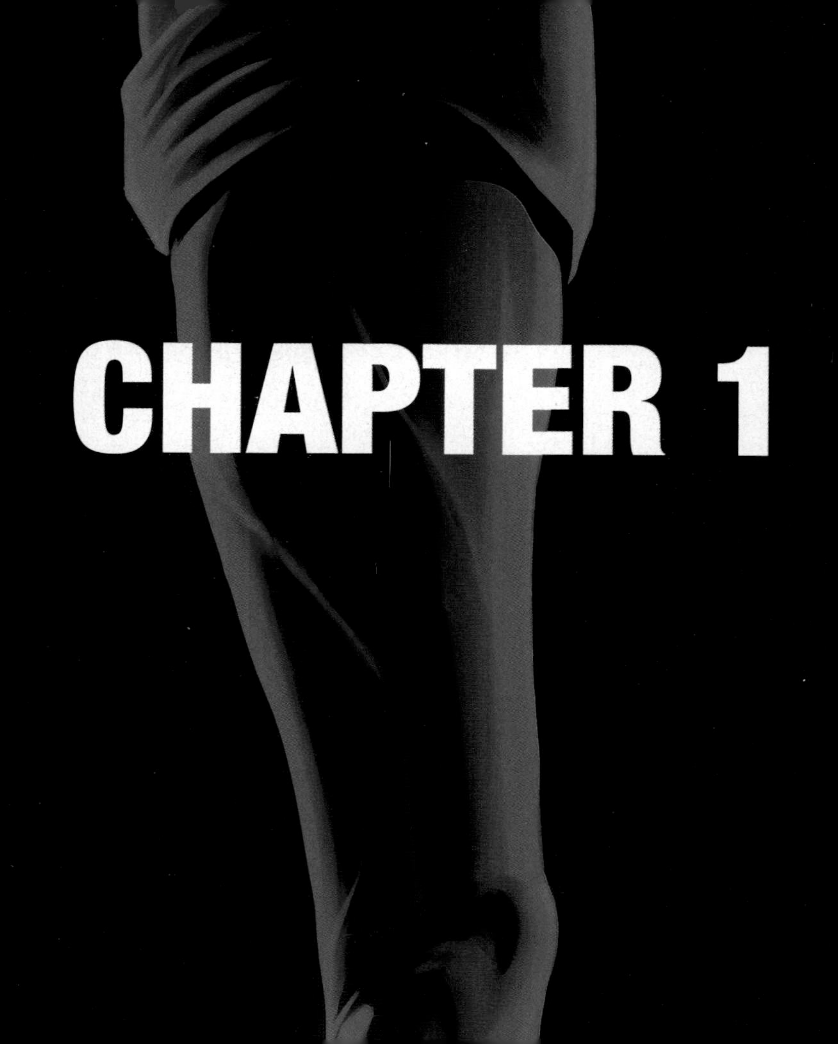

CHAPTER 1

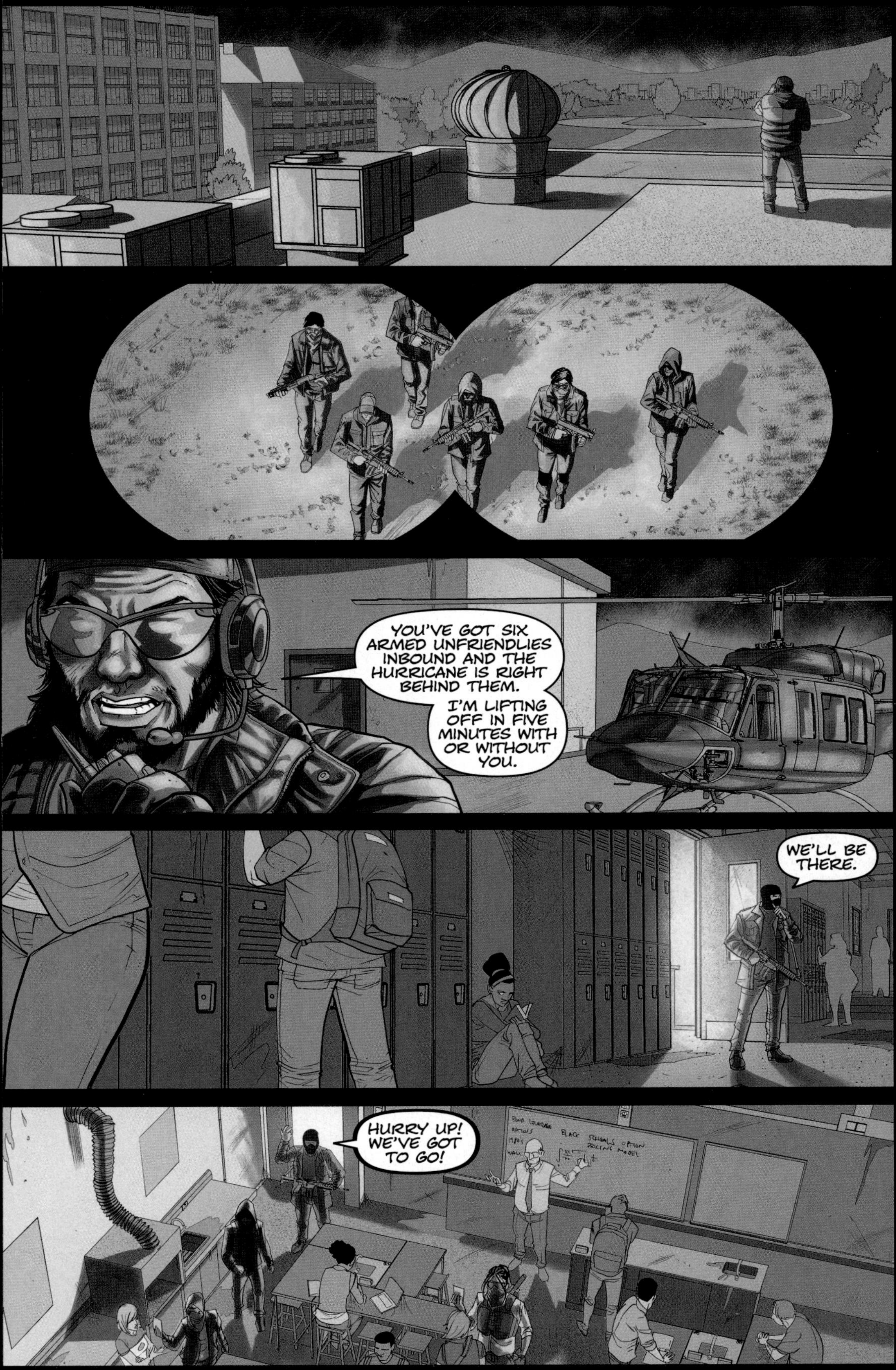
YOU'VE GOT SIX ARMED UNFRIENDLIES INBOUND AND THE HURRICANE IS RIGHT BEHIND THEM.
I'M LIFTING OFF IN FIVE MINUTES WITH OR WITHOUT YOU.
WE'LL BE THERE.
HURRY UP! WE'VE GOT TO GO!

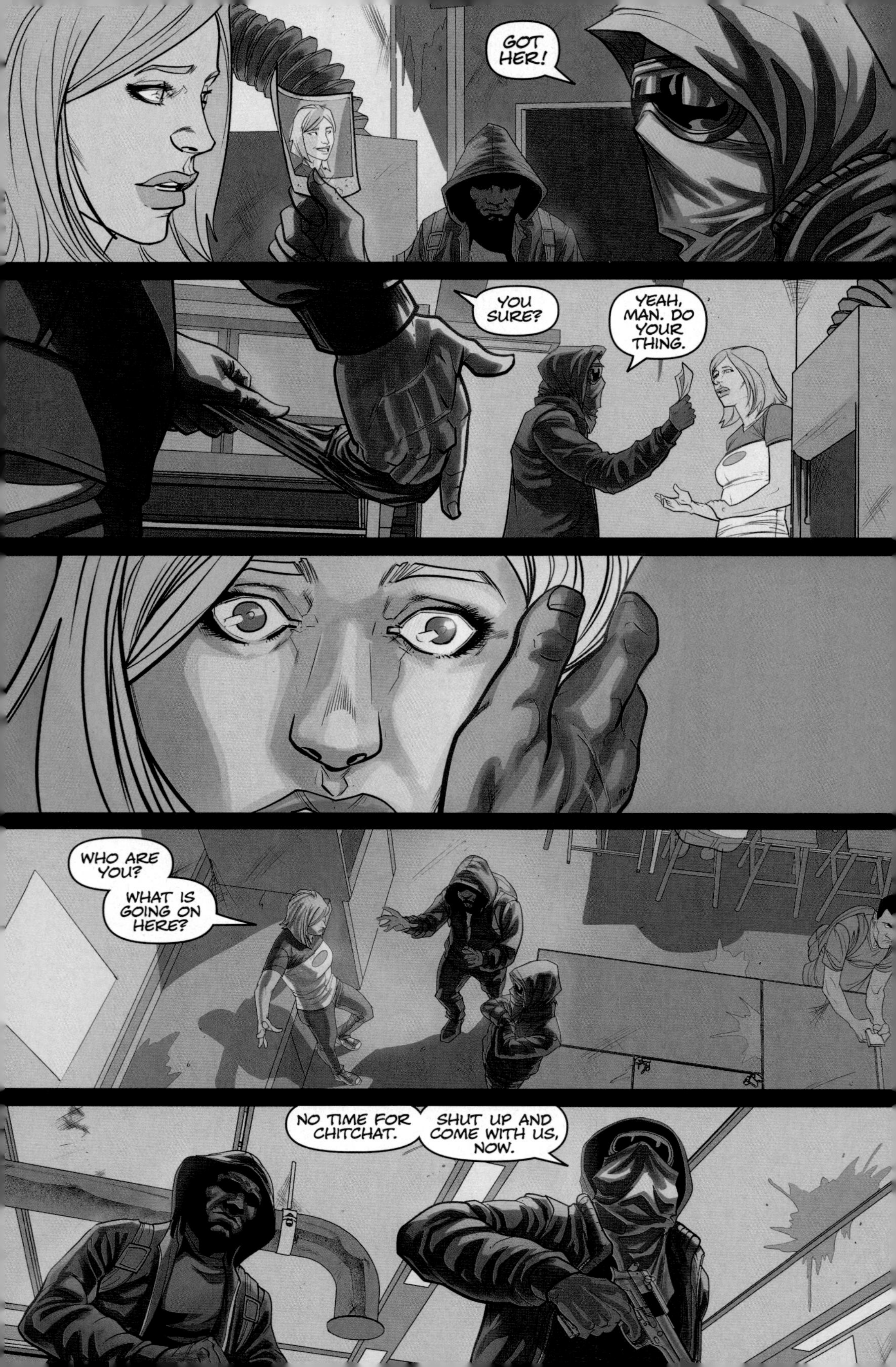
GOT HER!
YOU SURE?
YEAH, MAN. DO YOUR THING.
WHO ARE YOU?
WHAT IS GOING ON HERE?
NO TIME FOR CHITCHAT.
SHUT UP AND COME WITH US, NOW.

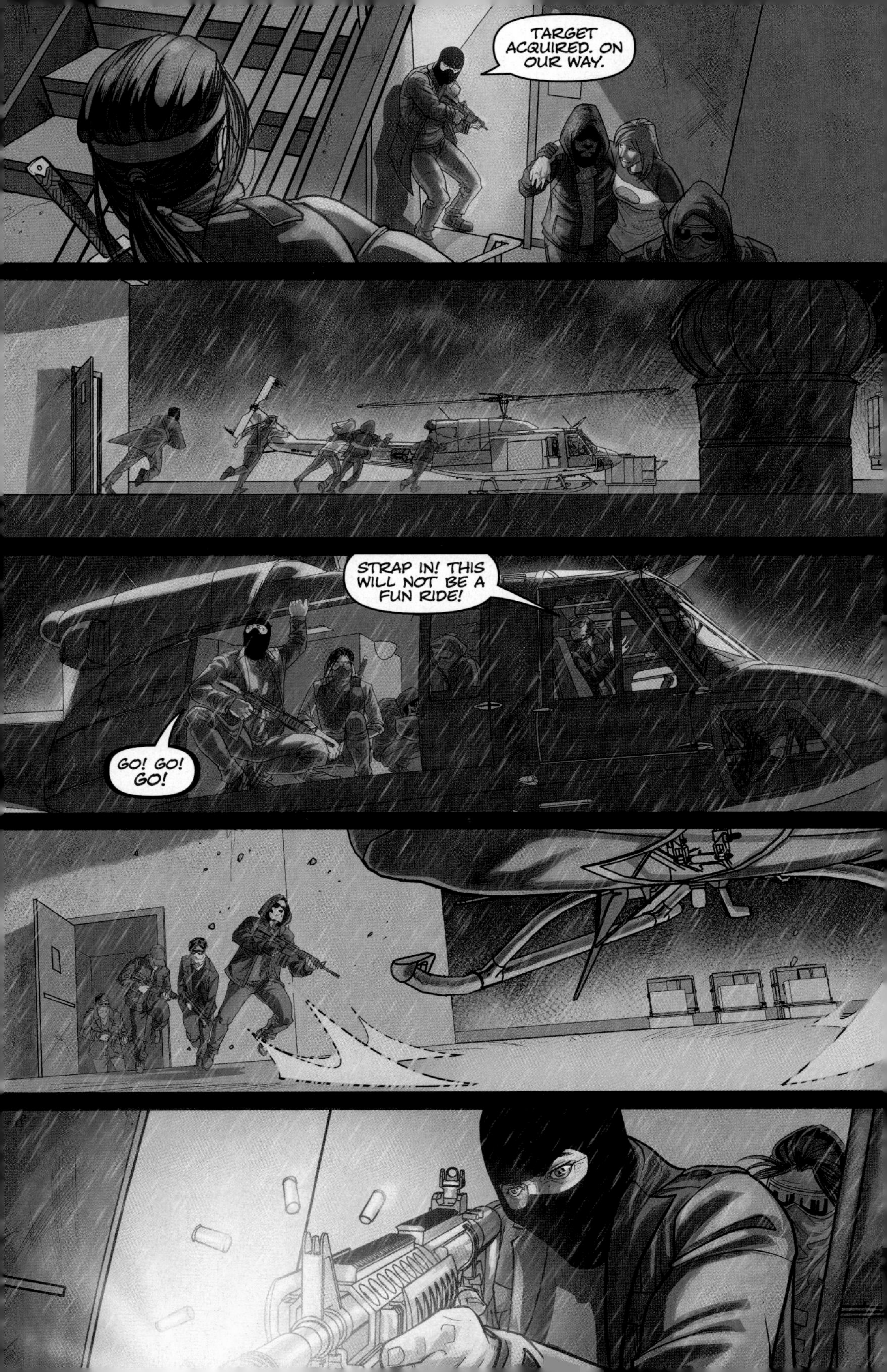
TARGET ACQUIRED. ON OUR WAY.
STRAP IN! THIS WILL NOT BE A FUN RIDE!
GO! GO! GO!

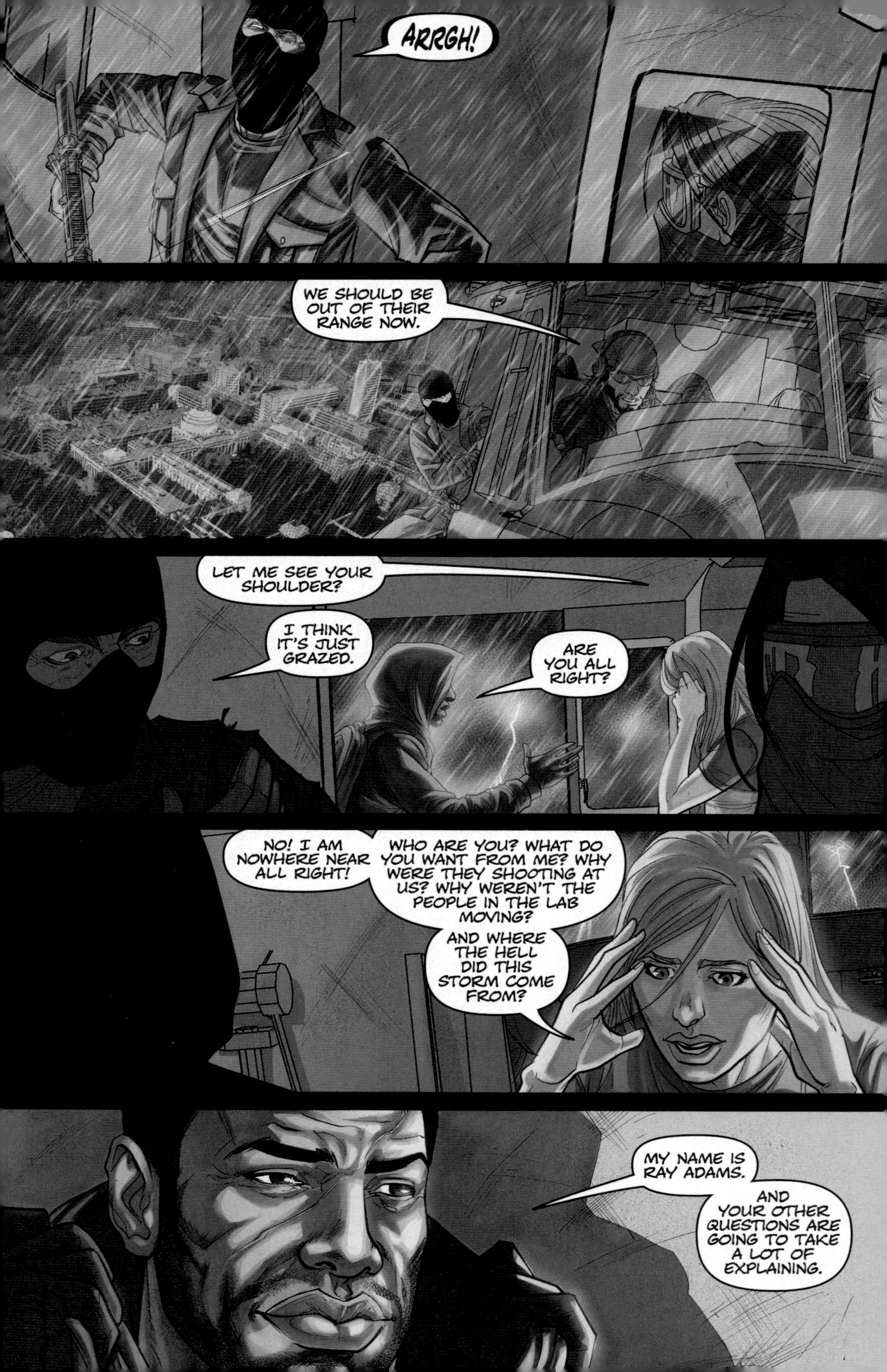
ARRGH!
WE SHOULD BE OUT OF THEIR RANGE NOW.
LET ME SEE YOUR SHOULDER?
I THINK IT'S JUST GRAZED.
ARE YOU ALL RIGHT?
NO! I AM NOWHERE NEAR ALL RIGHT!
WHO ARE YOU? WHAT DO YOU WANT FROM ME? WHY WERE THEY SHOOTING AT US? WHY WEREN'T THE PEOPLE IN THE LAB MOVING?
AND WHERE THE HELL DID THIS STORM COME FROM?
MY NAME IS RAY ADAMS.
AND YOUR OTHER QUESTIONS ARE GOING TO TAKE A LOT OF EXPLAINING.

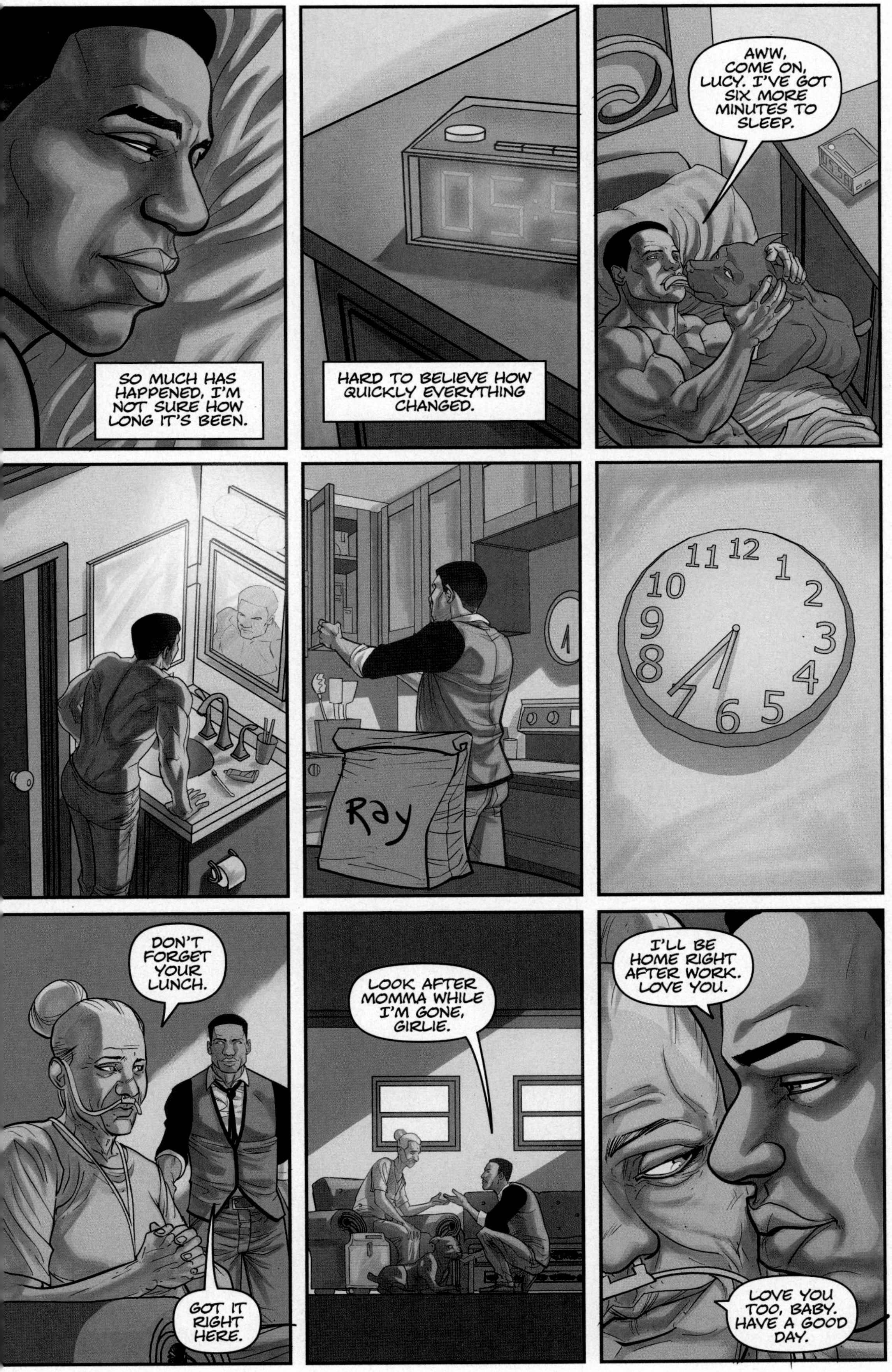
SO MUCH HAS HAPPENED, I'M NOT SURE HOW LONG IT'S BEEN.
HARD TO BELIEVE HOW QUICKLY EVERYTHING CHANGED.
AWW, COME ON, LUCY. I'VE GOT SIX MORE MINUTES TO SLEEP.
Ray
DON'T FORGET YOUR LUNCH.
GOT IT RIGHT HERE.
LOOK AFTER MOMMA WHILE I'M GONE, GIRLIE.
I'LL BE HOME RIGHT AFTER WORK. LOVE YOU.
LOVE YOU TOO, BABY. HAVE A GOOD DAY.

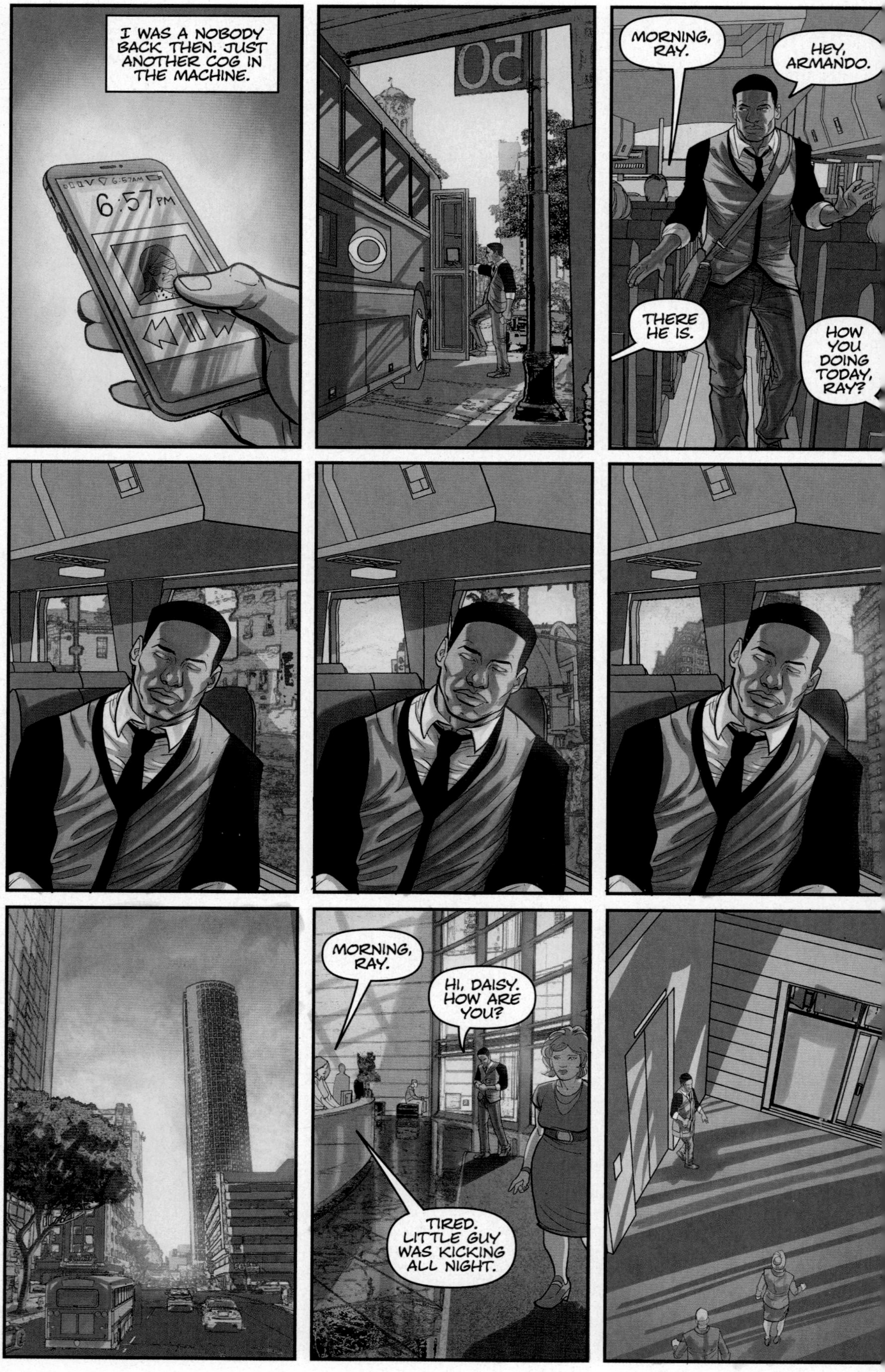
I WAS A NOBODY BACK THEN. JUST ANOTHER COG IN THE MACHINE.
6:57AM
6:57PM
50
MORNING, RAY.
HEY, ARMANDO.
THERE HE IS.
HOW YOU DOING TODAY, RAY?
MORNING, RAY.
HI, DAISY. HOW ARE YOU?
TIRED. LITTLE GUY WAS KICKING ALL NIGHT.

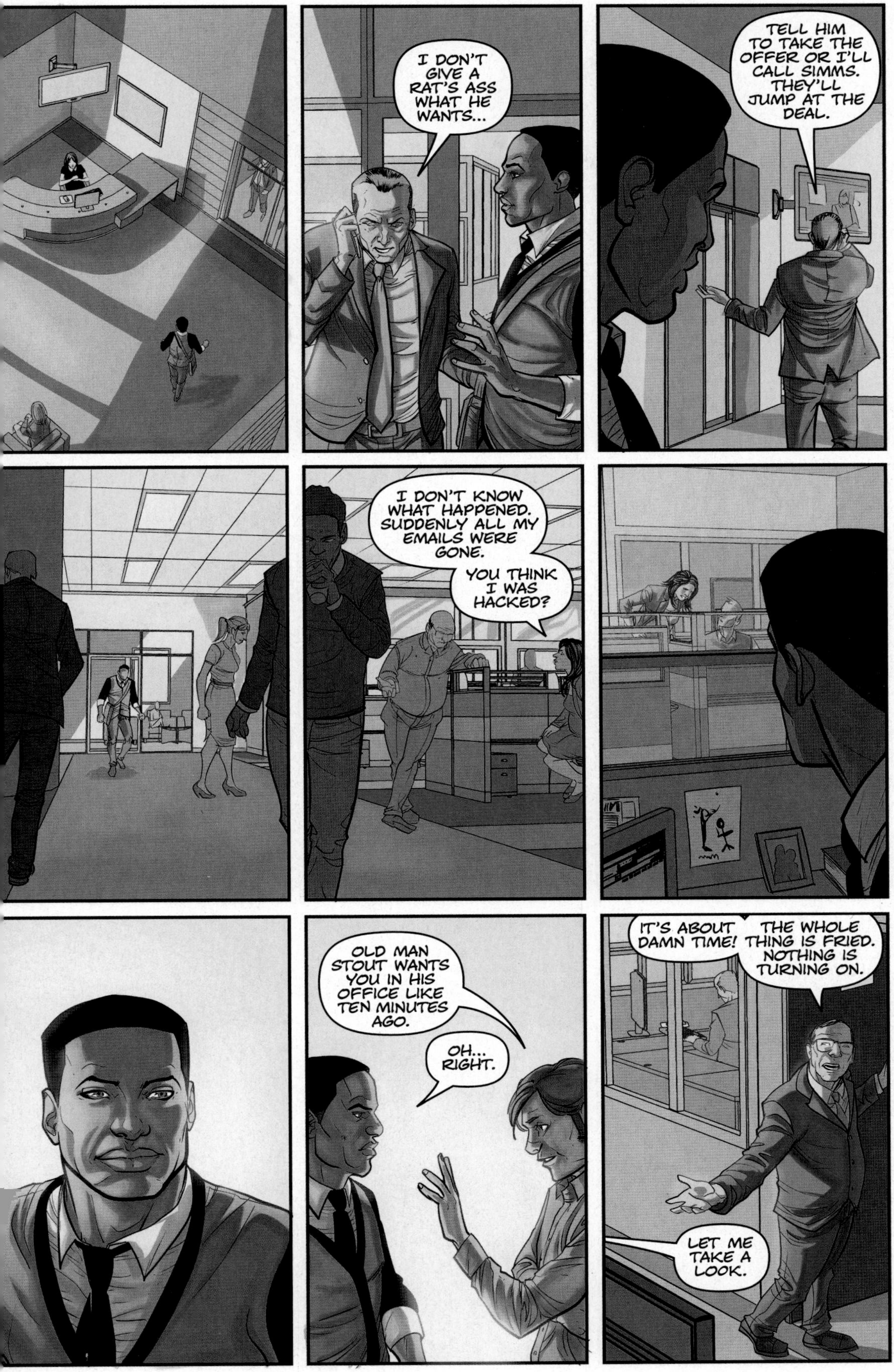
I DON'T GIVE A RAT'S ASS WHAT HE WANTS...
TELL HIM TO TAKE THE OFFER OR I'LL CALL SIMMS. THEY'LL JUMP AT THE DEAL.
I DON'T KNOW WHAT HAPPENED. SUDDENLY ALL MY EMAILS WERE GONE.
YOU THINK I WAS HACKED?
OLD MAN STOUT WANTS YOU IN HIS OFFICE LIKE TEN MINUTES AGO.
OH... RIGHT.
IT'S ABOUT DAMN TIME!
THE WHOLE THING IS FRIED. NOTHING IS TURNING ON.
LET ME TAKE A LOOK.

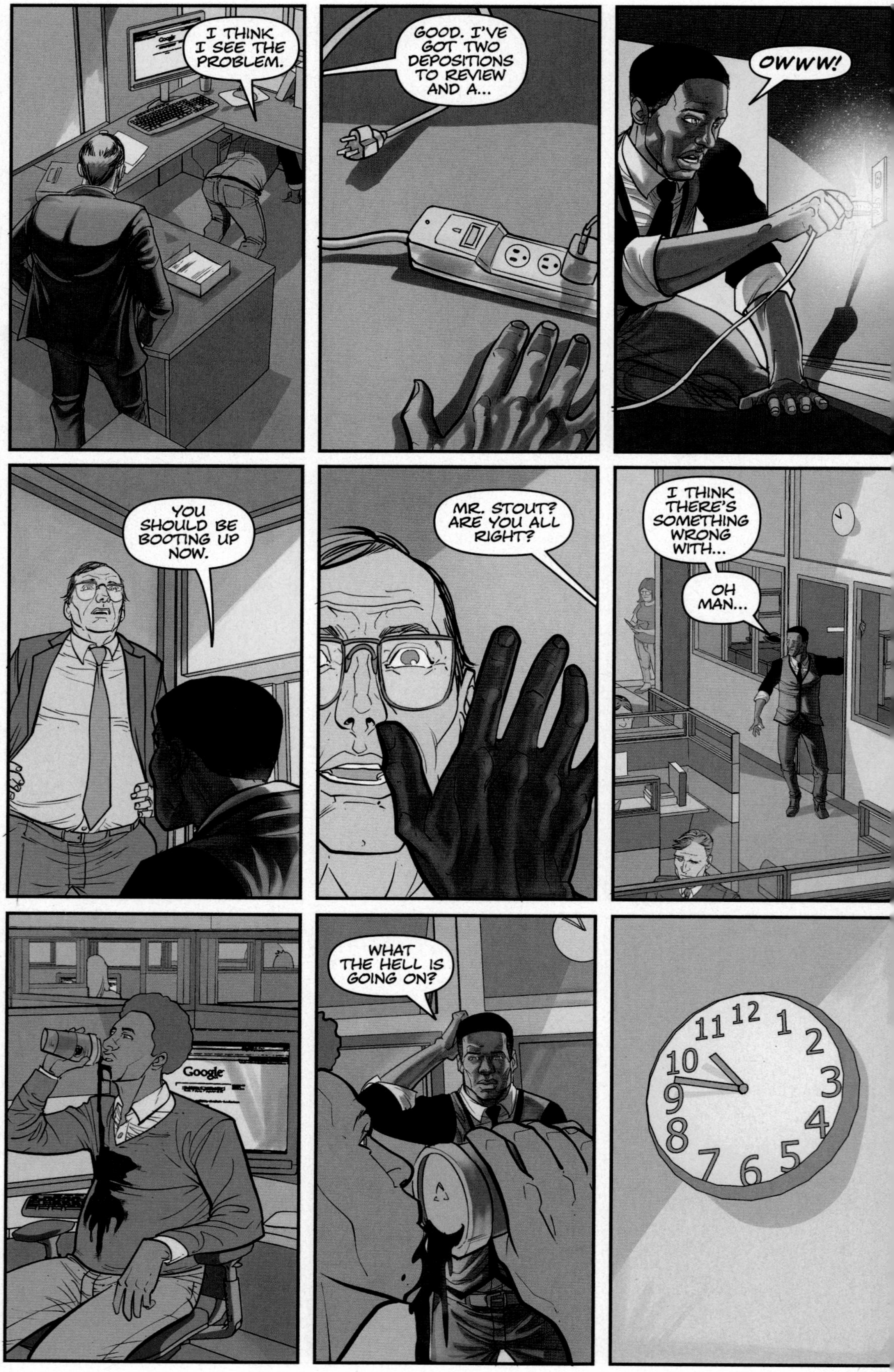
I THINK I SEE THE PROBLEM.
GOOD. I'VE GOT TWO DEPOSITIONS TO REVIEW AND A...
OWWW!
YOU SHOULD BE BOOTING UP NOW.
MR. STOUT? ARE YOU ALL RIGHT?
I THINK THERE'S SOMETHING WRONG WITH...
OH MAN...
Google
WHAT THE HELL IS GOING ON?

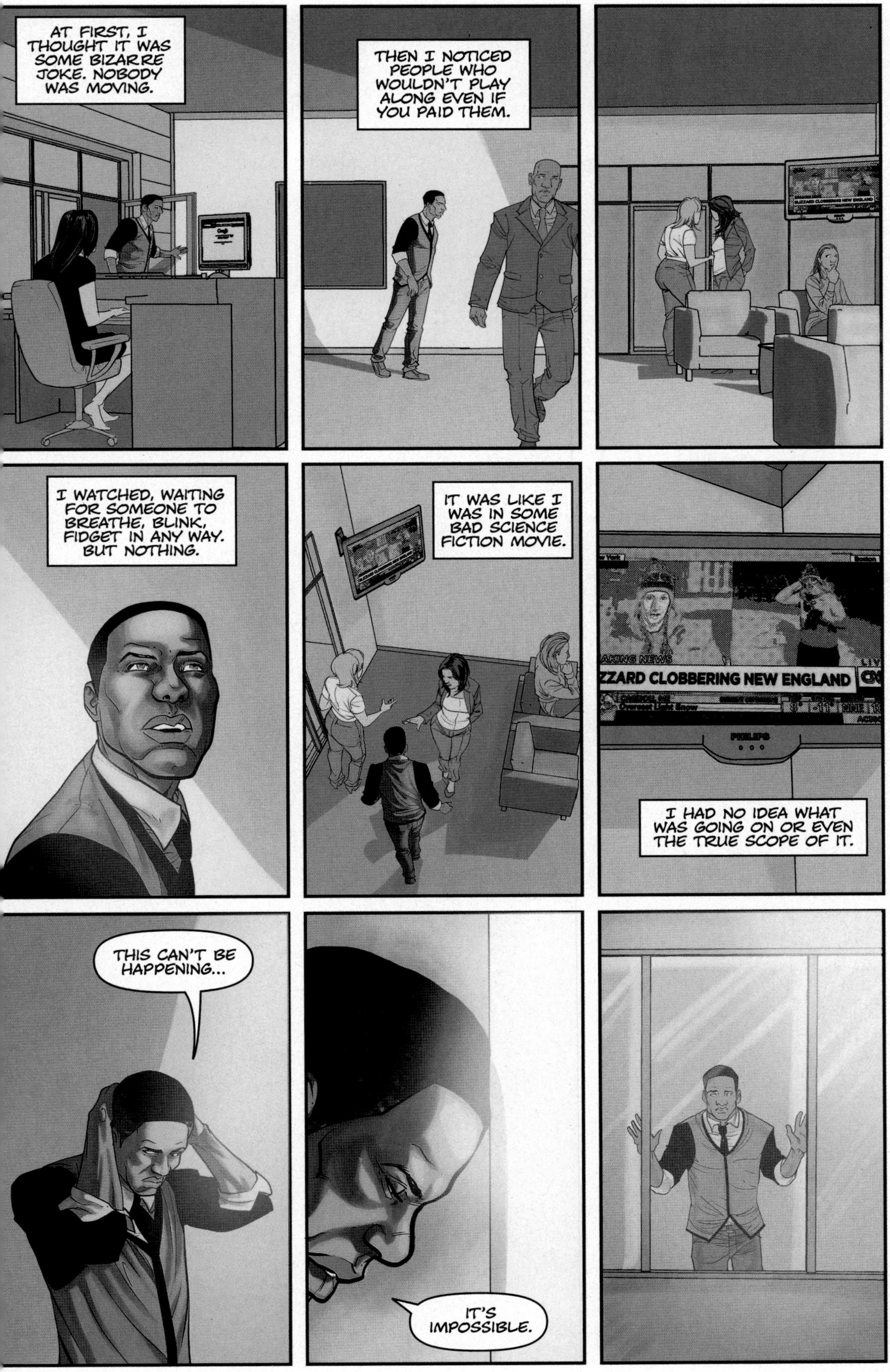
AT FIRST, I THOUGHT IT WAS SOME BIZARRE JOKE. NOBODY WAS MOVING.
THEN I NOTICED PEOPLE WHO WOULDN'T PLAY ALONG EVEN IF YOU PAID THEM.
I WATCHED, WAITING FOR SOMEONE TO BREATHE, BLINK, FIDGET IN ANY WAY. BUT NOTHING.
IT WAS LIKE I WAS IN SOME BAD SCIENCE FICTION MOVIE.
ZZARD CLOBBERING NEW ENGLAND
I HAD NO IDEA WHAT WAS GOING ON OR EVEN THE TRUE SCOPE OF IT.
THIS CAN'T BE HAPPENING...
IT'S IMPOSSIBLE.

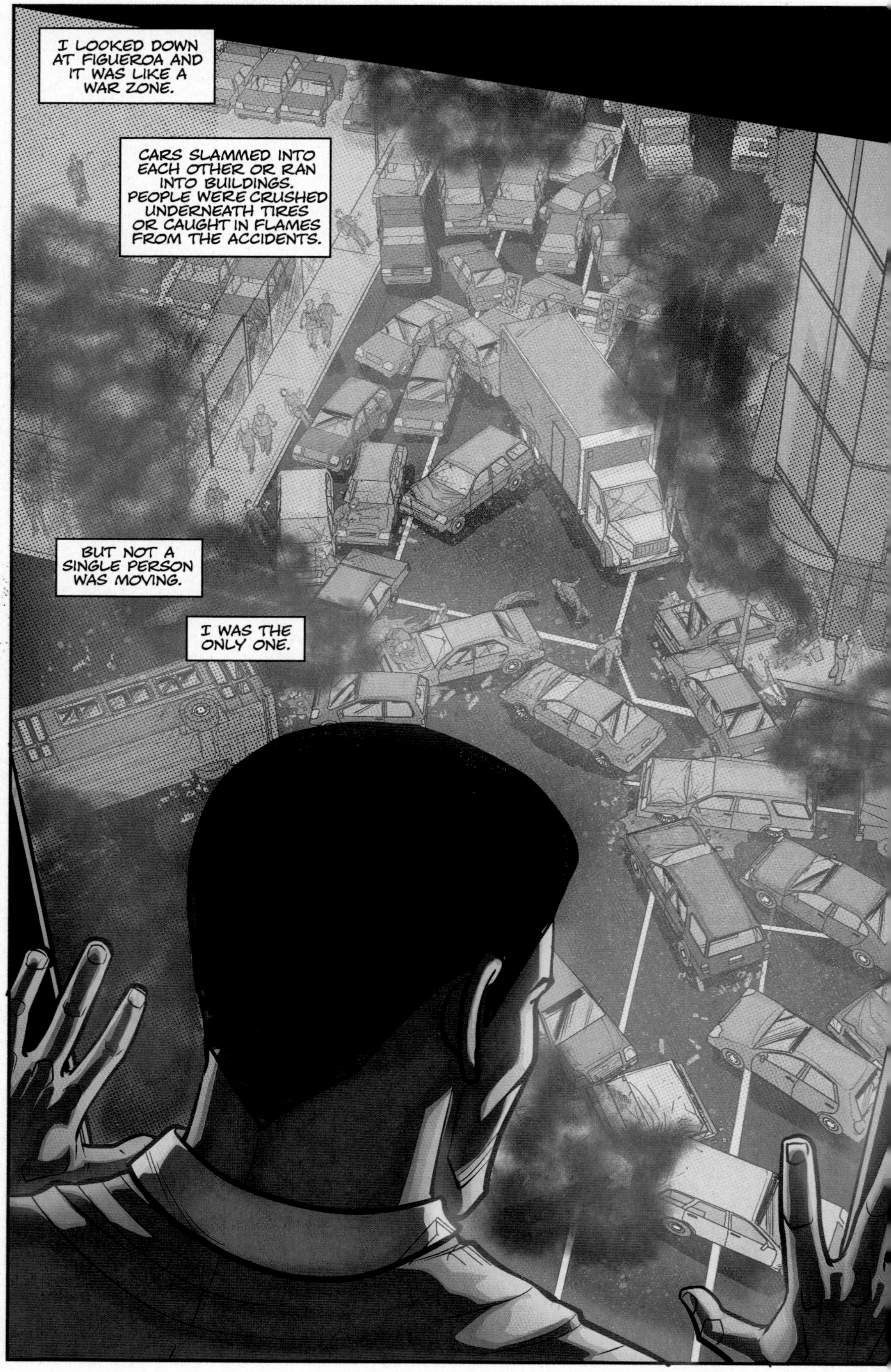

I LOOKED DOWN AT FIGUEROA AND IT WAS LIKE A WAR ZONE.
CARS SLAMMED INTO EACH OTHER OR RAN INTO BUILDINGS. PEOPLE WERE CRUSHED UNDERNEATH TIRES OR CAUGHT IN FLAMES FROM THE ACCIDENTS.
BUT NOT A SINGLE PERSON WAS MOVING.
I WAS THE ONLY ONE.

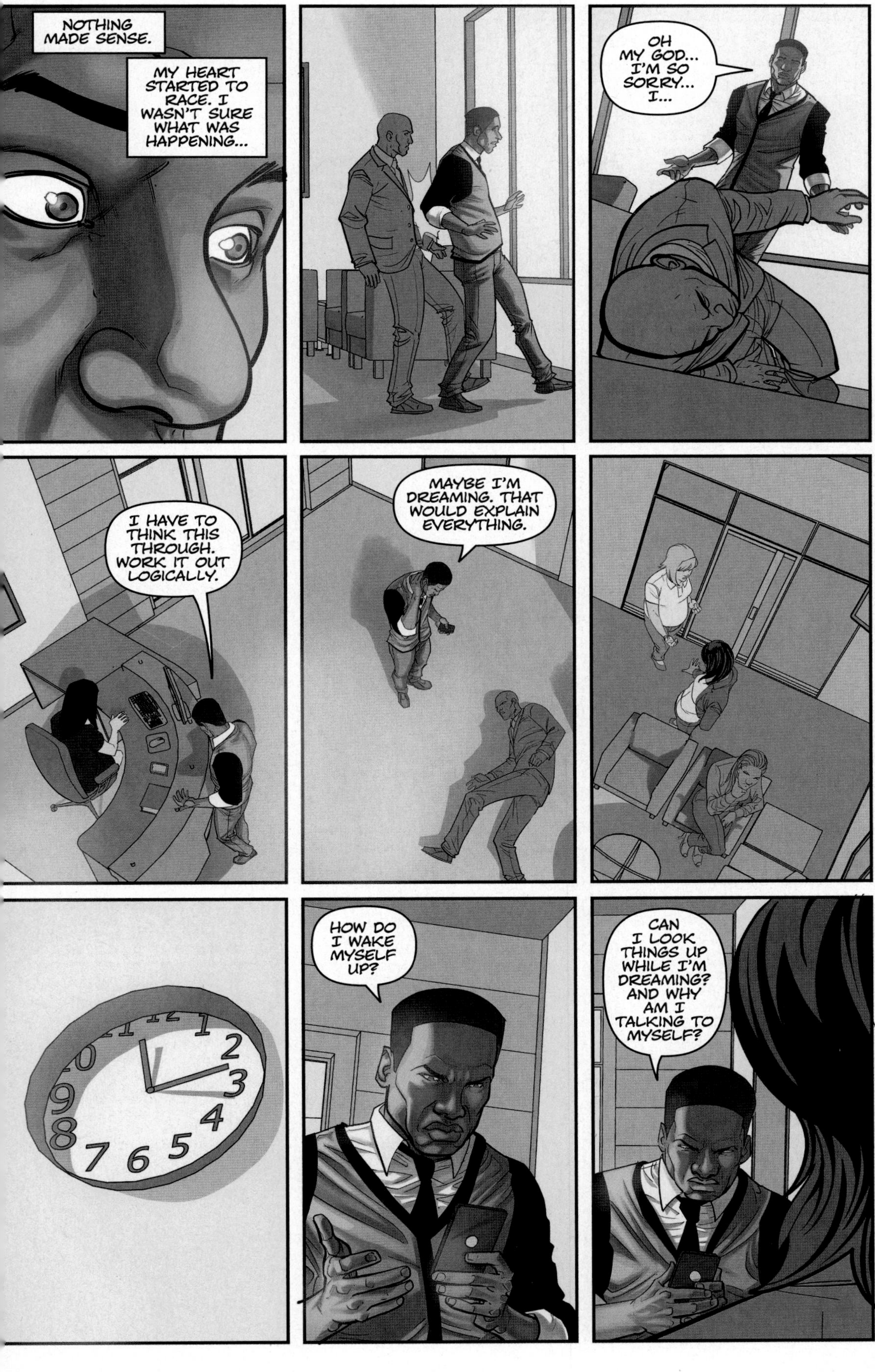
NOTHING MADE SENSE.
MY HEART STARTED TO RACE. I WASN'T SURE WHAT WAS HAPPENING...
OH MY GOD... I'M SO SORRY... I...
I HAVE TO THINK THIS THROUGH. WORK IT OUT LOGICALLY.
MAYBE I'M DREAMING. THAT WOULD EXPLAIN EVERYTHING.
HOW DO I WAKE MYSELF UP?
CAN I LOOK THINGS UP WHILE I'M DREAMING? AND WHY AM I TALKING TO MYSELF?

I WAS ON THE VERGE OF LOSING IT. IT WAS TOO MUCH TO TAKE IN.

AND THEN I SAW LISA.

THIS IS DEFINITELY A DREAM.

THAT'S WHEN I NOTICED THE PHYSICAL DIFFERENCE. HER SKIN HAD A BLUEISH HUE TO IT.

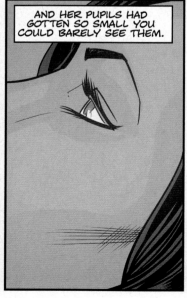

AND HER PUPILS HAD GOTTEN SO SMALL YOU COULD BARELY SEE THEM.

IT WAS ALSO WHEN I MADE THE MOST IMPORTANT DISCOVERY.

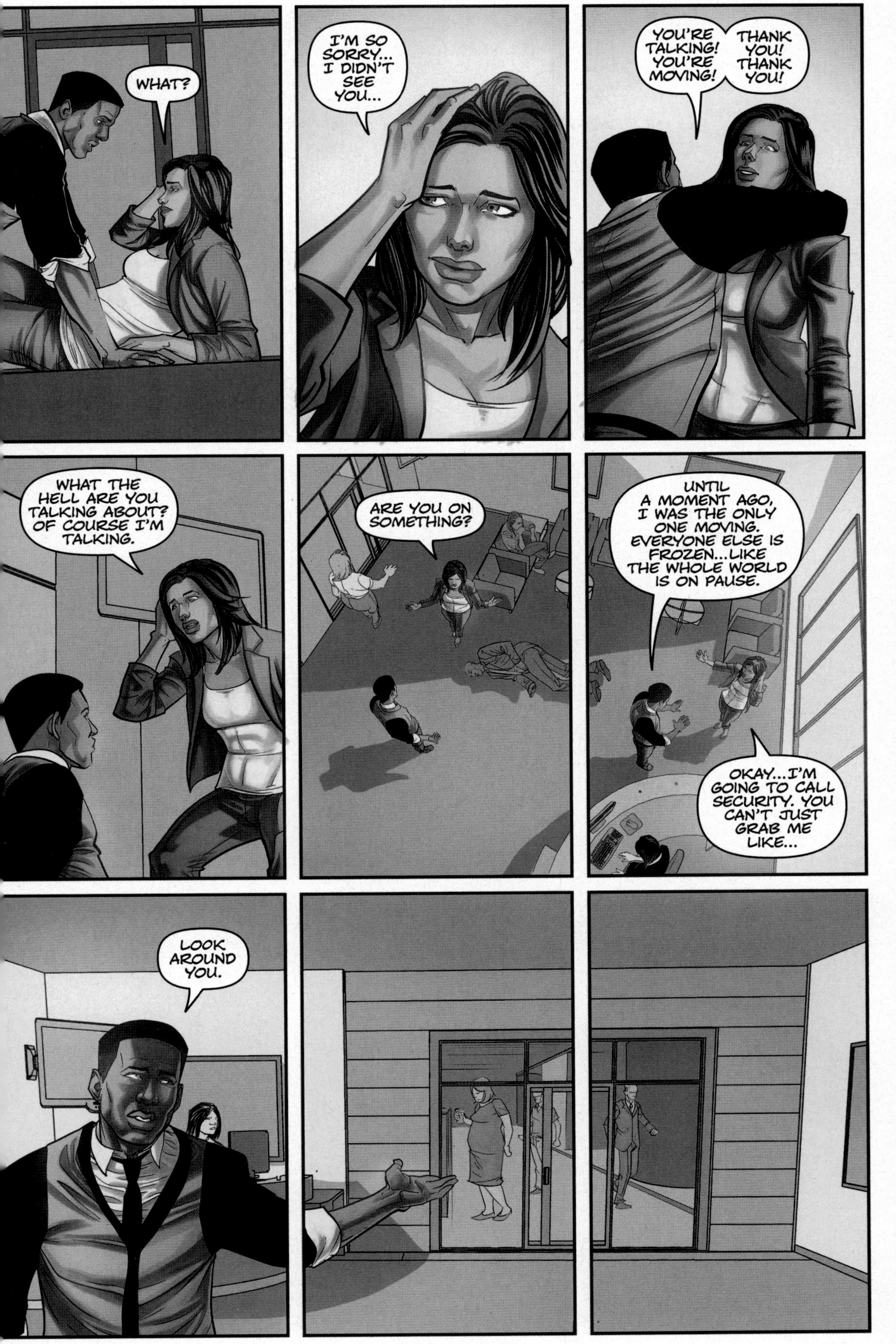
WHAT?
I'M SO SORRY... I DIDN'T SEE YOU...
YOU'RE TALKING! YOU'RE MOVING!
THANK YOU! THANK YOU!
WHAT THE HELL ARE YOU TALKING ABOUT? OF COURSE I'M TALKING.
ARE YOU ON SOMETHING?
UNTIL A MOMENT AGO, I WAS THE ONLY ONE MOVING. EVERYONE ELSE IS FROZEN...LIKE THE WHOLE WORLD IS ON PAUSE.
OKAY...I'M GOING TO CALL SECURITY. YOU CAN'T JUST GRAB ME LIKE...
LOOK AROUND YOU.

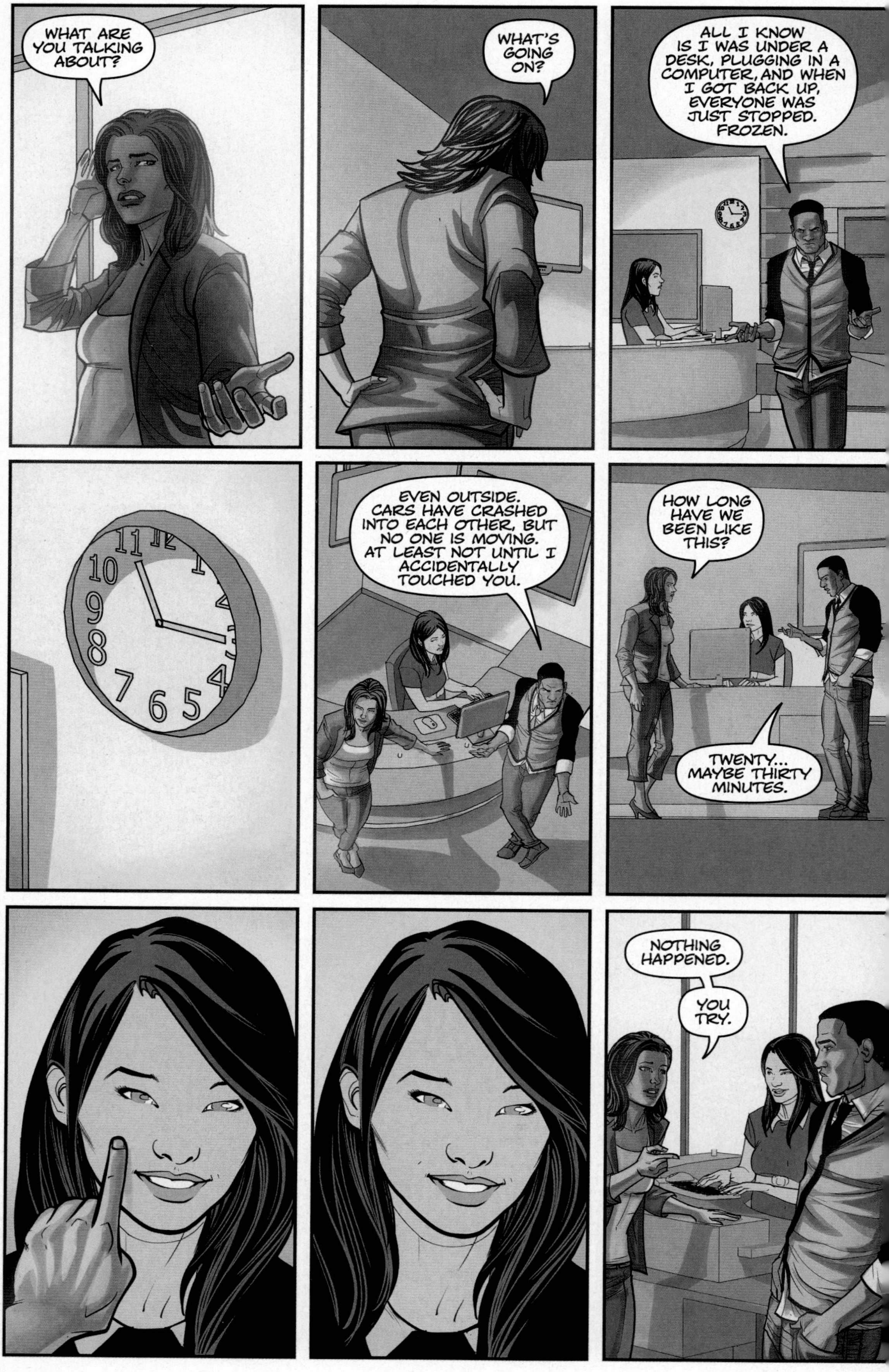
WHAT ARE YOU TALKING ABOUT?
WHAT'S GOING ON?
ALL I KNOW IS I WAS UNDER A DESK, PLUGGING IN A COMPUTER, AND WHEN I GOT BACK UP, EVERYONE WAS JUST STOPPED. FROZEN.
EVEN OUTSIDE. CARS HAVE CRASHED INTO EACH OTHER, BUT NO ONE IS MOVING. AT LEAST NOT UNTIL I ACCIDENTALLY TOUCHED YOU.
HOW LONG HAVE WE BEEN LIKE THIS?
TWENTY... MAYBE THIRTY MINUTES.
NOTHING HAPPENED.
YOU TRY.

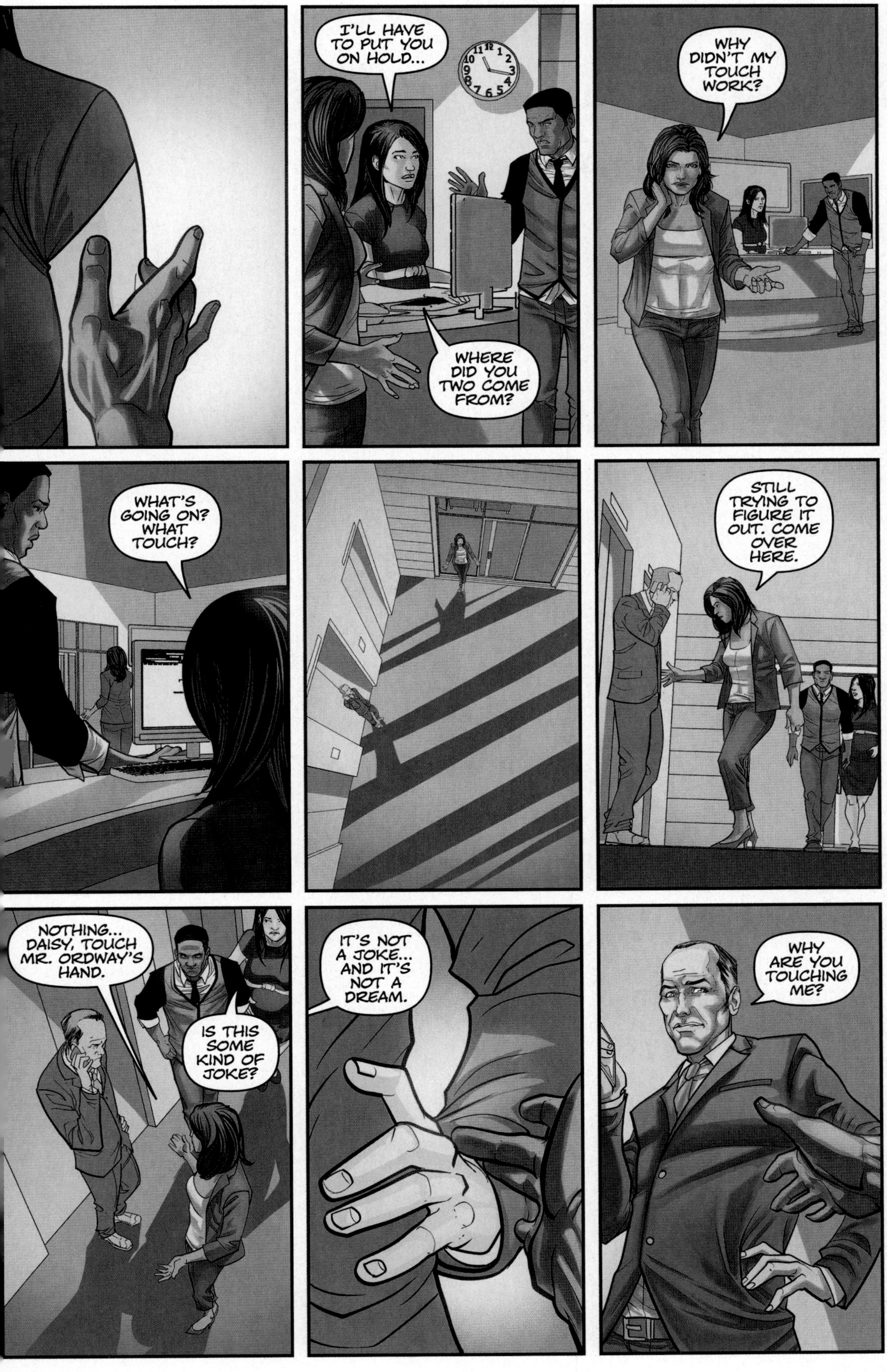
I'LL HAVE TO PUT YOU ON HOLD...
WHERE DID YOU TWO COME FROM?
WHY DIDN'T MY TOUCH WORK?
WHAT'S GOING ON? WHAT TOUCH?
STILL TRYING TO FIGURE IT OUT. COME OVER HERE.
NOTHING... DAISY, TOUCH MR. ORDWAY'S HAND.
IS THIS SOME KIND OF JOKE?
IT'S NOT A JOKE... AND IT'S NOT A DREAM.
WHY ARE YOU TOUCHING ME?

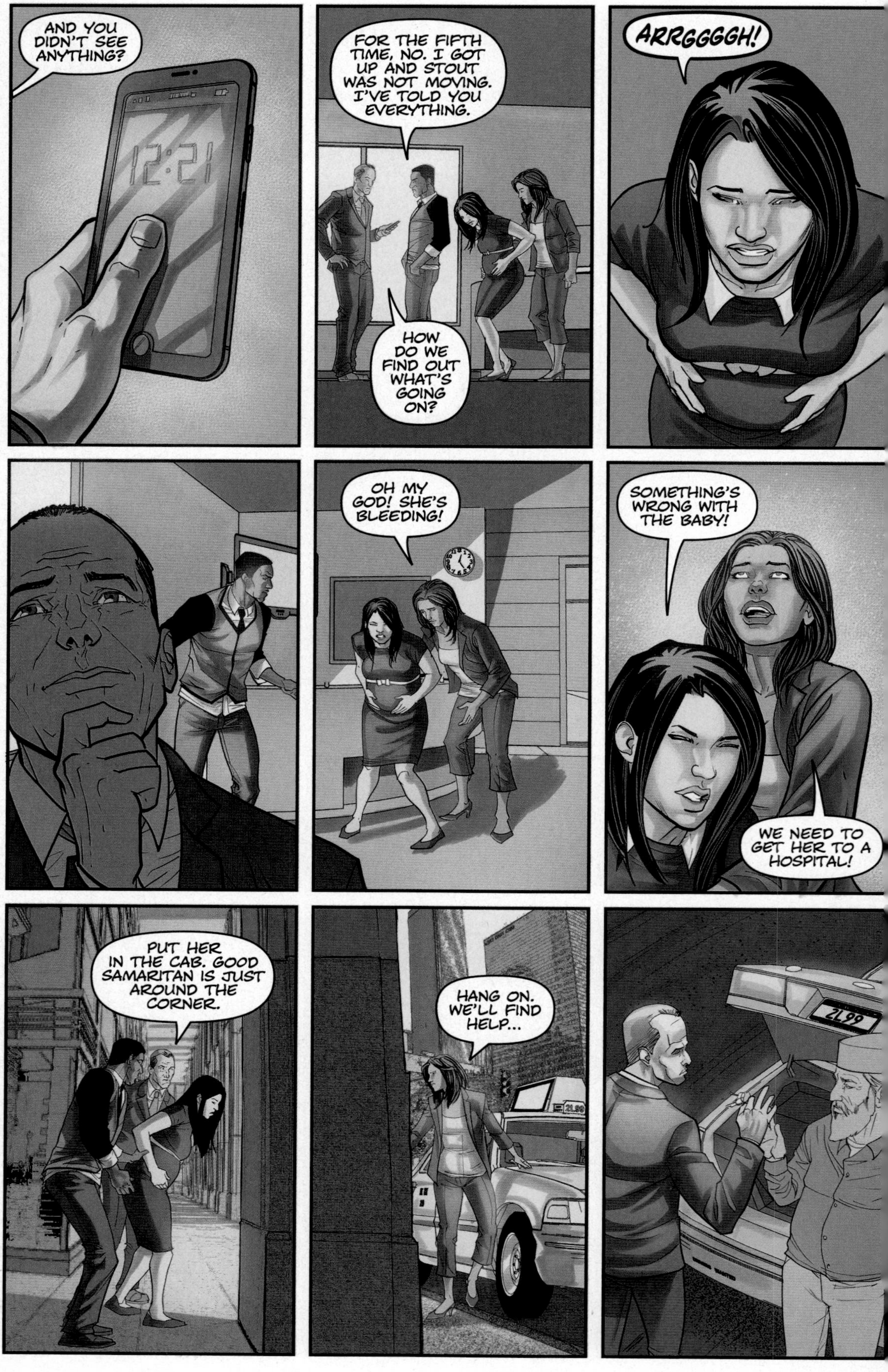
AND YOU DIDN'T SEE ANYTHING?
12:21
FOR THE FIFTH TIME, NO. I GOT UP AND STOUT WAS NOT MOVING. I'VE TOLD YOU EVERYTHING.
HOW DO WE FIND OUT WHAT'S GOING ON?
ARRGGGGH!
OH MY GOD! SHE'S BLEEDING!
SOMETHING'S WRONG WITH THE BABY!
WE NEED TO GET HER TO A HOSPITAL!
PUT HER IN THE CAB. GOOD SAMARITAN IS JUST AROUND THE CORNER.
HANG ON. WE'LL FIND HELP...
2L99

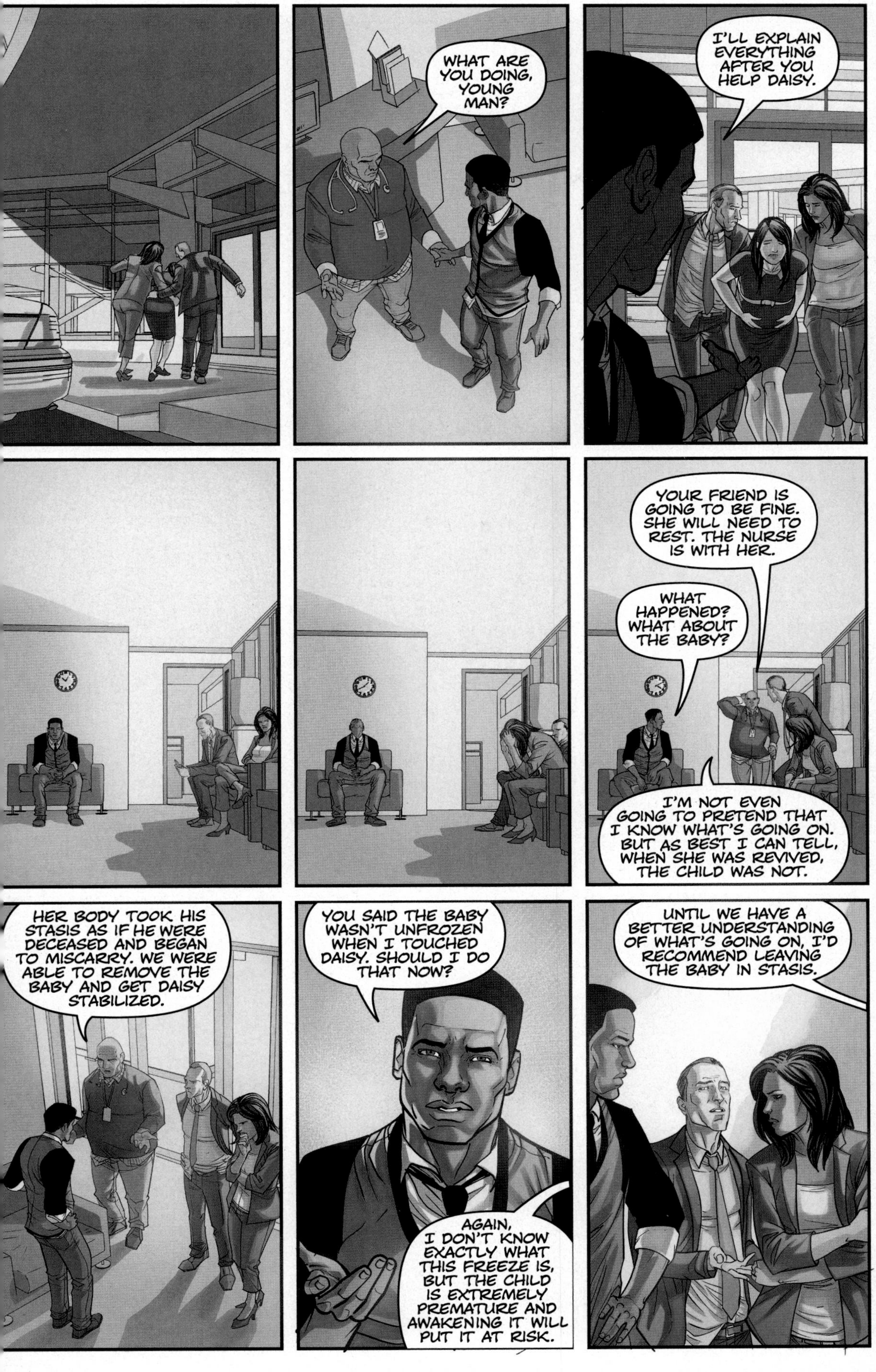
WHAT ARE YOU DOING, YOUNG MAN?
I'LL EXPLAIN EVERYTHING AFTER YOU HELP DAISY.
YOUR FRIEND IS GOING TO BE FINE. SHE WILL NEED TO REST. THE NURSE IS WITH HER.
WHAT HAPPENED? WHAT ABOUT THE BABY?
I'M NOT EVEN GOING TO PRETEND THAT I KNOW WHAT'S GOING ON. BUT AS BEST I CAN TELL, WHEN SHE WAS REVIVED, THE CHILD WAS NOT.
HER BODY TOOK HIS STASIS AS IF HE WERE DECEASED AND BEGAN TO MISCARRY. WE WERE ABLE TO REMOVE THE BABY AND GET DAISY STABILIZED.
YOU SAID THE BABY WASN'T UNFROZEN WHEN I TOUCHED DAISY. SHOULD I DO THAT NOW?
AGAIN, I DON'T KNOW EXACTLY WHAT THIS FREEZE IS, BUT THE CHILD IS EXTREMELY PREMATURE AND AWAKENING IT WILL PUT IT AT RISK.
UNTIL WE HAVE A BETTER UNDERSTANDING OF WHAT'S GOING ON, I'D RECOMMEND LEAVING THE BABY IN STASIS.

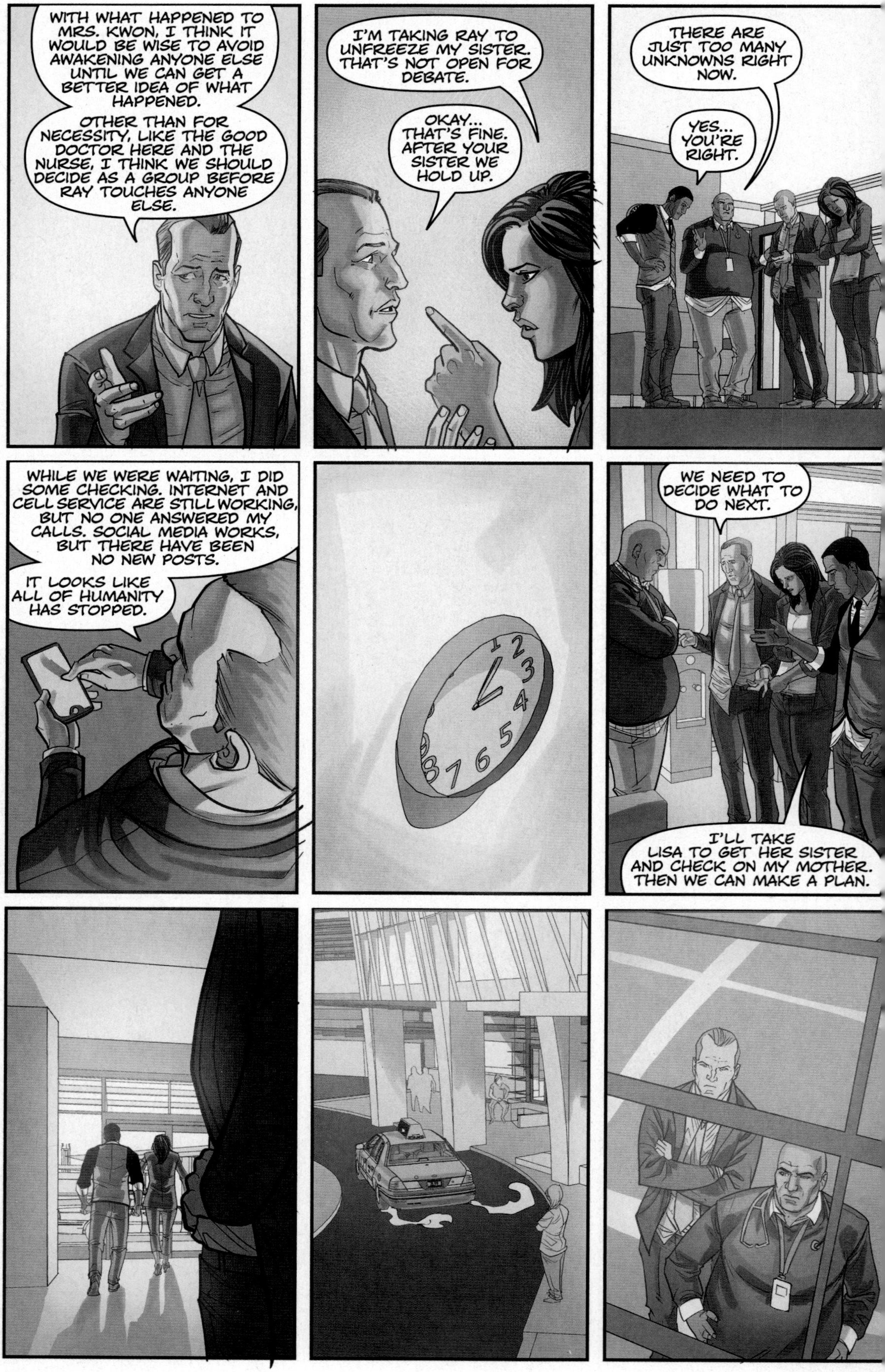
WITH WHAT HAPPENED TO MRS. KWON, I THINK IT WOULD BE WISE TO AVOID AWAKENING ANYONE ELSE UNTIL WE CAN GET A BETTER IDEA OF WHAT HAPPENED.
OTHER THAN FOR NECESSITY, LIKE THE GOOD DOCTOR HERE AND THE NURSE, I THINK WE SHOULD DECIDE AS A GROUP BEFORE RAY TOUCHES ANYONE ELSE.
I'M TAKING RAY TO UNFREEZE MY SISTER. THAT'S NOT OPEN FOR DEBATE.
OKAY... THAT'S FINE. AFTER YOUR SISTER WE HOLD UP.
THERE ARE JUST TOO MANY UNKNOWNS RIGHT NOW.
YES... YOU'RE RIGHT.
WHILE WE WERE WAITING, I DID SOME CHECKING. INTERNET AND CELL SERVICE ARE STILL WORKING, BUT NO ONE ANSWERED MY CALLS. SOCIAL MEDIA WORKS, BUT THERE HAVE BEEN NO NEW POSTS.
IT LOOKS LIKE ALL OF HUMANITY HAS STOPPED.
WE NEED TO DECIDE WHAT TO DO NEXT.
I'LL TAKE LISA TO GET HER SISTER AND CHECK ON MY MOTHER. THEN WE CAN MAKE A PLAN.

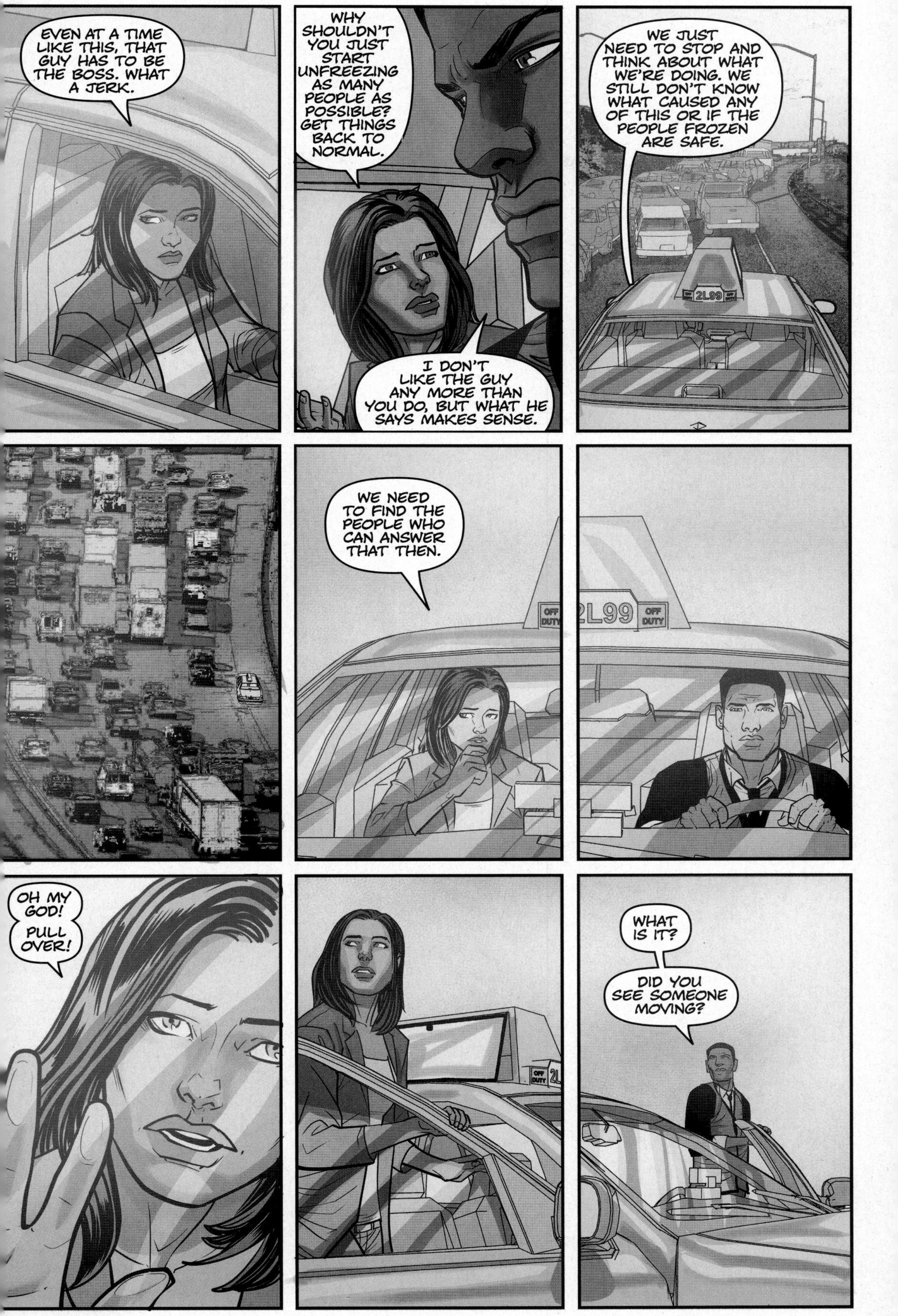

EVEN AT A TIME LIKE THIS, THAT GUY HAS TO BE THE BOSS. WHAT A JERK.
WHY SHOULDN'T YOU JUST START UNFREEZING AS MANY PEOPLE AS POSSIBLE? GET THINGS BACK TO NORMAL.
I DON'T LIKE THE GUY ANY MORE THAN YOU DO, BUT WHAT HE SAYS MAKES SENSE.
WE JUST NEED TO STOP AND THINK ABOUT WHAT WE'RE DOING. WE STILL DON'T KNOW WHAT CAUSED ANY OF THIS OR IF THE PEOPLE FROZEN ARE SAFE.
2L99
WE NEED TO FIND THE PEOPLE WHO CAN ANSWER THAT THEN.
OFF DUTY
2L99
OFF DUTY
OH MY GOD! PULL OVER!
WHAT IS IT?
DID YOU SEE SOMEONE MOVING?

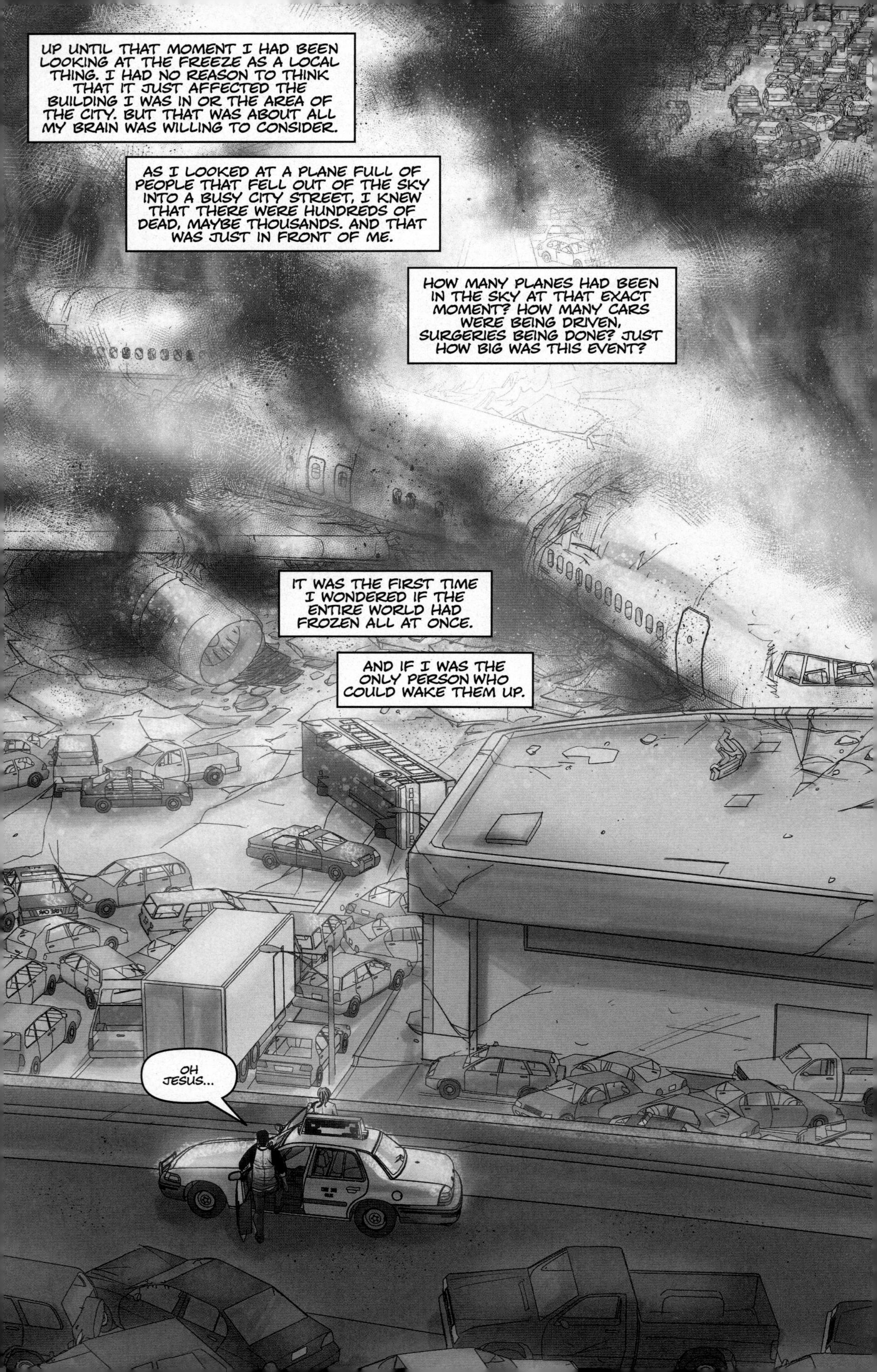
UP UNTIL THAT MOMENT I HAD BEEN LOOKING AT THE FREEZE AS A LOCAL THING. I HAD NO REASON TO THINK THAT IT JUST AFFECTED THE BUILDING I WAS IN OR THE AREA OF THE CITY. BUT THAT WAS ABOUT ALL MY BRAIN WAS WILLING TO CONSIDER.
AS I LOOKED AT A PLANE FULL OF PEOPLE THAT FELL OUT OF THE SKY INTO A BUSY CITY STREET, I KNEW THAT THERE WERE HUNDREDS OF DEAD, MAYBE THOUSANDS. AND THAT WAS JUST IN FRONT OF ME.
HOW MANY PLANES HAD BEEN IN THE SKY AT THAT EXACT MOMENT? HOW MANY CARS WERE BEING DRIVEN, SURGERIES BEING DONE? JUST HOW BIG WAS THIS EVENT?
IT WAS THE FIRST TIME I WONDERED IF THE ENTIRE WORLD HAD FROZEN ALL AT ONCE.
AND IF I WAS THE ONLY PERSON WHO COULD WAKE THEM UP.
OH JESUS...

CHAPTER 2

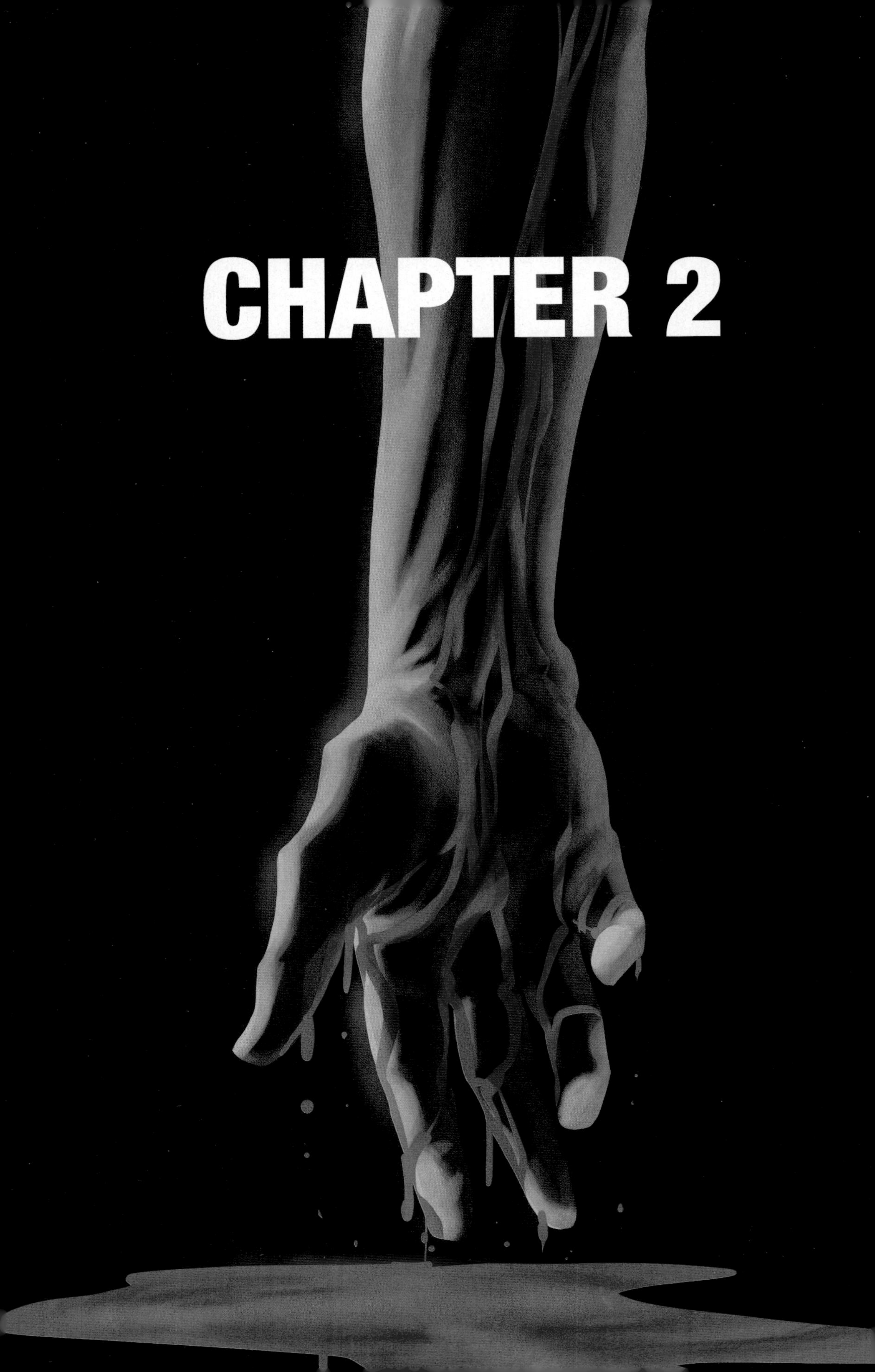

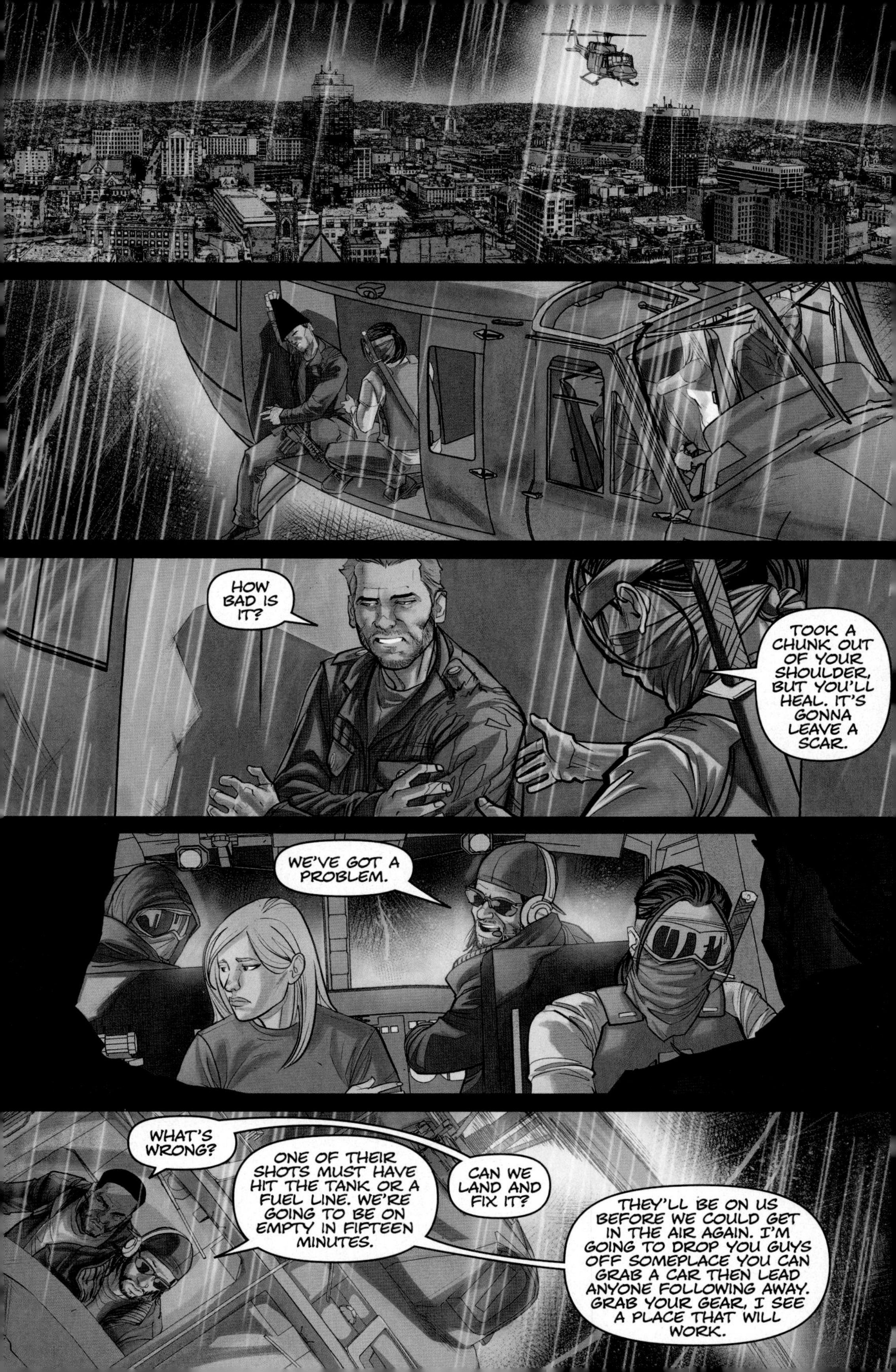
HOW BAD IS IT?
TOOK A CHUNK OUT OF YOUR SHOULDER, BUT YOU'LL HEAL. IT'S GONNA LEAVE A SCAR.
WE'VE GOT A PROBLEM.
WHAT'S WRONG?
ONE OF THEIR SHOTS MUST HAVE HIT THE TANK OR A FUEL LINE. WE'RE GOING TO BE ON EMPTY IN FIFTEEN MINUTES.
CAN WE LAND AND FIX IT?
THEY'LL BE ON US BEFORE WE COULD GET IN THE AIR AGAIN. I'M GOING TO DROP YOU GUYS OFF SOMEPLACE YOU CAN GRAB A CAR THEN LEAD ANYONE FOLLOWING AWAY. GRAB YOUR GEAR, I SEE A PLACE THAT WILL WORK.

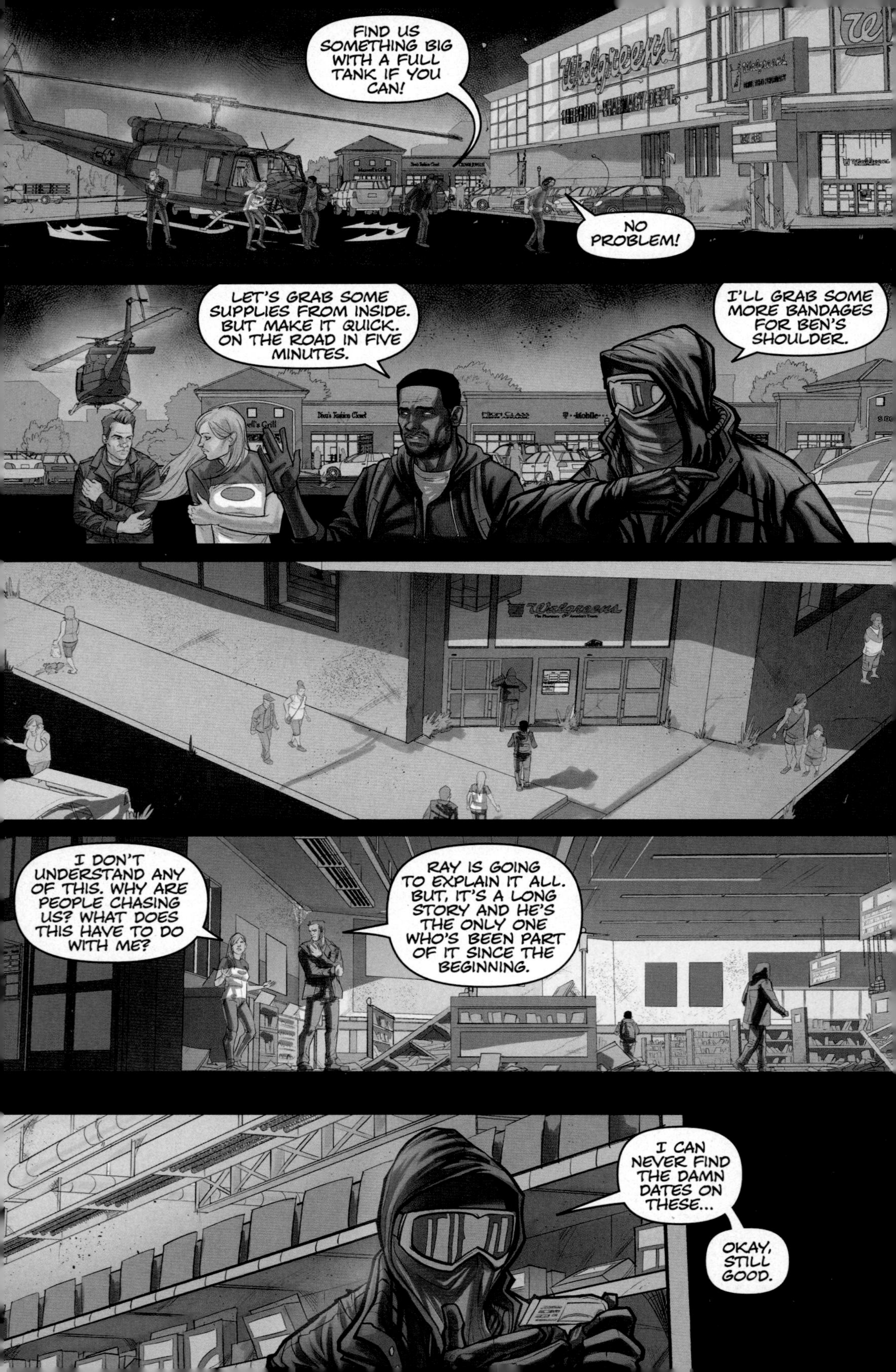
FIND US SOMETHING BIG WITH A FULL TANK IF YOU CAN!
NO PROBLEM!
LET'S GRAB SOME SUPPLIES FROM INSIDE. BUT MAKE IT QUICK. ON THE ROAD IN FIVE MINUTES.
I'LL GRAB SOME MORE BANDAGES FOR BEN'S SHOULDER.
I DON'T UNDERSTAND ANY OF THIS. WHY ARE PEOPLE CHASING US? WHAT DOES THIS HAVE TO DO WITH ME?
RAY IS GOING TO EXPLAIN IT ALL. BUT, IT'S A LONG STORY AND HE'S THE ONLY ONE WHO'S BEEN PART OF IT SINCE THE BEGINNING.
I CAN NEVER FIND THE DAMN DATES ON THESE...
OKAY, STILL GOOD.

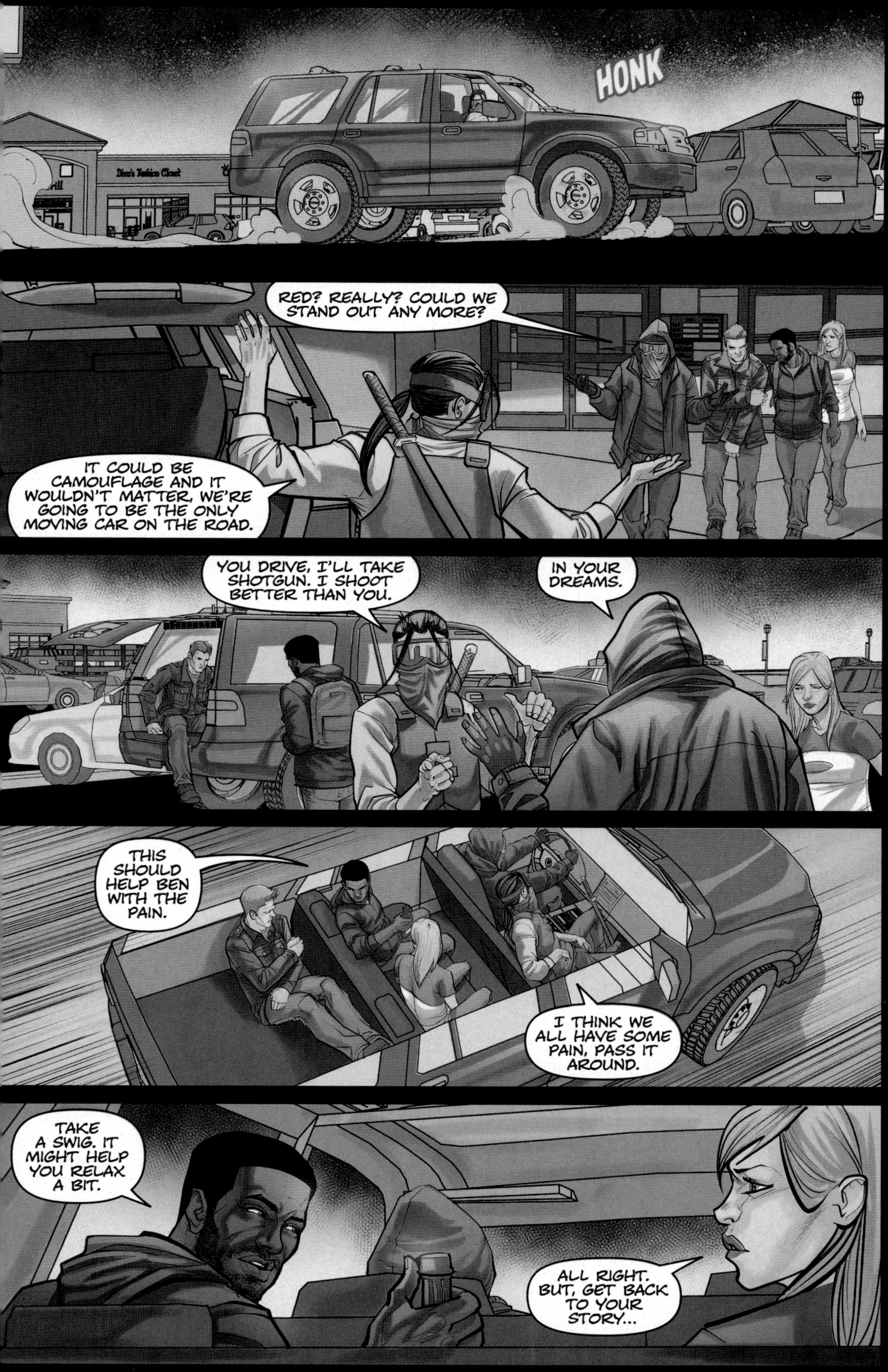
HONK
RED? REALLY? COULD WE STAND OUT ANY MORE?
IT COULD BE CAMOUFLAGE AND IT WOULDN'T MATTER, WE'RE GOING TO BE THE ONLY MOVING CAR ON THE ROAD.
YOU DRIVE, I'LL TAKE SHOTGUN. I SHOOT BETTER THAN YOU.
IN YOUR DREAMS.
THIS SHOULD HELP BEN WITH THE PAIN.
I THINK WE ALL HAVE SOME PAIN, PASS IT AROUND.
TAKE A SWIG. IT MIGHT HELP YOU RELAX A BIT.
ALL RIGHT. BUT, GET BACK TO YOUR STORY...

AFTER SOME TIME HAD PASSED AND IT BECAME OBVIOUS THAT PEOPLE WEREN'T JUST GOING TO SUDDENLY WAKE UP ON THEIR OWN, GAVIN SUGGESTED WE MOVE OUT OF THE DOWNTOWN AREA.

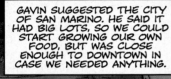

GAVIN SUGGESTED THE CITY OF SAN MARINO. HE SAID IT HAD BIG LOTS, SO WE COULD START GROWING OUR OWN FOOD, BUT WAS CLOSE ENOUGH TO DOWNTOWN IN CASE WE NEEDED ANYTHING.

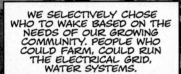

WE SELECTIVELY CHOSE WHO TO WAKE BASED ON THE NEEDS OF OUR GROWING COMMUNITY. PEOPLE WHO COULD FARM, COULD RUN THE ELECTRICAL GRID, WATER SYSTEMS.

IT BECAME QUITE A SYSTEM. WHEN WE DISCOVERED A NEED, WE WOULD FIND A FEW LIKELY CANDIDATES, LOOK THEM UP THE BEST WE COULD AND CHOOSE THE ONE MOST LIKELY TO JOIN WITH THE OTHERS WITH THE LEAST AMOUNT OF PROBLEMS.

I PICKED OUT A PLACE I THOUGHT MOMMA WOULD LIKE, THEN HAD HER BROUGHT OVER. I STILL HADN'T WOKEN HER. THERE WERE JUST TOO MANY UNKNOWNS FOR ME TO RISK IT.

LISA AND MARIA MOVED IN WITH ME. SAID THEY DIDN'T WANT TO LIVE ON THEIR OWN. THEY EACH HAD THEIR OWN ROOMS. WHICH STILL LEFT SIX EMPTY AFTER WE PUT MOMMA IN ONE AND I TOOK THE OTHER. LUCY HAD THE RUN OF THE PLACE AS USUAL.

I WASN'T SURE WHICH I WAS LESS COMFORTABLE WITH, KNOWING THAT I WAS THE ONLY ONE THAT COULD BRING PEOPLE BACK TO LIFE,

OR THAT LISA, DAISY, GAVIN, NIZAM AND I HAD THE FINAL SAY ON EVERY DECISION. WE WERE, FOR ALL INTENTS AND PURPOSES, THE DEFACTO GOVERNMENT.

GAVIN SEEMED TO RELISH IN HIS NEW POWER. NIZAM LOOKED AT THE COMMUNITY AS A PATIENT AND TRIED TO DO WHAT WAS BEST FOR THE PATIENT'S HEALTH.

LISA WOULD FIND OUT AS MUCH AS SHE COULD ABOUT THINGS BEFORE MAKING A DECISION. DAISY DIDN'T SEEM TO CARE, JUST WENT ALONG WITH THE MAJORITY MOST OF THE TIME.

I HATED IT. I WAS AFRAID OF MAKING THE WRONG CHOICE AND WHO IT MIGHT HURT.

I DIDN'T SIGN UP FOR ANY OF IT. AND I JUST WANTED EVERYTHING TO GO BACK TO NORMAL.

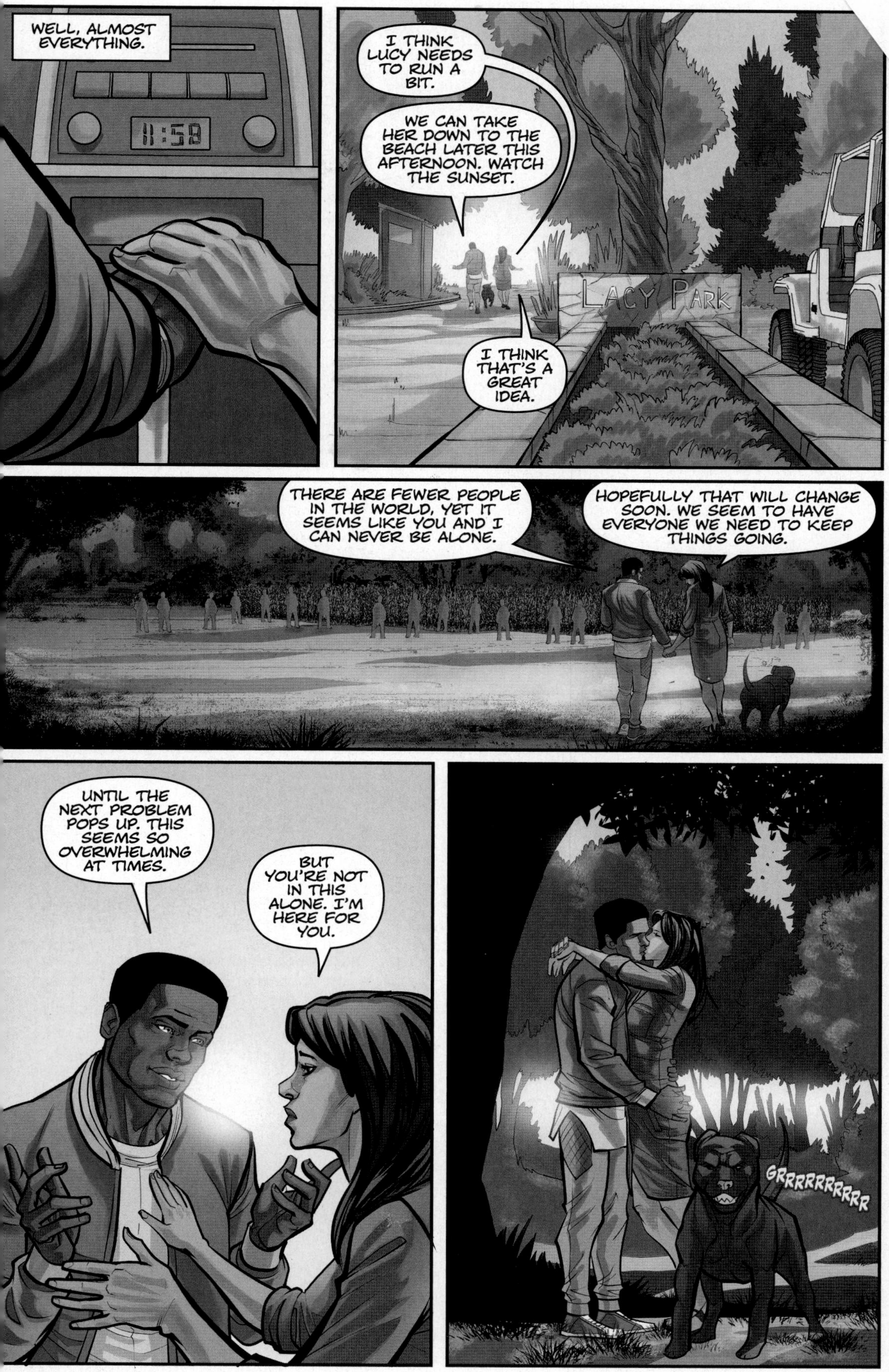
WELL, ALMOST EVERYTHING.
11:58
I THINK LUCY NEEDS TO RUN A BIT.
WE CAN TAKE HER DOWN TO THE BEACH LATER THIS AFTERNOON. WATCH THE SUNSET.
LACY PARK
I THINK THAT'S A GREAT IDEA.
THERE ARE FEWER PEOPLE IN THE WORLD, YET IT SEEMS LIKE YOU AND I CAN NEVER BE ALONE.
HOPEFULLY THAT WILL CHANGE SOON. WE SEEM TO HAVE EVERYONE WE NEED TO KEEP THINGS GOING.
UNTIL THE NEXT PROBLEM POPS UP. THIS SEEMS SO OVERWHELMING AT TIMES.
BUT YOU'RE NOT IN THIS ALONE. I'M HERE FOR YOU.
GRRRRRRRRRR

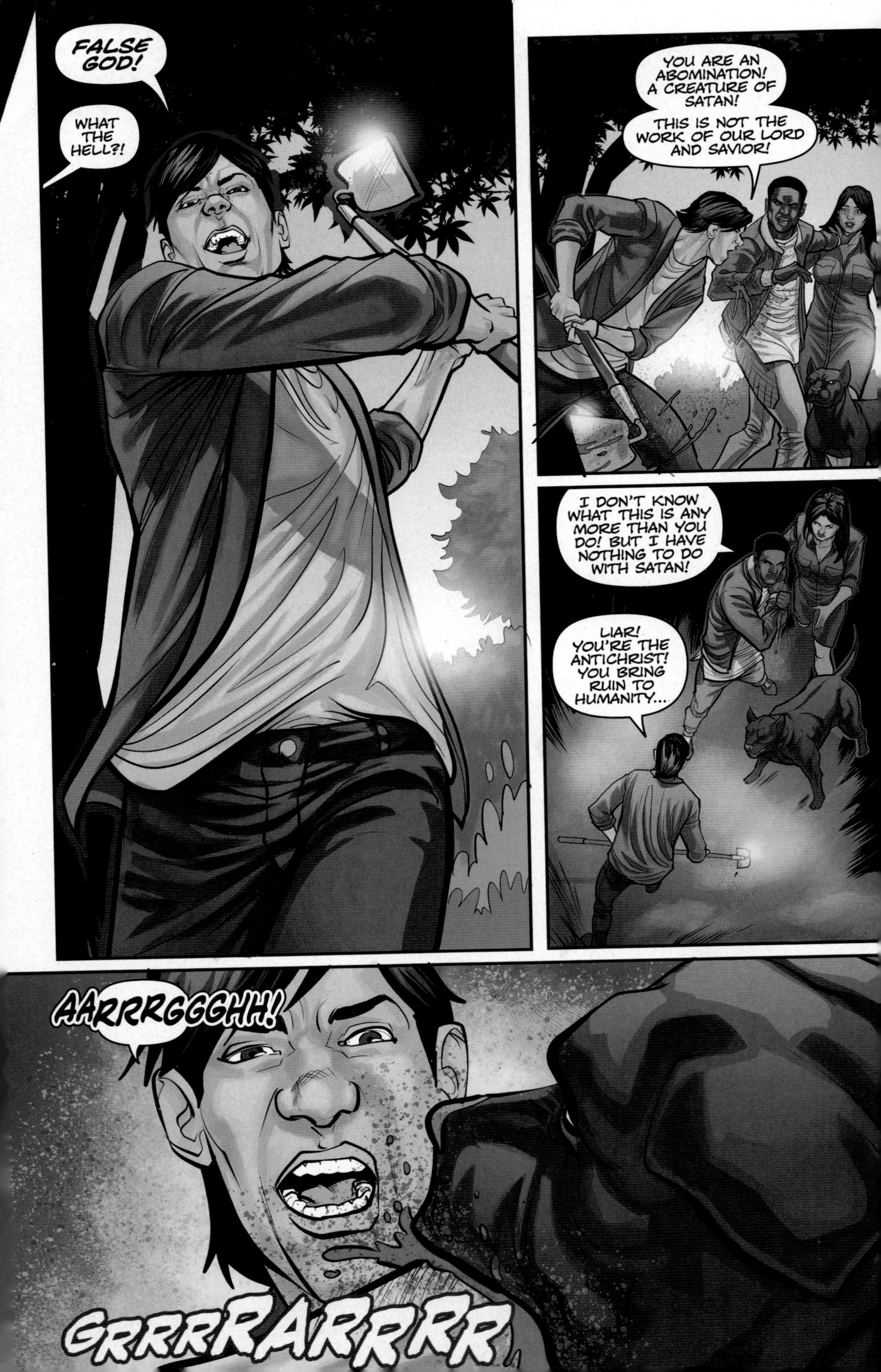
FALSE GOD!
WHAT THE HELL?!
YOU ARE AN ABOMINATION! A CREATURE OF SATAN!
THIS IS NOT THE WORK OF OUR LORD AND SAVIOR!
I DON'T KNOW WHAT THIS IS ANY MORE THAN YOU DO! BUT I HAVE NOTHING TO DO WITH SATAN!
LIAR! YOU'RE THE ANTICHRIST! YOU BRING RUIN TO HUMANITY...
AARRRGGGHH!
GRRRRARRRRR

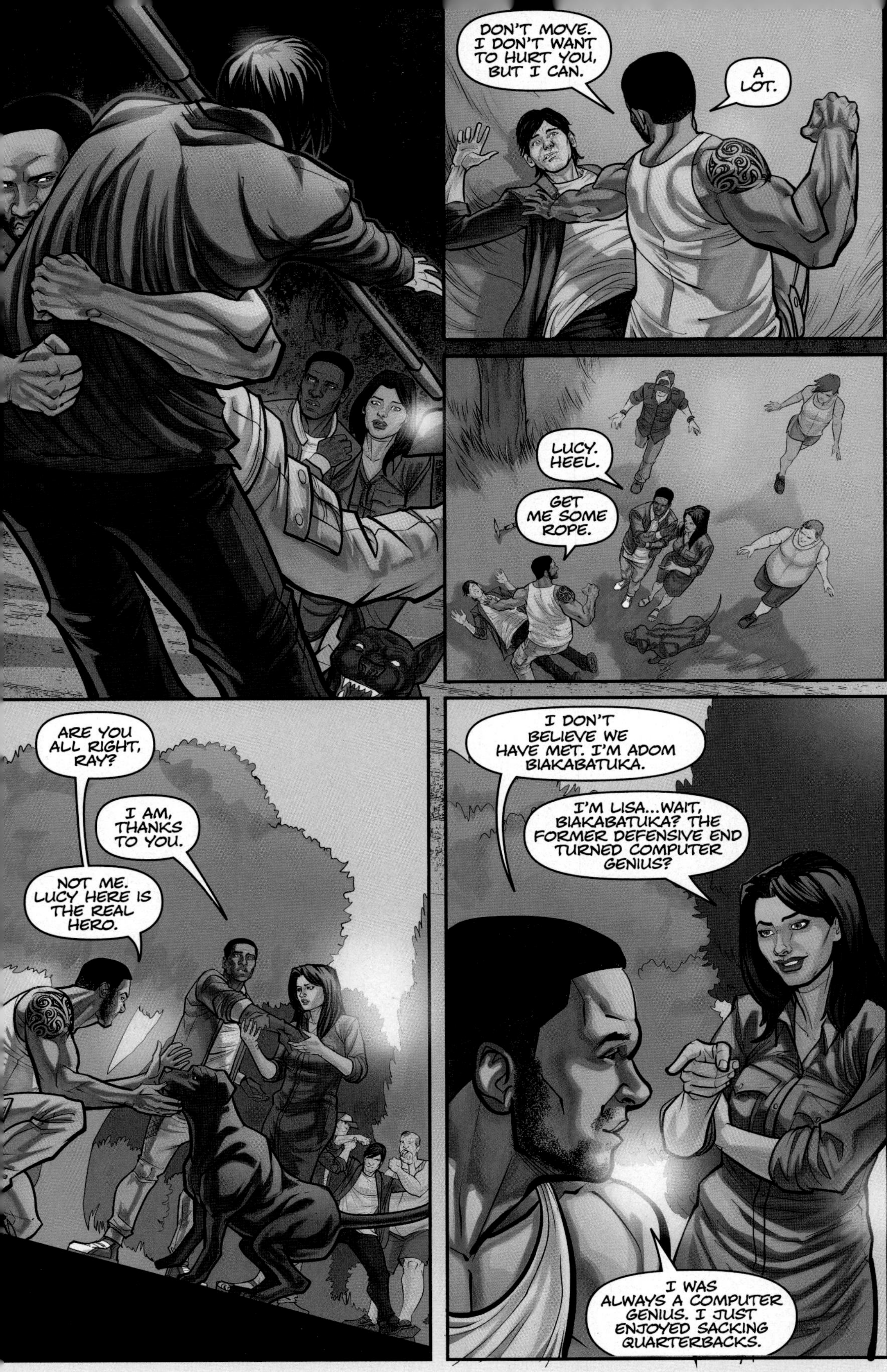
DON'T MOVE. I DON'T WANT TO HURT YOU, BUT I CAN.
A LOT.
LUCY. HEEL.
GET ME SOME ROPE.
ARE YOU ALL RIGHT, RAY?
I AM, THANKS TO YOU.
NOT ME. LUCY HERE IS THE REAL HERO.
I DON'T BELIEVE WE HAVE MET. I'M ADOM BIAKABATUKA.
I'M LISA...WAIT, BIAKABATUKA? THE FORMER DEFENSIVE END TURNED COMPUTER GENIUS?
I WAS ALWAYS A COMPUTER GENIUS. I JUST ENJOYED SACKING QUARTERBACKS.

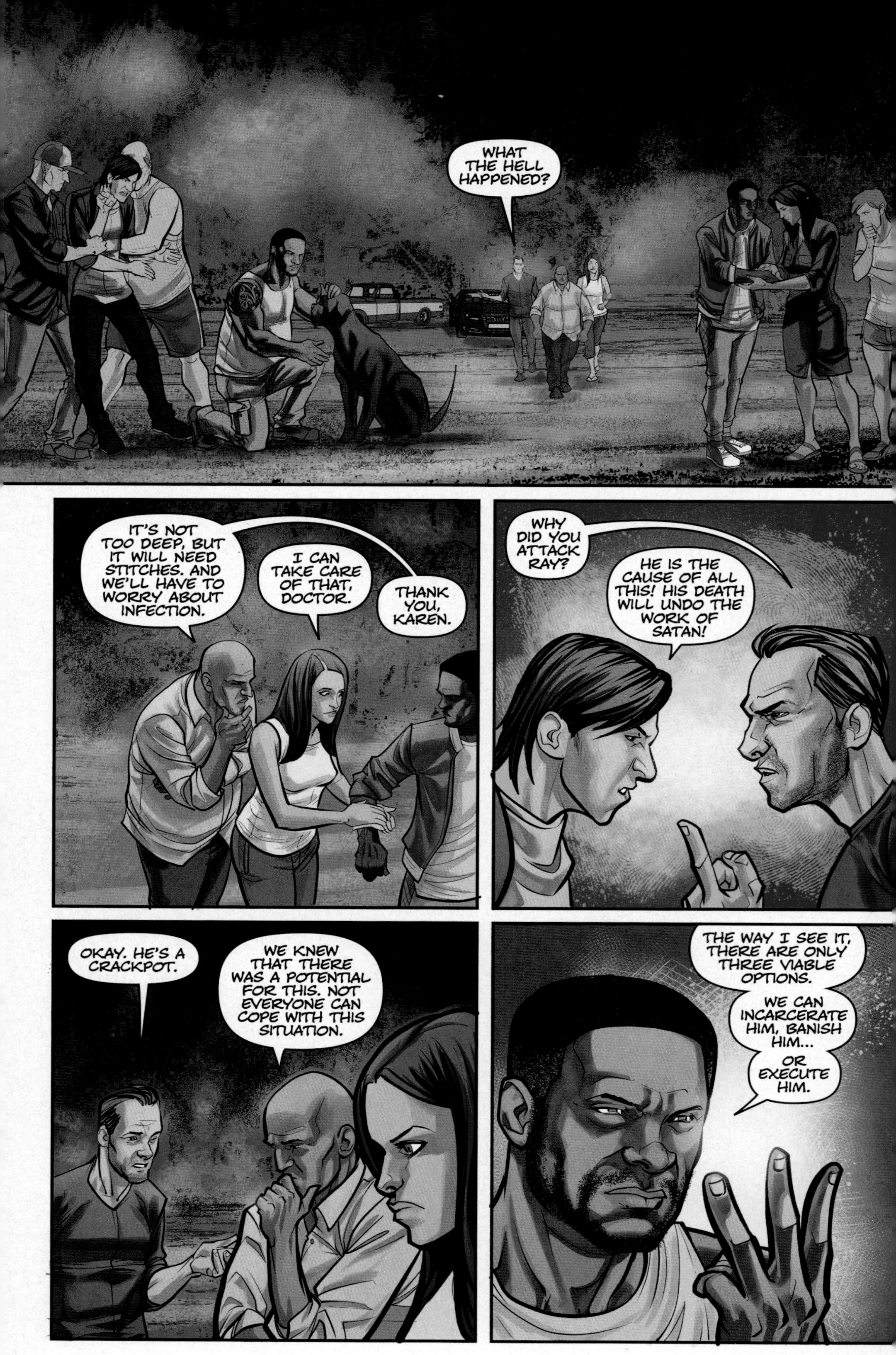
WHAT THE HELL HAPPENED?
IT'S NOT TOO DEEP, BUT IT WILL NEED STITCHES. AND WE'LL HAVE TO WORRY ABOUT INFECTION.
I CAN TAKE CARE OF THAT, DOCTOR.
THANK YOU, KAREN.
WHY DID YOU ATTACK RAY?
HE IS THE CAUSE OF ALL THIS! HIS DEATH WILL UNDO THE WORK OF SATAN!
OKAY. HE'S A CRACKPOT.
WE KNEW THAT THERE WAS A POTENTIAL FOR THIS. NOT EVERYONE CAN COPE WITH THIS SITUATION.
THE WAY I SEE IT, THERE ARE ONLY THREE VIABLE OPTIONS.
WE CAN INCARCERATE HIM, BANISH HIM...
OR EXECUTE HIM.

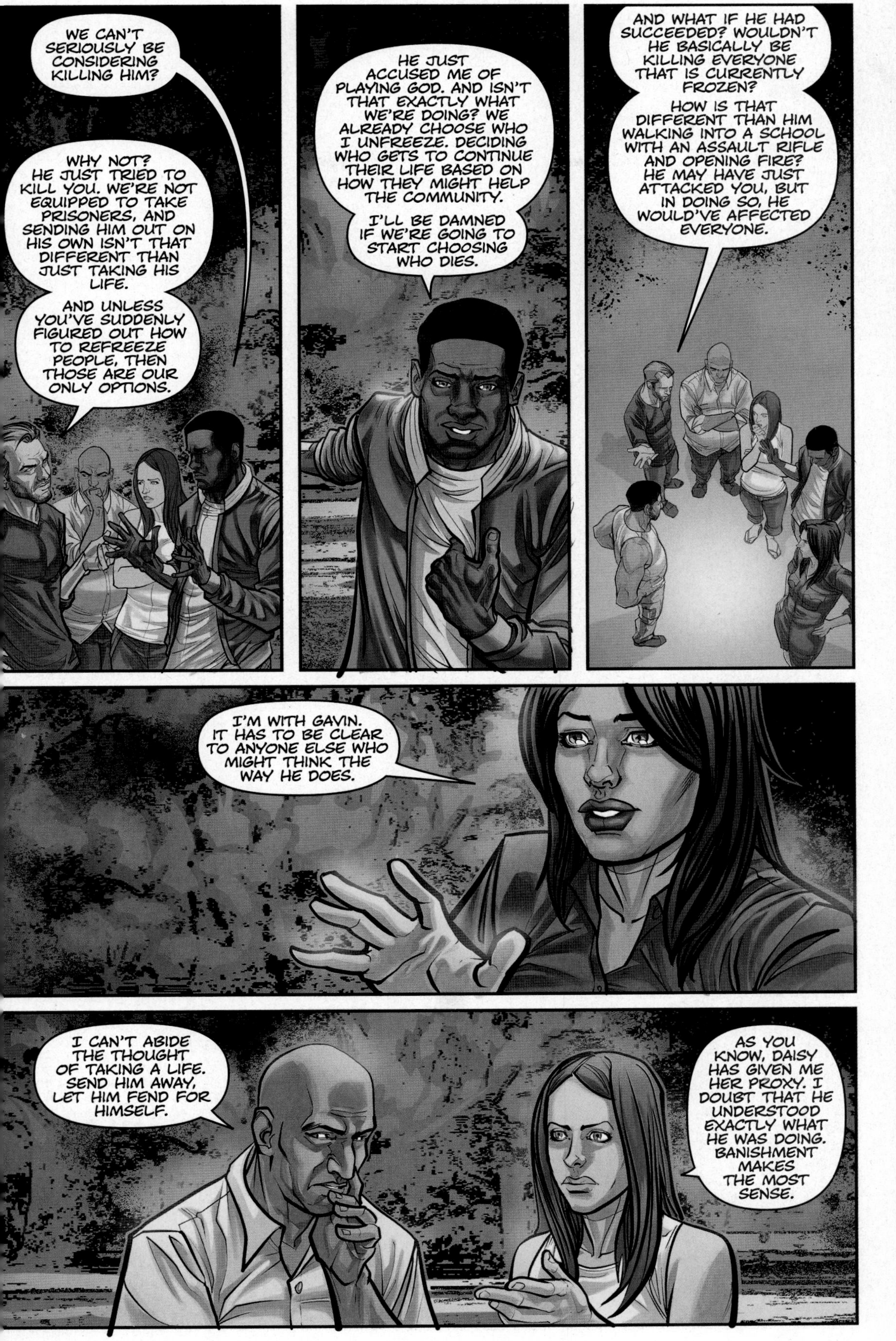
WE CAN'T SERIOUSLY BE CONSIDERING KILLING HIM?
WHY NOT? HE JUST TRIED TO KILL YOU. WE'RE NOT EQUIPPED TO TAKE PRISONERS, AND SENDING HIM OUT ON HIS OWN ISN'T THAT DIFFERENT THAN JUST TAKING HIS LIFE.
AND UNLESS YOU'VE SUDDENLY FIGURED OUT HOW TO REFREEZE PEOPLE, THEN THOSE ARE OUR ONLY OPTIONS.
HE JUST ACCUSED ME OF PLAYING GOD. AND ISN'T THAT EXACTLY WHAT WE'RE DOING? WE ALREADY CHOOSE WHO I UNFREEZE. DECIDING WHO GETS TO CONTINUE THEIR LIFE BASED ON HOW THEY MIGHT HELP THE COMMUNITY.
I'LL BE DAMNED IF WE'RE GOING TO START CHOOSING WHO DIES.
AND WHAT IF HE HAD SUCCEEDED? WOULDN'T HE BASICALLY BE KILLING EVERYONE THAT IS CURRENTLY FROZEN?
HOW IS THAT DIFFERENT THAN HIM WALKING INTO A SCHOOL WITH AN ASSAULT RIFLE AND OPENING FIRE? HE MAY HAVE JUST ATTACKED YOU, BUT IN DOING SO, HE WOULD'VE AFFECTED EVERYONE.
I'M WITH GAVIN. IT HAS TO BE CLEAR TO ANYONE ELSE WHO MIGHT THINK THE WAY HE DOES.
I CAN'T ABIDE THE THOUGHT OF TAKING A LIFE. SEND HIM AWAY, LET HIM FEND FOR HIMSELF.
AS YOU KNOW, DAISY HAS GIVEN ME HER PROXY. I DOUBT THAT HE UNDERSTOOD EXACTLY WHAT HE WAS DOING. BANISHMENT MAKES THE MOST SENSE.

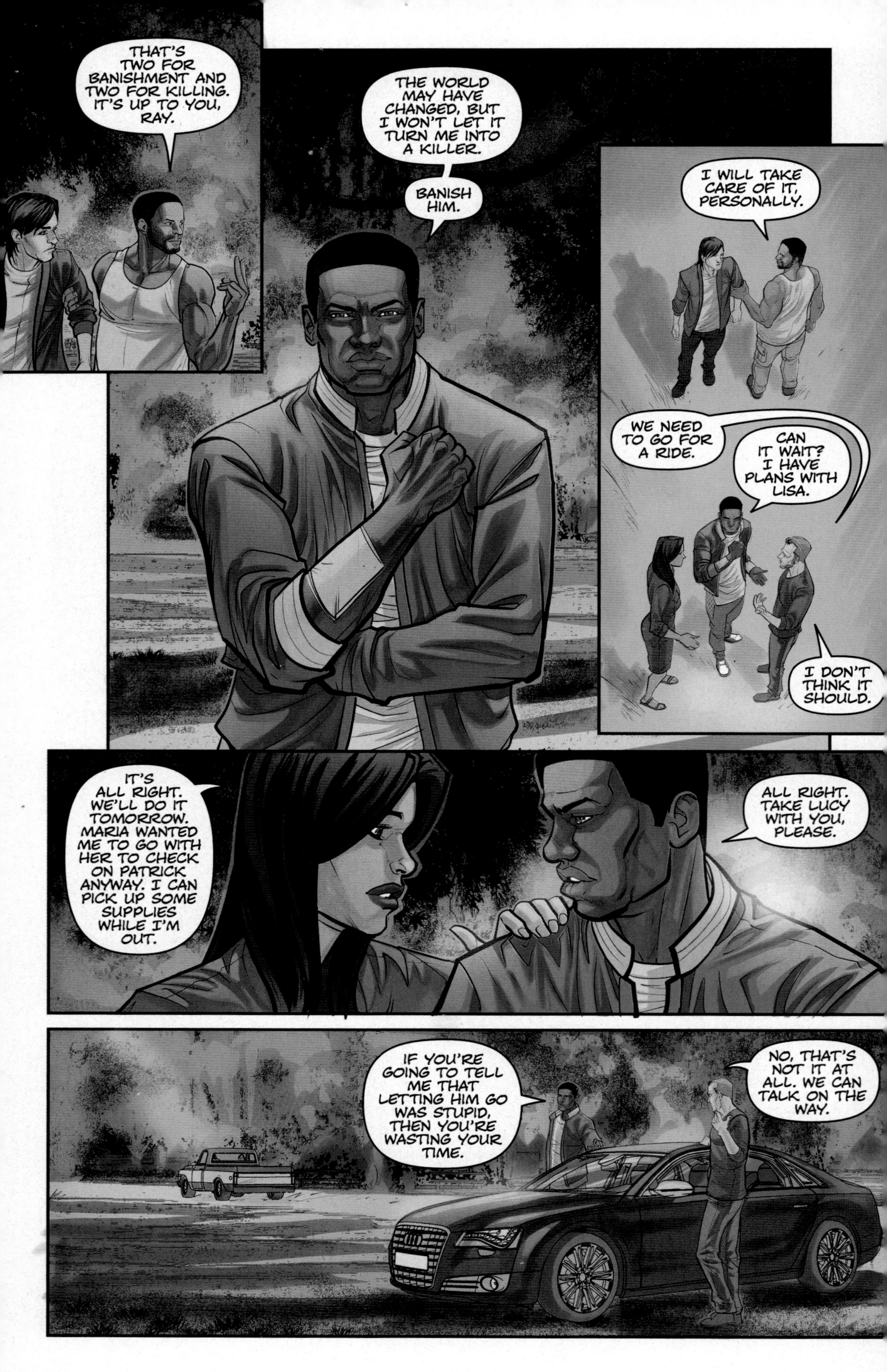
THAT'S TWO FOR BANISHMENT AND TWO FOR KILLING. IT'S UP TO YOU, RAY.
THE WORLD MAY HAVE CHANGED, BUT I WON'T LET IT TURN ME INTO A KILLER.
BANISH HIM.
I WILL TAKE CARE OF IT, PERSONALLY.
WE NEED TO GO FOR A RIDE.
CAN IT WAIT? I HAVE PLANS WITH LISA.
I DON'T THINK IT SHOULD.
IT'S ALL RIGHT. WE'LL DO IT TOMORROW. MARIA WANTED ME TO GO WITH HER TO CHECK ON PATRICK ANYWAY. I CAN PICK UP SOME SUPPLIES WHILE I'M OUT.
ALL RIGHT. TAKE LUCY WITH YOU, PLEASE.
IF YOU'RE GOING TO TELL ME THAT LETTING HIM GO WAS STUPID, THEN YOU'RE WASTING YOUR TIME.
NO, THAT'S NOT IT AT ALL. WE CAN TALK ON THE WAY.

END OF THE LINE, MY FRIEND.

YOU DO HIS BIDDING, THEN YOU'RE NO FRIEND OF MINE.

I APPRECIATE YOUR FAITH. I TOO FOLLOW THE PATH OF THE LORD.

THEN YOU MUST SEE THE ABOMINATION AS I DO. THAT HE HAS BROUGHT A PLAGUE TO THIS WORLD AND ONLY HIS DEATH CAN END IT.

THAT, MY FRIEND, IS WHERE WE DIFFER. I SEE THIS EVENT AS GOD CLEANSING THE WORLD OF THE SAVAGES.

AND RAY IS HIS PROPHET, CHOOSING THE RIGHTEOUS TO REBUILD SOCIETY. HE IS A TOOL OF OUR LORD AND HE MUST BE PROTECTED AT ALL COSTS.

YOU WERE NOT WORTHY TO SEE THE LIGHT.

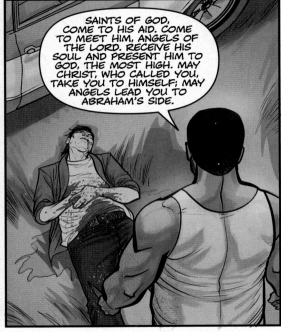

SAINTS OF GOD, COME TO HIS AID. COME TO MEET HIM, ANGELS OF THE LORD. RECEIVE HIS SOUL AND PRESENT HIM TO GOD, THE MOST HIGH. MAY CHRIST, WHO CALLED YOU, TAKE YOU TO HIMSELF; MAY ANGELS LEAD YOU TO ABRAHAM'S SIDE.

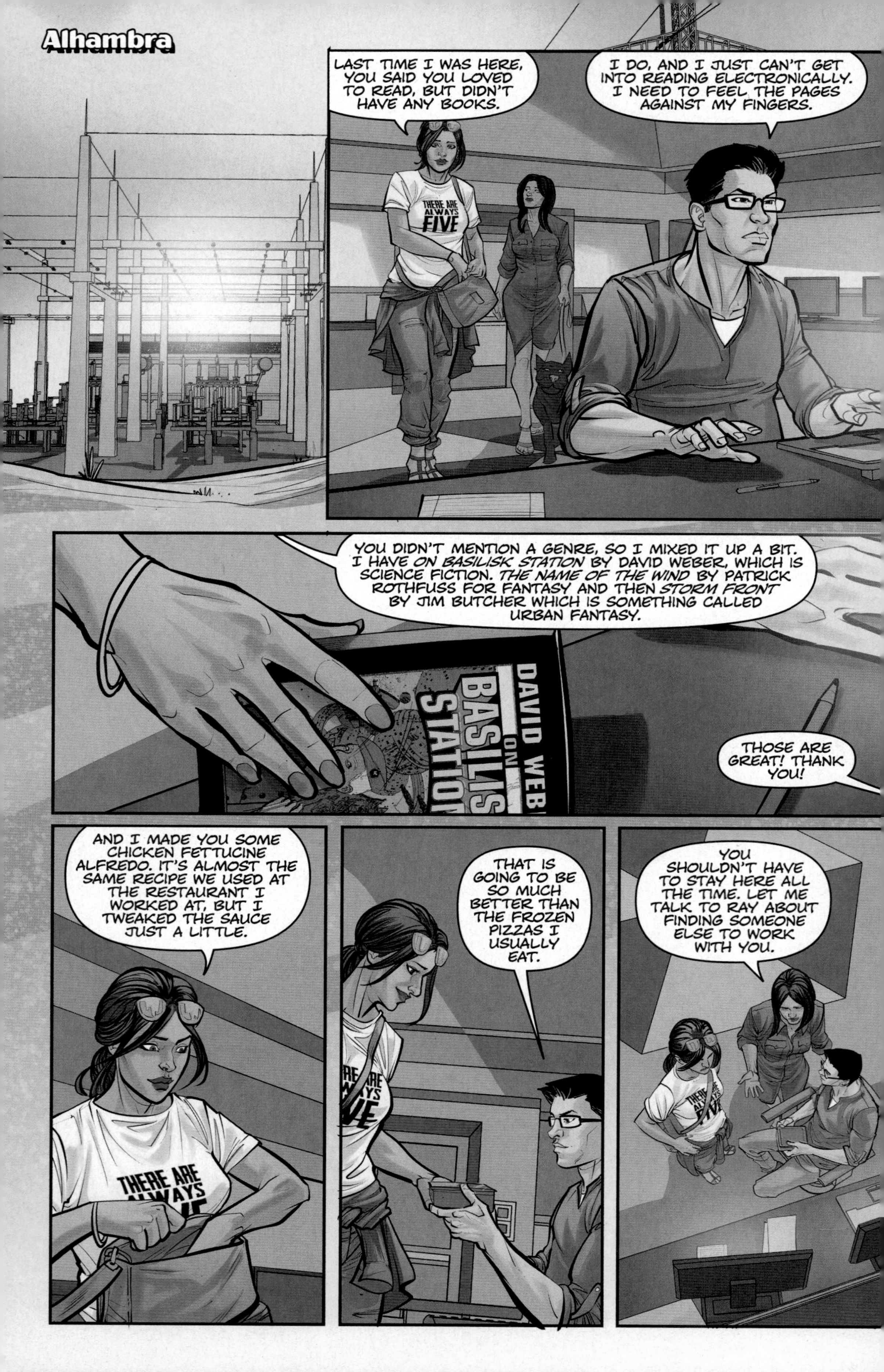
LAST TIME I WAS HERE, YOU SAID YOU LOVED TO READ, BUT DIDN'T HAVE ANY BOOKS.
I DO, AND I JUST CAN'T GET INTO READING ELECTRONICALLY. I NEED TO FEEL THE PAGES AGAINST MY FINGERS.
THERE ARE ALWAYS FIVE
YOU DIDN'T MENTION A GENRE, SO I MIXED IT UP A BIT. I HAVE *ON BASILISK STATION* BY DAVID WEBER, WHICH IS SCIENCE FICTION. *THE NAME OF THE WIND* BY PATRICK ROTHFUSS FOR FANTASY AND THEN *STORM FRONT* BY JIM BUTCHER WHICH IS SOMETHING CALLED URBAN FANTASY.
DAVID WEBER
ON BASILISK STATION
THOSE ARE GREAT! THANK YOU!
AND I MADE YOU SOME CHICKEN FETTUCINE ALFREDO. IT'S ALMOST THE SAME RECIPE WE USED AT THE RESTAURANT I WORKED AT, BUT I TWEAKED THE SAUCE JUST A LITTLE.
THERE ARE ALWAYS
THAT IS GOING TO BE SO MUCH BETTER THAN THE FROZEN PIZZAS I USUALLY EAT.
YOU SHOULDN'T HAVE TO STAY HERE ALL THE TIME. LET ME TALK TO RAY ABOUT FINDING SOMEONE ELSE TO WORK WITH YOU.

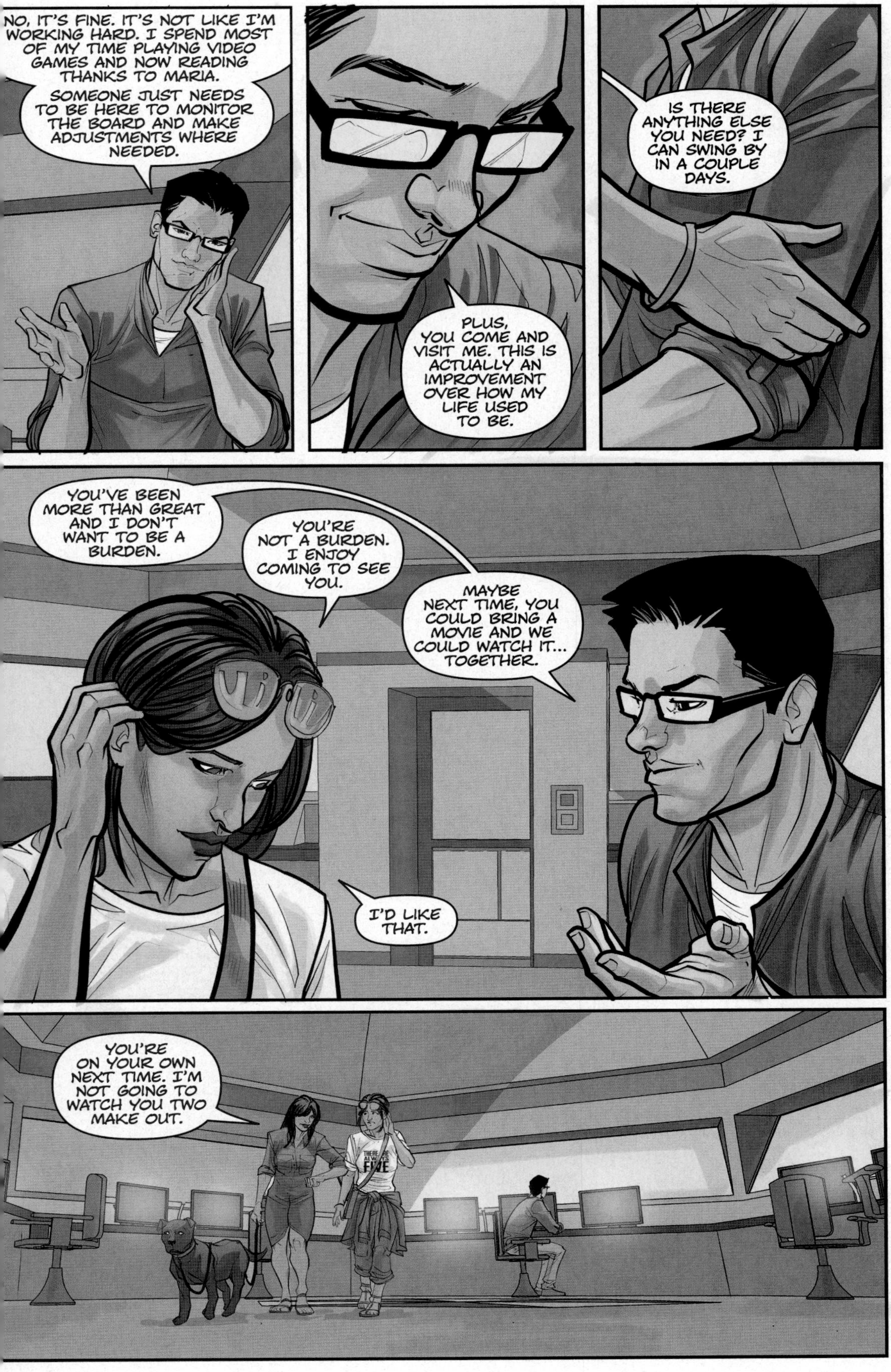
NO, IT'S FINE. IT'S NOT LIKE I'M WORKING HARD. I SPEND MOST OF MY TIME PLAYING VIDEO GAMES AND NOW READING THANKS TO MARIA.
SOMEONE JUST NEEDS TO BE HERE TO MONITOR THE BOARD AND MAKE ADJUSTMENTS WHERE NEEDED.
PLUS, YOU COME AND VISIT ME. THIS IS ACTUALLY AN IMPROVEMENT OVER HOW MY LIFE USED TO BE.
IS THERE ANYTHING ELSE YOU NEED? I CAN SWING BY IN A COUPLE DAYS.
YOU'VE BEEN MORE THAN GREAT AND I DON'T WANT TO BE A BURDEN.
YOU'RE NOT A BURDEN. I ENJOY COMING TO SEE YOU.
MAYBE NEXT TIME, YOU COULD BRING A MOVIE AND WE COULD WATCH IT... TOGETHER.
I'D LIKE THAT.
YOU'RE ON YOUR OWN NEXT TIME. I'M NOT GOING TO WATCH YOU TWO MAKE OUT.

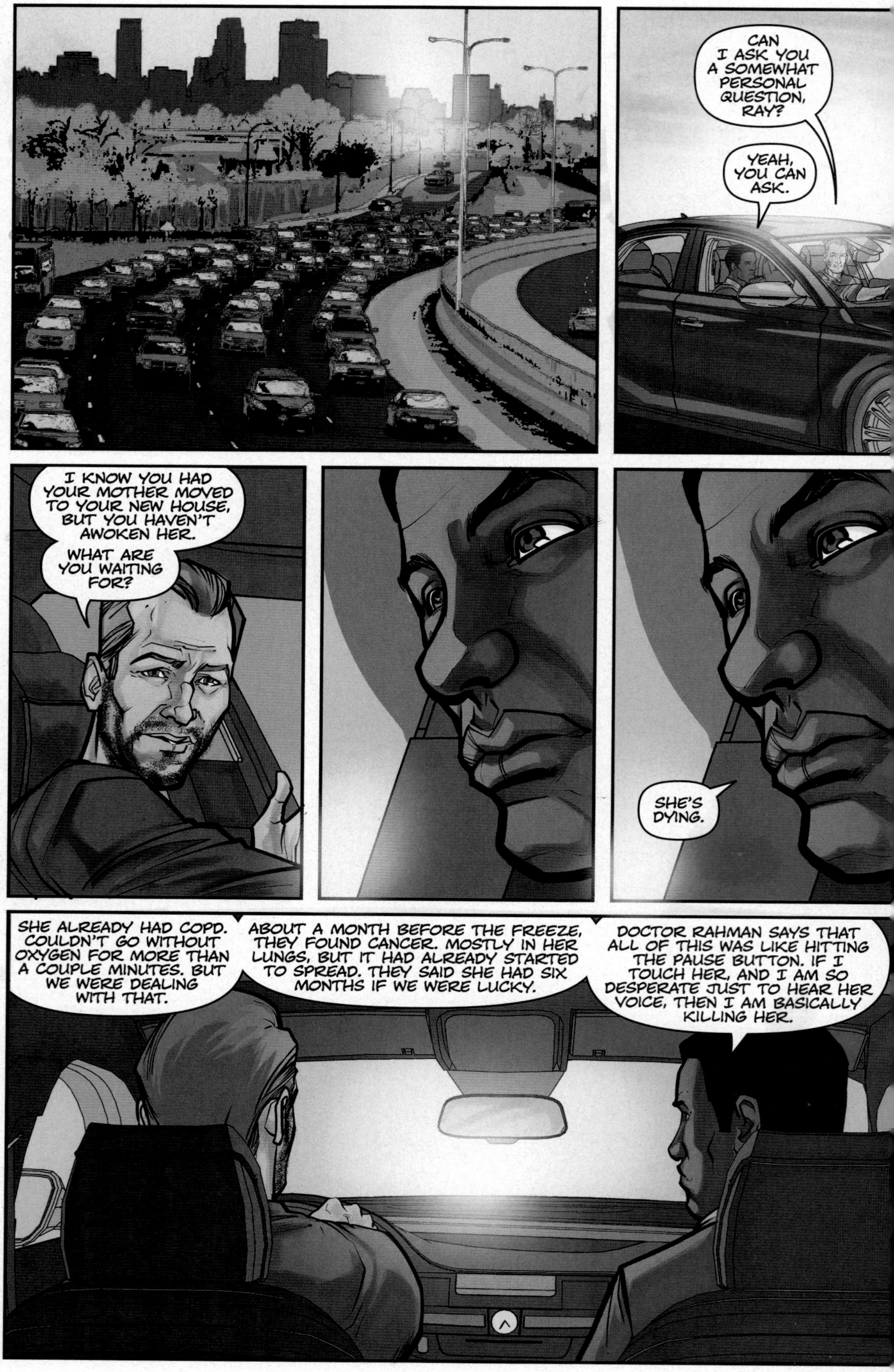
CAN I ASK YOU A SOMEWHAT PERSONAL QUESTION, RAY?
YEAH, YOU CAN ASK.
I KNOW YOU HAD YOUR MOTHER MOVED TO YOUR NEW HOUSE, BUT YOU HAVEN'T AWOKEN HER.
WHAT ARE YOU WAITING FOR?
SHE'S DYING.
SHE ALREADY HAD COPD. COULDN'T GO WITHOUT OXYGEN FOR MORE THAN A COUPLE MINUTES. BUT WE WERE DEALING WITH THAT.
ABOUT A MONTH BEFORE THE FREEZE, THEY FOUND CANCER. MOSTLY IN HER LUNGS, BUT IT HAD ALREADY STARTED TO SPREAD. THEY SAID SHE HAD SIX MONTHS IF WE WERE LUCKY.
DOCTOR RAHMAN SAYS THAT ALL OF THIS WAS LIKE HITTING THE PAUSE BUTTON. IF I TOUCH HER, AND I AM SO DESPERATE JUST TO HEAR HER VOICE, THEN I AM BASICALLY KILLING HER.

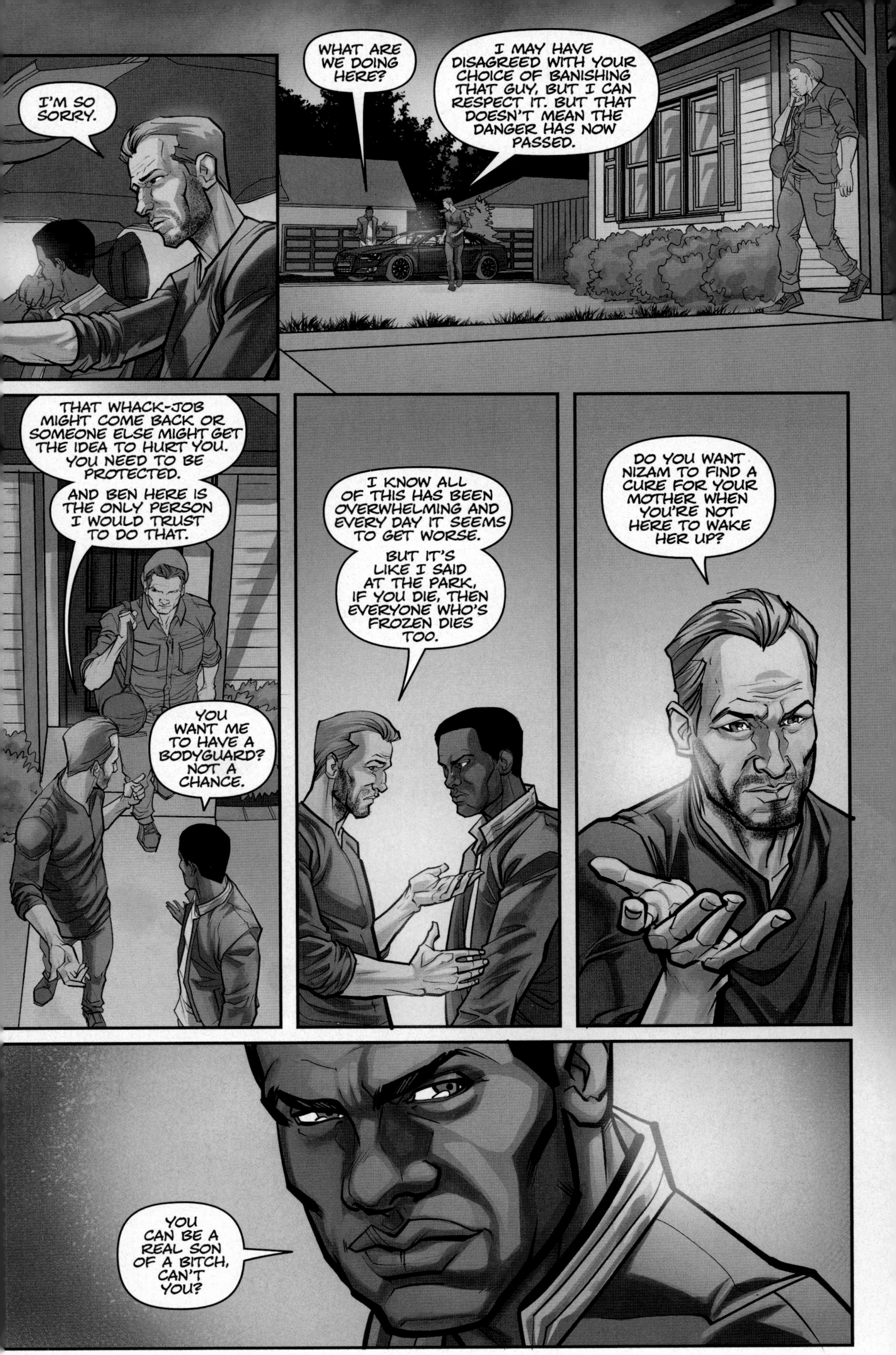
I'M SO SORRY.
WHAT ARE WE DOING HERE?
I MAY HAVE DISAGREED WITH YOUR CHOICE OF BANISHING THAT GUY, BUT I CAN RESPECT IT. BUT THAT DOESN'T MEAN THE DANGER HAS NOW PASSED.
THAT WHACK-JOB MIGHT COME BACK OR SOMEONE ELSE MIGHT GET THE IDEA TO HURT YOU. YOU NEED TO BE PROTECTED.
AND BEN HERE IS THE ONLY PERSON I WOULD TRUST TO DO THAT.
YOU WANT ME TO HAVE A BODYGUARD? NOT A CHANCE.
I KNOW ALL OF THIS HAS BEEN OVERWHELMING AND EVERY DAY IT SEEMS TO GET WORSE.
BUT IT'S LIKE I SAID AT THE PARK, IF YOU DIE, THEN EVERYONE WHO'S FROZEN DIES TOO.
DO YOU WANT NIZAM TO FIND A CURE FOR YOUR MOTHER WHEN YOU'RE NOT HERE TO WAKE HER UP?
YOU CAN BE A REAL SON OF A BITCH, CAN'T YOU?

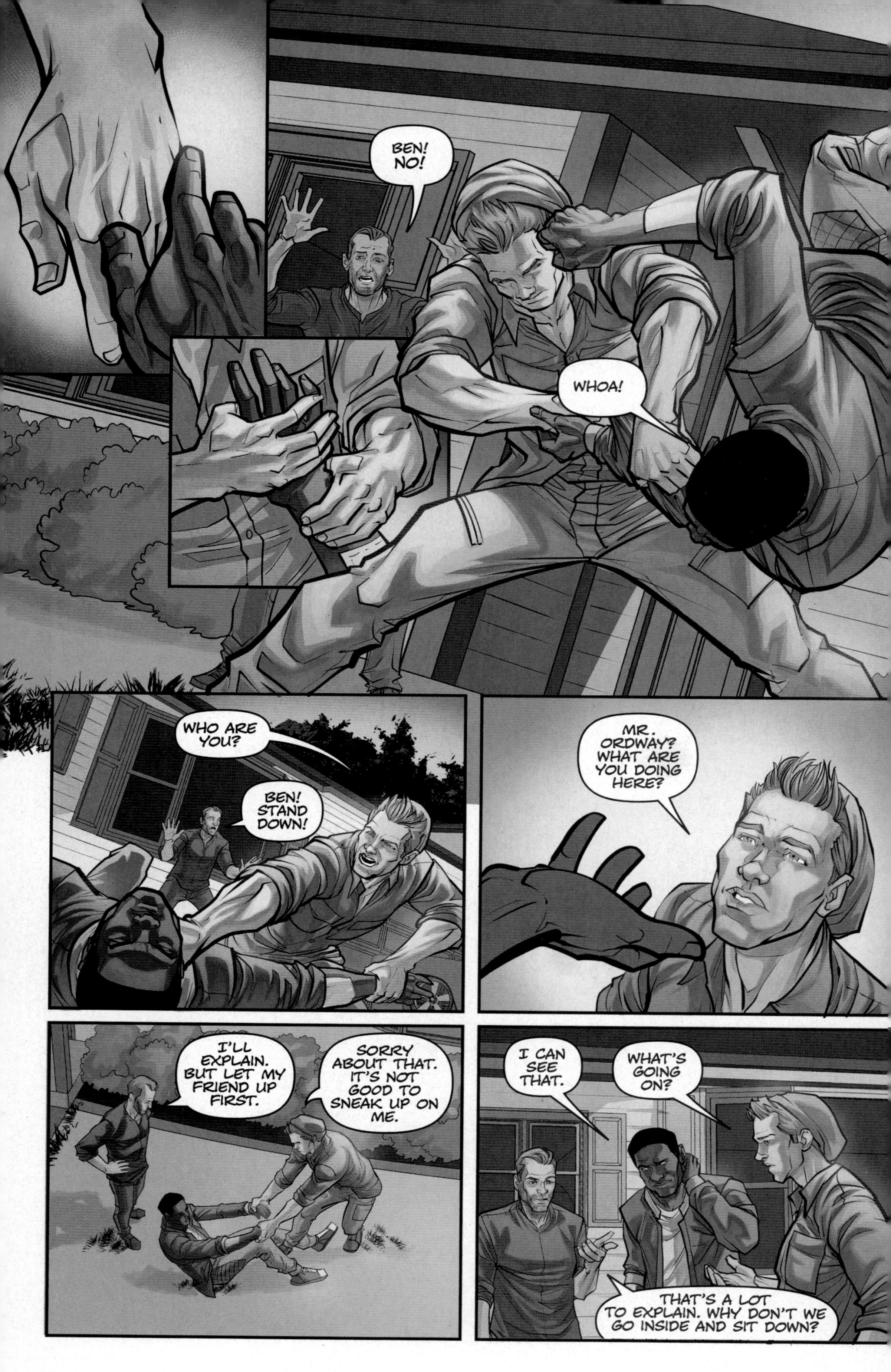
BEN! NO!
WHOA!
WHO ARE YOU?
BEN! STAND DOWN!
MR. ORDWAY? WHAT ARE YOU DOING HERE?
I'LL EXPLAIN. BUT LET MY FRIEND UP FIRST.
SORRY ABOUT THAT. IT'S NOT GOOD TO SNEAK UP ON ME.
I CAN SEE THAT.
WHAT'S GOING ON?
THAT'S A LOT TO EXPLAIN. WHY DON'T WE GO INSIDE AND SIT DOWN?

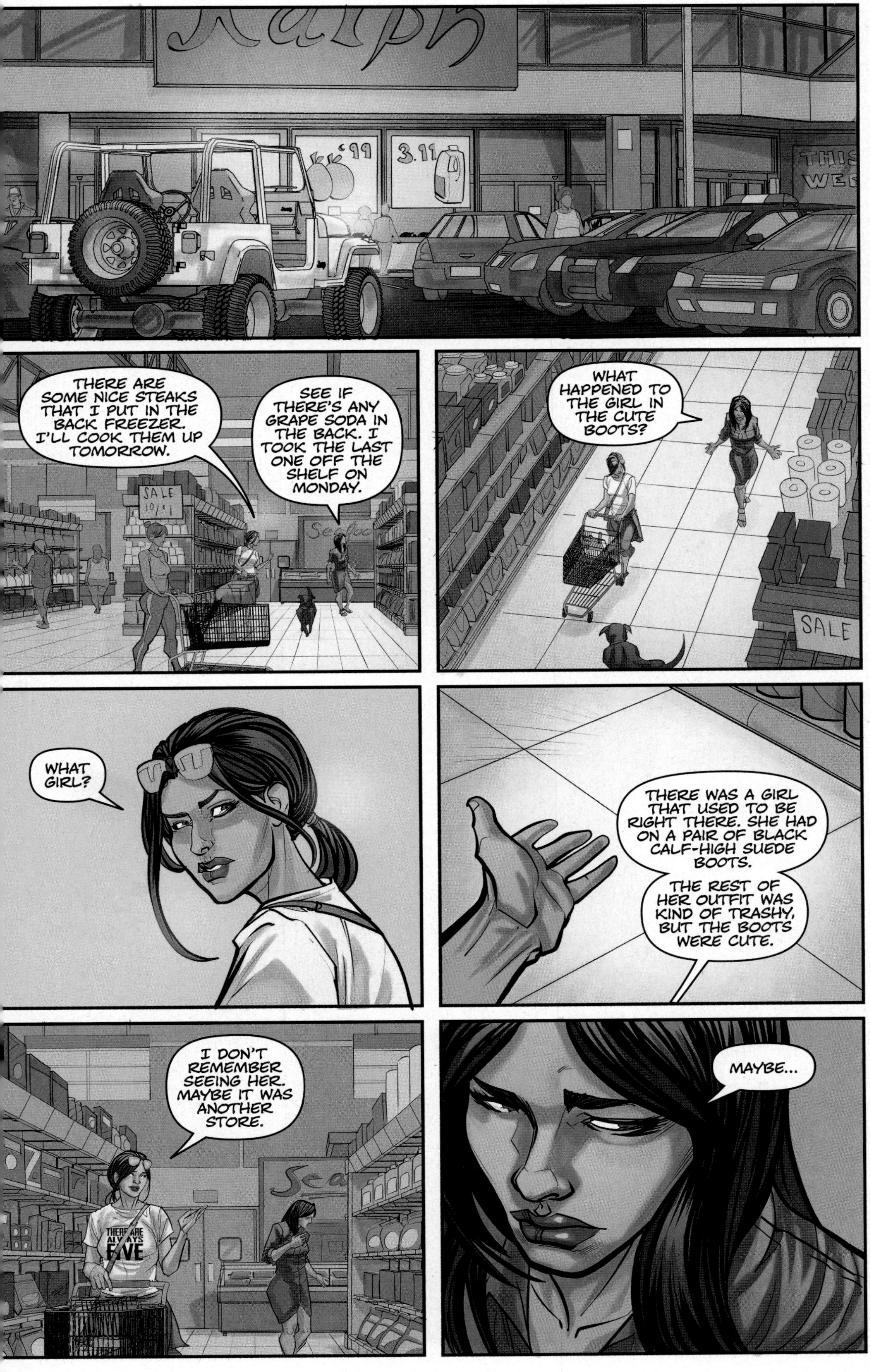
Ralph
'99
3.11
THIS WE
THERE ARE SOME NICE STEAKS THAT I PUT IN THE BACK FREEZER. I'LL COOK THEM UP TOMORROW.
SEE IF THERE'S ANY GRAPE SODA IN THE BACK. I TOOK THE LAST ONE OFF THE SHELF ON MONDAY.
SALE
WHAT HAPPENED TO THE GIRL IN THE CUTE BOOTS?
SALE
WHAT GIRL?
THERE WAS A GIRL THAT USED TO BE RIGHT THERE. SHE HAD ON A PAIR OF BLACK CALF-HIGH SUEDE BOOTS.
THE REST OF HER OUTFIT WAS KIND OF TRASHY, BUT THE BOOTS WERE CUTE.
I DON'T REMEMBER SEEING HER. MAYBE IT WAS ANOTHER STORE.
THERE ARE ALWAYS FIVE
MAYBE...

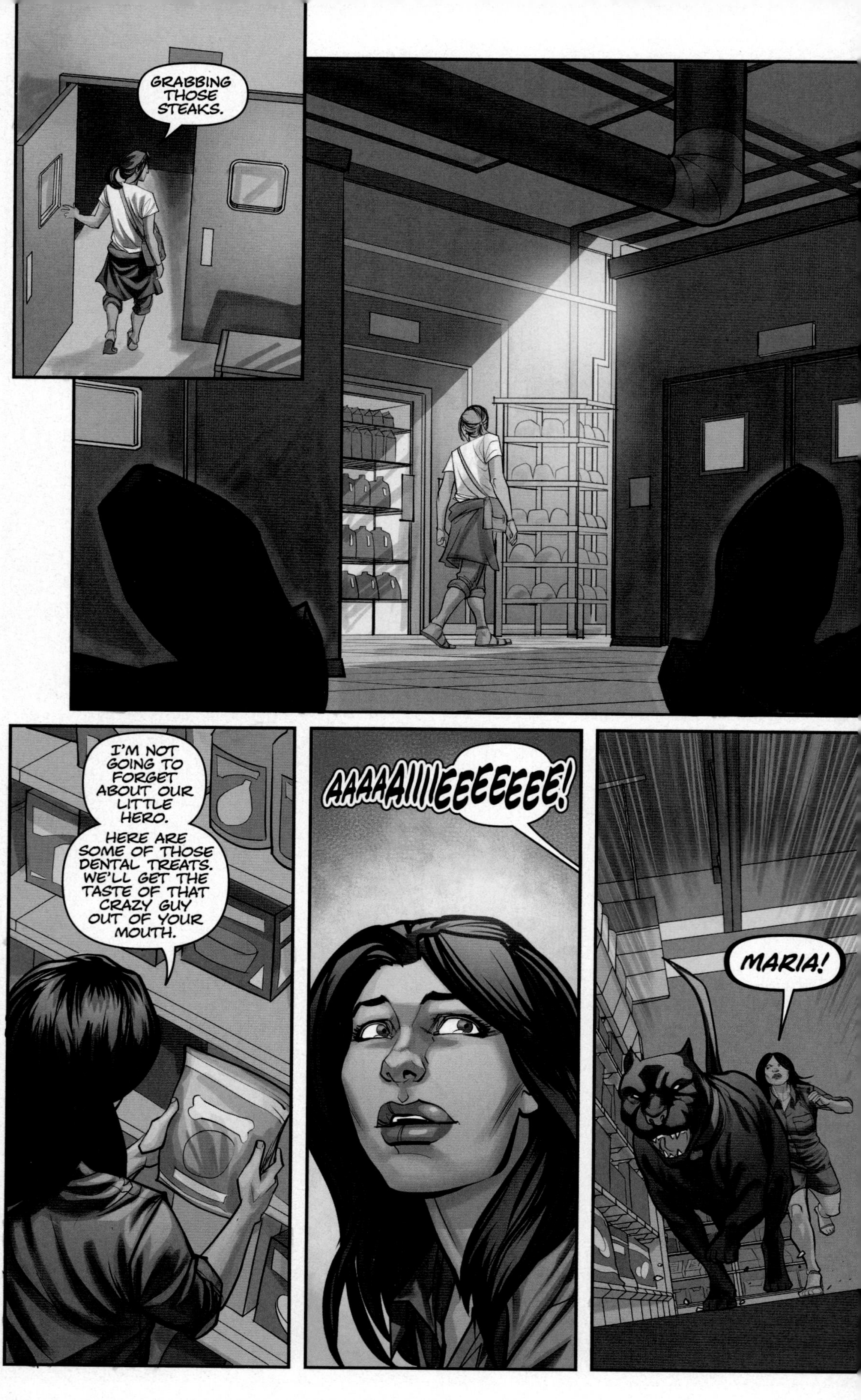
GRABBING THOSE STEAKS.
I'M NOT GOING TO FORGET ABOUT OUR LITTLE HERO.
HERE ARE SOME OF THOSE DENTAL TREATS. WE'LL GET THE TASTE OF THAT CRAZY GUY OUT OF YOUR MOUTH.
AAAAAIIIIEEEEEEE!
MARIA!

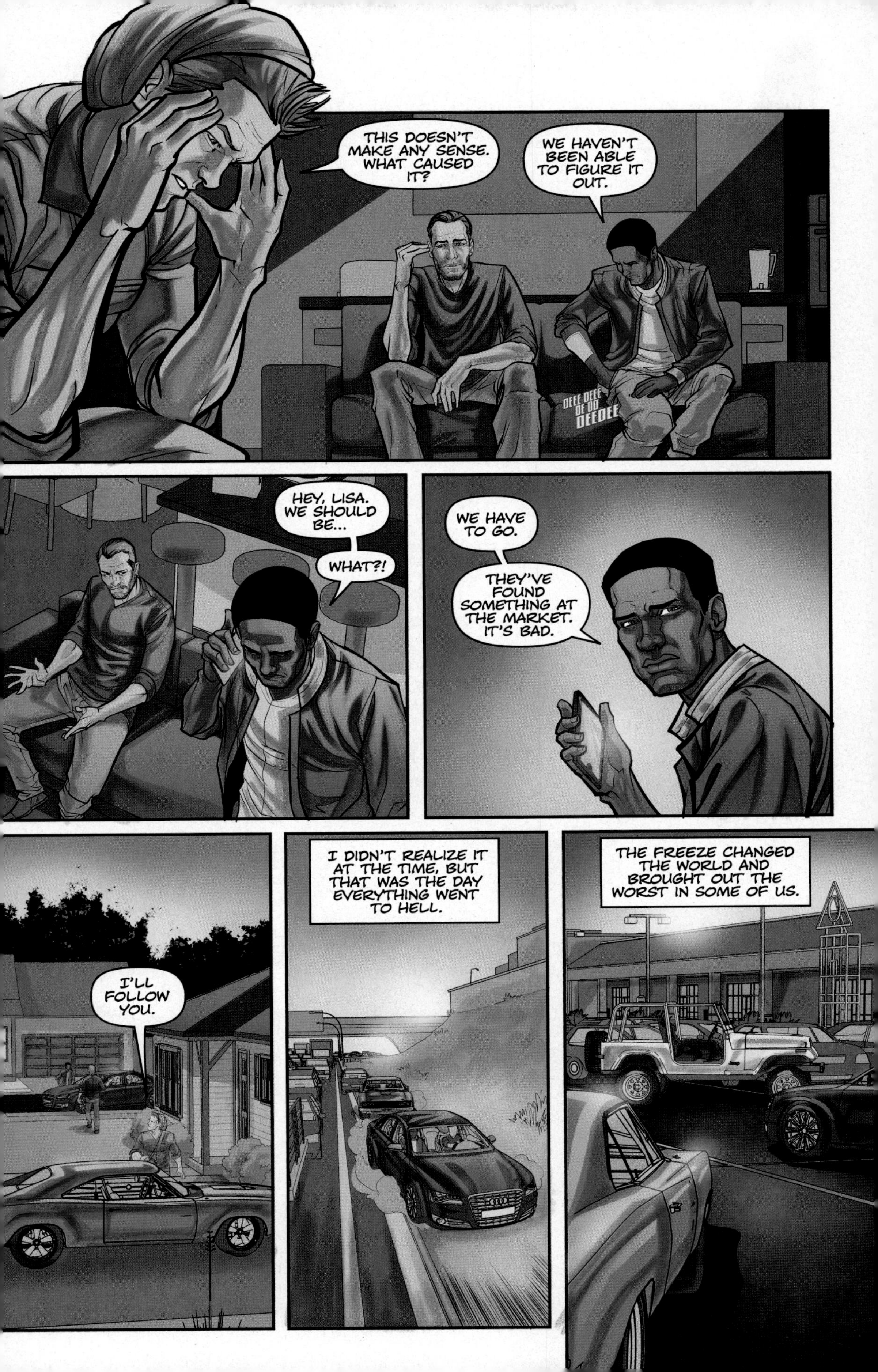
THIS DOESN'T MAKE ANY SENSE. WHAT CAUSED IT?
WE HAVEN'T BEEN ABLE TO FIGURE IT OUT.
DEEE DEEE DE DO DEEDEE
HEY, LISA. WE SHOULD BE...
WHAT?!
WE HAVE TO GO.
THEY'VE FOUND SOMETHING AT THE MARKET. IT'S BAD.
I'LL FOLLOW YOU.
I DIDN'T REALIZE IT AT THE TIME, BUT THAT WAS THE DAY EVERYTHING WENT TO HELL.
THE FREEZE CHANGED THE WORLD AND BROUGHT OUT THE WORST IN SOME OF US.

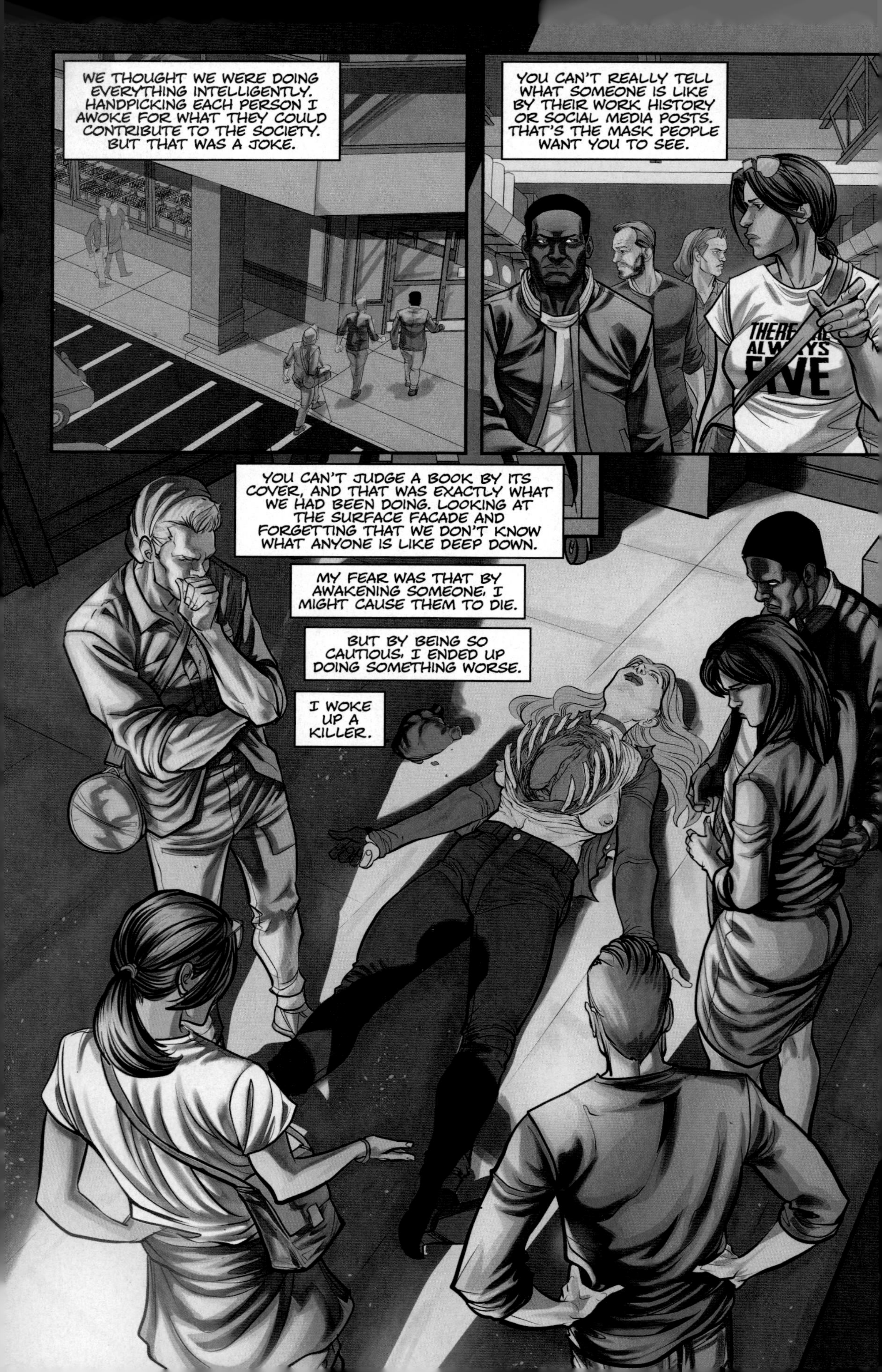
WE THOUGHT WE WERE DOING EVERYTHING INTELLIGENTLY. HANDPICKING EACH PERSON I AWOKE FOR WHAT THEY COULD CONTRIBUTE TO THE SOCIETY. BUT THAT WAS A JOKE.
YOU CAN'T REALLY TELL WHAT SOMEONE IS LIKE BY THEIR WORK HISTORY OR SOCIAL MEDIA POSTS. THAT'S THE MASK PEOPLE WANT YOU TO SEE.
YOU CAN'T JUDGE A BOOK BY ITS COVER, AND THAT WAS EXACTLY WHAT WE HAD BEEN DOING. LOOKING AT THE SURFACE FACADE AND FORGETTING THAT WE DON'T KNOW WHAT ANYONE IS LIKE DEEP DOWN.
MY FEAR WAS THAT BY AWAKENING SOMEONE, I MIGHT CAUSE THEM TO DIE.
BUT BY BEING SO CAUTIOUS, I ENDED UP DOING SOMETHING WORSE.
I WOKE UP A KILLER.

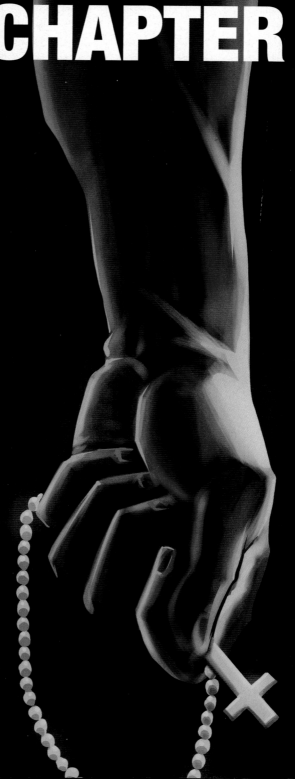

CHAPTER 3

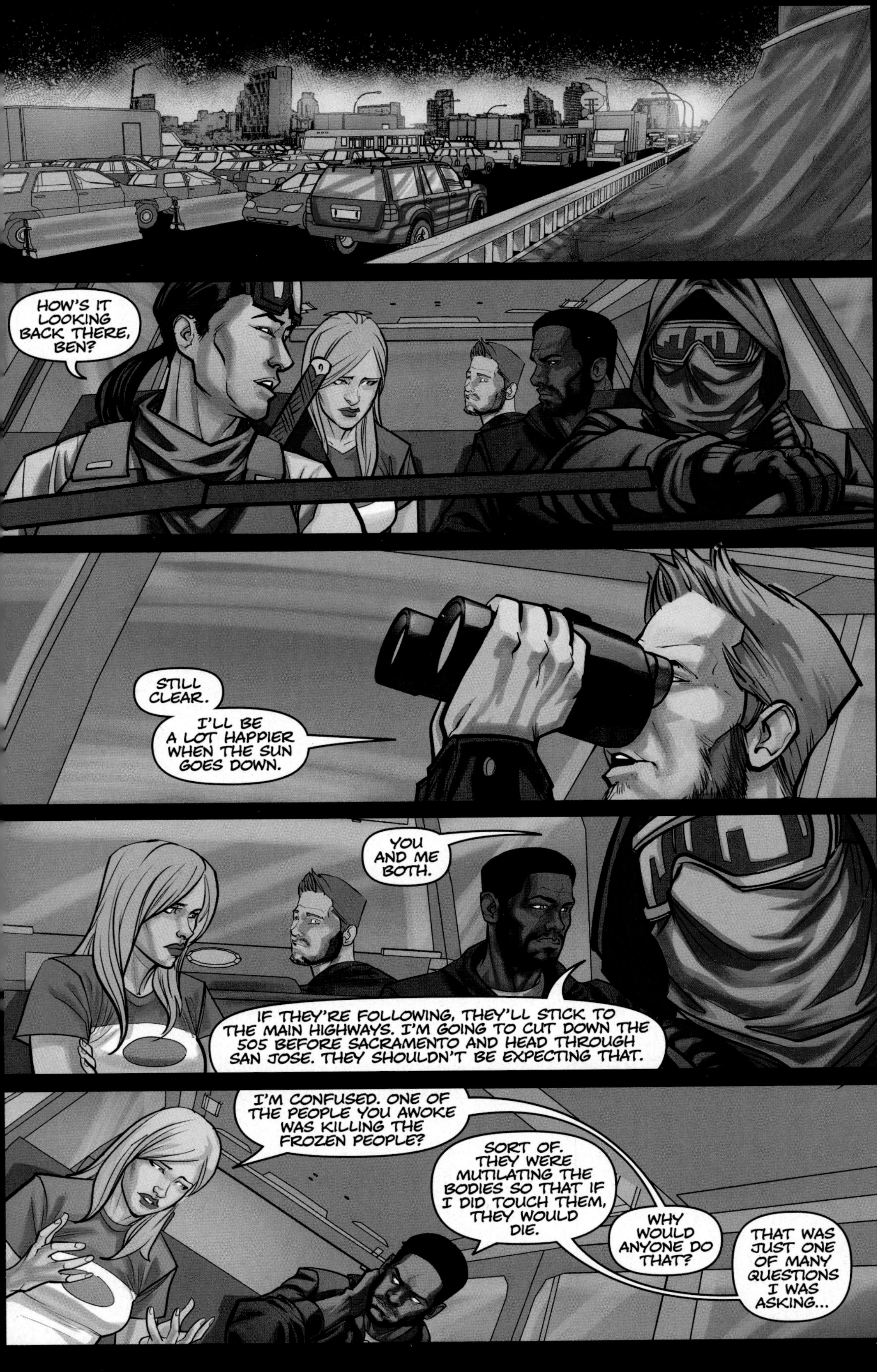
HOW'S IT LOOKING BACK THERE, BEN?
STILL CLEAR.
I'LL BE A LOT HAPPIER WHEN THE SUN GOES DOWN.
YOU AND ME BOTH.
IF THEY'RE FOLLOWING, THEY'LL STICK TO THE MAIN HIGHWAYS. I'M GOING TO CUT DOWN THE 505 BEFORE SACRAMENTO AND HEAD THROUGH SAN JOSE. THEY SHOULDN'T BE EXPECTING THAT.
I'M CONFUSED. ONE OF THE PEOPLE YOU AWOKE WAS KILLING THE FROZEN PEOPLE?
SORT OF. THEY WERE MUTILATING THE BODIES SO THAT IF I DID TOUCH THEM, THEY WOULD DIE.
WHY WOULD ANYONE DO THAT?
THAT WAS JUST ONE OF MANY QUESTIONS I WAS ASKING...

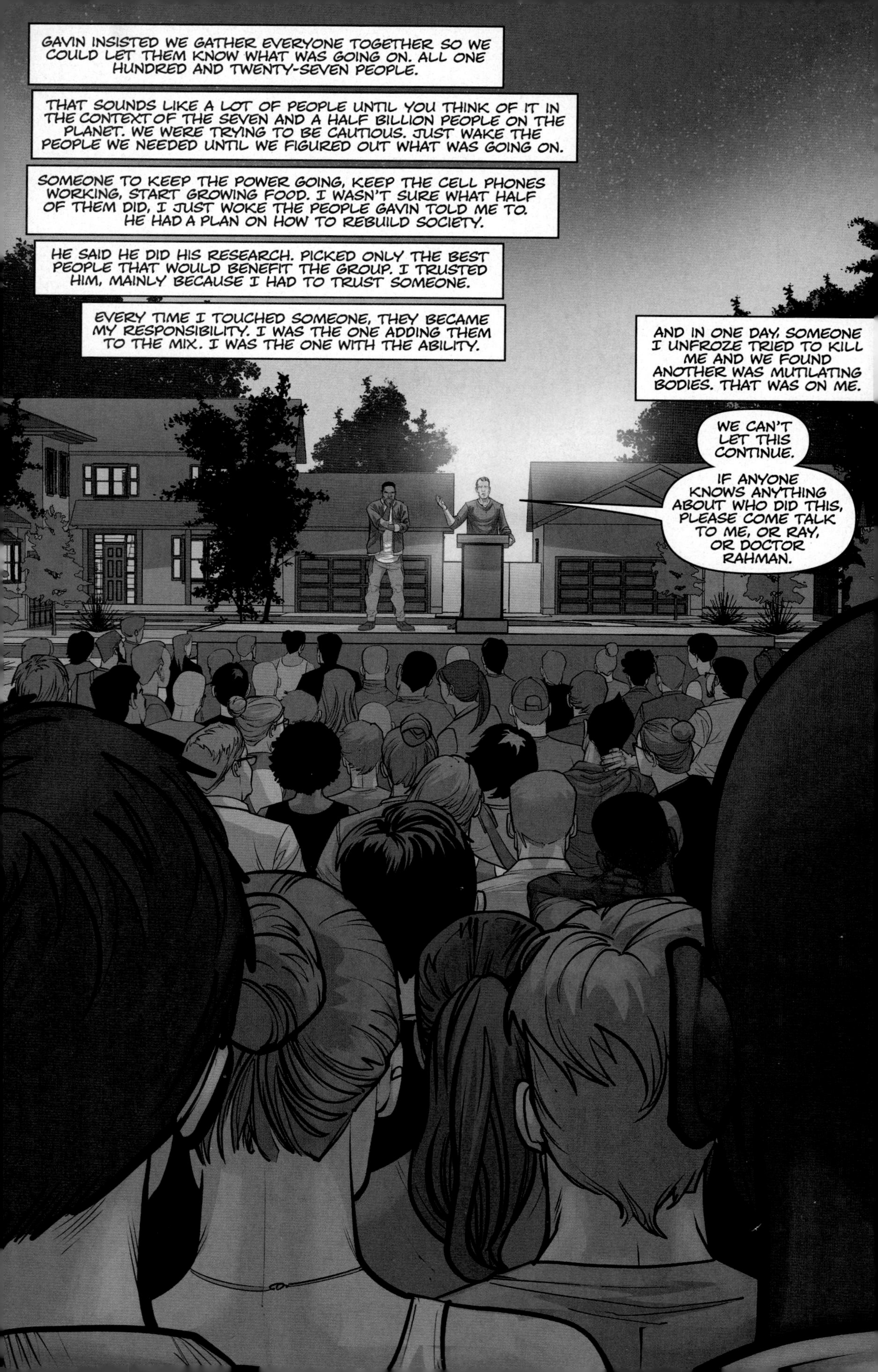
GAVIN INSISTED WE GATHER EVERYONE TOGETHER SO WE COULD LET THEM KNOW WHAT WAS GOING ON. ALL ONE HUNDRED AND TWENTY-SEVEN PEOPLE.
THAT SOUNDS LIKE A LOT OF PEOPLE UNTIL YOU THINK OF IT IN THE CONTEXT OF THE SEVEN AND A HALF BILLION PEOPLE ON THE PLANET. WE WERE TRYING TO BE CAUTIOUS. JUST WAKE THE PEOPLE WE NEEDED UNTIL WE FIGURED OUT WHAT WAS GOING ON.
SOMEONE TO KEEP THE POWER GOING, KEEP THE CELL PHONES WORKING, START GROWING FOOD. I WASN'T SURE WHAT HALF OF THEM DID, I JUST WOKE THE PEOPLE GAVIN TOLD ME TO. HE HAD A PLAN ON HOW TO REBUILD SOCIETY.
HE SAID HE DID HIS RESEARCH. PICKED ONLY THE BEST PEOPLE THAT WOULD BENEFIT THE GROUP. I TRUSTED HIM, MAINLY BECAUSE I HAD TO TRUST SOMEONE.
EVERY TIME I TOUCHED SOMEONE, THEY BECAME MY RESPONSIBILITY. I WAS THE ONE ADDING THEM TO THE MIX. I WAS THE ONE WITH THE ABILITY.
AND IN ONE DAY, SOMEONE I UNFROZE TRIED TO KILL ME AND WE FOUND ANOTHER WAS MUTILATING BODIES. THAT WAS ON ME.
WE CAN'T LET THIS CONTINUE.
IF ANYONE KNOWS ANYTHING ABOUT WHO DID THIS, PLEASE COME TALK TO ME, OR RAY, OR DOCTOR RAHMAN.

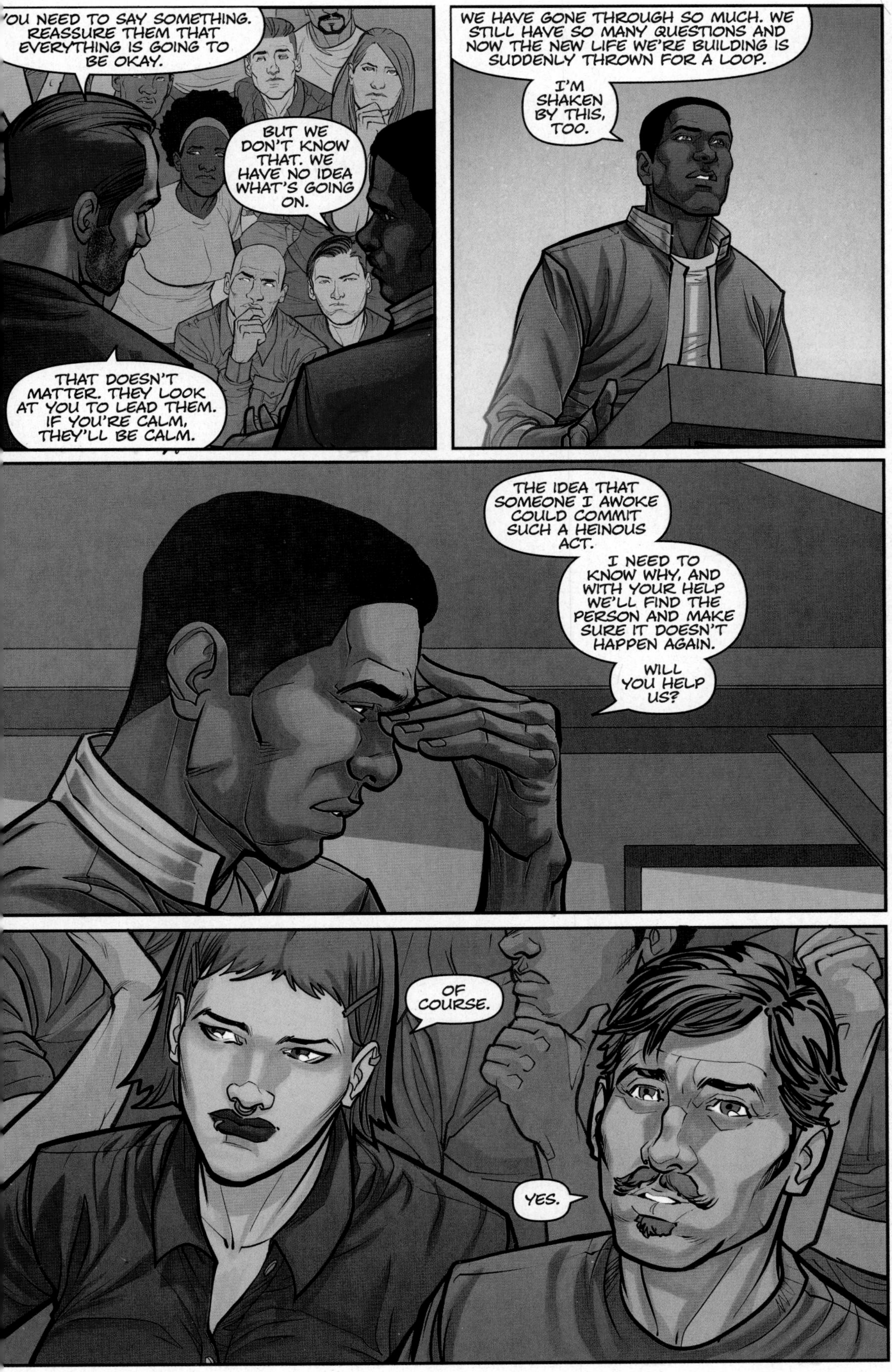
YOU NEED TO SAY SOMETHING. REASSURE THEM THAT EVERYTHING IS GOING TO BE OKAY.
BUT WE DON'T KNOW THAT. WE HAVE NO IDEA WHAT'S GOING ON.
THAT DOESN'T MATTER. THEY LOOK AT YOU TO LEAD THEM. IF YOU'RE CALM, THEY'LL BE CALM.
WE HAVE GONE THROUGH SO MUCH. WE STILL HAVE SO MANY QUESTIONS AND NOW THE NEW LIFE WE'RE BUILDING IS SUDDENLY THROWN FOR A LOOP.
I'M SHAKEN BY THIS, TOO.
THE IDEA THAT SOMEONE I AWOKE COULD COMMIT SUCH A HEINOUS ACT.
I NEED TO KNOW WHY, AND WITH YOUR HELP WE'LL FIND THE PERSON AND MAKE SURE IT DOESN'T HAPPEN AGAIN.
WILL YOU HELP US?
OF COURSE.
YES.

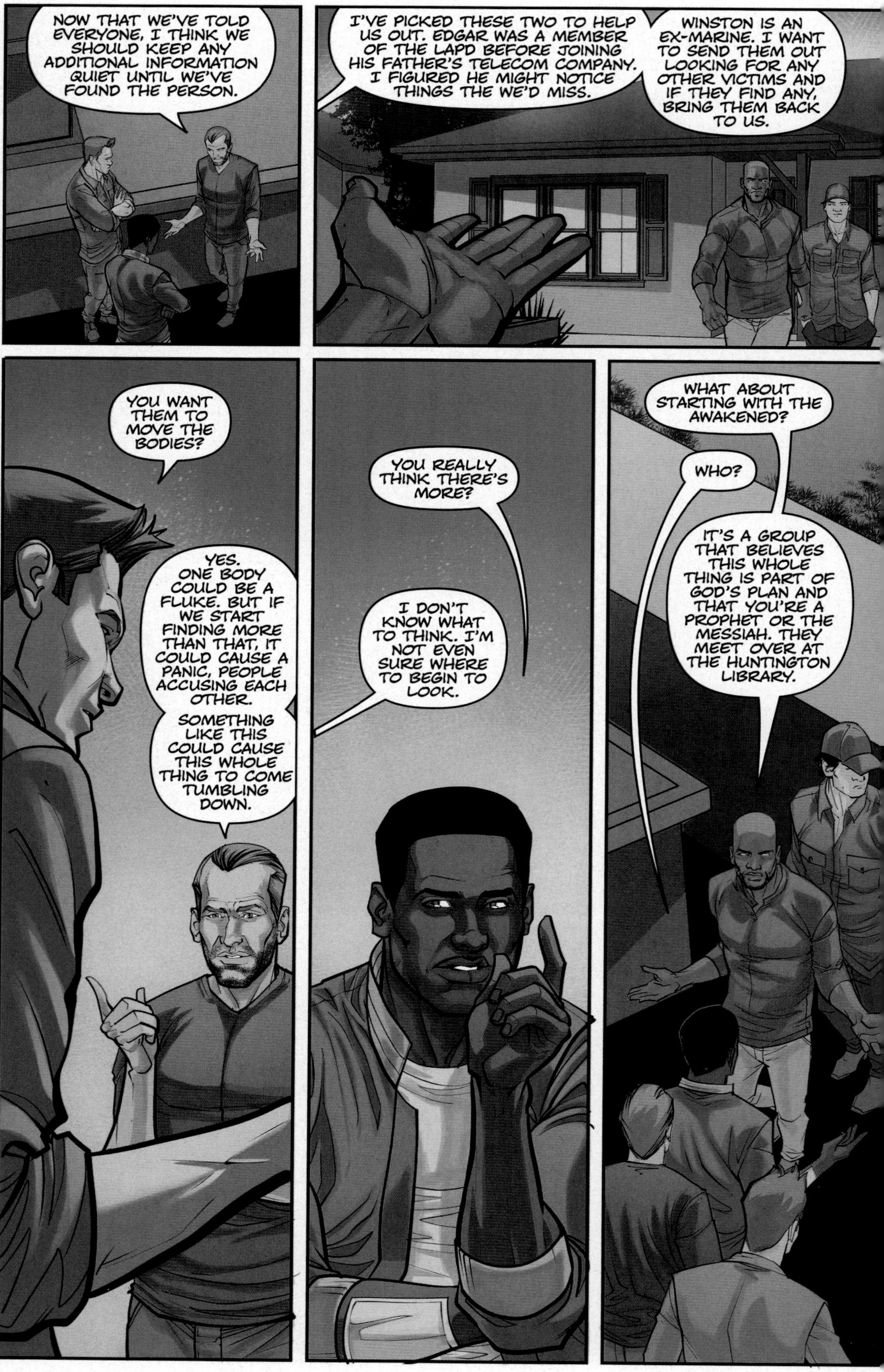
NOW THAT WE'VE TOLD EVERYONE, I THINK WE SHOULD KEEP ANY ADDITIONAL INFORMATION QUIET UNTIL WE'VE FOUND THE PERSON.
I'VE PICKED THESE TWO TO HELP US OUT. EDGAR WAS A MEMBER OF THE LAPD BEFORE JOINING HIS FATHER'S TELECOM COMPANY. I FIGURED HE MIGHT NOTICE THINGS THE WE'D MISS.
WINSTON IS AN EX-MARINE. I WANT TO SEND THEM OUT LOOKING FOR ANY OTHER VICTIMS AND IF THEY FIND ANY, BRING THEM BACK TO US.
YOU WANT THEM TO MOVE THE BODIES?
YES. ONE BODY COULD BE A FLUKE. BUT IF WE START FINDING MORE THAN THAT, IT COULD CAUSE A PANIC, PEOPLE ACCUSING EACH OTHER.
SOMETHING LIKE THIS COULD CAUSE THIS WHOLE THING TO COME TUMBLING DOWN.
YOU REALLY THINK THERE'S MORE?
I DON'T KNOW WHAT TO THINK. I'M NOT EVEN SURE WHERE TO BEGIN TO LOOK.
WHAT ABOUT STARTING WITH THE AWAKENED?
WHO?
IT'S A GROUP THAT BELIEVES THIS WHOLE THING IS PART OF GOD'S PLAN AND THAT YOU'RE A PROPHET OR THE MESSIAH. THEY MEET OVER AT THE HUNTINGTON LIBRARY.

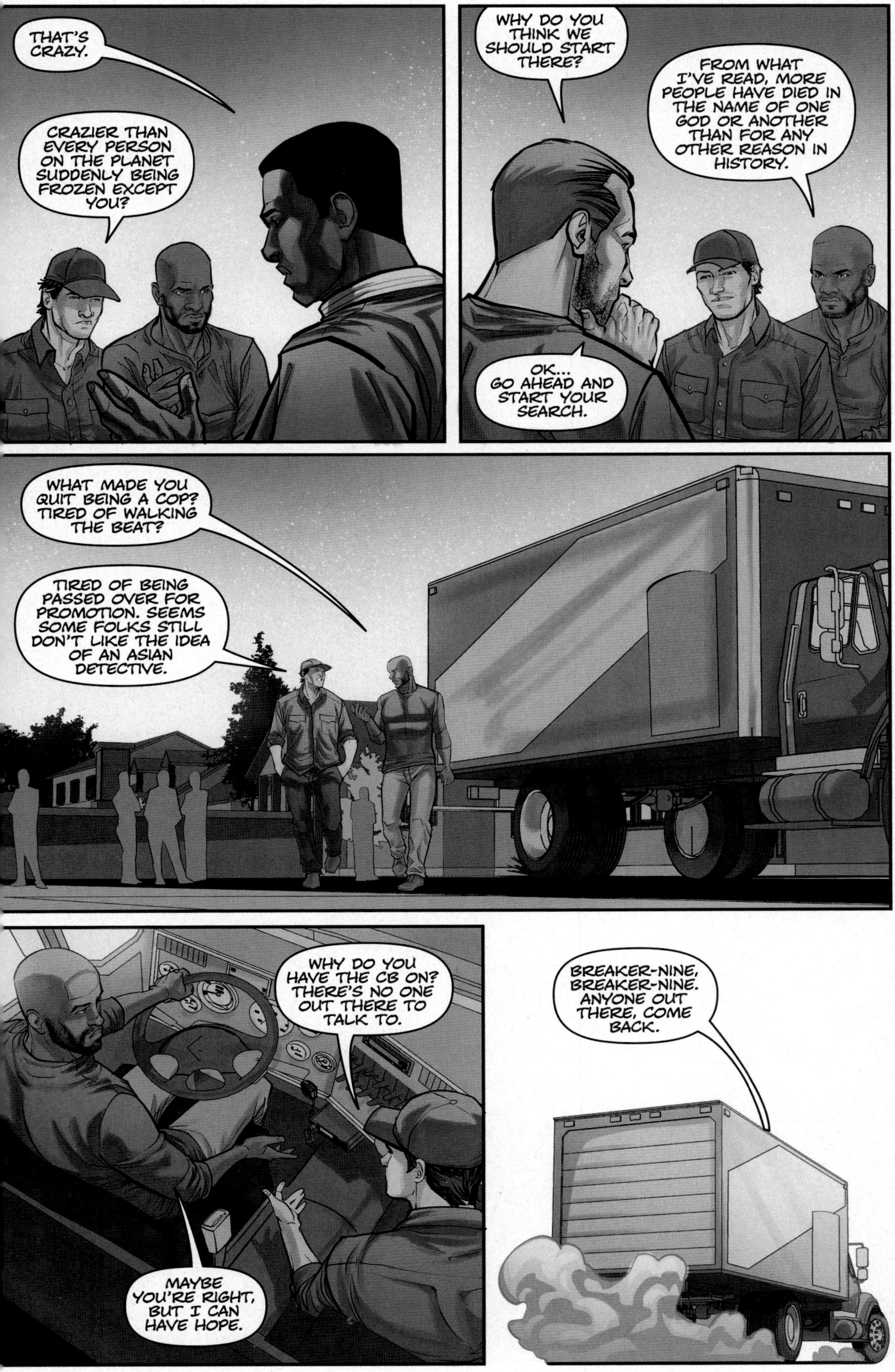
THAT'S CRAZY.
CRAZIER THAN EVERY PERSON ON THE PLANET SUDDENLY BEING FROZEN EXCEPT YOU?
WHY DO YOU THINK WE SHOULD START THERE?
FROM WHAT I'VE READ, MORE PEOPLE HAVE DIED IN THE NAME OF ONE GOD OR ANOTHER THAN FOR ANY OTHER REASON IN HISTORY.
OK... GO AHEAD AND START YOUR SEARCH.
WHAT MADE YOU QUIT BEING A COP? TIRED OF WALKING THE BEAT?
TIRED OF BEING PASSED OVER FOR PROMOTION. SEEMS SOME FOLKS STILL DON'T LIKE THE IDEA OF AN ASIAN DETECTIVE.
WHY DO YOU HAVE THE CB ON? THERE'S NO ONE OUT THERE TO TALK TO.
MAYBE YOU'RE RIGHT, BUT I CAN HAVE HOPE.
BREAKER-NINE, BREAKER-NINE. ANYONE OUT THERE, COME BACK.

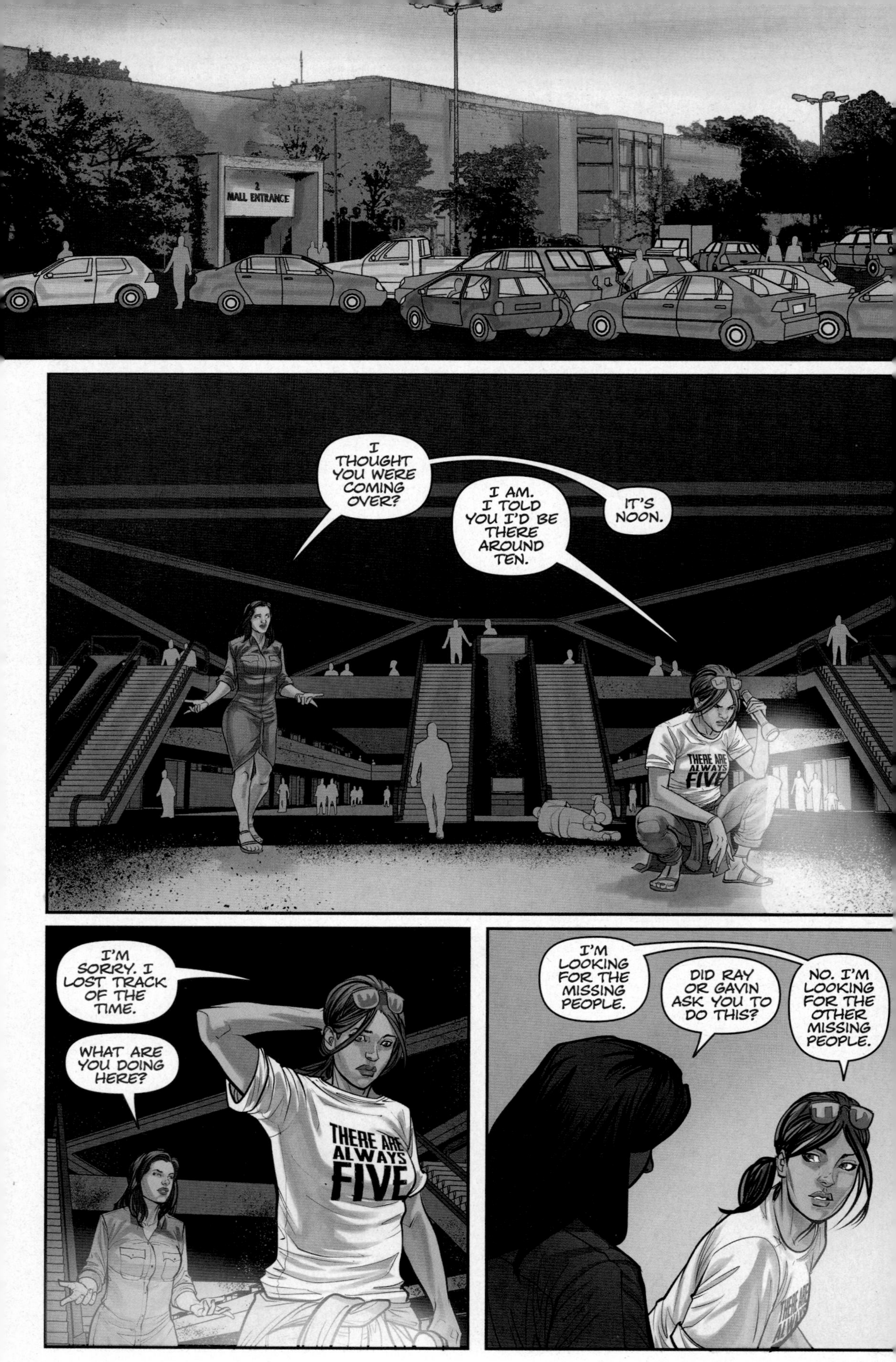

2
MALL ENTRANCE
I THOUGHT YOU WERE COMING OVER?
I AM. I TOLD YOU I'D BE THERE AROUND TEN.
IT'S NOON.
THERE ARE ALWAYS FIVE
I'M SORRY. I LOST TRACK OF THE TIME.
WHAT ARE YOU DOING HERE?
THERE ARE ALWAYS FIVE
I'M LOOKING FOR THE MISSING PEOPLE.
DID RAY OR GAVIN ASK YOU TO DO THIS?
NO. I'M LOOKING FOR THE OTHER MISSING PEOPLE.

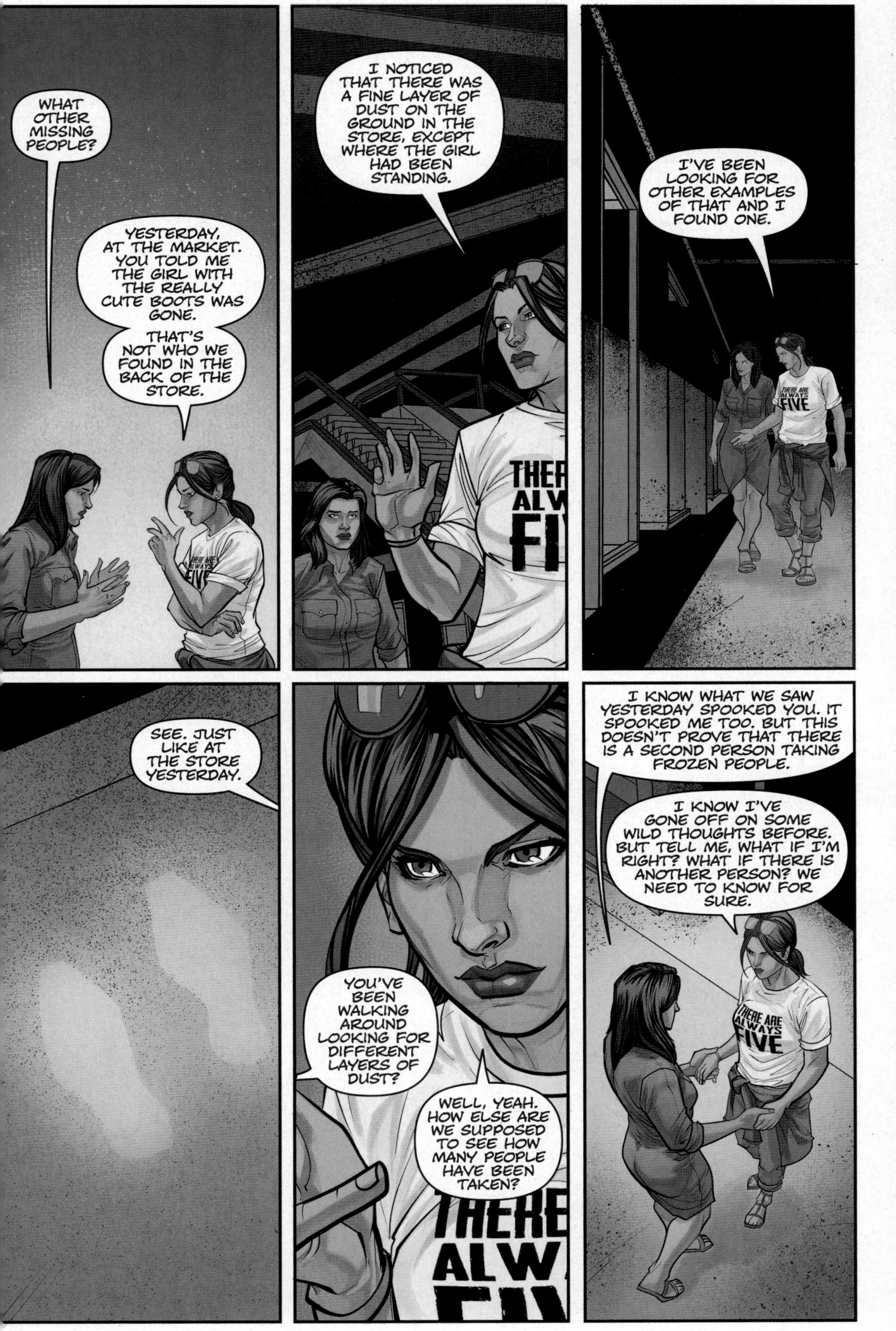
WHAT OTHER MISSING PEOPLE?
YESTERDAY, AT THE MARKET. YOU TOLD ME THE GIRL WITH THE REALLY CUTE BOOTS WAS GONE.
THAT'S NOT WHO WE FOUND IN THE BACK OF THE STORE.
I NOTICED THAT THERE WAS A FINE LAYER OF DUST ON THE GROUND IN THE STORE, EXCEPT WHERE THE GIRL HAD BEEN STANDING.
THERE ARE ALWAYS FIVE
I'VE BEEN LOOKING FOR OTHER EXAMPLES OF THAT AND I FOUND ONE.
SEE. JUST LIKE AT THE STORE YESTERDAY.
YOU'VE BEEN WALKING AROUND LOOKING FOR DIFFERENT LAYERS OF DUST?
WELL, YEAH. HOW ELSE ARE WE SUPPOSED TO SEE HOW MANY PEOPLE HAVE BEEN TAKEN?
I KNOW WHAT WE SAW YESTERDAY SPOOKED YOU. IT SPOOKED ME TOO. BUT THIS DOESN'T PROVE THAT THERE IS A SECOND PERSON TAKING FROZEN PEOPLE.
I KNOW I'VE GONE OFF ON SOME WILD THOUGHTS BEFORE. BUT TELL ME, WHAT IF I'M RIGHT? WHAT IF THERE IS ANOTHER PERSON? WE NEED TO KNOW FOR SURE.
THERE ARE ALWAYS FIVE

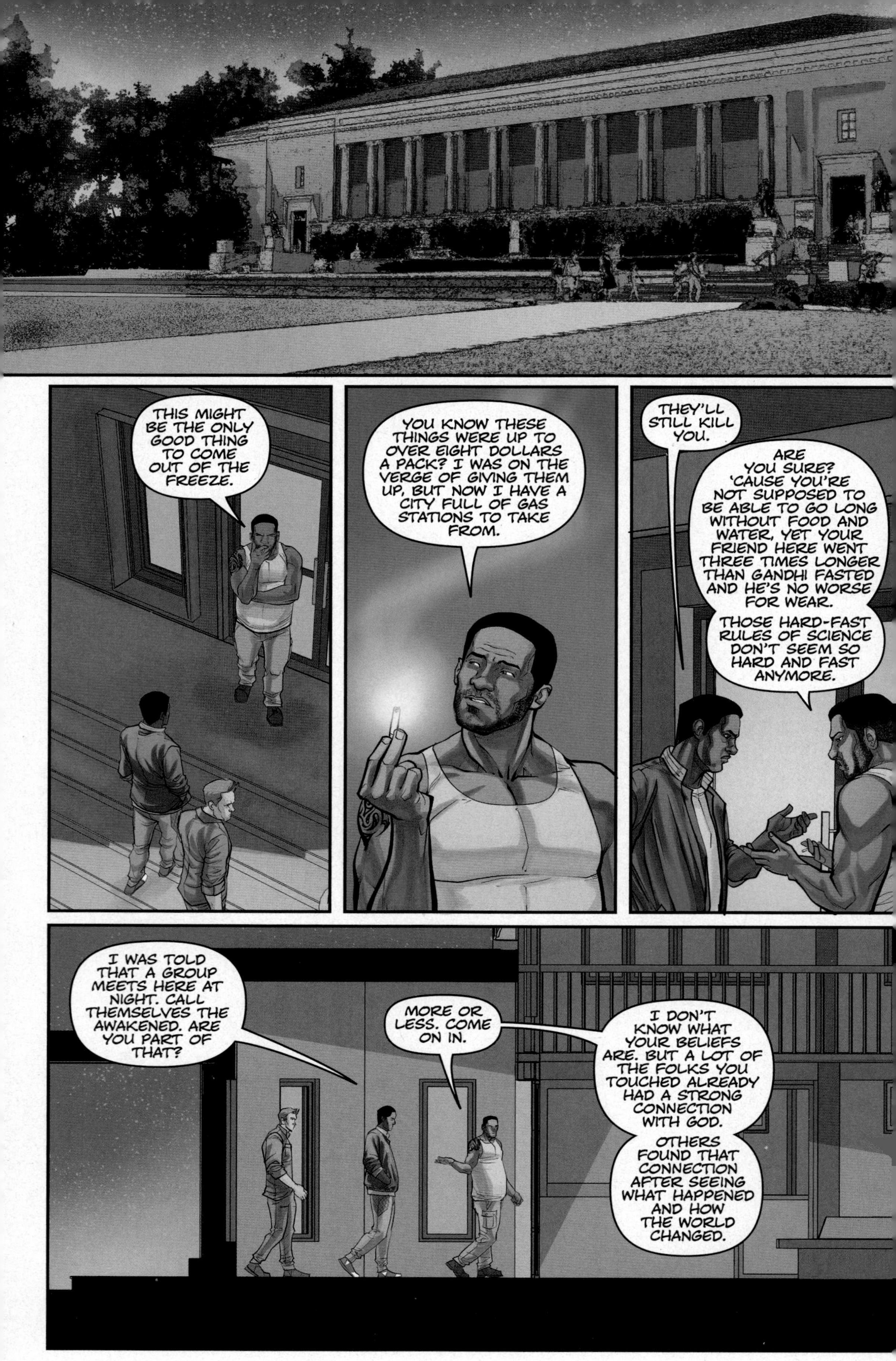
THIS MIGHT BE THE ONLY GOOD THING TO COME OUT OF THE FREEZE.
YOU KNOW THESE THINGS WERE UP TO OVER EIGHT DOLLARS A PACK? I WAS ON THE VERGE OF GIVING THEM UP, BUT NOW I HAVE A CITY FULL OF GAS STATIONS TO TAKE FROM.
THEY'LL STILL KILL YOU.
ARE YOU SURE? 'CAUSE YOU'RE NOT SUPPOSED TO BE ABLE TO GO LONG WITHOUT FOOD AND WATER, YET YOUR FRIEND HERE WENT THREE TIMES LONGER THAN GANDHI FASTED AND HE'S NO WORSE FOR WEAR.
THOSE HARD-FAST RULES OF SCIENCE DON'T SEEM SO HARD AND FAST ANYMORE.
I WAS TOLD THAT A GROUP MEETS HERE AT NIGHT. CALL THEMSELVES THE AWAKENED. ARE YOU PART OF THAT?
MORE OR LESS. COME ON IN.
I DON'T KNOW WHAT YOUR BELIEFS ARE. BUT A LOT OF THE FOLKS YOU TOUCHED ALREADY HAD A STRONG CONNECTION WITH GOD.
OTHERS FOUND THAT CONNECTION AFTER SEEING WHAT HAPPENED AND HOW THE WORLD CHANGED.

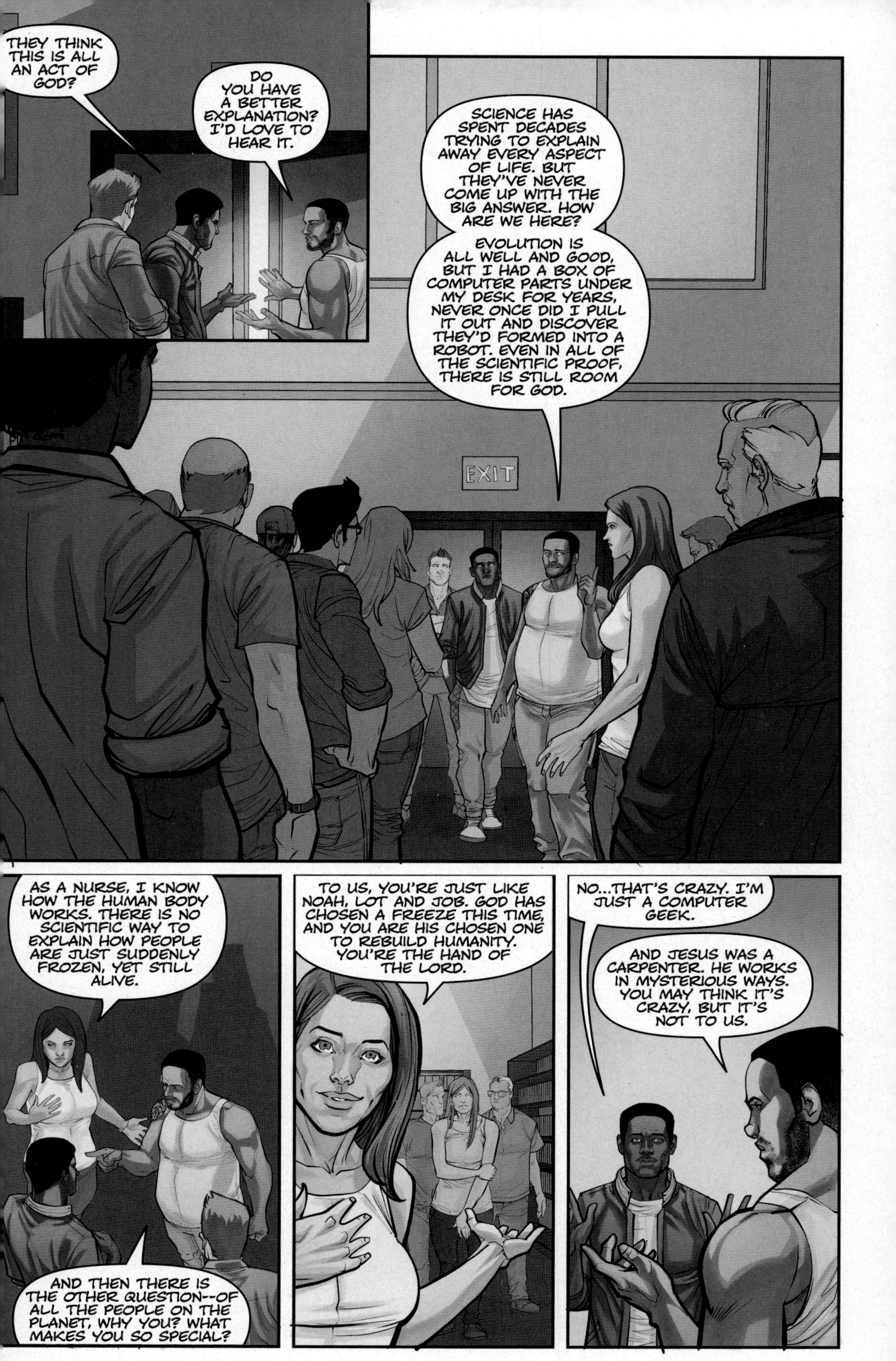
THEY THINK THIS IS ALL AN ACT OF GOD?
DO YOU HAVE A BETTER EXPLANATION? I'D LOVE TO HEAR IT.
SCIENCE HAS SPENT DECADES TRYING TO EXPLAIN AWAY EVERY ASPECT OF LIFE. BUT THEY'VE NEVER COME UP WITH THE BIG ANSWER. HOW ARE WE HERE?
EVOLUTION IS ALL WELL AND GOOD, BUT I HAD A BOX OF COMPUTER PARTS UNDER MY DESK FOR YEARS, NEVER ONCE DID I PULL IT OUT AND DISCOVER THEY'D FORMED INTO A ROBOT. EVEN IN ALL OF THE SCIENTIFIC PROOF, THERE IS STILL ROOM FOR GOD.
EXIT
AS A NURSE, I KNOW HOW THE HUMAN BODY WORKS. THERE IS NO SCIENTIFIC WAY TO EXPLAIN HOW PEOPLE ARE JUST SUDDENLY FROZEN, YET STILL ALIVE.
AND THEN THERE IS THE OTHER QUESTION--OF ALL THE PEOPLE ON THE PLANET, WHY YOU? WHAT MAKES YOU SO SPECIAL?
TO US, YOU'RE JUST LIKE NOAH, LOT AND JOB. GOD HAS CHOSEN A FREEZE THIS TIME, AND YOU ARE HIS CHOSEN ONE TO REBUILD HUMANITY. YOU'RE THE HAND OF THE LORD.
NO...THAT'S CRAZY. I'M JUST A COMPUTER GEEK.
AND JESUS WAS A CARPENTER. HE WORKS IN MYSTERIOUS WAYS. YOU MAY THINK IT'S CRAZY, BUT IT'S NOT TO US.

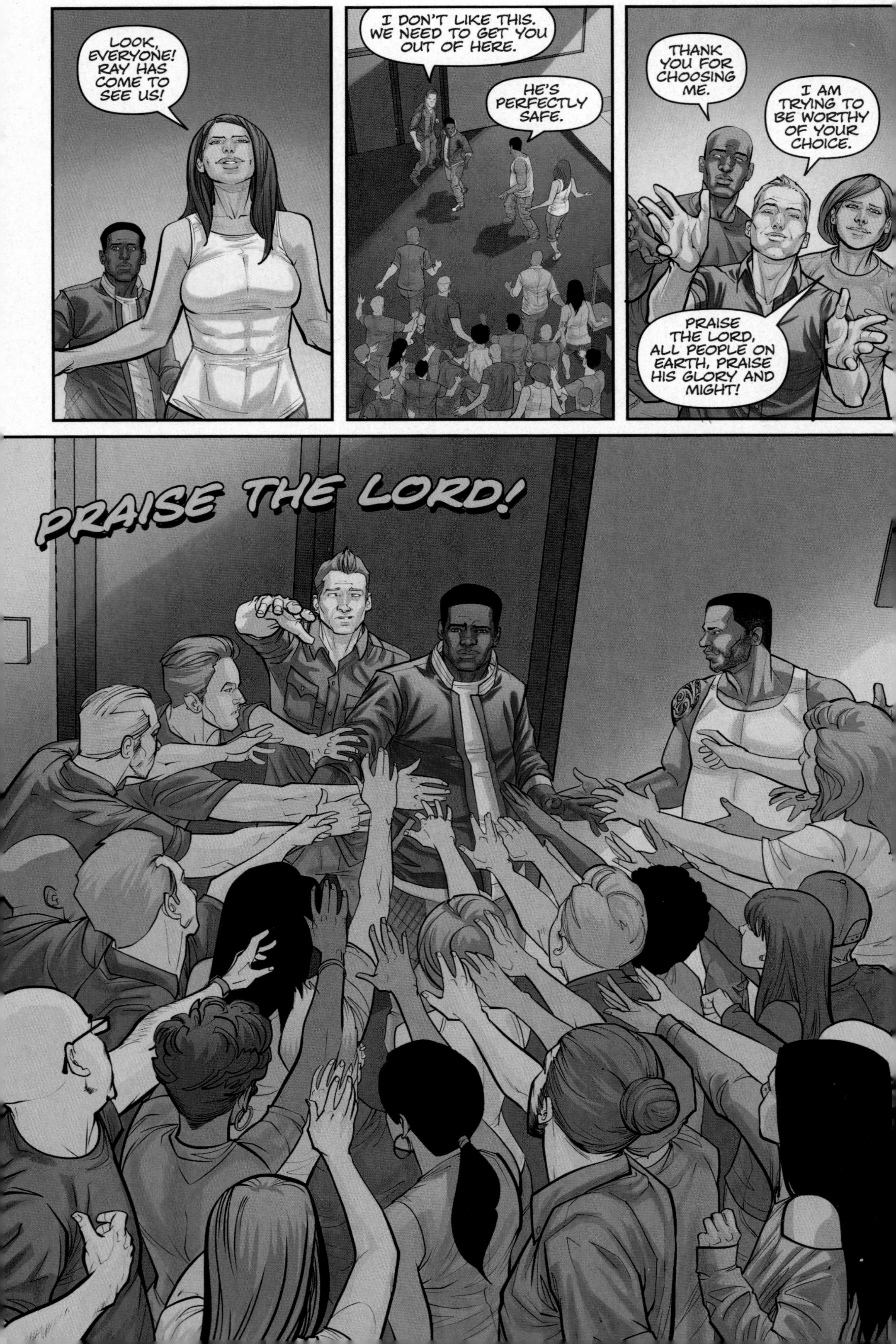
LOOK, EVERYONE! RAY HAS COME TO SEE US!
I DON'T LIKE THIS. WE NEED TO GET YOU OUT OF HERE.
HE'S PERFECTLY SAFE.
THANK YOU FOR CHOOSING ME.
I AM TRYING TO BE WORTHY OF YOUR CHOICE.
PRAISE THE LORD, ALL PEOPLE ON EARTH, PRAISE HIS GLORY AND MIGHT!
PRAISE THE LORD!

TIME TO GO.

THEY WEREN'T GOING TO HURT YOU!

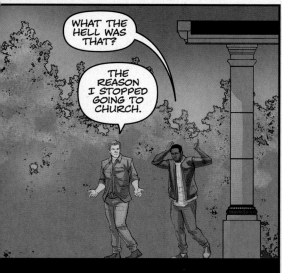

WHAT THE HELL WAS THAT?

THE REASON I STOPPED GOING TO CHURCH.

I'M SO SORRY ABOUT THAT.

THEY'VE CALMED DOWN NOW IF YOU'D LIKE TO COME BACK IN.

I DON'T THINK THAT'S A GOOD IDEA.

HE'LL BE PERFECTLY SAFE.

LIKE HE WAS WHEN THE ZEALOT TRIED TO KILL HIM THE OTHER DAY? GO ON BACK TO YOUR BIBLE THUMPING. I'M TAKING RAY HOME.

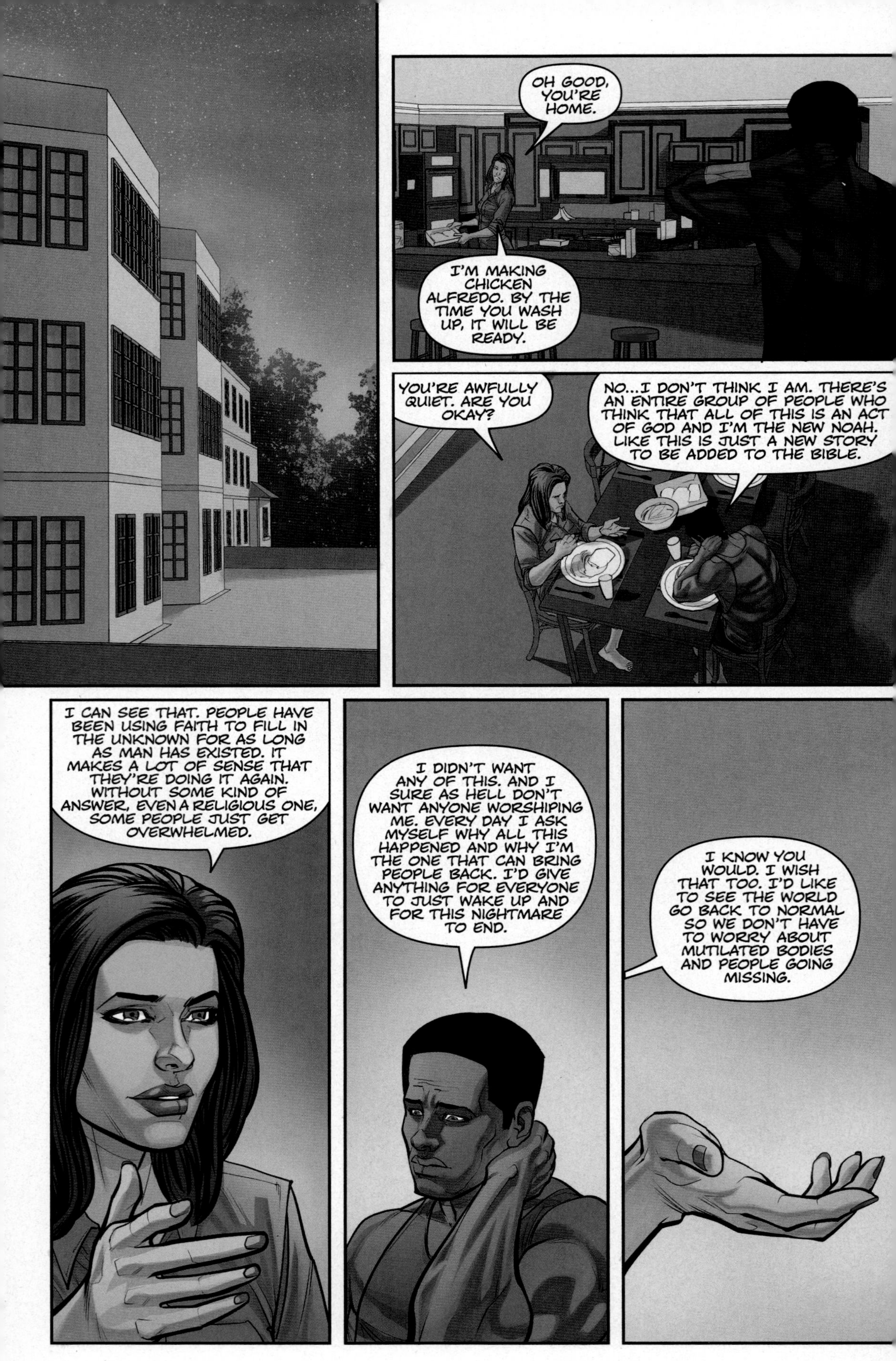
OH GOOD, YOU'RE HOME.
I'M MAKING CHICKEN ALFREDO. BY THE TIME YOU WASH UP, IT WILL BE READY.
YOU'RE AWFULLY QUIET. ARE YOU OKAY?
NO...I DON'T THINK I AM. THERE'S AN ENTIRE GROUP OF PEOPLE WHO THINK THAT ALL OF THIS IS AN ACT OF GOD AND I'M THE NEW NOAH. LIKE THIS IS JUST A NEW STORY TO BE ADDED TO THE BIBLE.
I CAN SEE THAT. PEOPLE HAVE BEEN USING FAITH TO FILL IN THE UNKNOWN FOR AS LONG AS MAN HAS EXISTED. IT MAKES A LOT OF SENSE THAT THEY'RE DOING IT AGAIN. WITHOUT SOME KIND OF ANSWER, EVEN A RELIGIOUS ONE, SOME PEOPLE JUST GET OVERWHELMED.
I DIDN'T WANT ANY OF THIS. AND I SURE AS HELL DON'T WANT ANYONE WORSHIPING ME. EVERY DAY I ASK MYSELF WHY ALL THIS HAPPENED AND WHY I'M THE ONE THAT CAN BRING PEOPLE BACK. I'D GIVE ANYTHING FOR EVERYONE TO JUST WAKE UP AND FOR THIS NIGHTMARE TO END.
I KNOW YOU WOULD. I WISH THAT TOO. I'D LIKE TO SEE THE WORLD GO BACK TO NORMAL SO WE DON'T HAVE TO WORRY ABOUT MUTILATED BODIES AND PEOPLE GOING MISSING.

PEOPLE GOING MISSING?

IT'S MY SISTER'S THEORY. SHE THINKS THAT BESIDES THE BODY WE FOUND, ONE OF THE FROZEN WENT MISSING AND SHE'S NOW GOING AROUND TOWN TRYING TO FIND PROOF OF OTHERS.

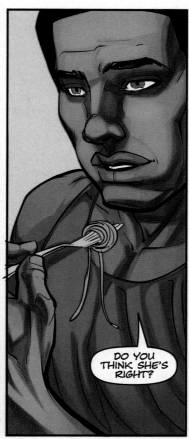

DO YOU THINK SHE'S RIGHT?

I DON'T KNOW. AS A KID SHE WOULD MAKE UP STORIES TO GET ATTENTION. SHE GOT IN TROUBLE A LOT. BUT I CAN'T SEE HER DOING THAT NOW.

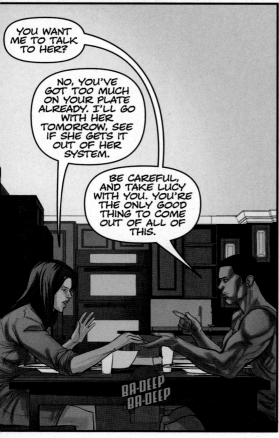

YOU WANT ME TO TALK TO HER?

NO, YOU'VE GOT TOO MUCH ON YOUR PLATE ALREADY. I'LL GO WITH HER TOMORROW, SEE IF SHE GETS IT OUT OF HER SYSTEM.

BE CAREFUL, AND TAKE LUCY WITH YOU. YOU'RE THE ONLY GOOD THING TO COME OUT OF ALL OF THIS.

BA-DEEP BA-DEEP

NO REST FOR THE WICKED.

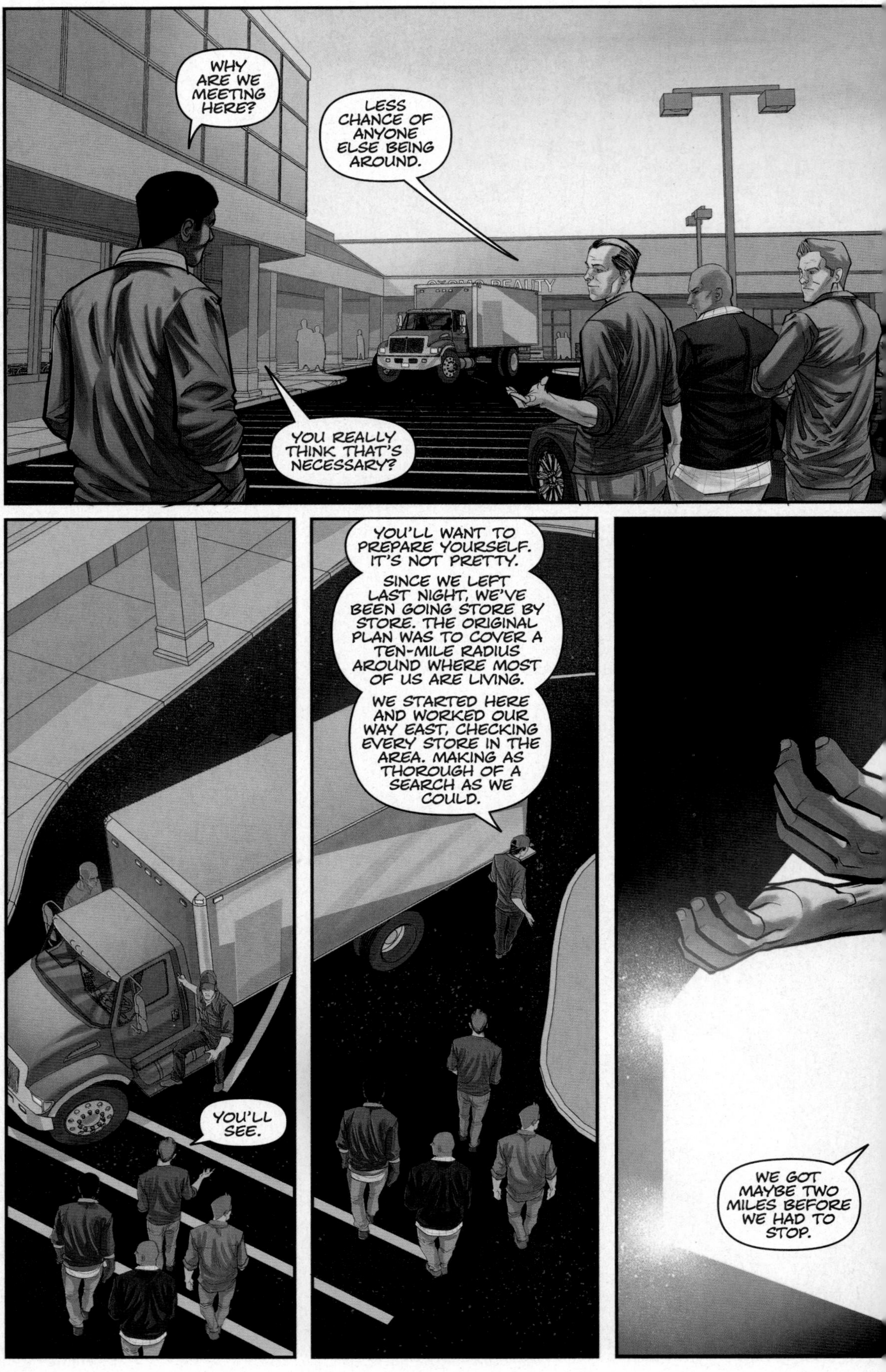
WHY ARE WE MEETING HERE?
LESS CHANCE OF ANYONE ELSE BEING AROUND.
YOU REALLY THINK THAT'S NECESSARY?
YOU'LL SEE.
YOU'LL WANT TO PREPARE YOURSELF. IT'S NOT PRETTY.
SINCE WE LEFT LAST NIGHT, WE'VE BEEN GOING STORE BY STORE. THE ORIGINAL PLAN WAS TO COVER A TEN-MILE RADIUS AROUND WHERE MOST OF US ARE LIVING.
WE STARTED HERE AND WORKED OUR WAY EAST, CHECKING EVERY STORE IN THE AREA. MAKING AS THOROUGH OF A SEARCH AS WE COULD.
WE GOT MAYBE TWO MILES BEFORE WE HAD TO STOP.

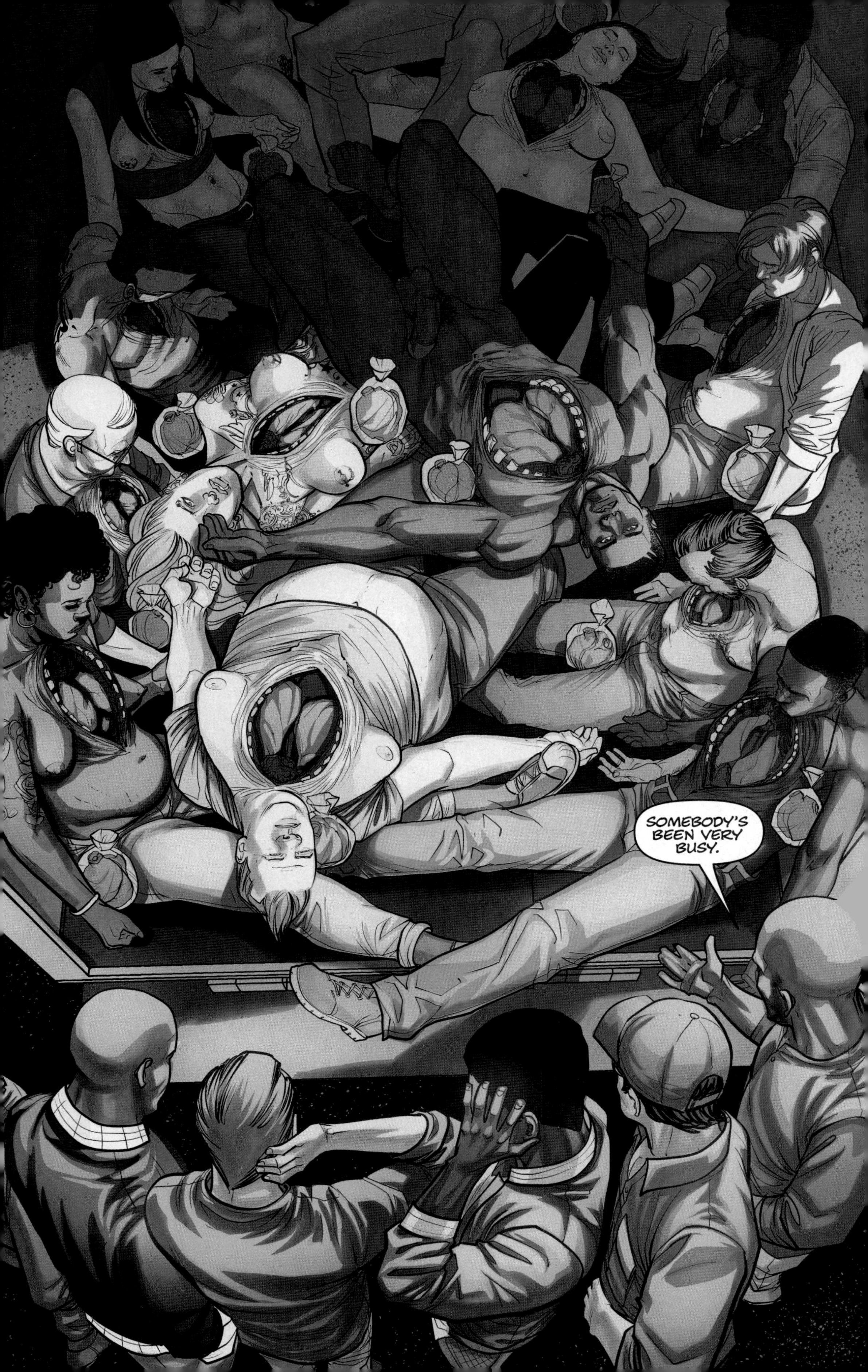
SOMEBODY'S BEEN VERY BUSY.

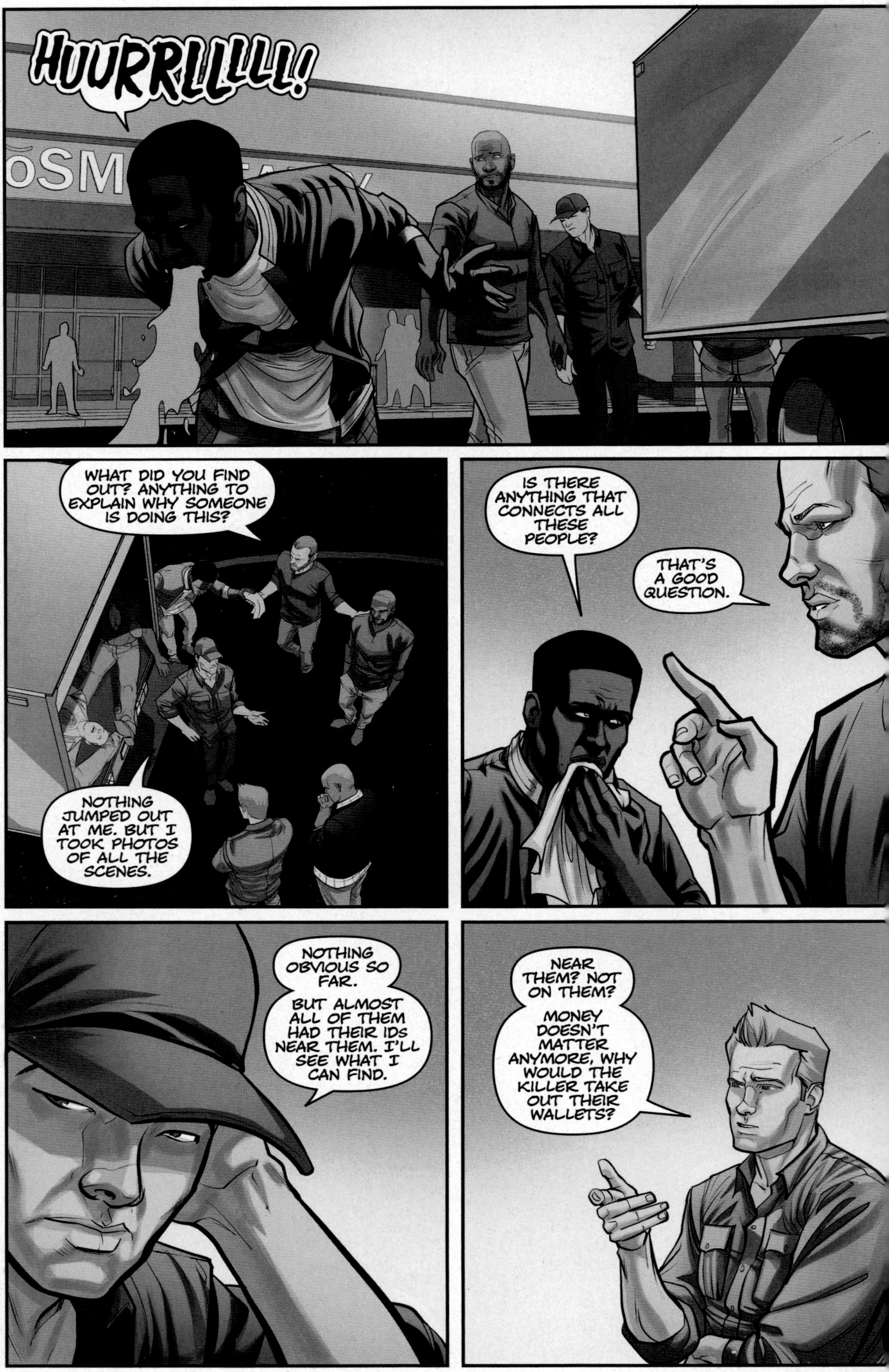
HUURRLLLLL!
WHAT DID YOU FIND OUT? ANYTHING TO EXPLAIN WHY SOMEONE IS DOING THIS?
NOTHING JUMPED OUT AT ME. BUT I TOOK PHOTOS OF ALL THE SCENES.
IS THERE ANYTHING THAT CONNECTS ALL THESE PEOPLE?
THAT'S A GOOD QUESTION.
NOTHING OBVIOUS SO FAR.
BUT ALMOST ALL OF THEM HAD THEIR IDS NEAR THEM. I'LL SEE WHAT I CAN FIND.
NEAR THEM? NOT ON THEM?
MONEY DOESN'T MATTER ANYMORE, WHY WOULD THE KILLER TAKE OUT THEIR WALLETS?

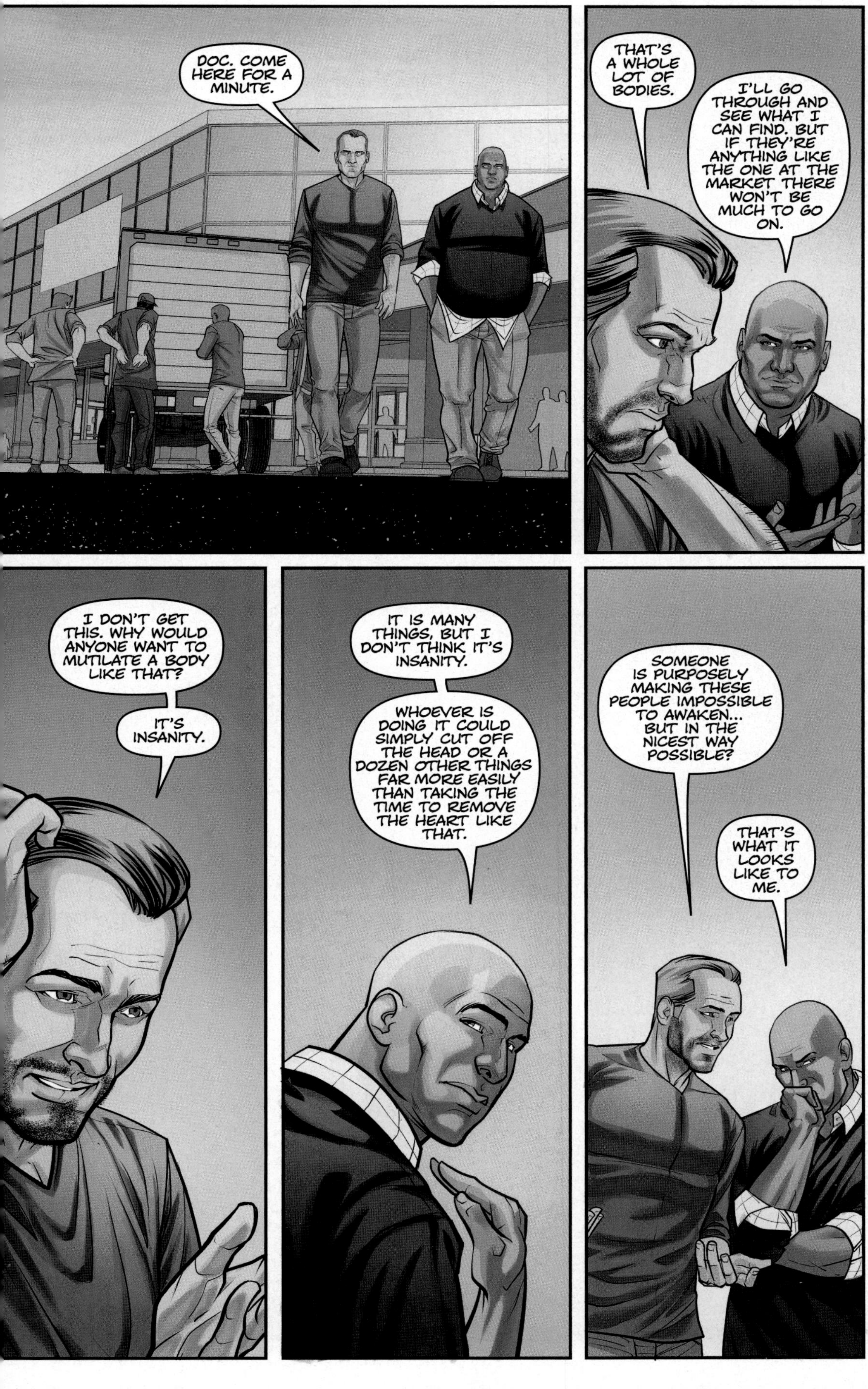
DOC. COME HERE FOR A MINUTE.
THAT'S A WHOLE LOT OF BODIES.
I'LL GO THROUGH AND SEE WHAT I CAN FIND. BUT IF THEY'RE ANYTHING LIKE THE ONE AT THE MARKET THERE WON'T BE MUCH TO GO ON.
I DON'T GET THIS. WHY WOULD ANYONE WANT TO MUTILATE A BODY LIKE THAT?
IT'S INSANITY.
IT IS MANY THINGS, BUT I DON'T THINK IT'S INSANITY.
WHOEVER IS DOING IT COULD SIMPLY CUT OFF THE HEAD OR A DOZEN OTHER THINGS FAR MORE EASILY THAN TAKING THE TIME TO REMOVE THE HEART LIKE THAT.
SOMEONE IS PURPOSELY MAKING THESE PEOPLE IMPOSSIBLE TO AWAKEN... BUT IN THE NICEST WAY POSSIBLE?
THAT'S WHAT IT LOOKS LIKE TO ME.

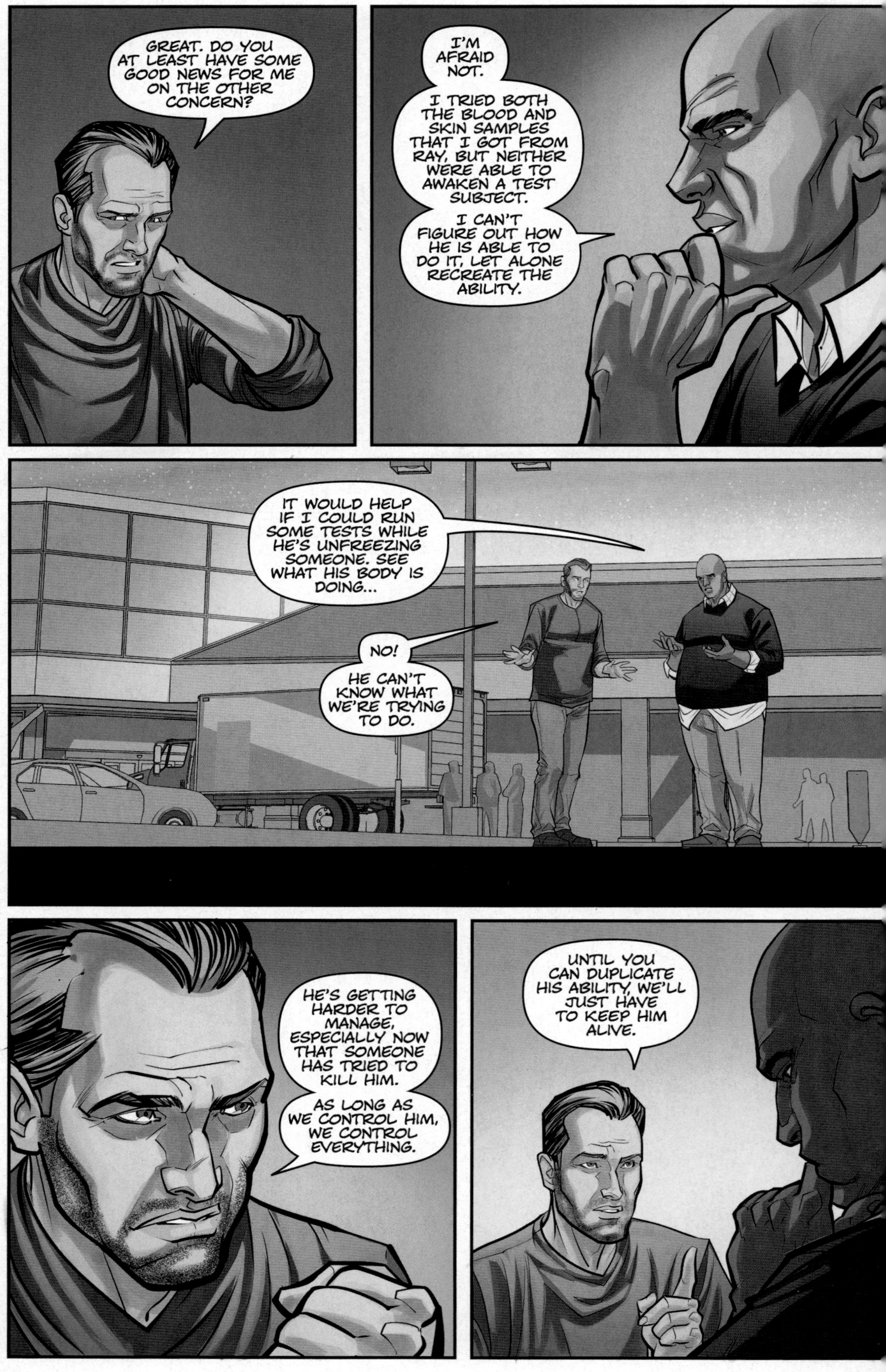
GREAT. DO YOU AT LEAST HAVE SOME GOOD NEWS FOR ME ON THE OTHER CONCERN?
I'M AFRAID NOT.
I TRIED BOTH THE BLOOD AND SKIN SAMPLES THAT I GOT FROM RAY, BUT NEITHER WERE ABLE TO AWAKEN A TEST SUBJECT.
I CAN'T FIGURE OUT HOW HE IS ABLE TO DO IT, LET ALONE RECREATE THE ABILITY.
IT WOULD HELP IF I COULD RUN SOME TESTS WHILE HE'S UNFREEZING SOMEONE. SEE WHAT HIS BODY IS DOING...
NO!
HE CAN'T KNOW WHAT WE'RE TRYING TO DO.
HE'S GETTING HARDER TO MANAGE, ESPECIALLY NOW THAT SOMEONE HAS TRIED TO KILL HIM.
AS LONG AS WE CONTROL HIM, WE CONTROL EVERYTHING.
UNTIL YOU CAN DUPLICATE HIS ABILITY, WE'LL JUST HAVE TO KEEP HIM ALIVE.

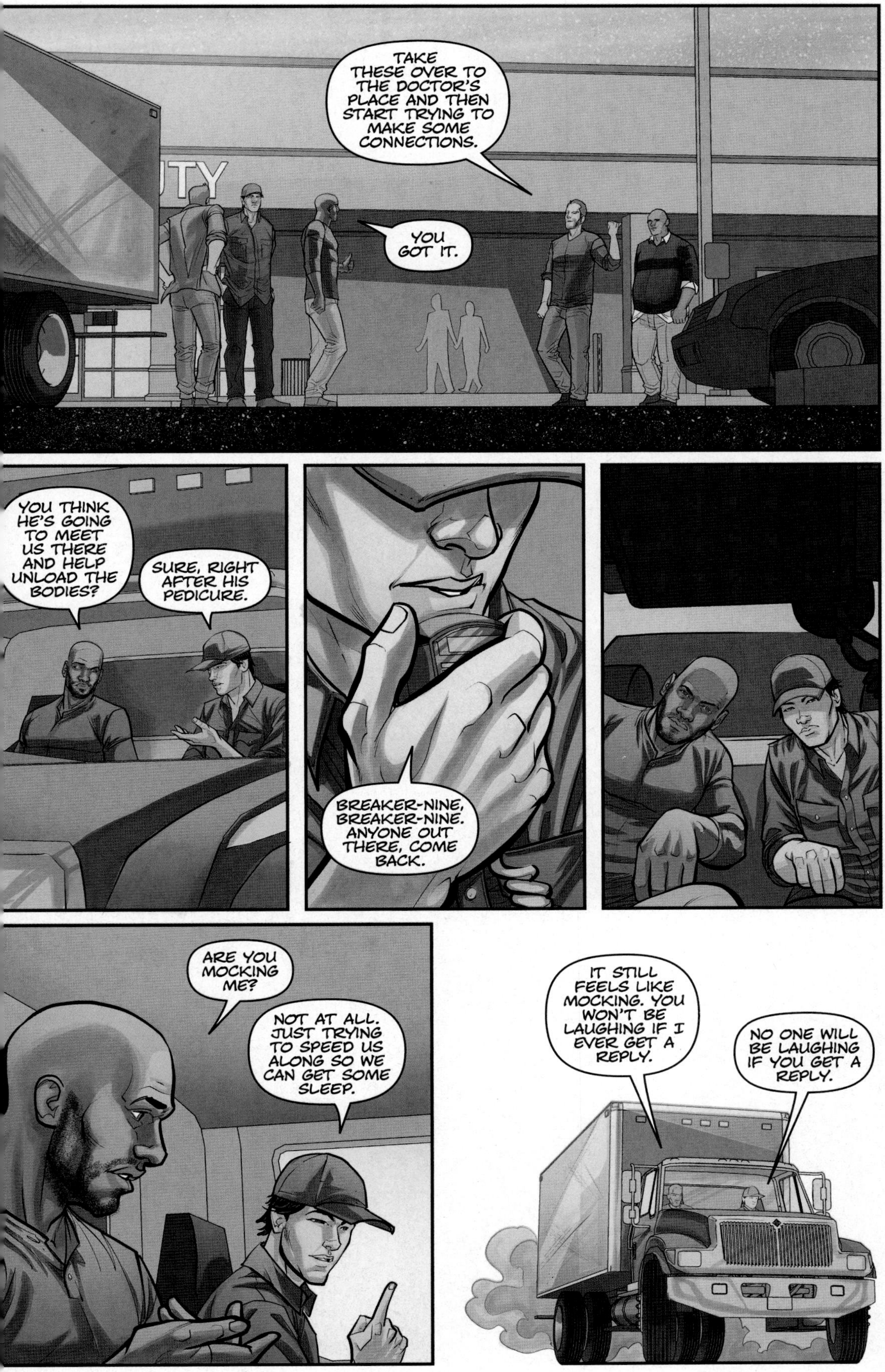
UTY
TAKE THESE OVER TO THE DOCTOR'S PLACE AND THEN START TRYING TO MAKE SOME CONNECTIONS.
YOU GOT IT.
YOU THINK HE'S GOING TO MEET US THERE AND HELP UNLOAD THE BODIES?
SURE, RIGHT AFTER HIS PEDICURE.
BREAKER-NINE, BREAKER-NINE. ANYONE OUT THERE, COME BACK.
ARE YOU MOCKING ME?
NOT AT ALL. JUST TRYING TO SPEED US ALONG SO WE CAN GET SOME SLEEP.
IT STILL FEELS LIKE MOCKING. YOU WON'T BE LAUGHING IF I EVER GET A REPLY.
NO ONE WILL BE LAUGHING IF YOU GET A REPLY.

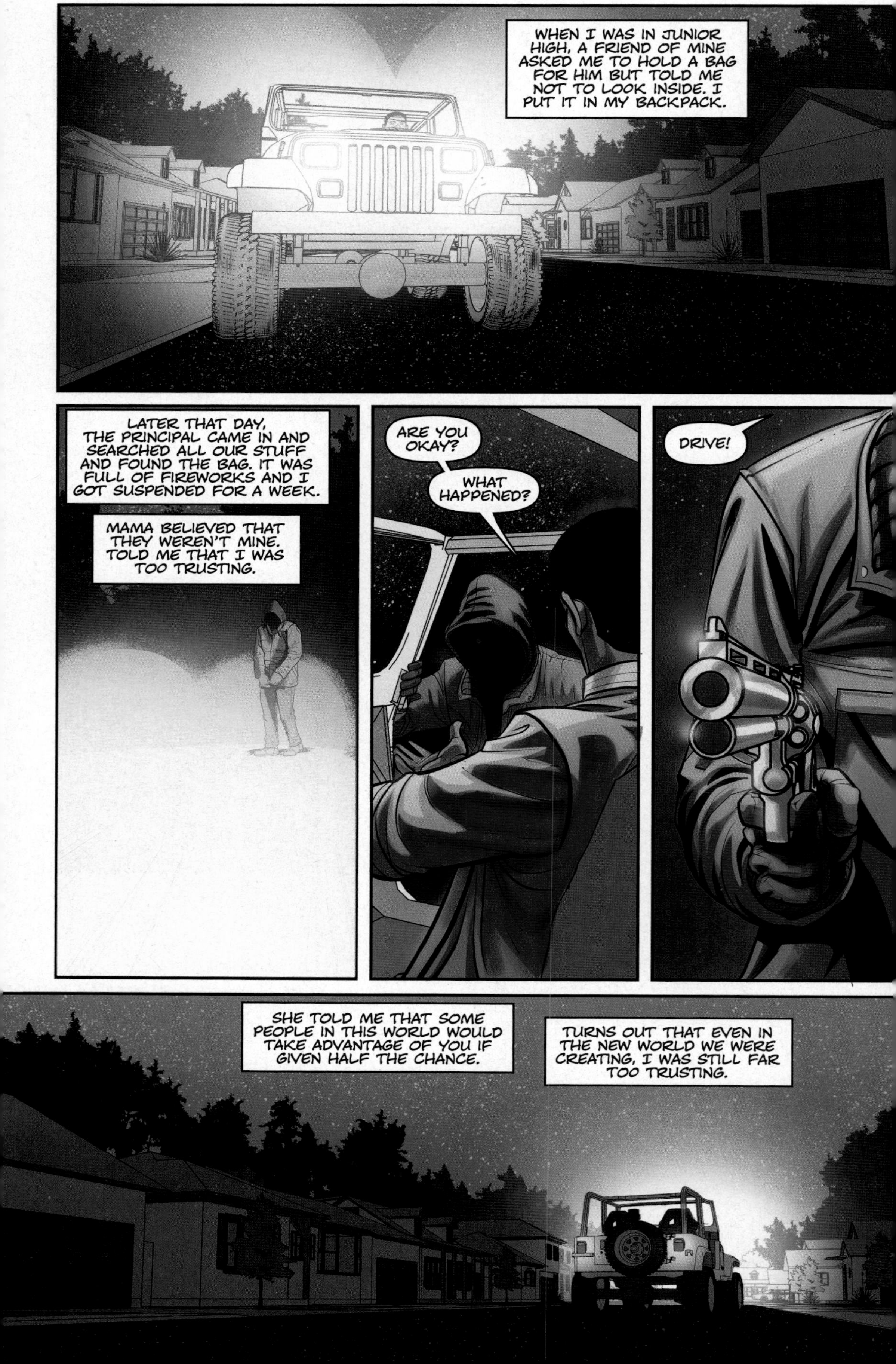
WHEN I WAS IN JUNIOR HIGH, A FRIEND OF MINE ASKED ME TO HOLD A BAG FOR HIM BUT TOLD ME NOT TO LOOK INSIDE. I PUT IT IN MY BACKPACK.
LATER THAT DAY, THE PRINCIPAL CAME IN AND SEARCHED ALL OUR STUFF AND FOUND THE BAG. IT WAS FULL OF FIREWORKS AND I GOT SUSPENDED FOR A WEEK.
MAMA BELIEVED THAT THEY WEREN'T MINE. TOLD ME THAT I WAS TOO TRUSTING.
ARE YOU OKAY?
WHAT HAPPENED?
DRIVE!
SHE TOLD ME THAT SOME PEOPLE IN THIS WORLD WOULD TAKE ADVANTAGE OF YOU IF GIVEN HALF THE CHANCE.
TURNS OUT THAT EVEN IN THE NEW WORLD WE WERE CREATING, I WAS STILL FAR TOO TRUSTING.

CHAPTER 4

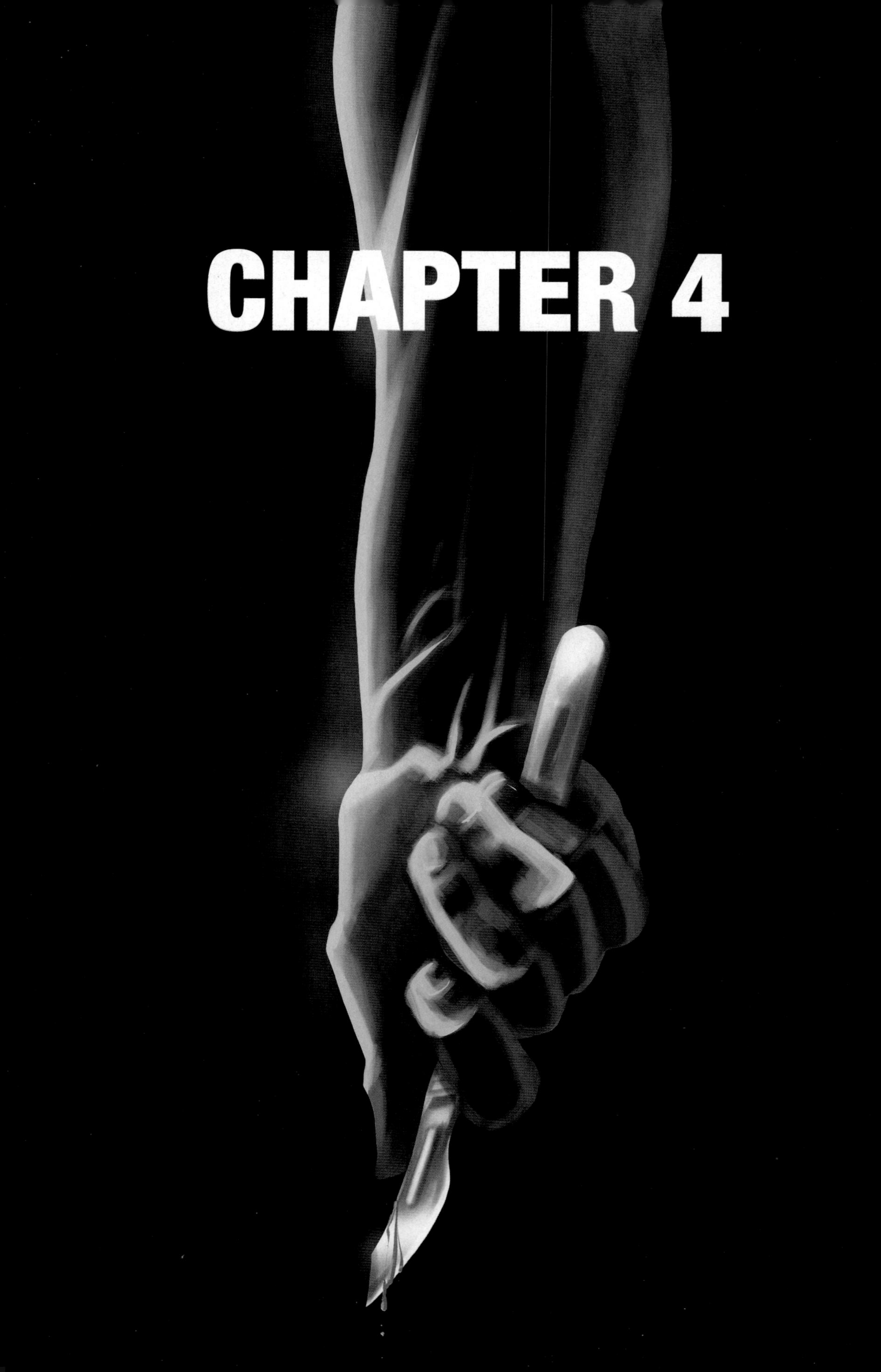

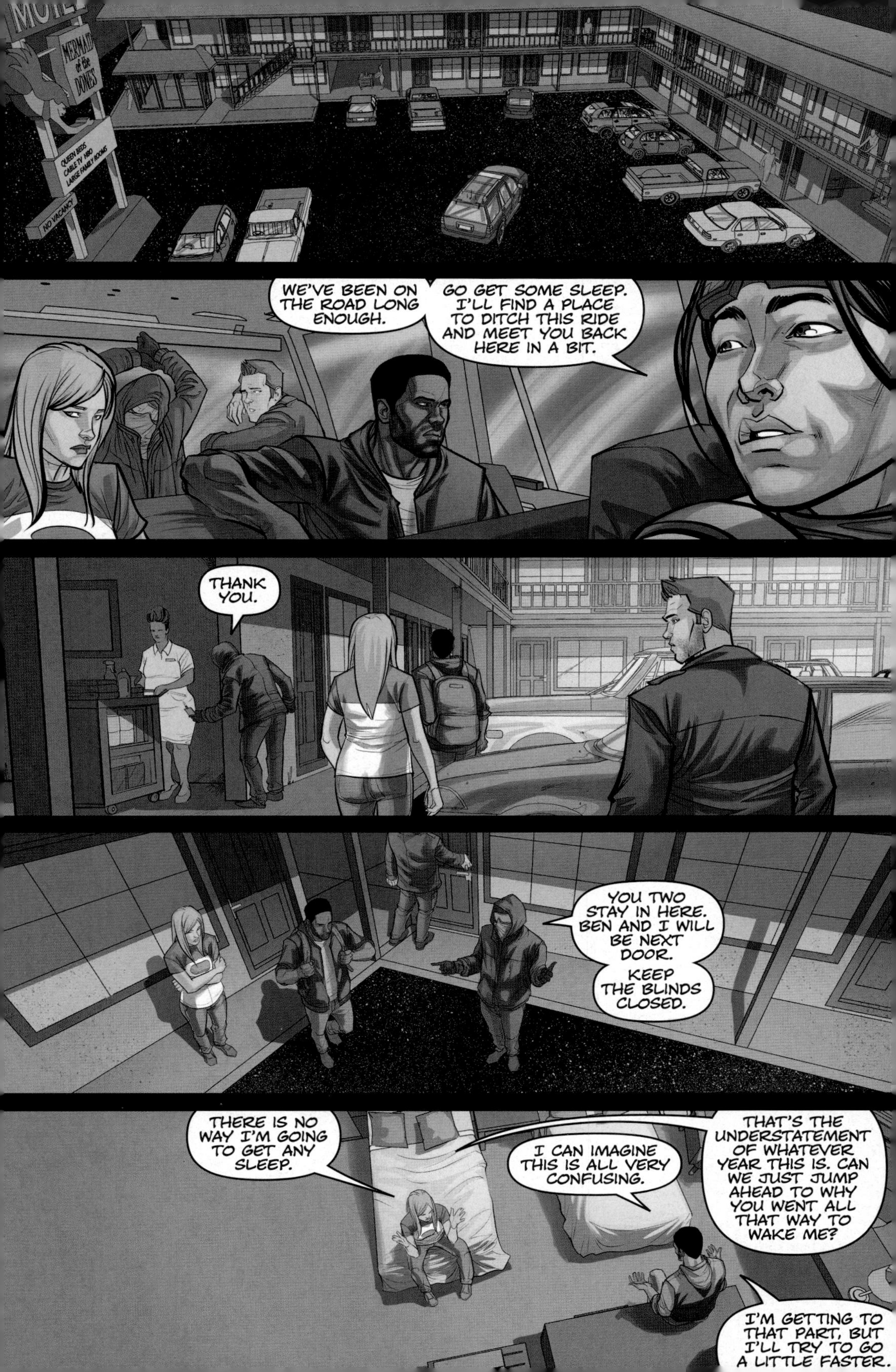
MOTEL
MERMAID of the DUNES
QUEEN BEDS
CABLE TV HBO
LARGE FAMILY ROOMS
NO VACANCY
WE'VE BEEN ON THE ROAD LONG ENOUGH.
GO GET SOME SLEEP. I'LL FIND A PLACE TO DITCH THIS RIDE AND MEET YOU BACK HERE IN A BIT.
THANK YOU.
YOU TWO STAY IN HERE. BEN AND I WILL BE NEXT DOOR.
KEEP THE BLINDS CLOSED.
THERE IS NO WAY I'M GOING TO GET ANY SLEEP.
I CAN IMAGINE THIS IS ALL VERY CONFUSING.
THAT'S THE UNDERSTATEMENT OF WHATEVER YEAR THIS IS. CAN WE JUST JUMP AHEAD TO WHY YOU WENT ALL THAT WAY TO WAKE ME?
I'M GETTING TO THAT PART, BUT I'LL TRY TO GO A LITTLE FASTER.

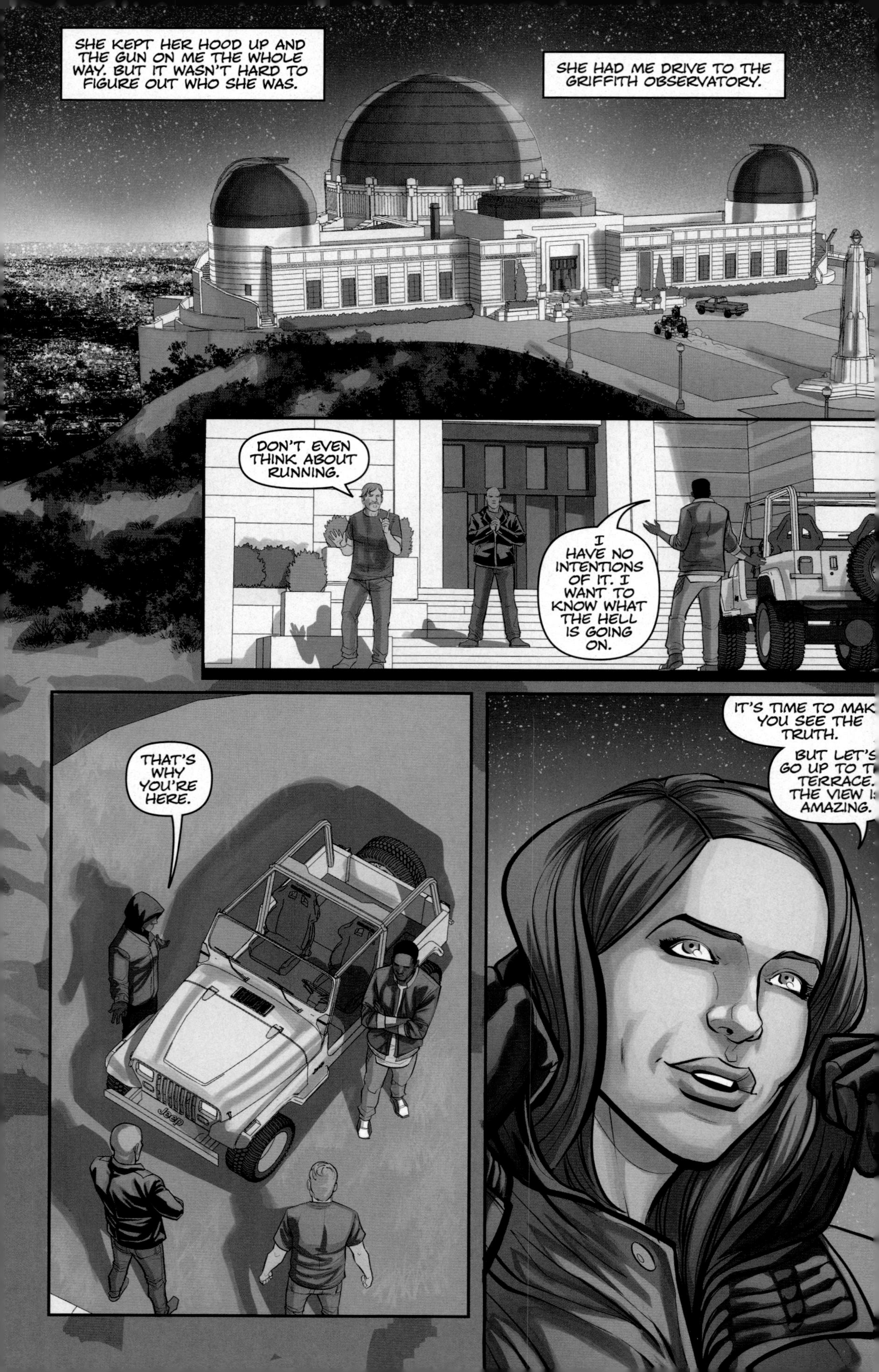

SHE KEPT HER HOOD UP AND THE GUN ON ME THE WHOLE WAY. BUT IT WASN'T HARD TO FIGURE OUT WHO SHE WAS.
SHE HAD ME DRIVE TO THE GRIFFITH OBSERVATORY.
DON'T EVEN THINK ABOUT RUNNING.
I HAVE NO INTENTIONS OF IT. I WANT TO KNOW WHAT THE HELL IS GOING ON.
THAT'S WHY YOU'RE HERE.
IT'S TIME TO MAK YOU SEE THE TRUTH.
BUT LET'S GO UP TO T TERRACE. THE VIEW I AMAZING.

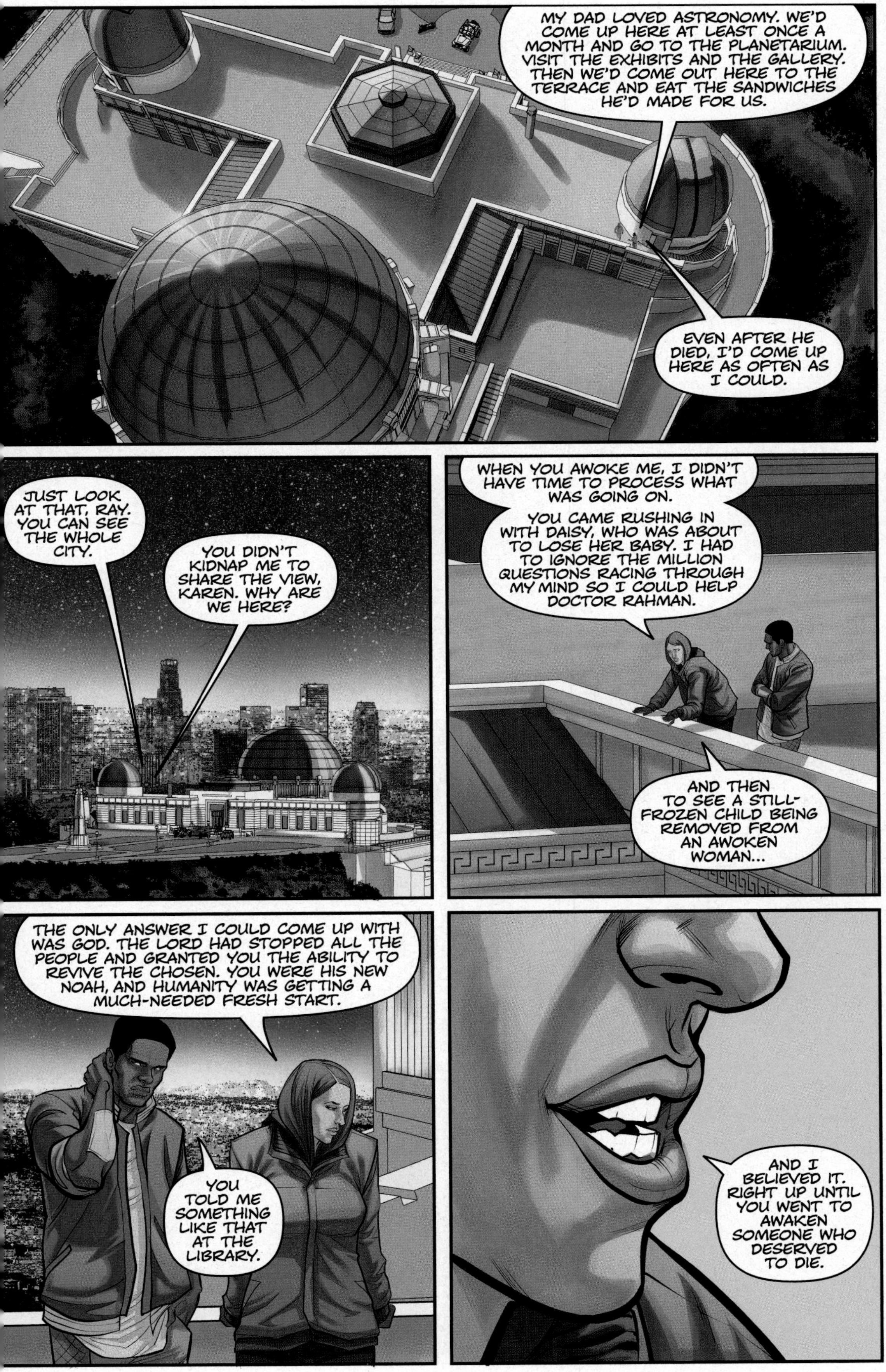

MY DAD LOVED ASTRONOMY. WE'D COME UP HERE AT LEAST ONCE A MONTH AND GO TO THE PLANETARIUM. VISIT THE EXHIBITS AND THE GALLERY. THEN WE'D COME OUT HERE TO THE TERRACE AND EAT THE SANDWICHES HE'D MADE FOR US.
EVEN AFTER HE DIED, I'D COME UP HERE AS OFTEN AS I COULD.
JUST LOOK AT THAT, RAY. YOU CAN SEE THE WHOLE CITY.
YOU DIDN'T KIDNAP ME TO SHARE THE VIEW, KAREN. WHY ARE WE HERE?
WHEN YOU AWOKE ME, I DIDN'T HAVE TIME TO PROCESS WHAT WAS GOING ON.
YOU CAME RUSHING IN WITH DAISY, WHO WAS ABOUT TO LOSE HER BABY. I HAD TO IGNORE THE MILLION QUESTIONS RACING THROUGH MY MIND SO I COULD HELP DOCTOR RAHMAN.
AND THEN TO SEE A STILL-FROZEN CHILD BEING REMOVED FROM AN AWOKEN WOMAN...
THE ONLY ANSWER I COULD COME UP WITH WAS GOD. THE LORD HAD STOPPED ALL THE PEOPLE AND GRANTED YOU THE ABILITY TO REVIVE THE CHOSEN. YOU WERE HIS NEW NOAH, AND HUMANITY WAS GETTING A MUCH-NEEDED FRESH START.
YOU TOLD ME SOMETHING LIKE THAT AT THE LIBRARY.
AND I BELIEVED IT. RIGHT UP UNTIL YOU WENT TO AWAKEN SOMEONE WHO DESERVED TO DIE.

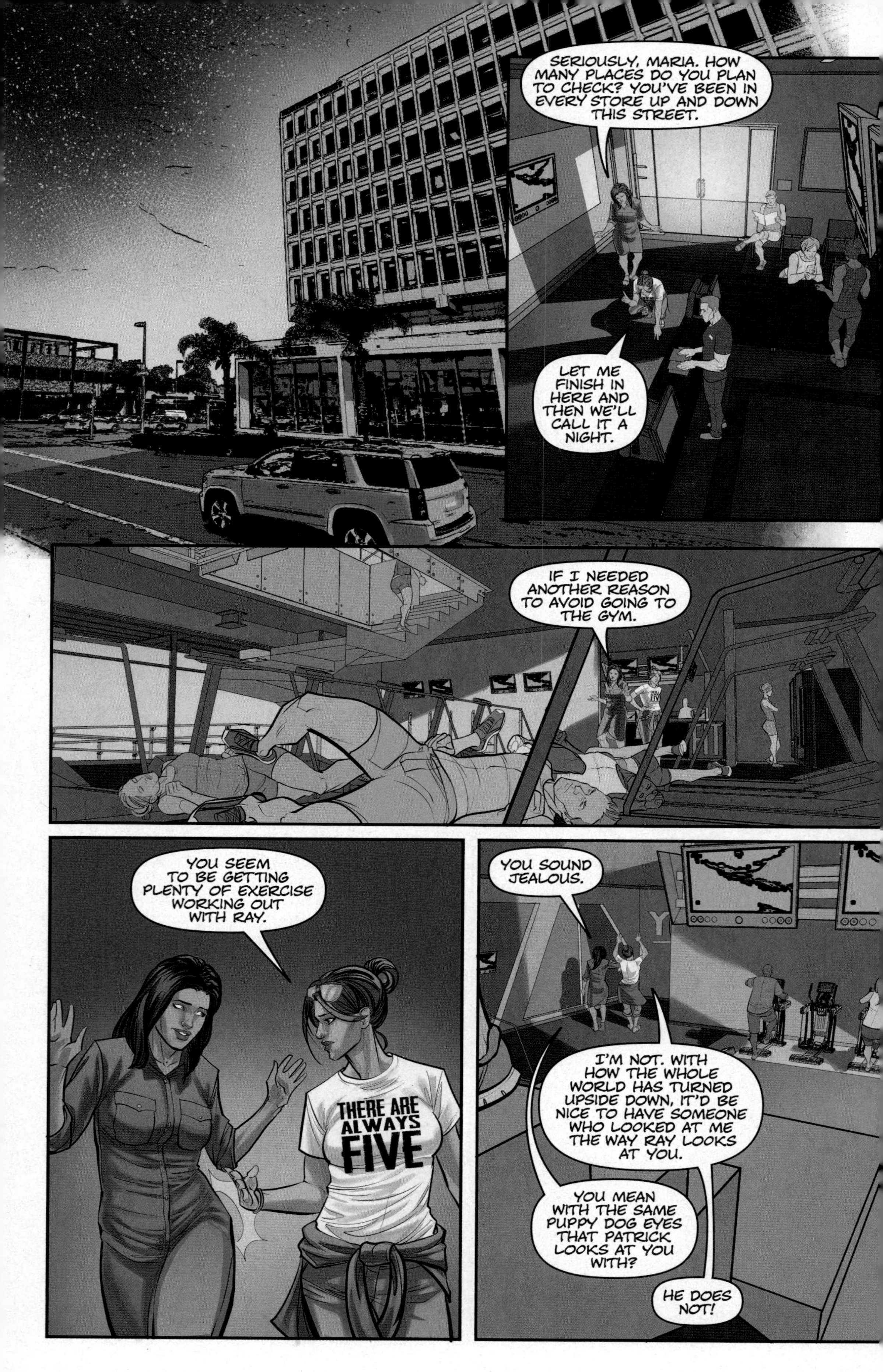
SERIOUSLY, MARIA. HOW MANY PLACES DO YOU PLAN TO CHECK? YOU'VE BEEN IN EVERY STORE UP AND DOWN THIS STREET.
LET ME FINISH IN HERE AND THEN WE'LL CALL IT A NIGHT.
IF I NEEDED ANOTHER REASON TO AVOID GOING TO THE GYM.
YOU SEEM TO BE GETTING PLENTY OF EXERCISE WORKING OUT WITH RAY.
THERE ARE ALWAYS FIVE
YOU SOUND JEALOUS.
I'M NOT. WITH HOW THE WHOLE WORLD HAS TURNED UPSIDE DOWN, IT'D BE NICE TO HAVE SOMEONE WHO LOOKED AT ME THE WAY RAY LOOKS AT YOU.
YOU MEAN WITH THE SAME PUPPY DOG EYES THAT PATRICK LOOKS AT YOU WITH?
HE DOES NOT!

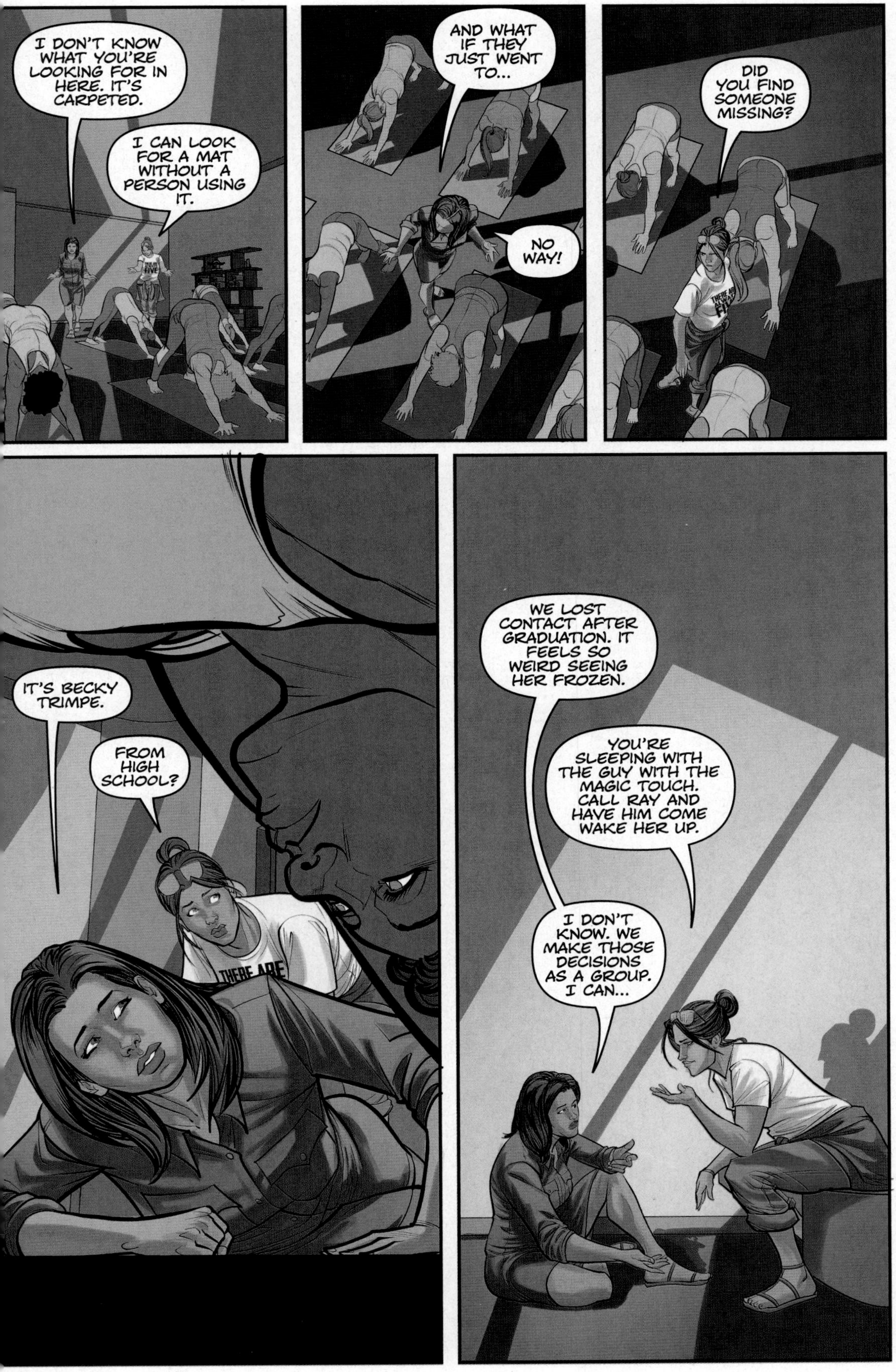
I DON'T KNOW WHAT YOU'RE LOOKING FOR IN HERE. IT'S CARPETED.
I CAN LOOK FOR A MAT WITHOUT A PERSON USING IT.
AND WHAT IF THEY JUST WENT TO...
NO WAY!
DID YOU FIND SOMEONE MISSING?
IT'S BECKY TRIMPE.
FROM HIGH SCHOOL?
WE LOST CONTACT AFTER GRADUATION. IT FEELS SO WEIRD SEEING HER FROZEN.
YOU'RE SLEEPING WITH THE GUY WITH THE MAGIC TOUCH. CALL RAY AND HAVE HIM COME WAKE HER UP.
I DON'T KNOW. WE MAKE THOSE DECISIONS AS A GROUP. I CAN...
THERE ARE

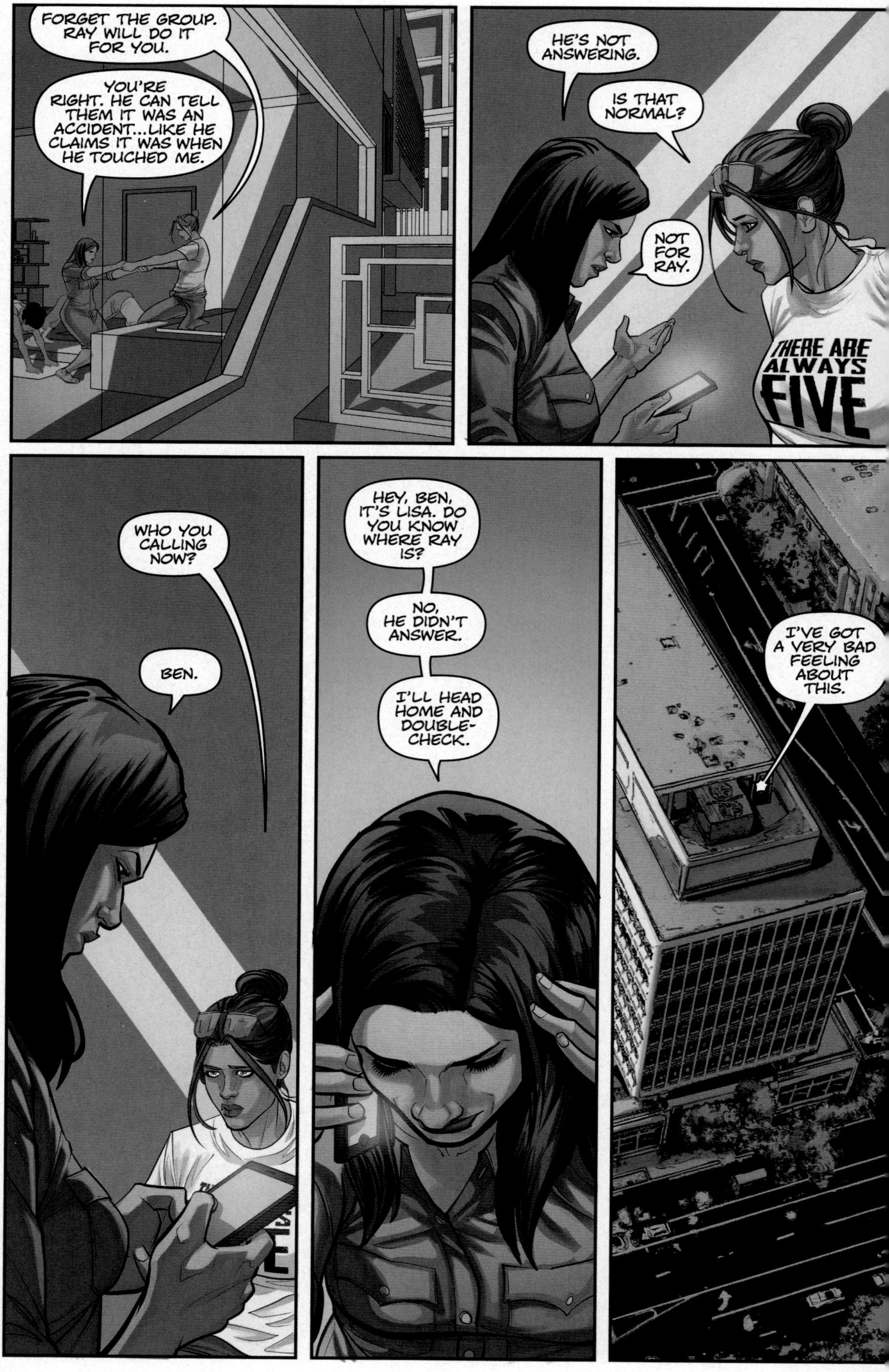
FORGET THE GROUP. RAY WILL DO IT FOR YOU.
YOU'RE RIGHT. HE CAN TELL THEM IT WAS AN ACCIDENT...LIKE HE CLAIMS IT WAS WHEN HE TOUCHED ME.
HE'S NOT ANSWERING.
IS THAT NORMAL?
NOT FOR RAY.
THERE ARE ALWAYS FIVE
WHO YOU CALLING NOW?
BEN.
HEY, BEN, IT'S LISA. DO YOU KNOW WHERE RAY IS?
NO, HE DIDN'T ANSWER.
I'LL HEAD HOME AND DOUBLE-CHECK.
I'VE GOT A VERY BAD FEELING ABOUT THIS.

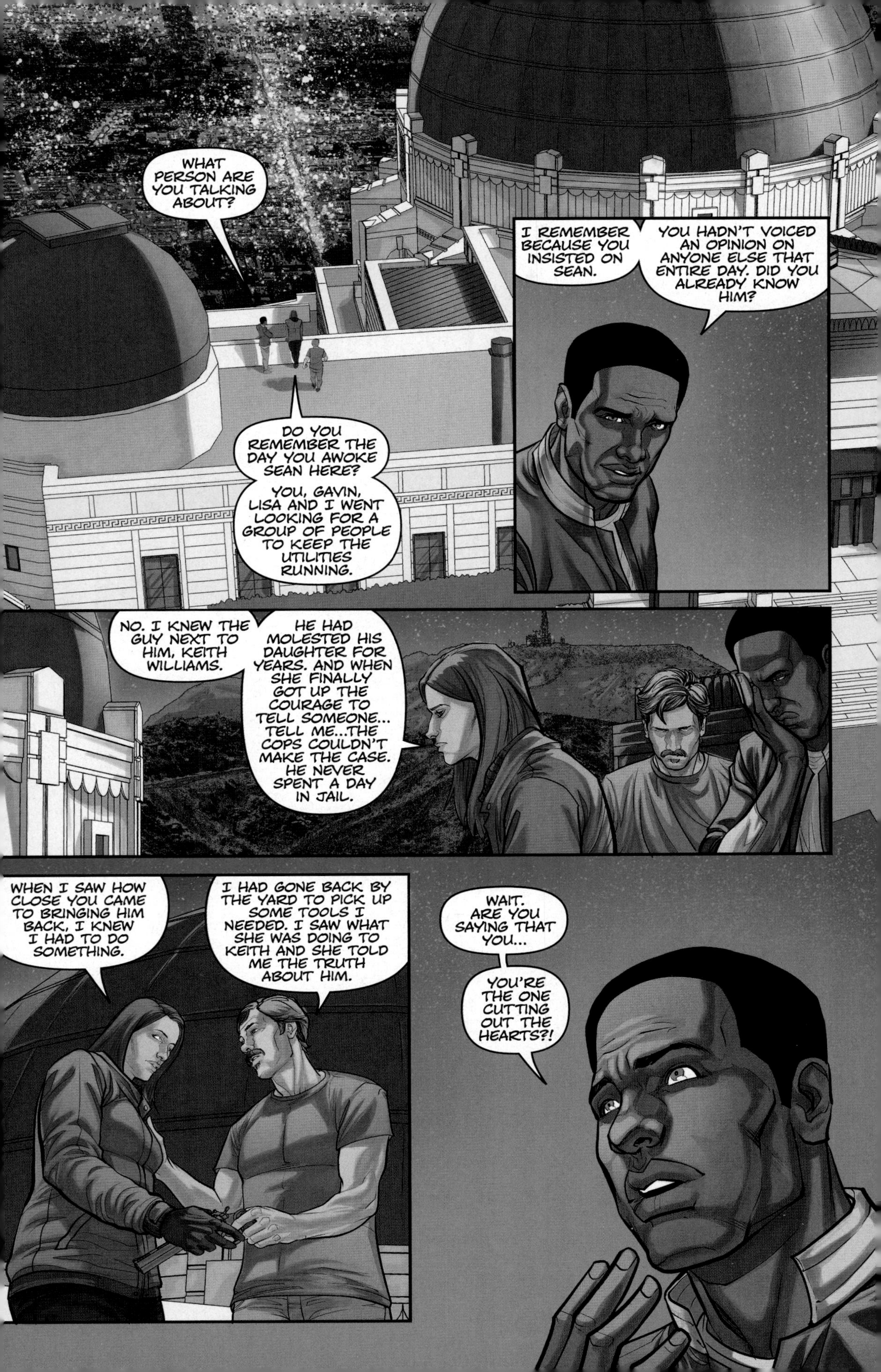
WHAT PERSON ARE YOU TALKING ABOUT?
DO YOU REMEMBER THE DAY YOU AWOKE SEAN HERE?
YOU, GAVIN, LISA AND I WENT LOOKING FOR A GROUP OF PEOPLE TO KEEP THE UTILITIES RUNNING.
I REMEMBER BECAUSE YOU INSISTED ON SEAN.
YOU HADN'T VOICED AN OPINION ON ANYONE ELSE THAT ENTIRE DAY. DID YOU ALREADY KNOW HIM?
NO. I KNEW THE GUY NEXT TO HIM, KEITH WILLIAMS.
HE HAD MOLESTED HIS DAUGHTER FOR YEARS. AND WHEN SHE FINALLY GOT UP THE COURAGE TO TELL SOMEONE... TELL ME...THE COPS COULDN'T MAKE THE CASE. HE NEVER SPENT A DAY IN JAIL.
WHEN I SAW HOW CLOSE YOU CAME TO BRINGING HIM BACK, I KNEW I HAD TO DO SOMETHING.
I HAD GONE BACK BY THE YARD TO PICK UP SOME TOOLS I NEEDED. I SAW WHAT SHE WAS DOING TO KEITH AND SHE TOLD ME THE TRUTH ABOUT HIM.
WAIT. ARE YOU SAYING THAT YOU...
YOU'RE THE ONE CUTTING OUT THE HEARTS?!

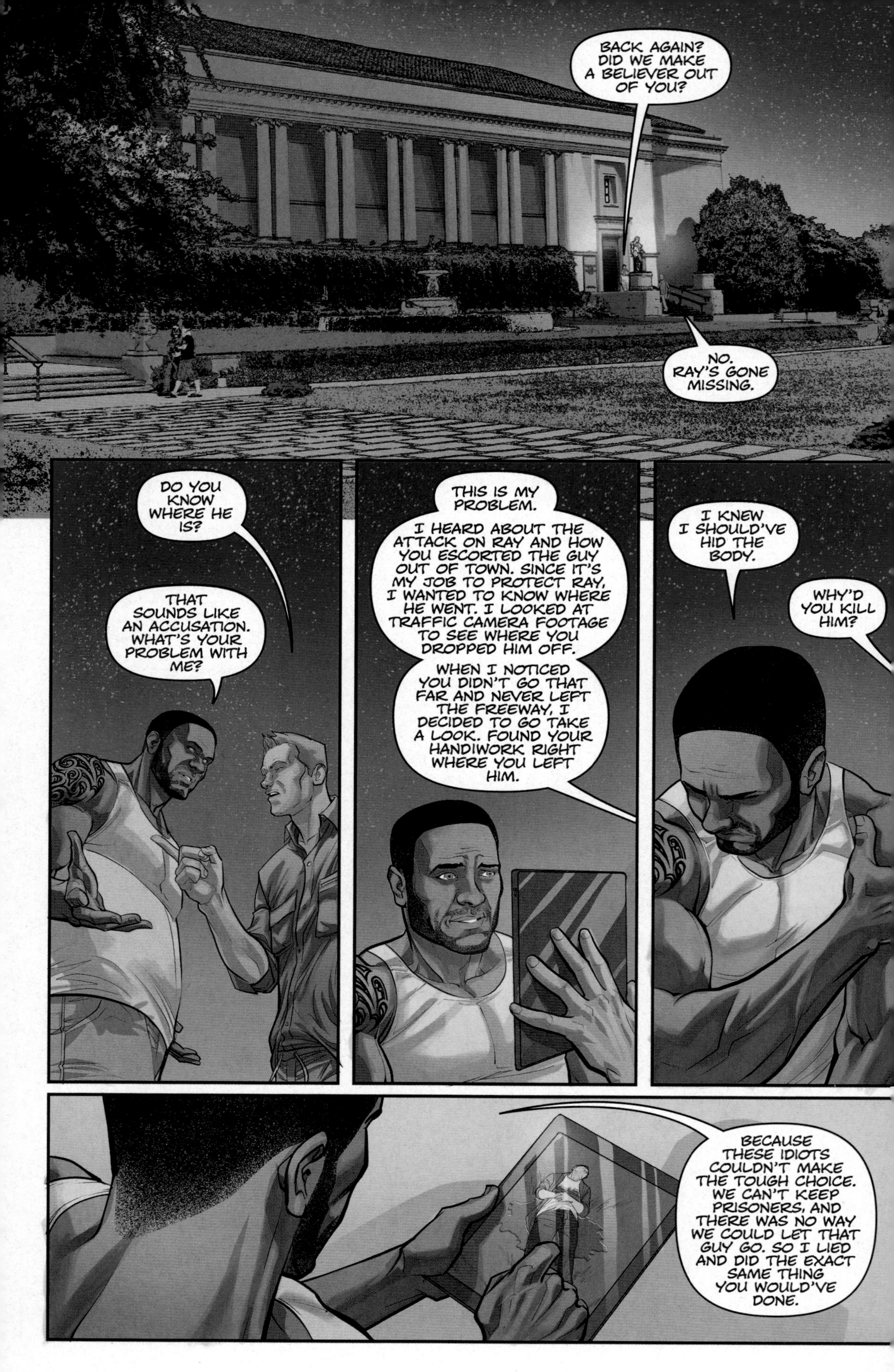
BACK AGAIN? DID WE MAKE A BELIEVER OUT OF YOU?
NO. RAY'S GONE MISSING.
DO YOU KNOW WHERE HE IS?
THAT SOUNDS LIKE AN ACCUSATION. WHAT'S YOUR PROBLEM WITH ME?
THIS IS MY PROBLEM.
I HEARD ABOUT THE ATTACK ON RAY AND HOW YOU ESCORTED THE GUY OUT OF TOWN. SINCE IT'S MY JOB TO PROTECT RAY, I WANTED TO KNOW WHERE HE WENT. I LOOKED AT TRAFFIC CAMERA FOOTAGE TO SEE WHERE YOU DROPPED HIM OFF.
WHEN I NOTICED YOU DIDN'T GO THAT FAR AND NEVER LEFT THE FREEWAY, I DECIDED TO GO TAKE A LOOK. FOUND YOUR HANDIWORK RIGHT WHERE YOU LEFT HIM.
I KNEW I SHOULD'VE HID THE BODY.
WHY'D YOU KILL HIM?
BECAUSE THESE IDIOTS COULDN'T MAKE THE TOUGH CHOICE. WE CAN'T KEEP PRISONERS, AND THERE WAS NO WAY WE COULD LET THAT GUY GO. SO I LIED AND DID THE EXACT SAME THING YOU WOULD'VE DONE.

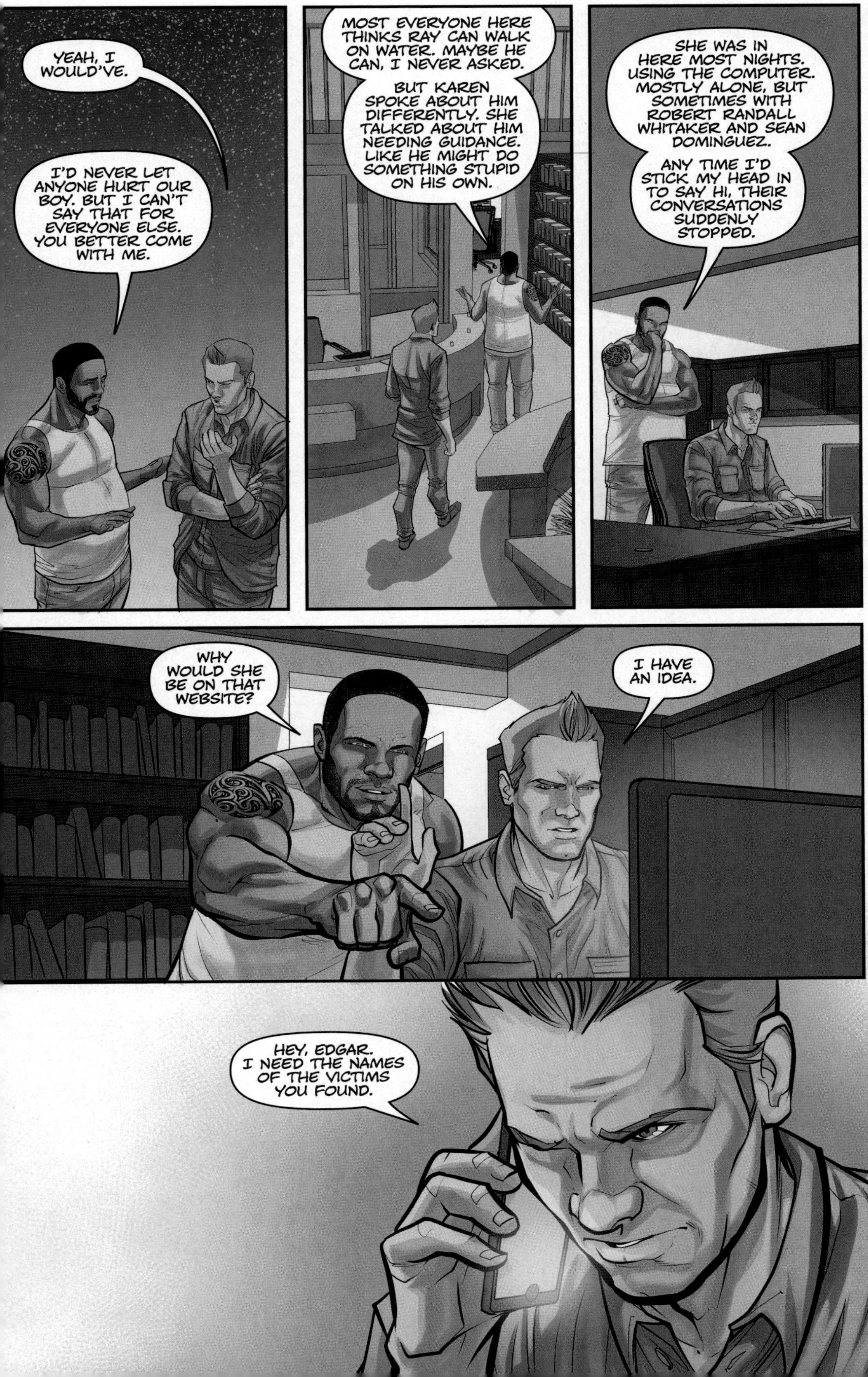
YEAH, I WOULD'VE.
I'D NEVER LET ANYONE HURT OUR BOY. BUT I CAN'T SAY THAT FOR EVERYONE ELSE. YOU BETTER COME WITH ME.
MOST EVERYONE HERE THINKS RAY CAN WALK ON WATER. MAYBE HE CAN, I NEVER ASKED.
BUT KAREN SPOKE ABOUT HIM DIFFERENTLY. SHE TALKED ABOUT HIM NEEDING GUIDANCE. LIKE HE MIGHT DO SOMETHING STUPID ON HIS OWN.
SHE WAS IN HERE MOST NIGHTS. USING THE COMPUTER. MOSTLY ALONE, BUT SOMETIMES WITH ROBERT RANDALL WHITAKER AND SEAN DOMINGUEZ.
ANY TIME I'D STICK MY HEAD IN TO SAY HI, THEIR CONVERSATIONS SUDDENLY STOPPED.
WHY WOULD SHE BE ON THAT WEBSITE?
I HAVE AN IDEA.
HEY, EDGAR. I NEED THE NAMES OF THE VICTIMS YOU FOUND.

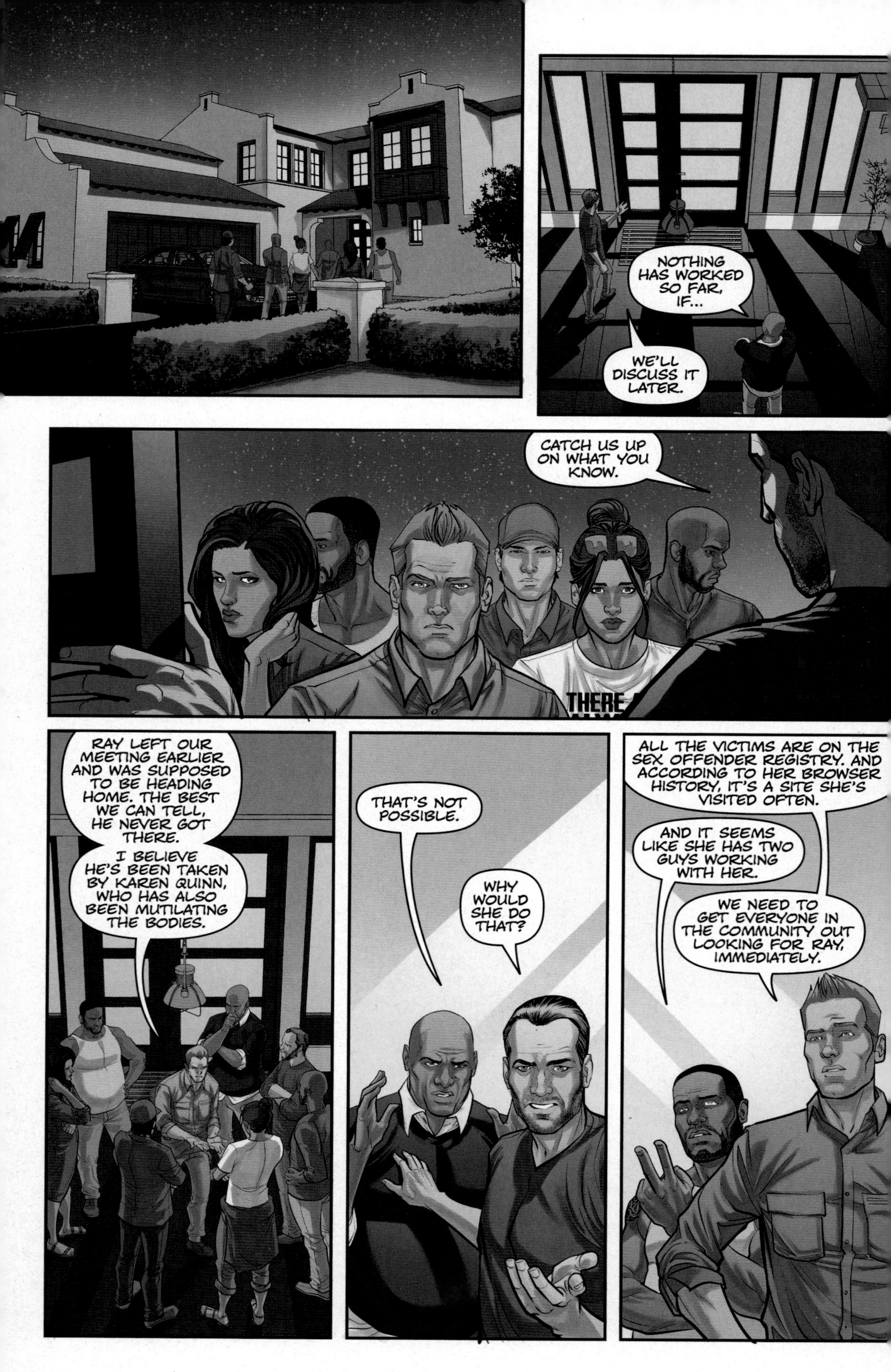
NOTHING HAS WORKED SO FAR, IF...
WE'LL DISCUSS IT LATER.
CATCH US UP ON WHAT YOU KNOW.
RAY LEFT OUR MEETING EARLIER AND WAS SUPPOSED TO BE HEADING HOME. THE BEST WE CAN TELL, HE NEVER GOT THERE.
I BELIEVE HE'S BEEN TAKEN BY KAREN QUINN, WHO HAS ALSO BEEN MUTILATING THE BODIES.
THAT'S NOT POSSIBLE.
WHY WOULD SHE DO THAT?
ALL THE VICTIMS ARE ON THE SEX OFFENDER REGISTRY. AND ACCORDING TO HER BROWSER HISTORY, IT'S A SITE SHE'S VISITED OFTEN.
AND IT SEEMS LIKE SHE HAS TWO GUYS WORKING WITH HER.
WE NEED TO GET EVERYONE IN THE COMMUNITY OUT LOOKING FOR RAY, IMMEDIATELY.

NO NEED TO DO THAT. IT WOULD JUST CAUSE A PANIC.

AND BESIDES, I CAN TRACK HIS PHONE.

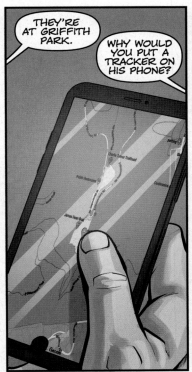

THEY'RE AT GRIFFITH PARK.

WHY WOULD YOU PUT A TRACKER ON HIS PHONE?

SOMEONE RECENTLY TRIED TO KILL HIM. BESIDES A BODYGUARD, I THOUGHT IT WOULD BE A GOOD IDEA TO BE ABLE TO FIND HIM IF HE WENT MISSING.

YOU'RE WELCOME.

ARGUE ABOUT THAT LATER. LET'S GO GET HIM.

BEN. THERE'S A MOTORCYCLE IN THE GARAGE, YOU'LL GET THERE FASTER.

IF SOMETHING HAPPENS TO RAY, WE'RE SCREWED.

WHAT IF I GET YOU HIS CORPSE?

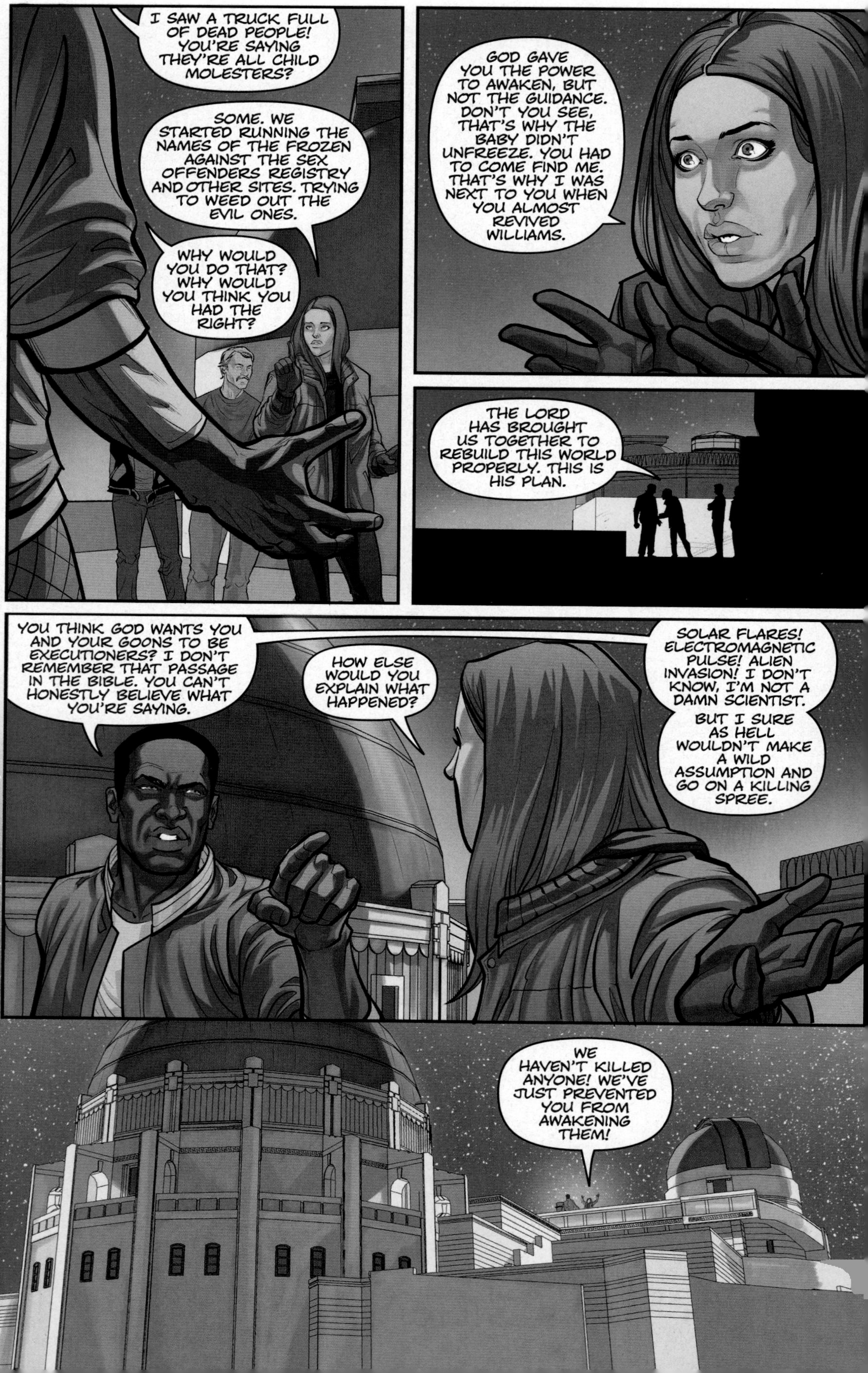
I SAW A TRUCK FULL OF DEAD PEOPLE! YOU'RE SAYING THEY'RE ALL CHILD MOLESTERS?
SOME. WE STARTED RUNNING THE NAMES OF THE FROZEN AGAINST THE SEX OFFENDERS REGISTRY AND OTHER SITES. TRYING TO WEED OUT THE EVIL ONES.
WHY WOULD YOU DO THAT? WHY WOULD YOU THINK YOU HAD THE RIGHT?
GOD GAVE YOU THE POWER TO AWAKEN, BUT NOT THE GUIDANCE. DON'T YOU SEE, THAT'S WHY THE BABY DIDN'T UNFREEZE. YOU HAD TO COME FIND ME. THAT'S WHY I WAS NEXT TO YOU WHEN YOU ALMOST REVIVED WILLIAMS.
THE LORD HAS BROUGHT US TOGETHER TO REBUILD THIS WORLD PROPERLY. THIS IS HIS PLAN.
YOU THINK GOD WANTS YOU AND YOUR GOONS TO BE EXECUTIONERS? I DON'T REMEMBER THAT PASSAGE IN THE BIBLE. YOU CAN'T HONESTLY BELIEVE WHAT YOU'RE SAYING.
HOW ELSE WOULD YOU EXPLAIN WHAT HAPPENED?
SOLAR FLARES! ELECTROMAGNETIC PULSE! ALIEN INVASION! I DON'T KNOW, I'M NOT A DAMN SCIENTIST.
BUT I SURE AS HELL WOULDN'T MAKE A WILD ASSUMPTION AND GO ON A KILLING SPREE.
WE HAVEN'T KILLED ANYONE! WE'VE JUST PREVENTED YOU FROM AWAKENING THEM!

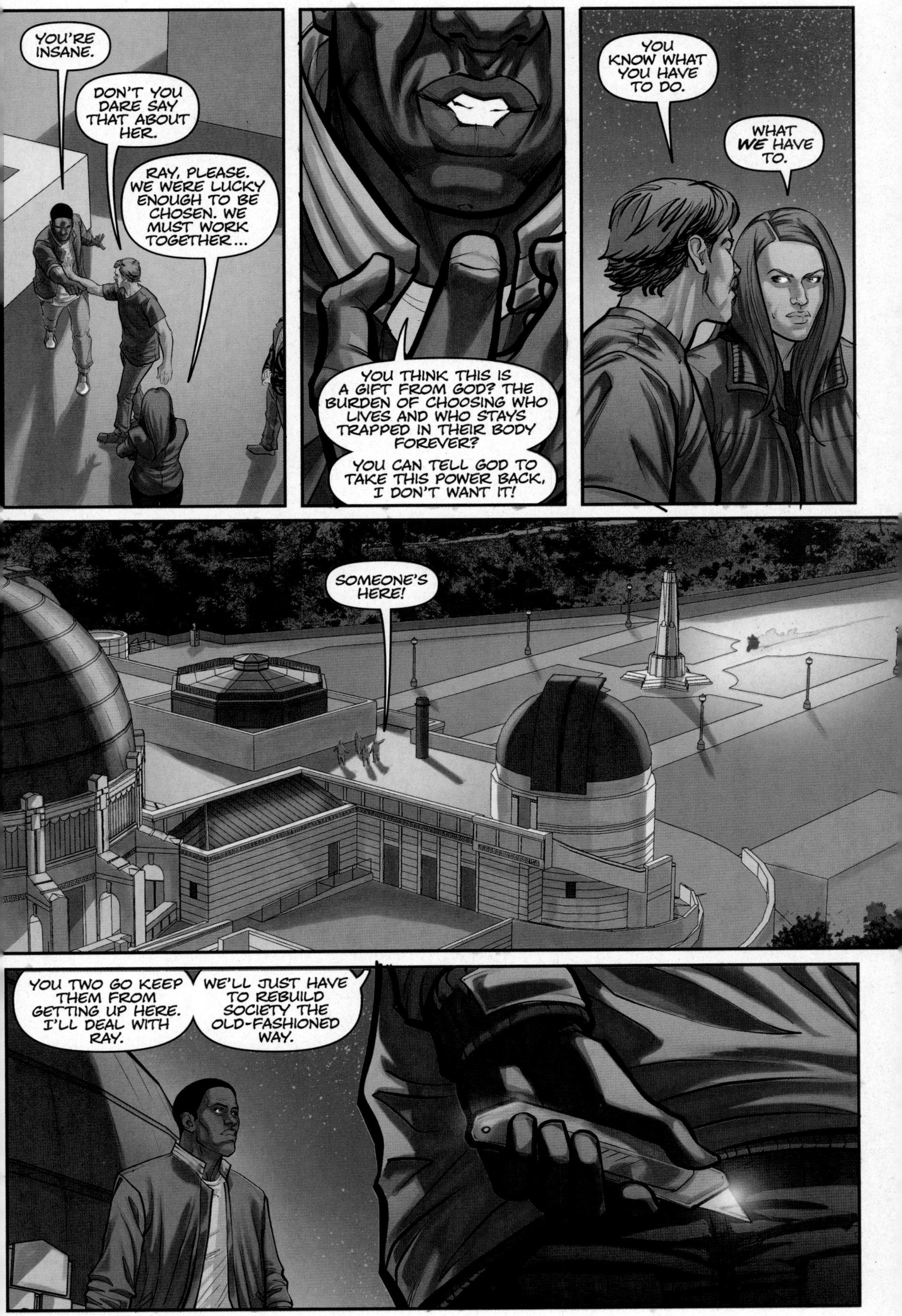

YOU'RE INSANE.
DON'T YOU DARE SAY THAT ABOUT HER.
RAY, PLEASE. WE WERE LUCKY ENOUGH TO BE CHOSEN. WE MUST WORK TOGETHER...
YOU THINK THIS IS A GIFT FROM GOD? THE BURDEN OF CHOOSING WHO LIVES AND WHO STAYS TRAPPED IN THEIR BODY FOREVER?
YOU CAN TELL GOD TO TAKE THIS POWER BACK, I DON'T WANT IT!
YOU KNOW WHAT YOU HAVE TO DO.
WHAT **WE** HAVE TO.
SOMEONE'S HERE!
YOU TWO GO KEEP THEM FROM GETTING UP HERE. I'LL DEAL WITH RAY.
WE'LL JUST HAVE TO REBUILD SOCIETY THE OLD-FASHIONED WAY.

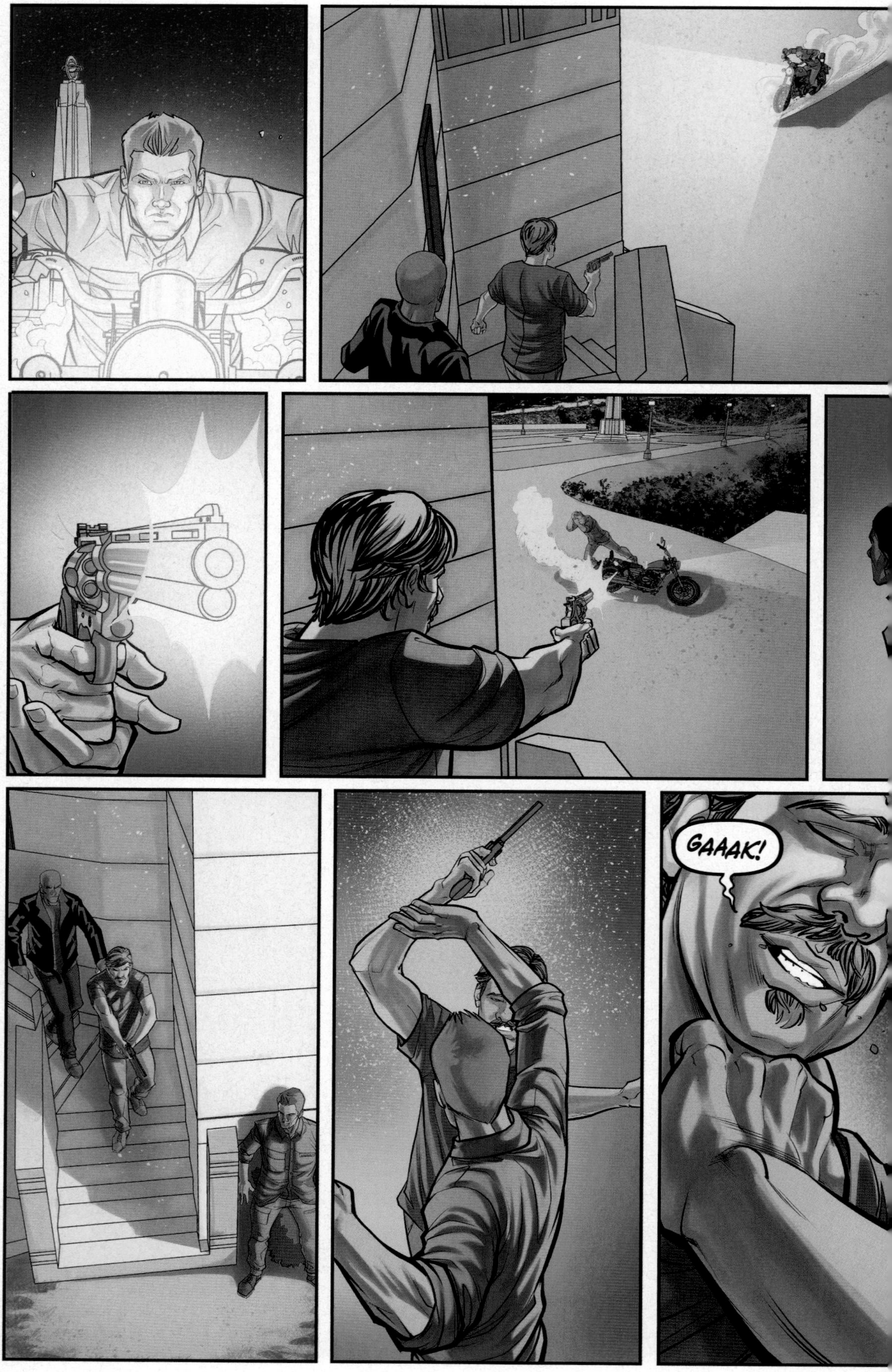
GAAAK!

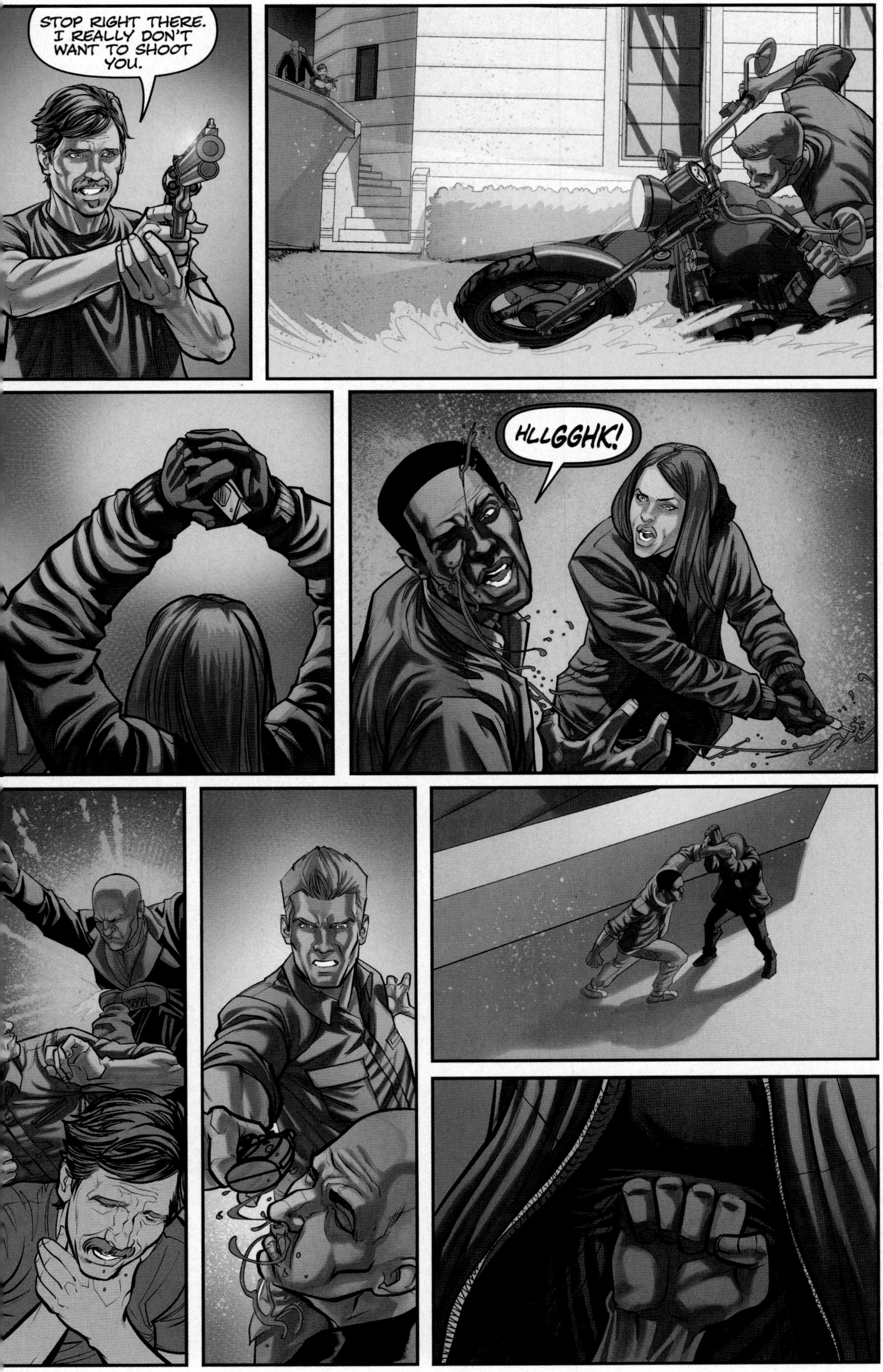
STOP RIGHT THERE. I REALLY DON'T WANT TO SHOOT YOU.
HLLGGHK!

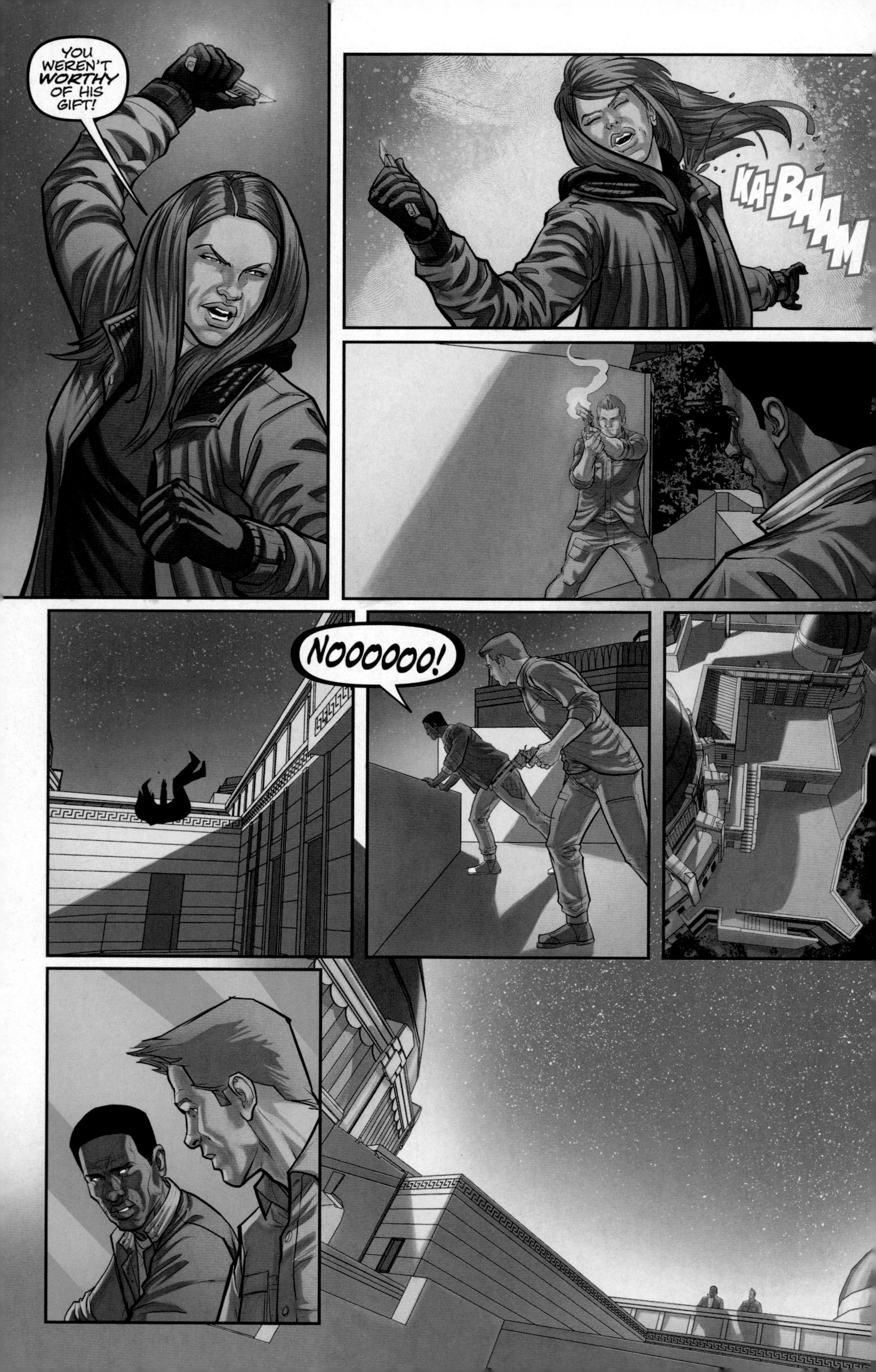

YOU WEREN'T WORTHY OF HIS GIFT!
KA-BAAAM
NOOOOOO!

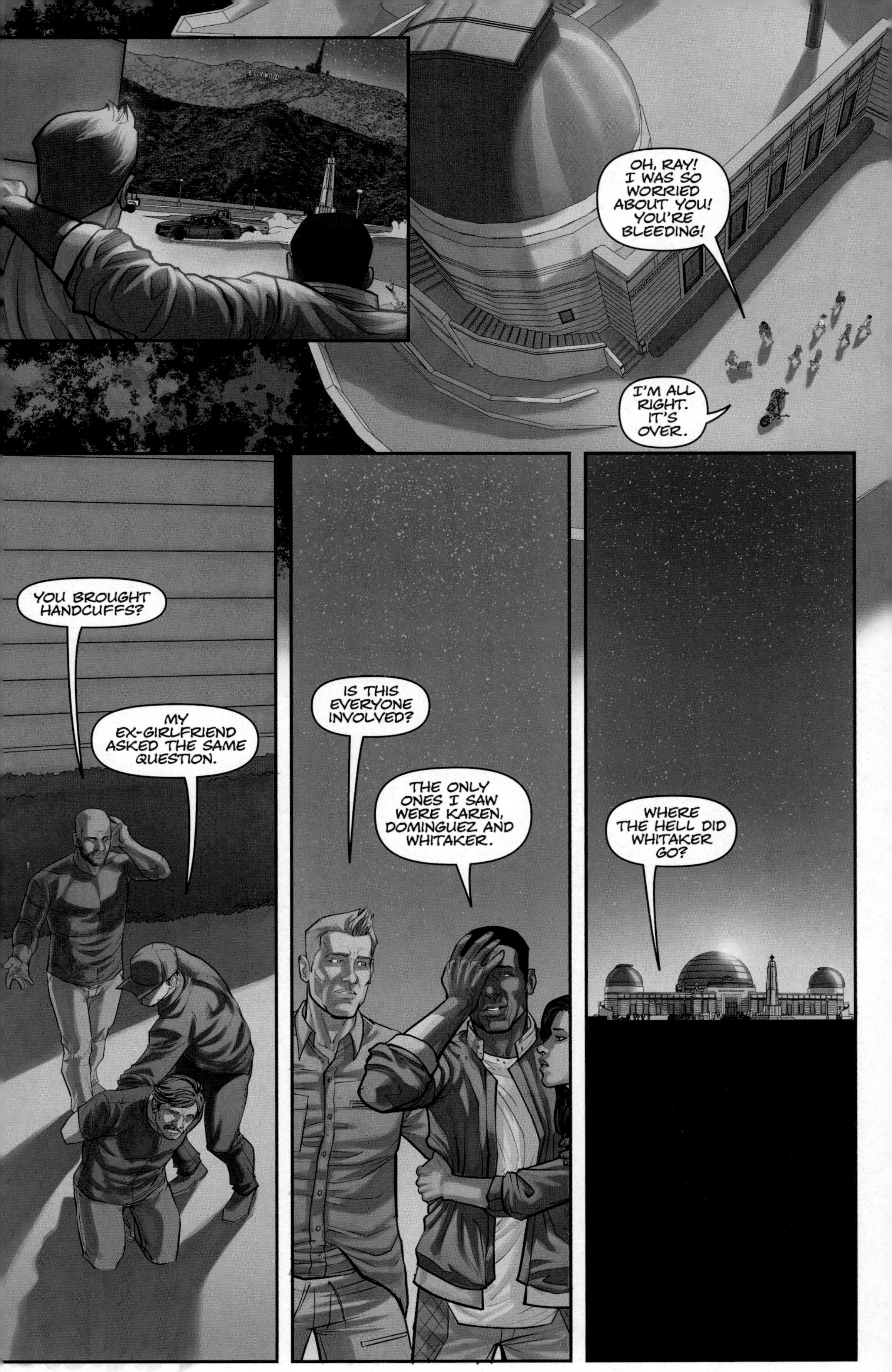
OH, RAY! I WAS SO WORRIED ABOUT YOU! YOU'RE BLEEDING!
I'M ALL RIGHT. IT'S OVER.
YOU BROUGHT HANDCUFFS?
MY EX-GIRLFRIEND ASKED THE SAME QUESTION.
IS THIS EVERYONE INVOLVED?
THE ONLY ONES I SAW WERE KAREN, DOMINGUEZ AND WHITAKER.
WHERE THE HELL DID WHITAKER GO?

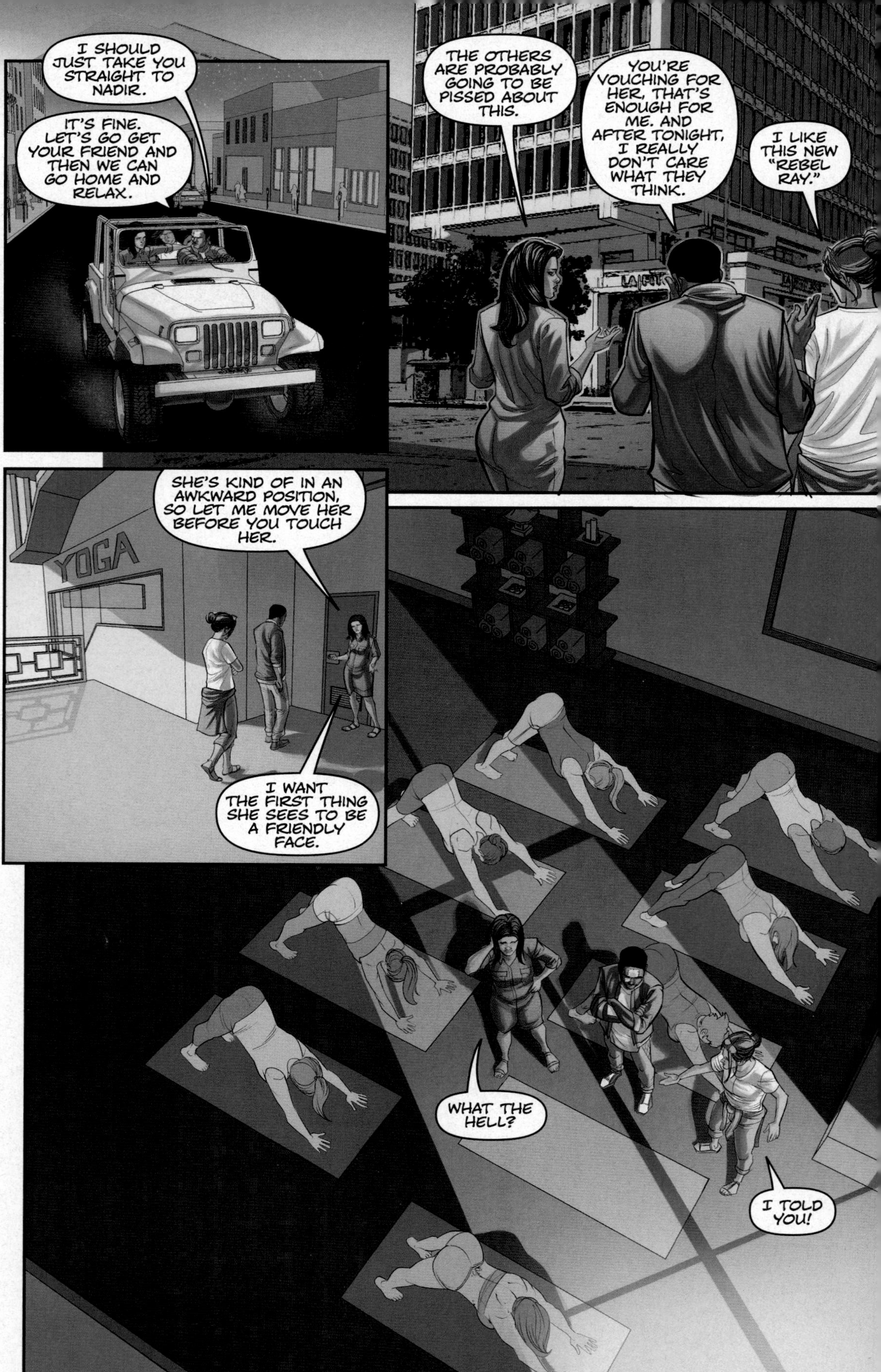
I SHOULD JUST TAKE YOU STRAIGHT TO NADIR.
IT'S FINE. LET'S GO GET YOUR FRIEND AND THEN WE CAN GO HOME AND RELAX.
THE OTHERS ARE PROBABLY GOING TO BE PISSED ABOUT THIS.
YOU'RE VOUCHING FOR HER, THAT'S ENOUGH FOR ME. AND AFTER TONIGHT, I REALLY DON'T CARE WHAT THEY THINK.
I LIKE THIS NEW "REBEL RAY."
YOGA
SHE'S KIND OF IN AN AWKWARD POSITION, SO LET ME MOVE HER BEFORE YOU TOUCH HER.
I WANT THE FIRST THING SHE SEES TO BE A FRIENDLY FACE.
WHAT THE HELL?
I TOLD YOU!

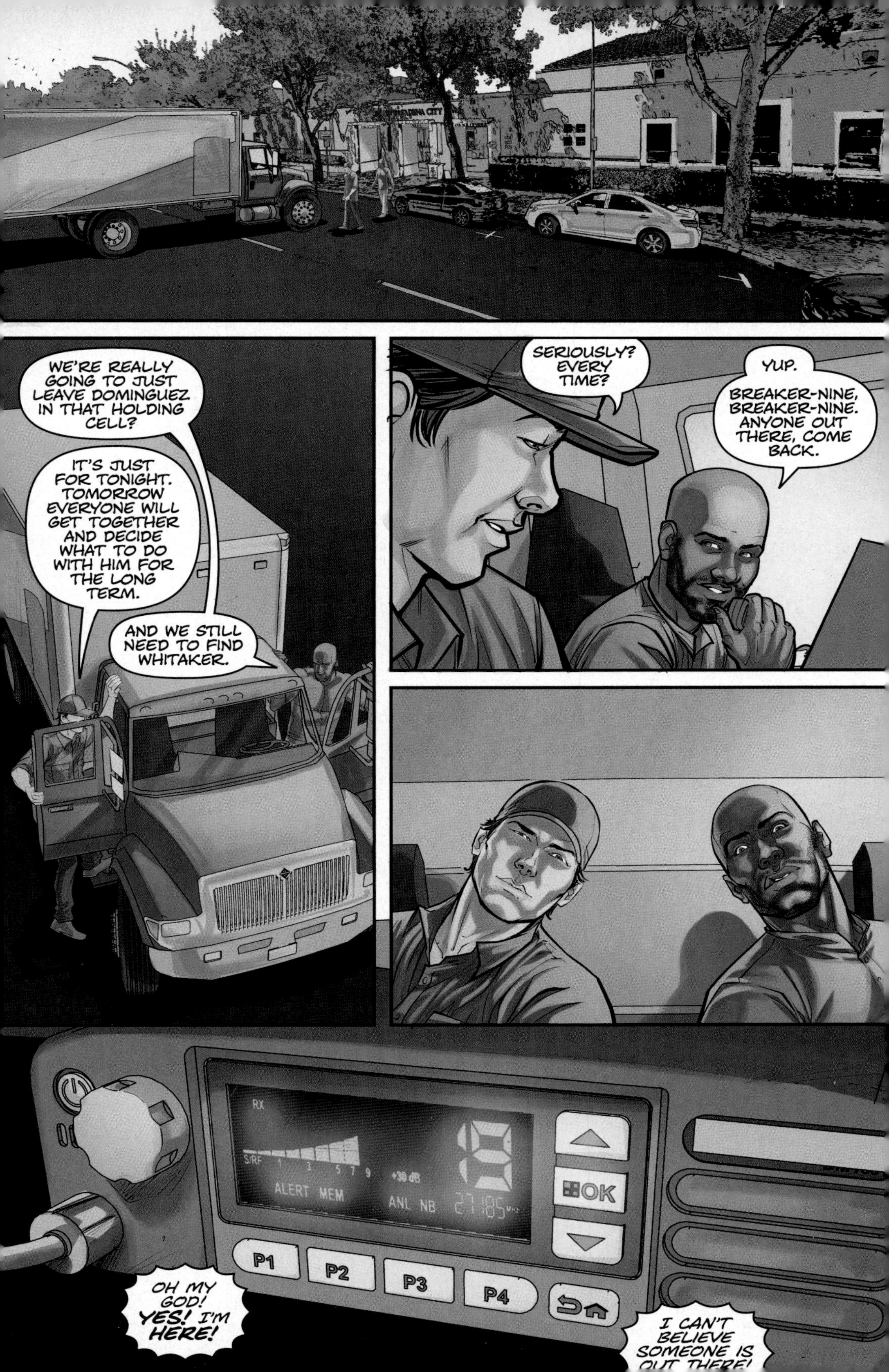
WE'RE REALLY GOING TO JUST LEAVE DOMINGUEZ IN THAT HOLDING CELL?
IT'S JUST FOR TONIGHT. TOMORROW EVERYONE WILL GET TOGETHER AND DECIDE WHAT TO DO WITH HIM FOR THE LONG TERM.
AND WE STILL NEED TO FIND WHITAKER.
SERIOUSLY? EVERY TIME?
YUP.
BREAKER-NINE, BREAKER-NINE. ANYONE OUT THERE, COME BACK.
RX
S/RF 1 3 5 7 9
+30 dB
ALERT MEM
ANL NB
OK
P1
P2
P3
P4
OH MY GOD! YES! I'M HERE!
I CAN'T BELIEVE SOMEONE IS OUT THERE!

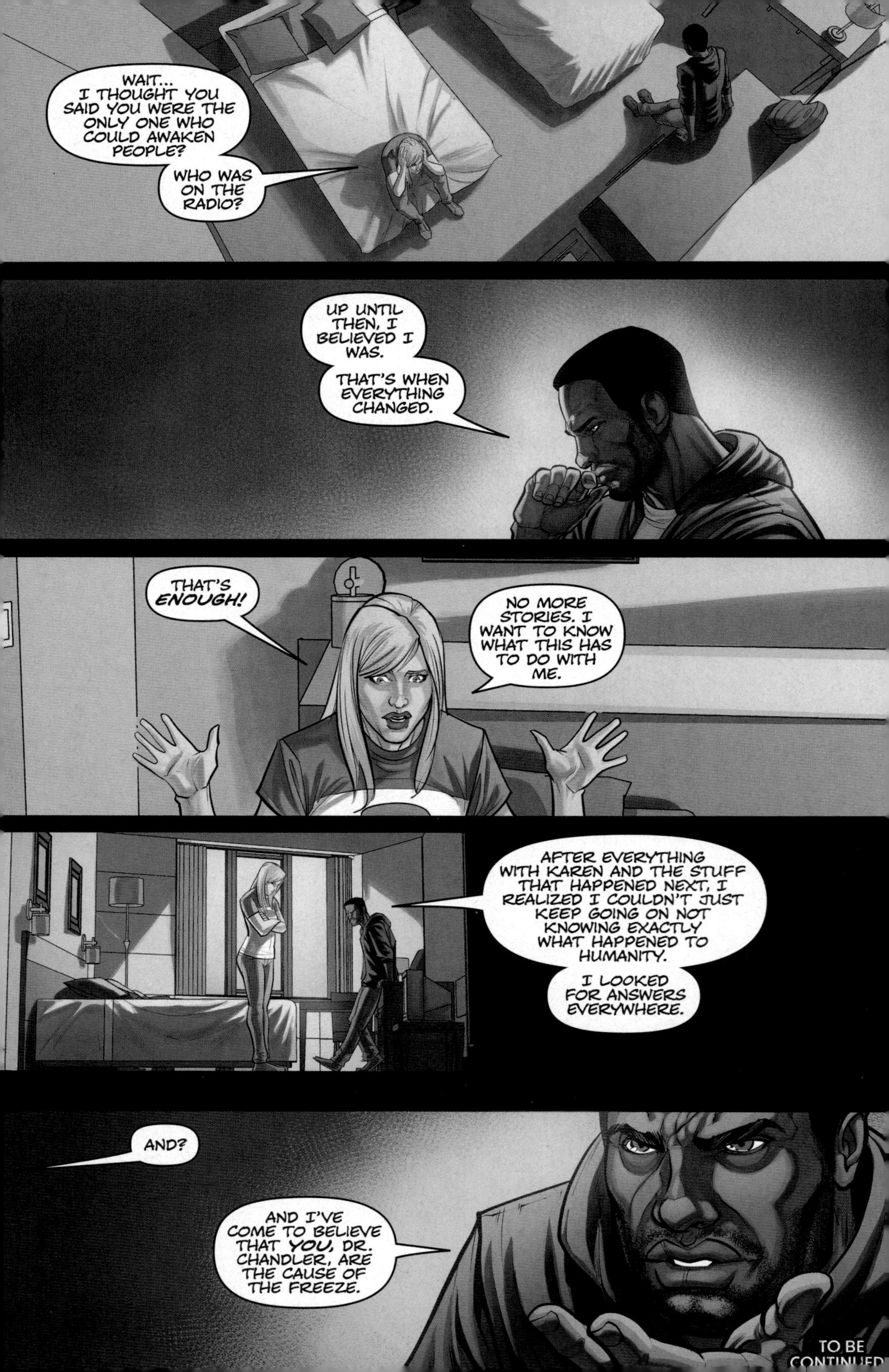
WAIT... I THOUGHT YOU SAID YOU WERE THE ONLY ONE WHO COULD AWAKEN PEOPLE?
WHO WAS ON THE RADIO?
UP UNTIL THEN, I BELIEVED I WAS.
THAT'S WHEN EVERYTHING CHANGED.
THAT'S *ENOUGH!*
NO MORE STORIES. I WANT TO KNOW WHAT THIS HAS TO DO WITH ME.
AFTER EVERYTHING WITH KAREN AND THE STUFF THAT HAPPENED NEXT, I REALIZED I COULDN'T JUST KEEP GOING ON NOT KNOWING EXACTLY WHAT HAPPENED TO HUMANITY.
I LOOKED FOR ANSWERS EVERYWHERE.
AND?
AND I'VE COME TO BELIEVE THAT *YOU,* DR. CHANDLER, ARE THE CAUSE OF THE FREEZE.
TO BE CONTINUED!

FREEZE FRAME

"We shall sell no comic before its time."

If you've been around for a while, you know that phrase is a play on an old wine slogan delivered by the great Orson Wells. It applies very well to THE FREEZE. I've been asked a lot lately about where the concept came from and how long it had been around. The idea goes back to my days as a computer programmer, sitting in my cubicle as my mind wandered as it was wont to do. I remember seeing a co-worker sitting at his desk and not moving. It was kind of eerie. Odds were he fell asleep, but I wasn't going to check. That was enough of a seed for my mind to take off and Ray Adams was quickly born.

As for the when, that's harder to nail down. Sometimes you come up with a story, you bounce it around a bit and then it's on its way to being a series. I did a book called *Blood-Stained Sword* with Ben Templesmith that was like that. From concept to beginning production was maybe a month. And then there are other books like the one you hold in your hand. It's been well over a decade since the original idea came to me. I can't say exactly how many years, but I know the second time I pitched it to a studio I remember seeing a bus stop ad for a new Nathan Fillion series called *Castle* that was debuting later that month. It wasn't the right time for the book then.

Flash-forward eight years and I pitch the story to Matt Hawkins, two days later I get the green light and I'm introduced to the talented Phillip Sevy who asks for the first script. Like a fine wine (I hope), THE FREEZE had found its time.

I've had a lot of fun promoting this book because of the concept. It sounds so simple at first and that's how people tend to react to it. "Oh, he just needs to run around and unfreeze people." As you see in this first issue, it's not as simple as that. Ray must ask himself what awakening someone means to them and to the new society that he's building. Will they be a positive addition or cause dissension or worse? How do you judge that?

I grew up loving science fiction, but not for the spaceships and laser guns... okay, some of it was for those things... but I really liked how authors could address major social issues that would be taboo if they weren't being told with aliens and robots. The best science fiction explores the true depth of humanity, both the good and the bad. And most of the time the real monsters in the story are the humans.

he concept of THE FREEZE is simple because the event that causes it is simple. People top moving. It's what happens next that brings the drama. Ray and the others have to rebuild ociety and each person they add changes things. But people don't change. They still have neir base emotions and are capable of acts of kindness or cruelty. They can be generous or elfish and do things for the group or for themselves. When talking to people about the book, love it when it clicks and they realize all the possibilities of this new universe.

hat's what this series is to me, endless possibilities. There's the overall mystery of what xactly caused the event and how to reverse it (if that's possible). But there are so many ther stories to tell with each new person awoken. What will they add to the world, what angers do they bring? And then there is the overall question you could ask yourself: if the eeze happened and you were the one who could bring people back, would you really want awaken everyone?

hanks for picking up this first issue and I hope you'll stick with Phillip and I as we take this urney. Would love to hear your thoughts, which you can email to **submissions@topcow. om with "Freeze Frame" as the subject line**, and if you mark it 'okay to print' it may just nd up in the back of an upcoming issue.

nd while you wait for issue #2, take a look at the people around you. If everyone stopped noving, who would you unfreeze?

– Dan Wickline

RAY ADAMS   LISA DUARTE   GAVIN ORDWAY   NIZAM RAHMAN   DAISY KWON   MARIA DUARTE

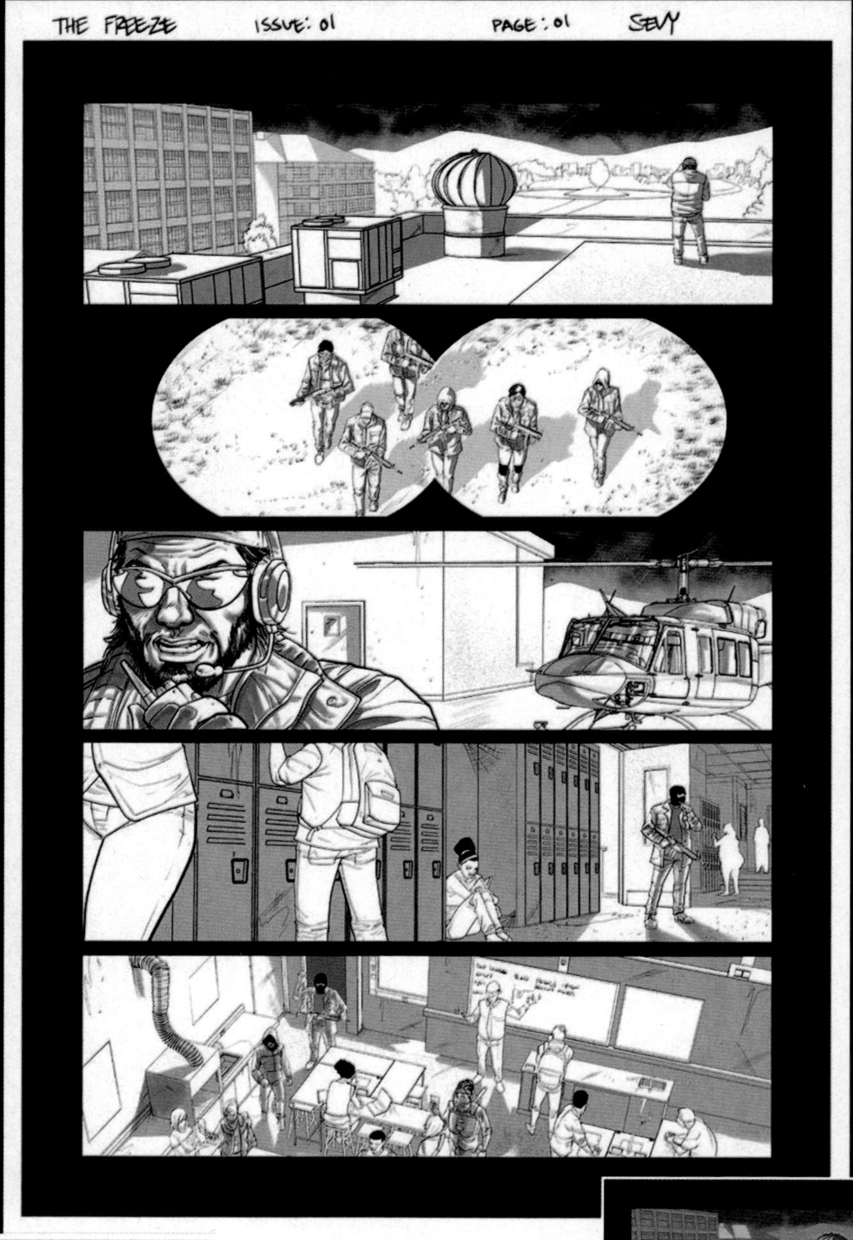
THE FREEZE
ISSUE: 01
PAGE: 01
SEVY

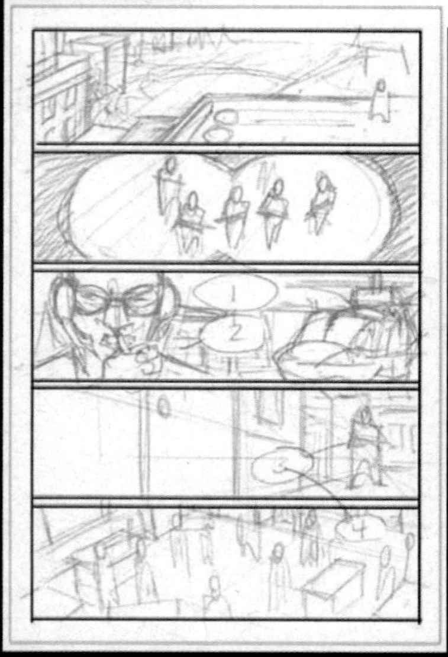

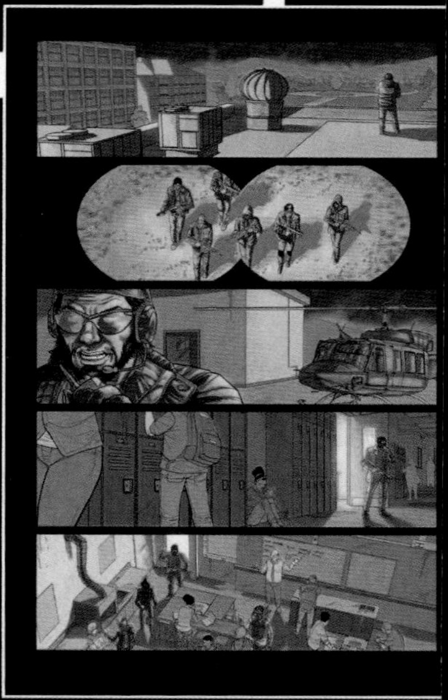

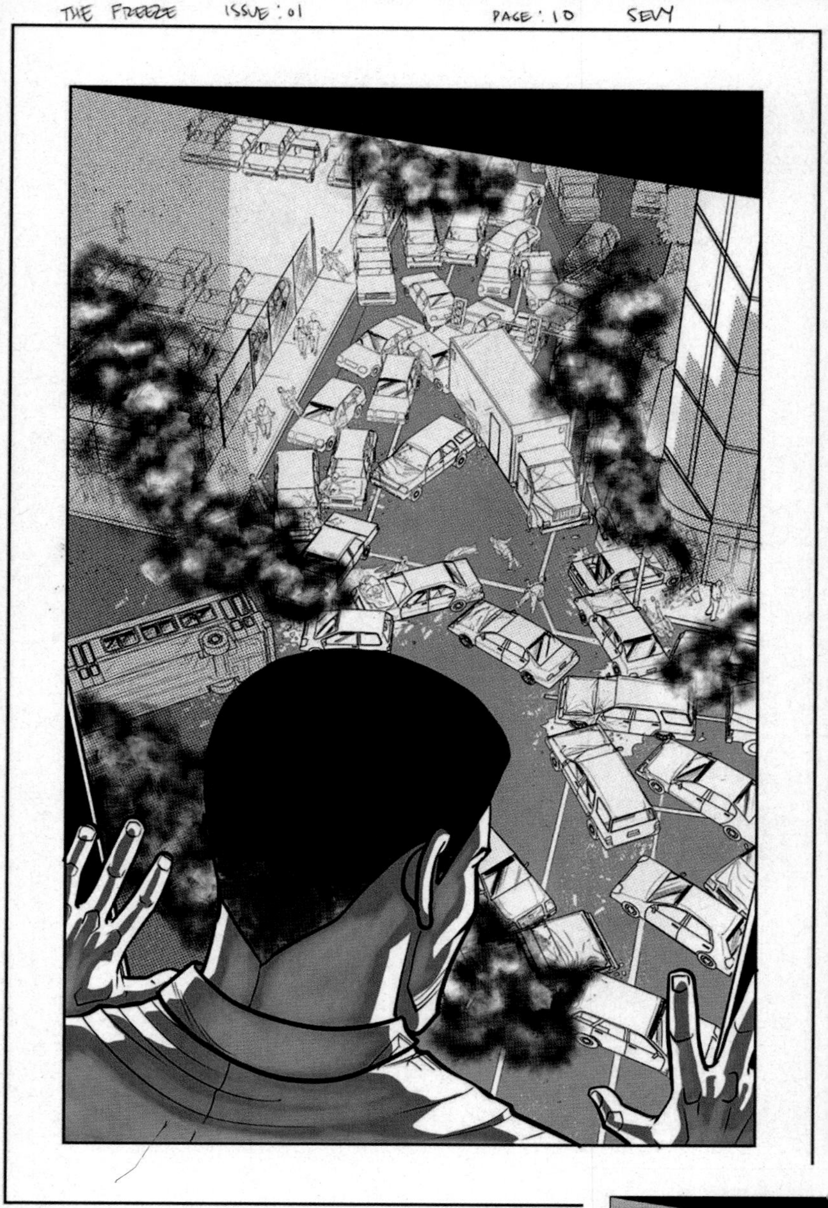
THE FREEZE ISSUE: 01 PAGE: 10 SEVY

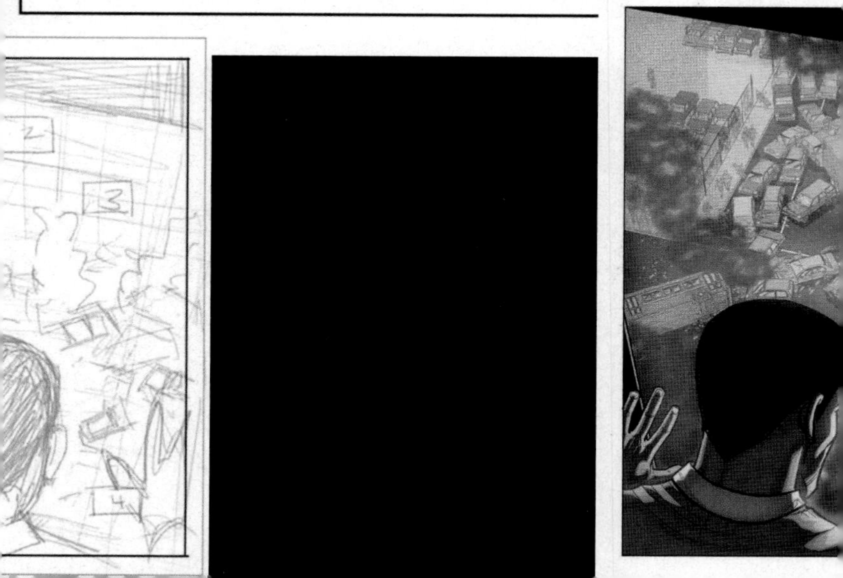

THE FREEZE ISSUE: 01 PAGE: 20 SEVY

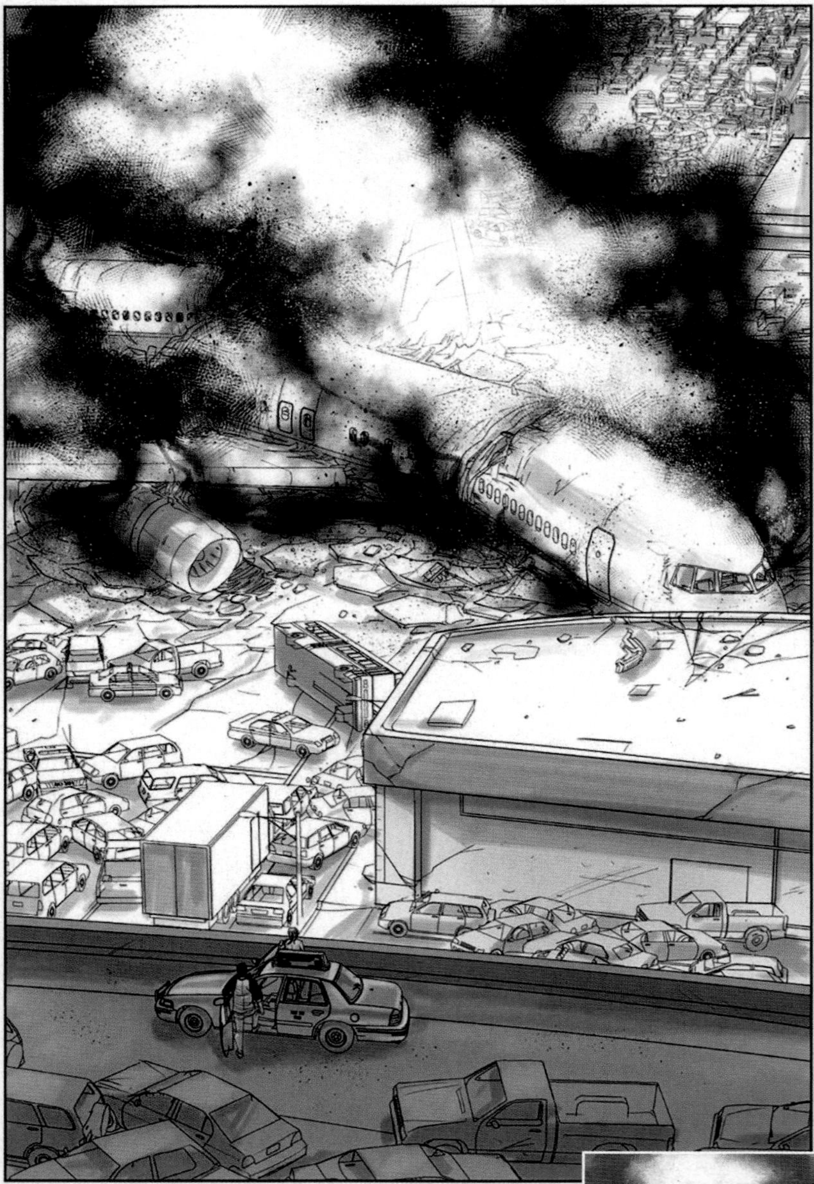

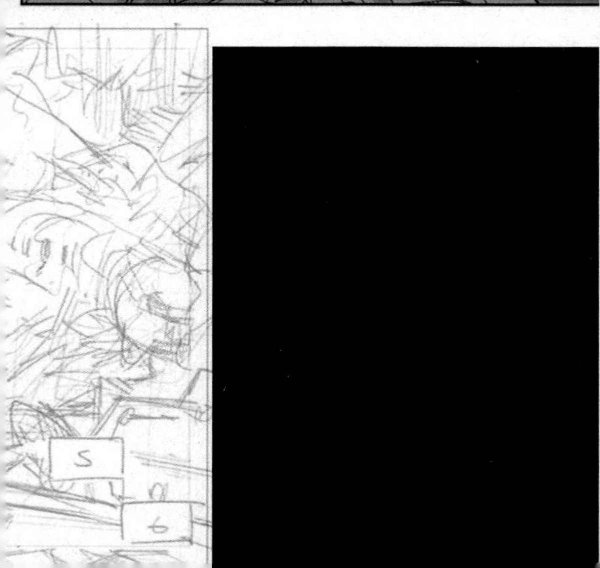
5
6

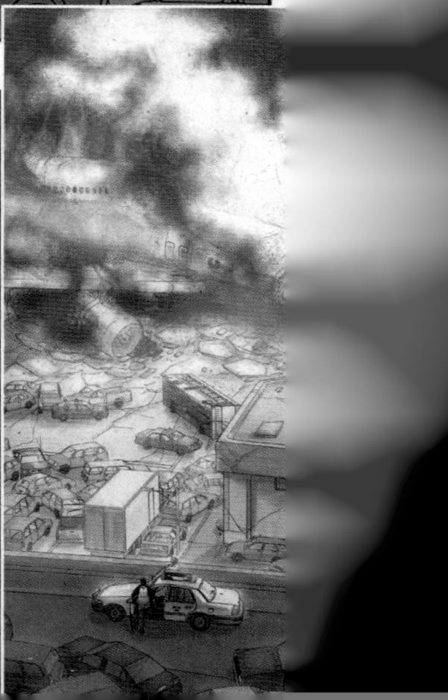

FREEZE FRAME

"Nature Abhors a Vacuum" –Aristotle

urns out, so do writers. We need an audience and feedback
n our work, both positive and negative. And while we get
ome of it from our editors and artists, the true test of a story
omes when the book is finally in readers' hands. As I type
o this article, I've already turned in the script for issue four
nd the first issue just hit the shelves five days ago. We're
nally hearing what you guys think and we really appreciate
l the kind words. Thank you to everyone who picked up the
rst issue and to all of you who got on social media or came
nd saw Phillip or I at our signings and let us know what you
ought. It means the world to us.

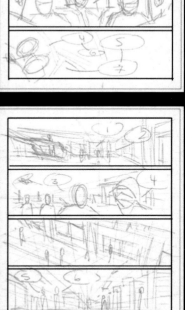

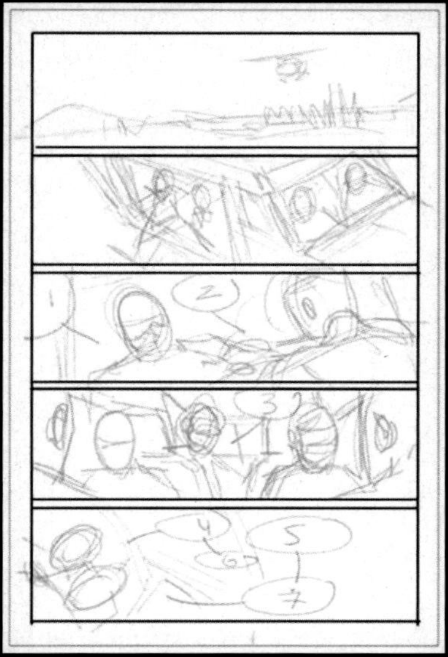

lso, welcome back to issue two. After the first issue, I could've
one a lot of different directions or spent time with Ray, Lisa
nd the crew dealing with putting out fires, deciding on how
eir new society would work and waking each person,
ut I felt moving ahead to the next big event would be the
est move. The story here is as much about Ray as it is
he Freeze. The Ray we see in the opening pages is very
fferent from the one who innocently went to work before
e event happened. We are going to see how he changes
nd just where he ends up when all is said and done.

all comes down to power and how it affects people. Some
ave it, others accept it while a few avoid it like a plague.
ut that is just part of it. How do these same people react
hen power is taken away? We see it around us every day.
orrible things are done in an effort to obtain power and
ven worse things are done in order to retain it. People
ecome obsessed with it. They become addicted to it and it
an take over their lives. Makes those that avoid it seem like
e wise ones sometimes.

nd the worst part is, someone must claim the power. We're
ack to the thing about nature abhorring a vacuum and in
is case a power vacuum will cause huge problems in a
ociety. Until someone takes charge there will be chaos.
here it seems that Gavin is being a bit power hungry and
etting himself up in a position of leadership, he also knows
e importance of having leaders in a society. Even in the
ost primitive cultures, tribes were formed, and leaders
ose. Rules began to be made whether through edict or
eligion. Humans create societies, it's what we do.

This episode picks up with the new society underway and groups forming within that societ[y]. People meeting up based on similar interests and beliefs like we do now. People are creature[s] of habit and they take comfort in those habits when everything else around them goes craz[y]. That's why we pick up with the group focused on rebuilding society and not as focused o[n] the cause as you might expect. They focus first on getting control of the situation.

Unless you're the type that reads the backmatter in a comic first, then you know that the[ir] attempt at getting some sense of normalcy goes out the window when Lisa and Maria go [to] the grocery store. This is where things start getting twisted… and fun.

And while you wait for issue #3, ask yourself what your priorities would be if you were in th[e] situation. Would you try to undo what happened and revive everyone, or would you focus o[n] getting control of your situation first? Would you want to be in charge? What would you do [if] someone else tried to take charge?

—Dan Wicklin[e]

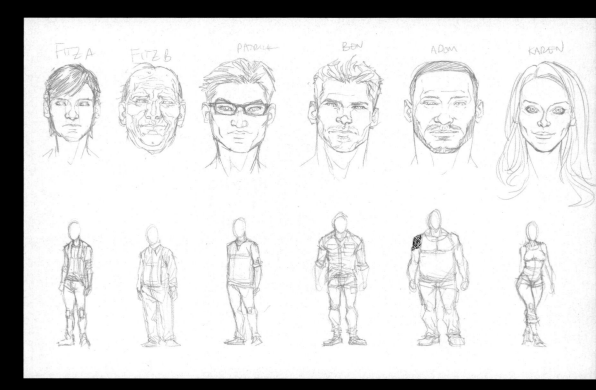

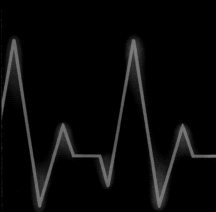

THE FREEZE ISSUE: 02 COVER SEVY

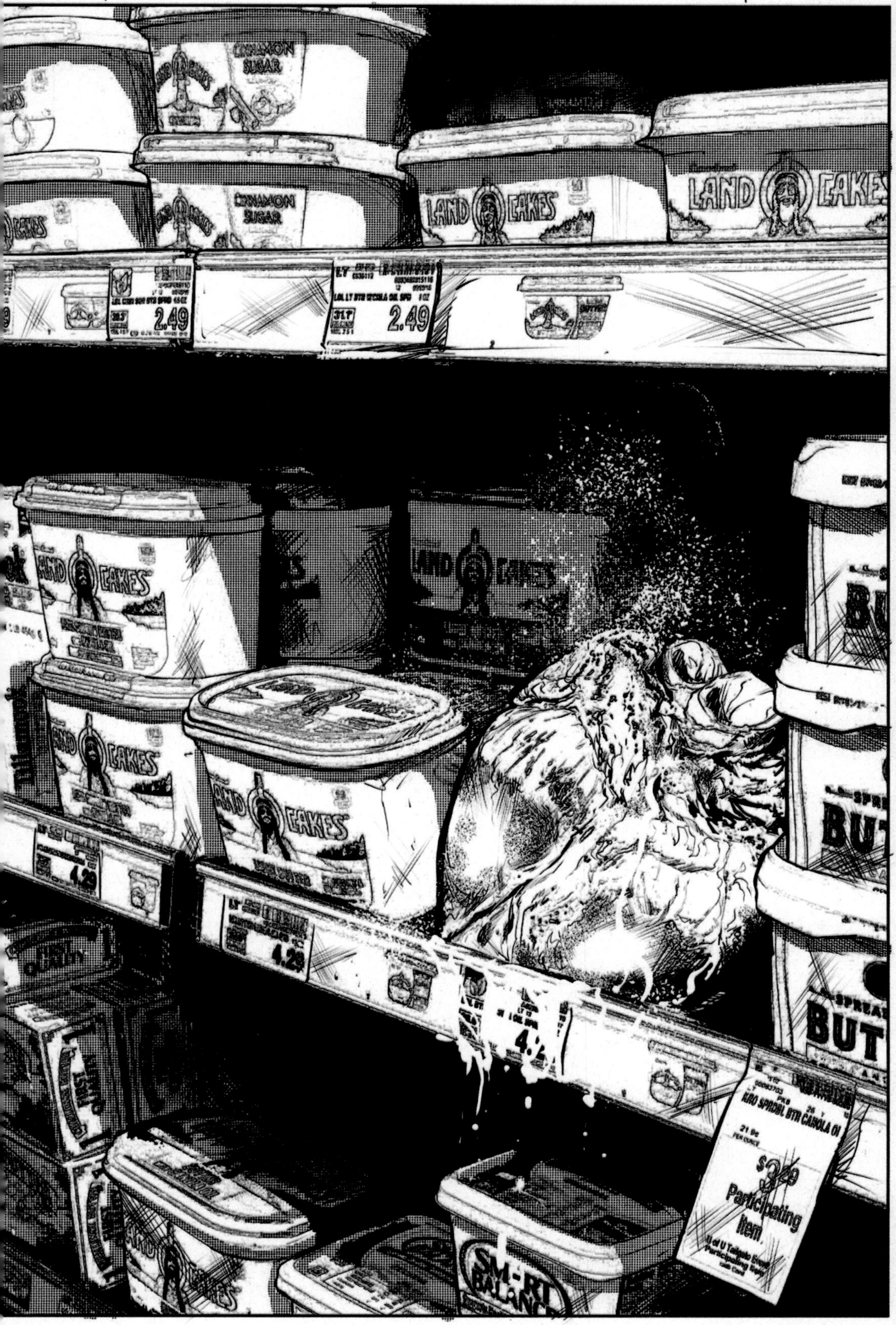
CINNAMON SUGAR
LAND O CAKES
CINNAMON SUGAR
LAND O CAKES
LAND O CAKES
2.49
2.49
LAND O CAKES
LAND O CAKES
LAND O CAKES
LAND O CAKES
4.29
4.29
BUT
BUT
$3.49
Participating Item
SM-RT BALANCE

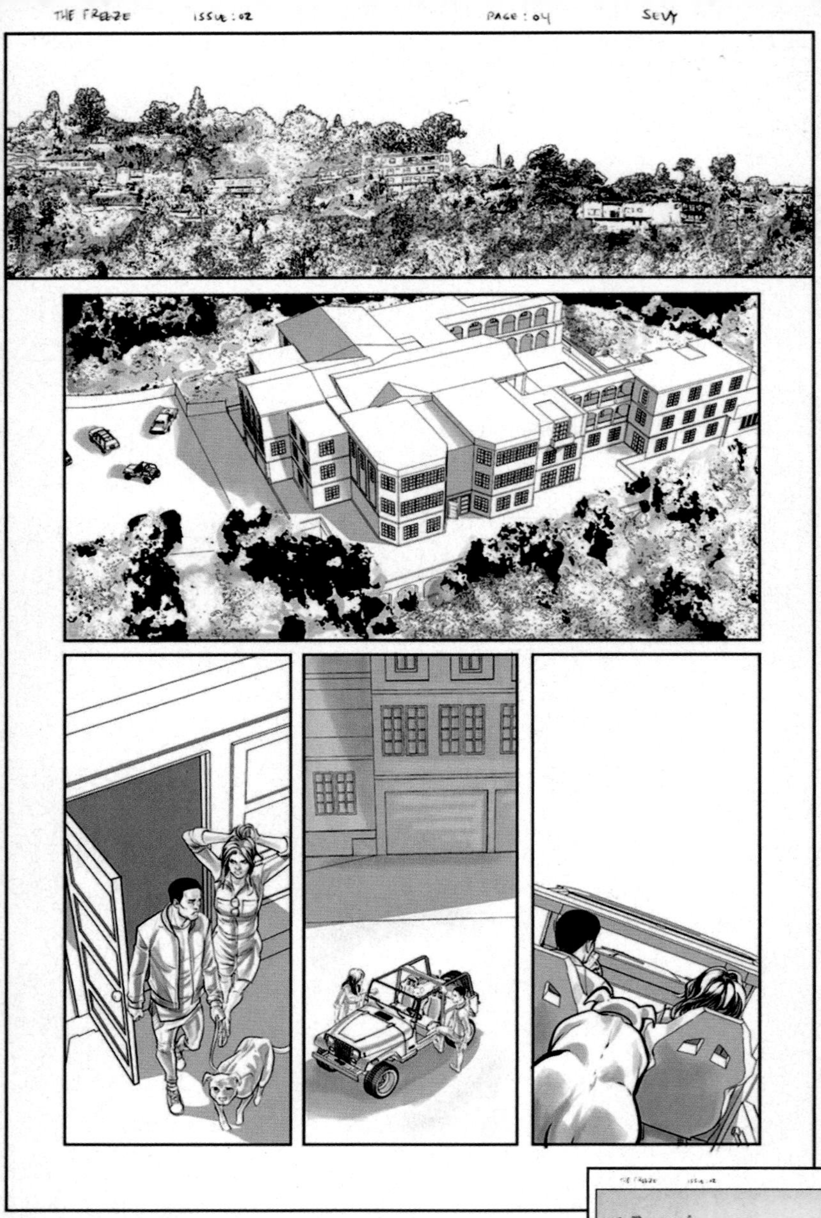
THE FREEZE
ISSUE:02
PAGE:04
SEVY

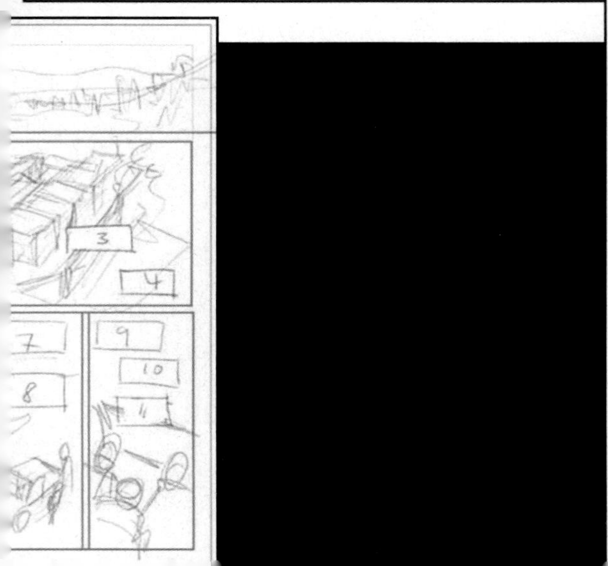

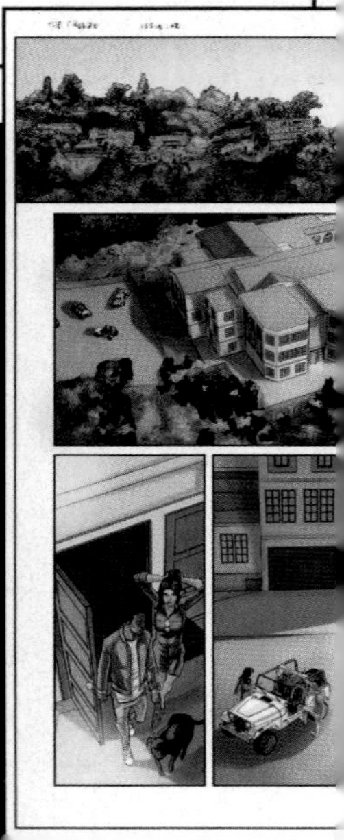

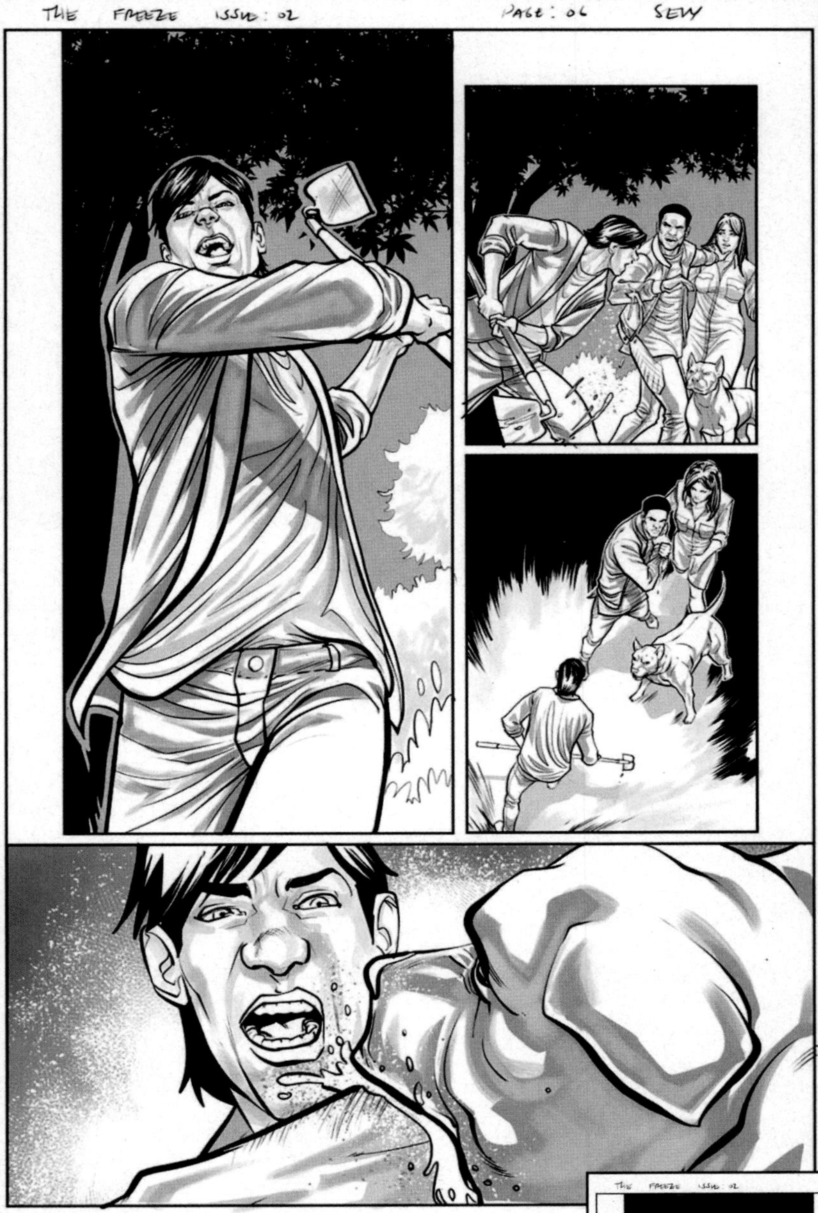
THE FREEZE ISSUE: 02
PAGE: 06 SEVY

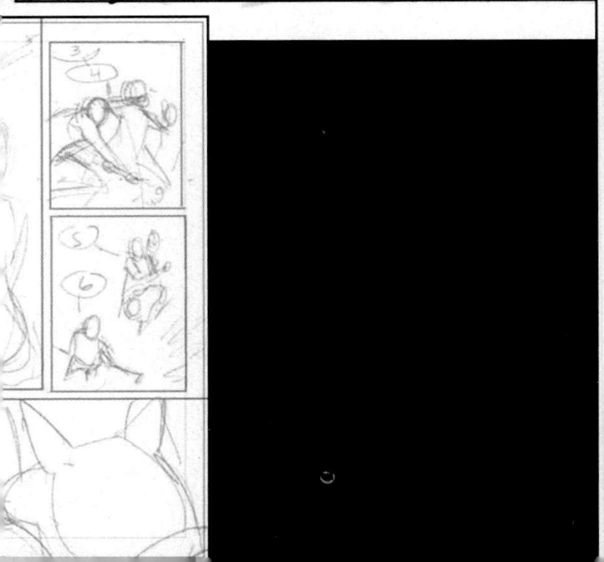

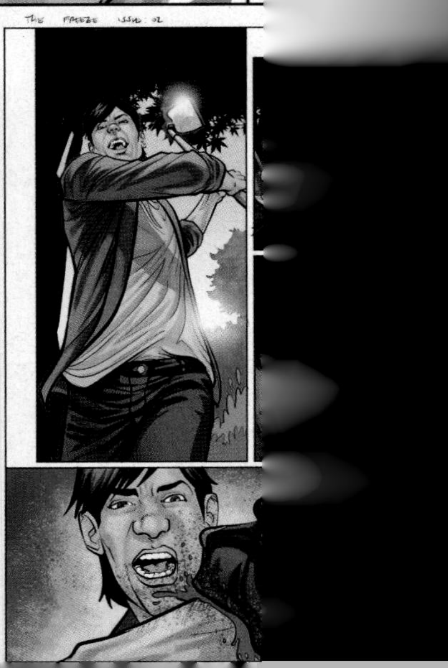
THE FREEZE ISSUE: 02

s! Phillip here. Dan and I were talking the other month and we de
e backmatter of issue 3 if I took over and gave you a tour of my
generally get a kick out of the BTS/WIP shots I post on my
hought I'd give some context.

gh the steps for issue 3, page 15 (the big bodies splash page
s very important, labor intensive, and my favorite page of this

---

PAGE FIFTEEN (1 Panels)

ill-page splash of the inside of the truck. It is filled with a bunch of bodies stacked on top of
here are bags of hearts tied to each body. This needs to be a really gruesome scene. Go to
page.

WINSTON
Somebody's been very busy.

---

n Dan's script. As you can see, Dan left a lot of the page up to me
three issues at this point, we're pretty comfortable with wha
ring to the table. Dan's very cool to generally give me space to
it up (hopefully you feel "my thing" more than me screwing it up
erpret the script to the best of my skills.

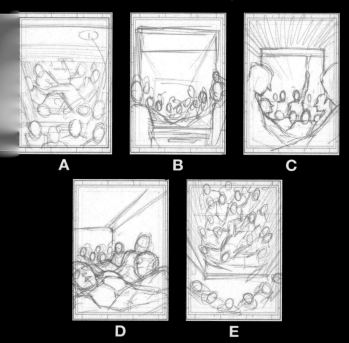

pt, I scribble up thumbnails and then layouts. Because this pac
ne, I went back to the drawing board and gave Dan five opti
d option E and I was cool with it too

ow, the part that makes everyone laugh. I nd to use a lot of reference when I draw. speeds up my process and allows me to et subtleties that I might not just drawing raight from my head. While working on book like *Tomb Raider*, I actually hired model to pose for my Lara shots, but r something like THE FREEZE (and other rojects) that are more grounded in reality, I st take reference photos of myself. I'll take e photos with my camera, on a poseable ipod, with a timer. I import the photos to my computer, then cut them up, copy nd paste them into Clip Studio Paint, and range them to match my layouts. What end up with (as you can see) is often a OT of Phillips interacting with each other. 's ridiculous. We've started calling them e "Council of Phils." This one particularly racked me up, because it's a van full of ead mes (I might have some issues).

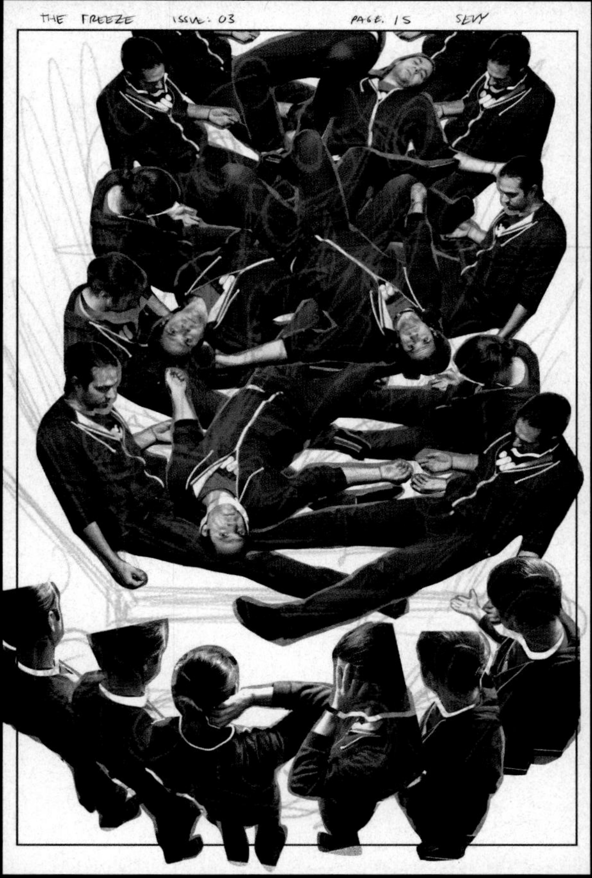
THE FREEZE
ISSUE: 03
PAGE. 15
SEVY

ext stage is pencils. The reference is the ase, but I draw all the different characters, enders, body types, clothing (or lack hereof) etc. from my imagination. I'll spare ou all my reference photos of open-heart urgeries and spread-open chest cavities hat I had to do for this page. It was gross. ake care of your cardiovascular systems, ids—you don't want that surgery if you an avoid it.

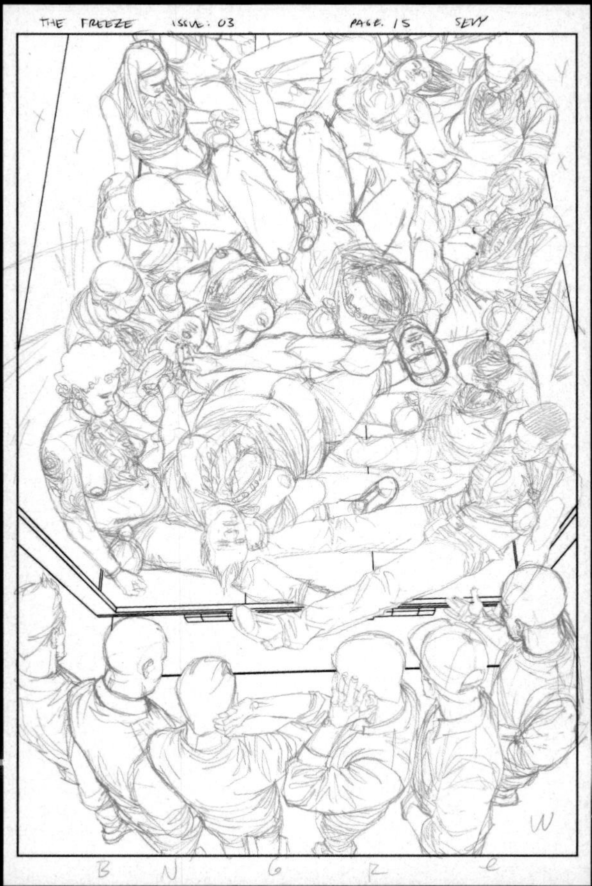
THE FREEZE
ISSUE: 03
PAGE. 15
SEVY

After that, inks! Working digitally, I pencil and ink in Clip Studio Paint using primarily Richard Frenden's amazing brushes. I keep my linework more open right now (and when I'm coloring myself) because of the next step:

THE FREEZE
ISSUE: 03
PAGE. 15
SEVY

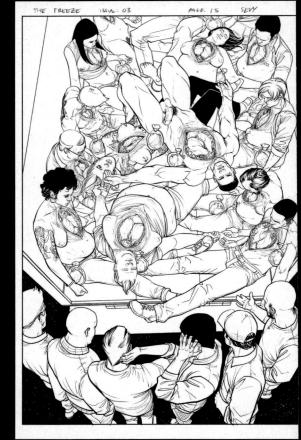

Gray tones. I digitally paint gray tones into my pages. It's an extra step that can be time consuming, but I like the control over the volumization of the shapes I've drawn. It also gives me some value control. In addition, when I color the pages, I use the gray tones as a shadow layer and it cuts down on my coloring time.

THE FREEZE
ISSUE: 03
PAGE. 15
SEVY

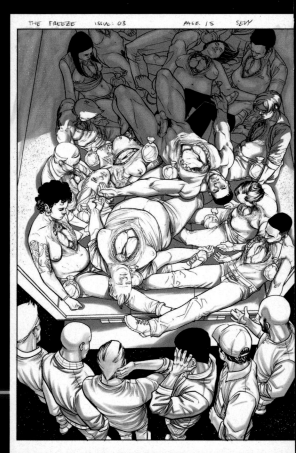

er the black and white work is done, nd my pages to my flatter. Fernando üello is my trusty and faithful flatter and ve him my life and sanity. He's flatted rly every page of this book. However, he n't flat this page. Because of his crazy kload and some holiday deadlines, I a former student (and amazing artist er own right), Lacey LeBlanc, flat a few es in this issue. She drew the short w and got this page. But as you can Lacey did a great job (she even flatted he little designs in character tattoos!). ting is the process of outlining shapes throwing in block colors. I take this e and change the colors and use it to t coloring.

THE FREEZE ISSUE: 03 PAGE. 15 SEVY

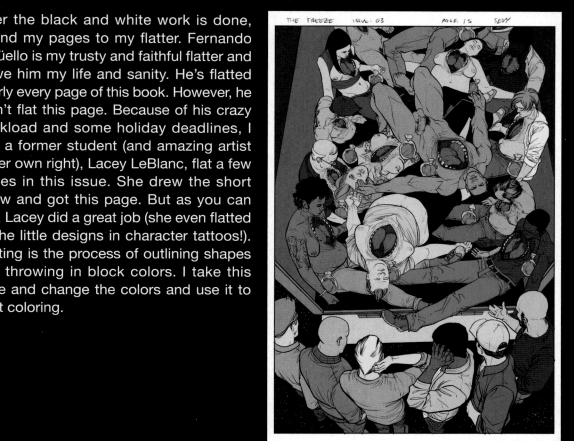

oring. THE FREEZE has been so fun d so much work) to do because Top v let me color myself. I take all the art put it in Photoshop. I then press the lor It" button and voila! It's done. Just ding. Hardly. There's even more work choices and thinking that goes into oring because it's a newer thing for me. there we go! The insane art process I to bring the book to you.

THE FREEZE ISSUE: 03 PAGE. 15 SEVY

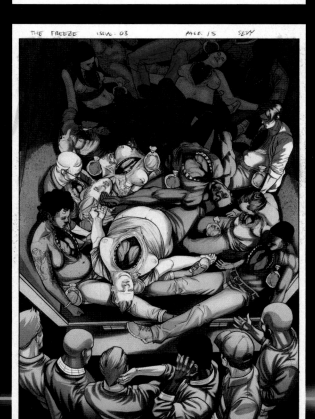

FREEZE FRAME

"Always make the audience suffer as much as possible." – **Alfred Hitchcock**

As you get to this page, you've seen the end of the first arc of *The Freeze* and gotten some answers. While other questions remain open. That's the nature of storytelling, always leave them wanting more. In the first issue I asked folks to write in and we appreciated every letter, email and social media comment. Here are a few of the ones got:

Hello Freeze Team,
 must say once I heard the synopsis of this book I was hooked. Instantly. I contacted my local comic book shop (9.9 Comics in Melbourne, FL) and made sure that they we going to put an issue on hold for me. I've always been interested in "what if" type stor especially the kind that changes just one small variable in our ordinary lives. Just like many episodes of *The Twilight Zone*, or most recently *The Leftovers*, these tales open mind to what may happen if things were another way. How quickly would things spira out of control in a world where the colors green and red instantly flipped for example. wouldn't take much for it to happen in my opinion.

So I just finished issue #1 and my expectations were met and I can't wait to see wher this story goes. I know I'm intrigued because I keep debating what I would do in Ray's shoes. Once I convince myself that it only makes sense to unfreeze everyone, I flip an start thinking what could be done with this power. It's a heavy burden for Ray regardle Also, can he freeze someone back? Is he the only one with this power? Why did this anomaly happen in the first place? I'll just have to keep reading I suppose.

Jonathan Hedrick

———

Dan,

Just finished reading *The Freeze #1* it has all the elements needed for a Post-Apocaly classic. I love the defrosted group of potential frenemies, hopefully they'll have to figh survival and possibly one another *Night of the Living Dead* - without the zombies - sty
 don't envy Ray "Uneasy lies the head that wears a crown" as The Bard said. The init solation, the social and ethnical implications of choosing who to unfreeze, this is goir be great.

Create wonder
Wes Chambers

eeze #1 is the only comic I have ever read two times in a row. I'm not sure what that eans, nonetheless I wanted to share. I've got a good feeling about this story. Did the imals get frozen too? Insects? Seems like even liquid got frozen mid air (coffee drinker page 8)! What will they eat if they can't chew or swallow stuff?! Ahhhh so many uestions!

ennis Harrison
ash. DC

There,
if you're reading this that means Ray has unfroze you. That was nice of him. d damn do I love the moral complications of Freeze. The concepts great and I've een thinking about where I'd draw the line if I was Ray. Do I never unfreeze a Trump upporter? Would that make the world a better place? What about all the Sharia law xtremists? How do you grapple with what makes the world a better place for you ersonally and what makes it better overall? I mean c'mon it's pretty presumptuous to ink you know "better". Anyway, you're probably going with "Freeze Frame" as a letters olumn name (which I despise because it sticks the J Geils Band song in my head) but I'd e to suggest "Thawing it out" or "Ray Adams Frozen Delicacies" or "Words that don't uck".
nyway, keep up the good work and I'm looking forward to what's hopefully a long run for e series.

anks
ake Ohlhausen

S. A big shout out to Mark and Francie at *Black Cat Comics* in rocking Milpitas, Ca for ulling the book for me. They're the best in the biz!!

y goal with THE FREEZE was to make the readers think… now you get to think about hat's going to happen next. A sincere thank you to the amazingly talented group of eople working on this book: Phillip Sevy, Troy Peteri, Elena Salcedo, Matt Hawkins and veryone at Top Cow. And a very special thank you to everyone who has picked up a opy of this series, you are our partners on this journey and we appreciate you coming ong for the ride.

Dan Wickline

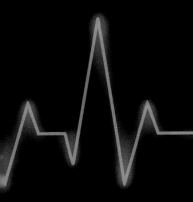

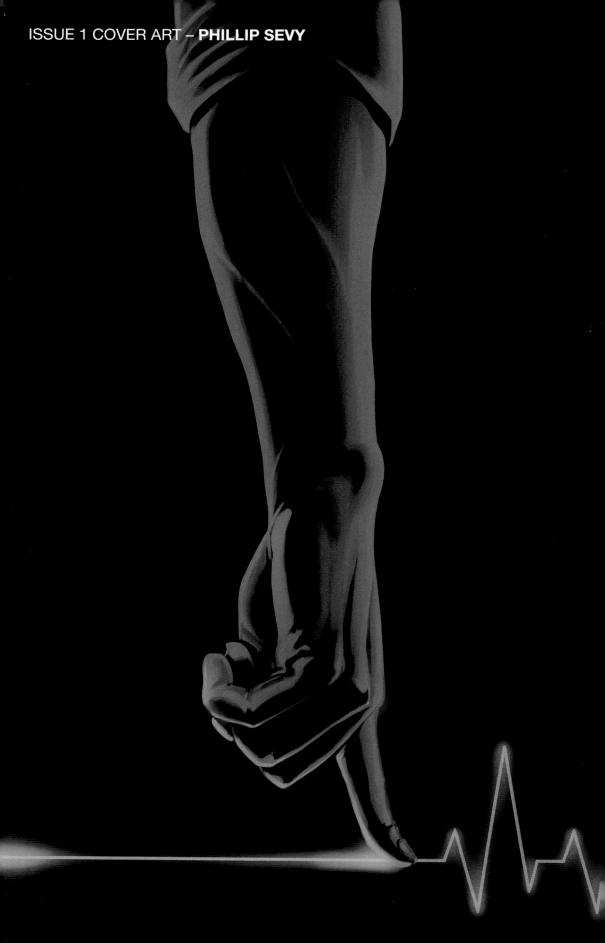

ISSUE 1 COVER ART – **PHILLIP SEVY**

ISSUE 1 HERO INITIATIVE VARIANT COVER – **RAFFAELE IENCO**

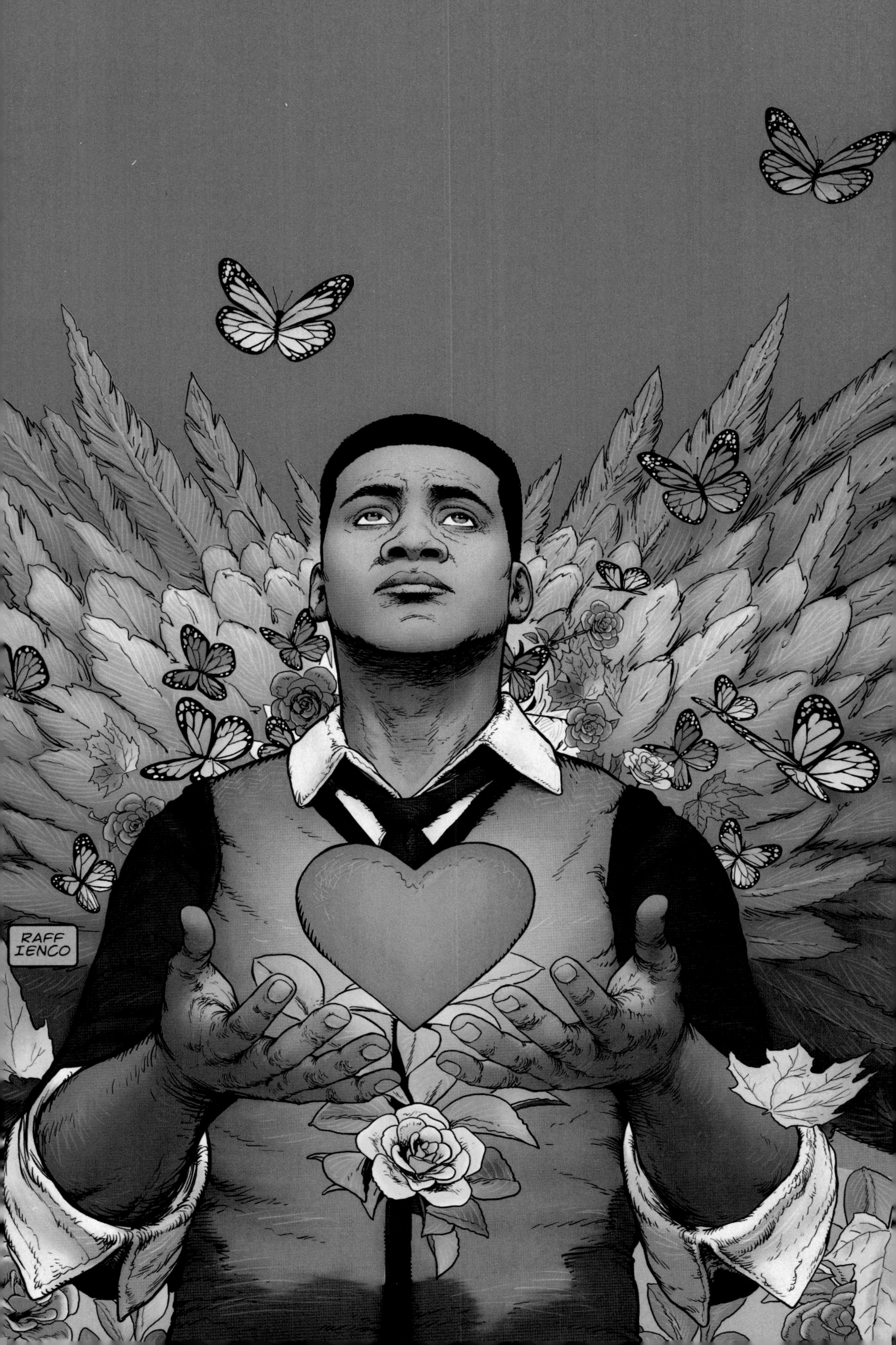
RAFF
IENCO

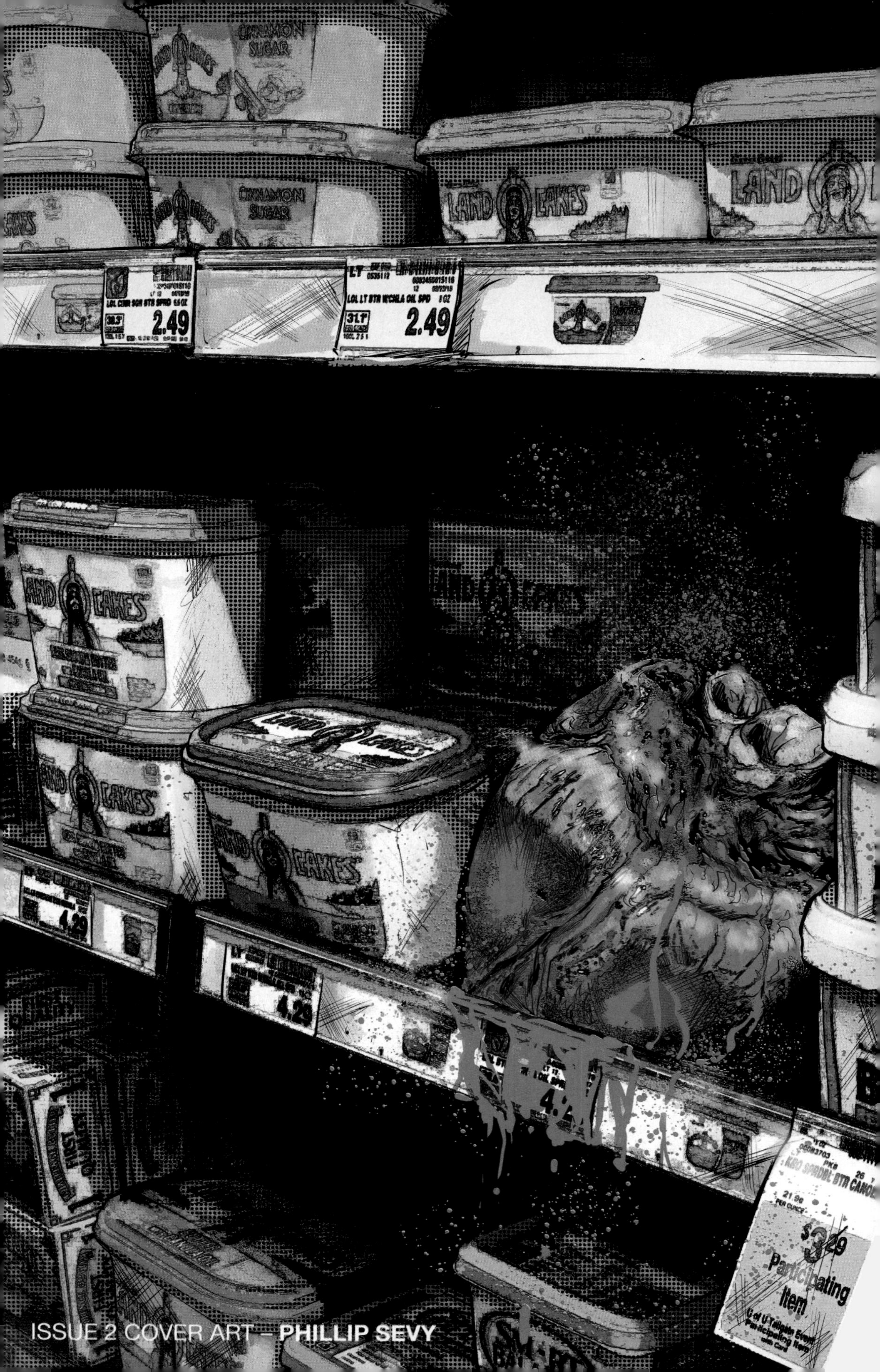
CINNAMON SUGAR
LAND O CAKES
2.49
2.49
4.29
4.29
Participating Item

ISSUE 2 COVER ART – **PHILLIP SEVY**

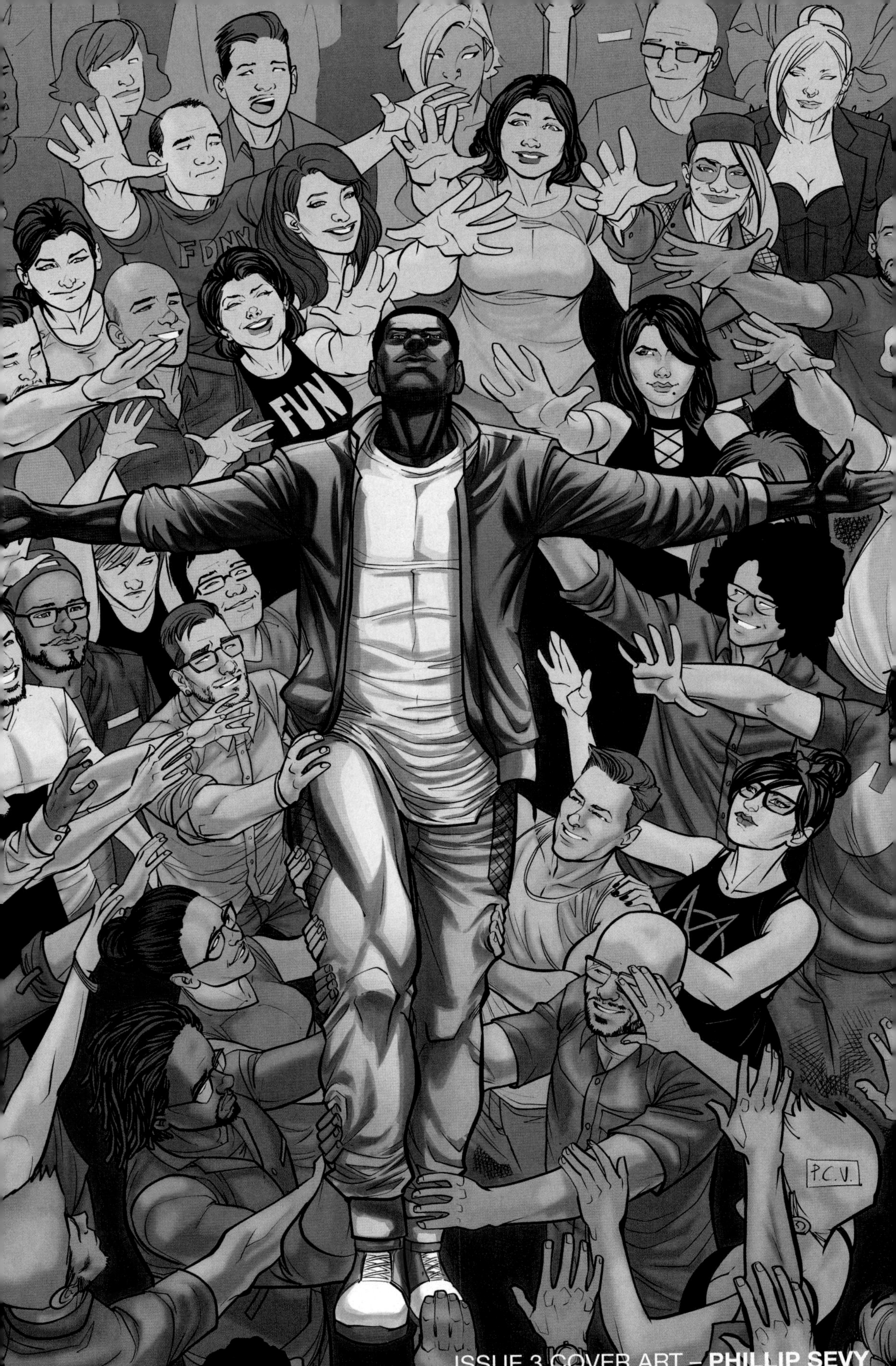
FDNY
FUN
P.C.V.
ISSUE 3 COVER ART – **PHILLIP SEVY**

ISSUE 4 COVER ART – **PHILLIP SEVY**

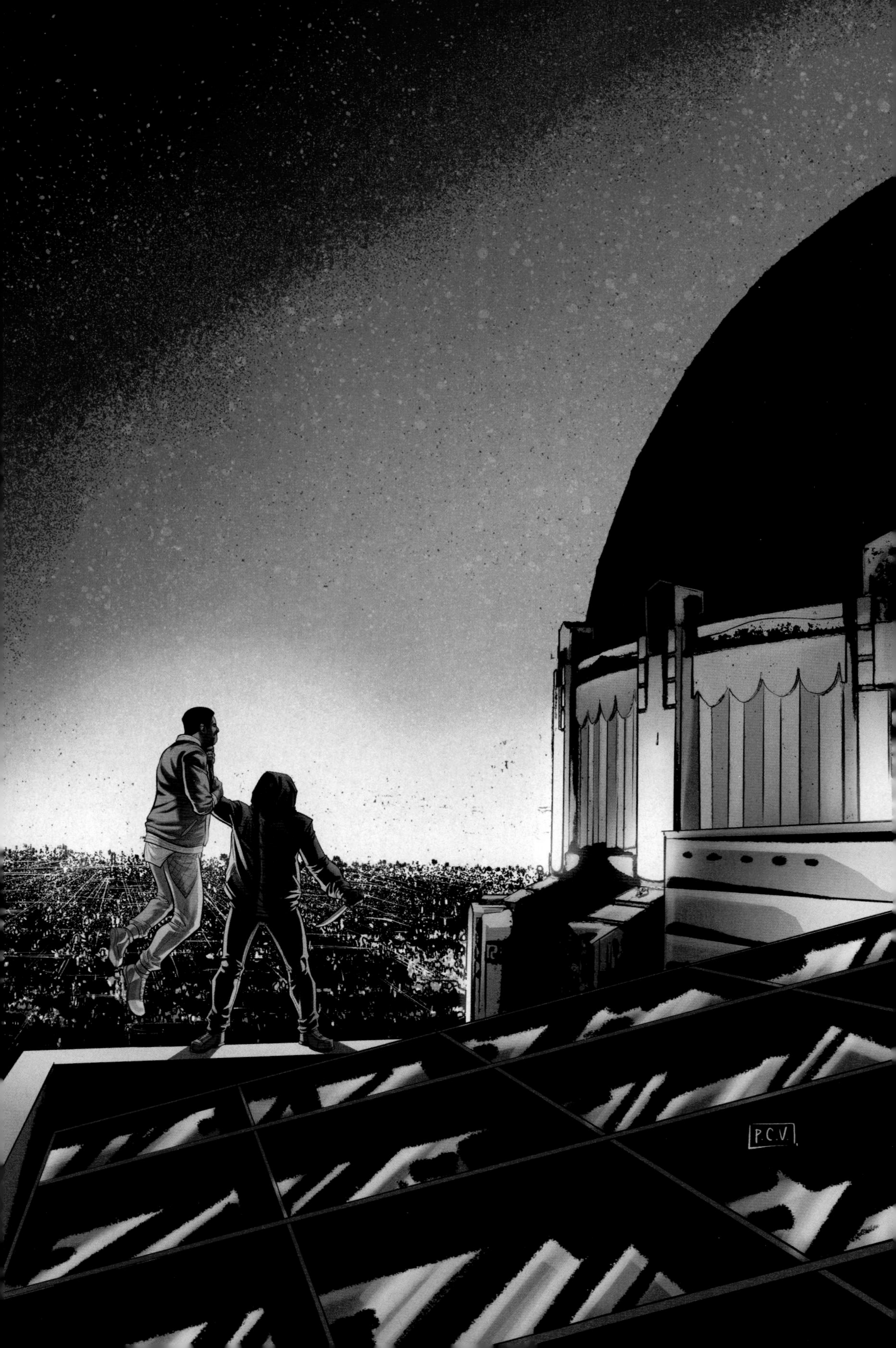
P.C.V.

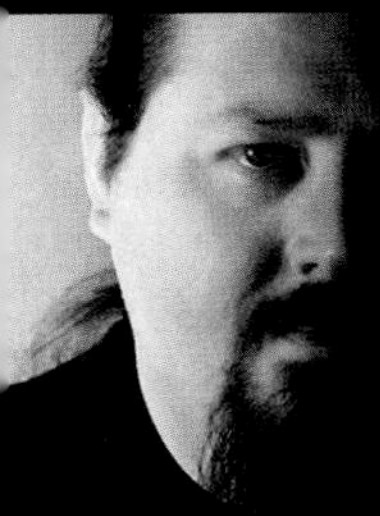

DAN WICKLINE has written for Image Comics, IDW Publishing, Humanoids Publishing, Zenescope Entertainment, Avatar Press, Top Cow and Dynamite Entertainment. He's also scripted for *The Metal Hurlant Chronicles* television series and has penned three novels featuring his character Lucius Fogg—*Deadly Creatures*, *Malicious Intent*, and *Educated Corpses*. He is currently finishing his next novel, *Blythe: the Trailer Park Knight Rises*.

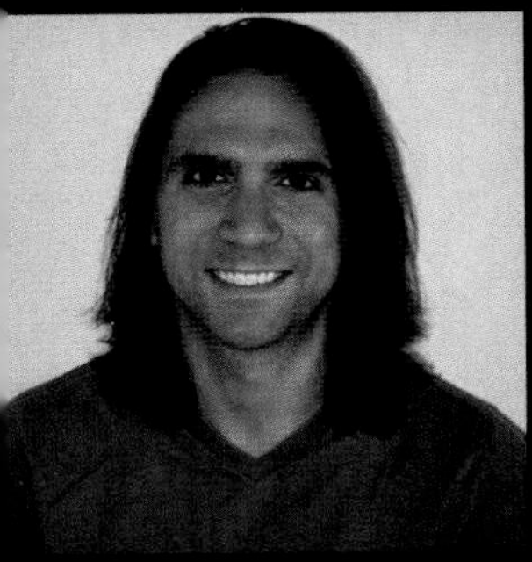

PHILLIP SEVY loves comics. Always has. Always will. He drew his first one at age 4. Over 25 years later, he was a runner-up in the Top Cow Talent Hunt 2013 and his career began. He graduated with an MFA in Sequential Art from SCAD and has worked for Top Cow, Black Mask, Valiant, Zenescope, Action Lab, and most notably on a long run of *Tomb Raider* for Dark Horse. In between drawing projects, he self-published *Paradox* and wrote *The House* (with artist Drew Zucker). Phillip lives in Utah with his wife (just one) and kids (only two). You can keep up with his work at **phillipsevy.com.**

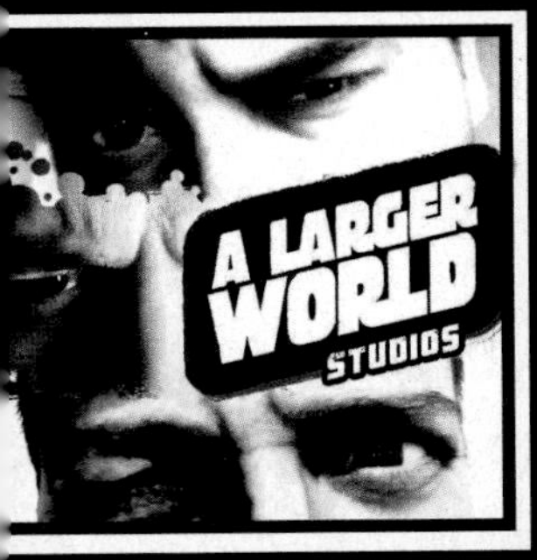
A LARGER WORLD
STUDIOS

TROY PETERI, Dave Lanphear and Joshua Cozine are collectively known as A Larger World Studios. They've lettered everything from *The Avengers*, *Iron Man*, *Wolverine*, *Amazing Spider-Man*, and *X-Men* to more recent titles such as WITCHBLADE, CYBERFORCE, and *Batman/Wonder Woman: The Brave & The Bold*. They can be reached at studio@alargerworld.com for your lettering and design needs. (Hooray, commerce!)

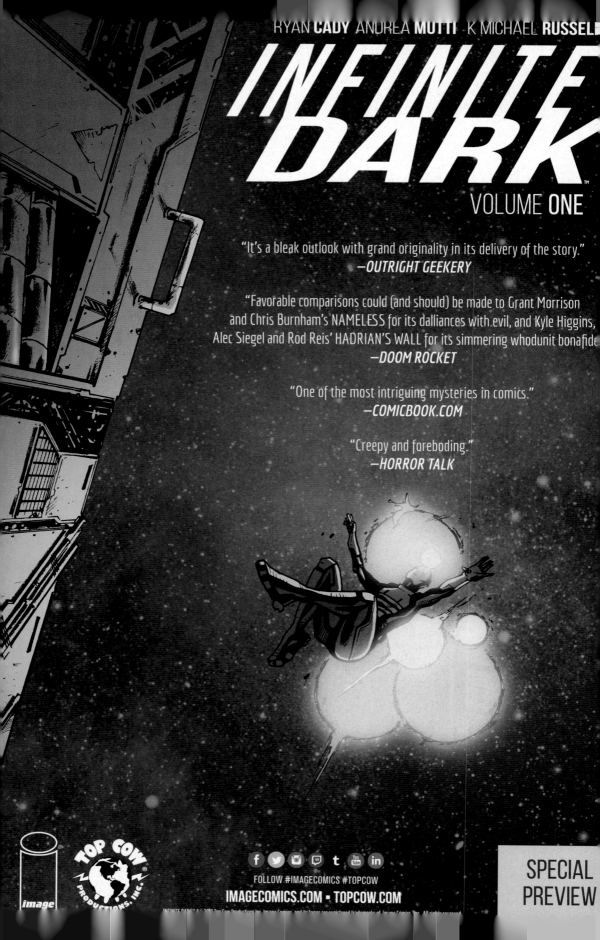

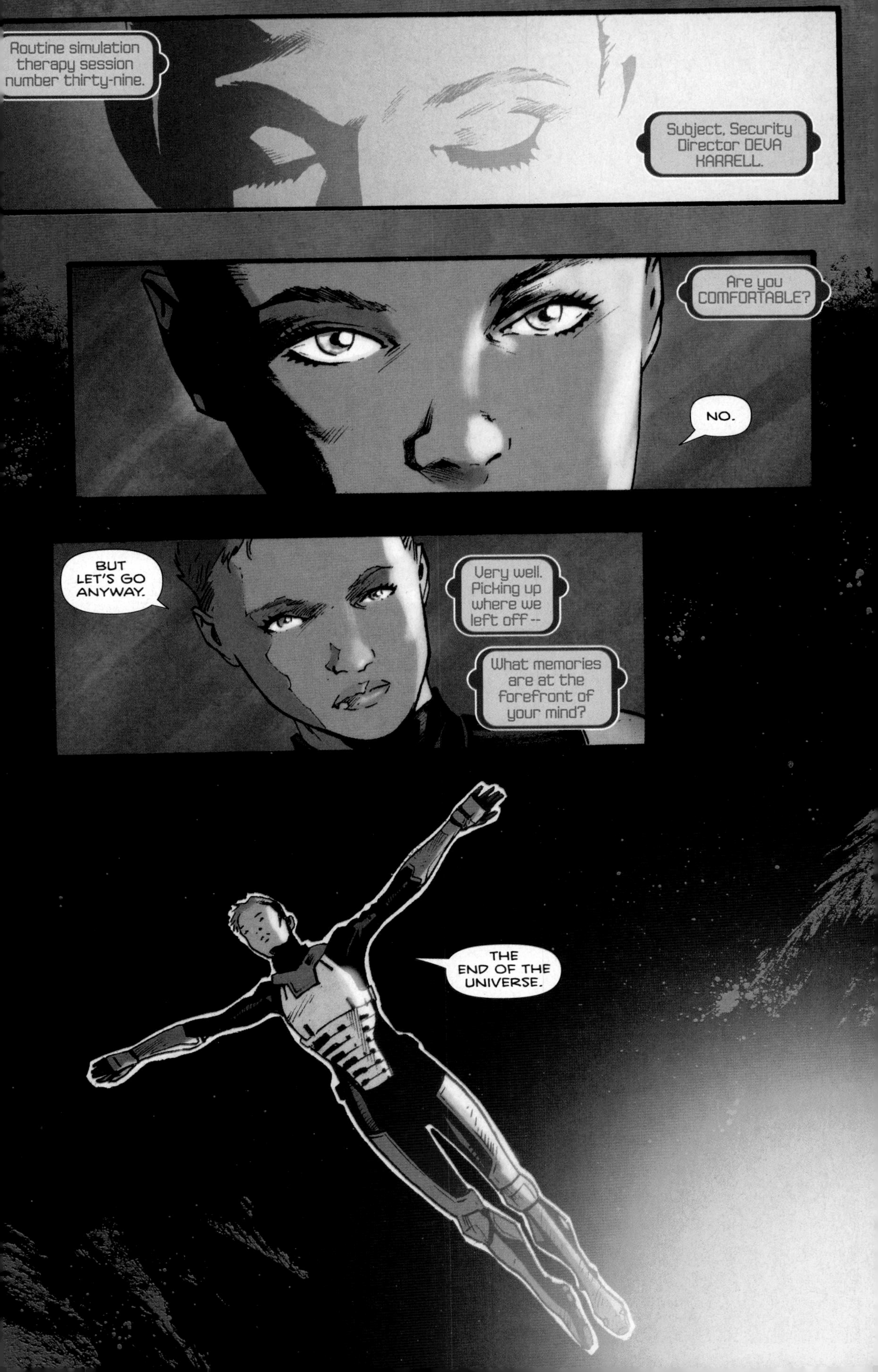
Routine simulation therapy session number thirty-nine.
Subject, Security Director DEVA KARRELL.
Are you COMFORTABLE?
NO.
BUT LET'S GO ANYWAY.
Very well. Picking up where we left off --
What memories are at the forefront of your mind?
THE END OF THE UNIVERSE.

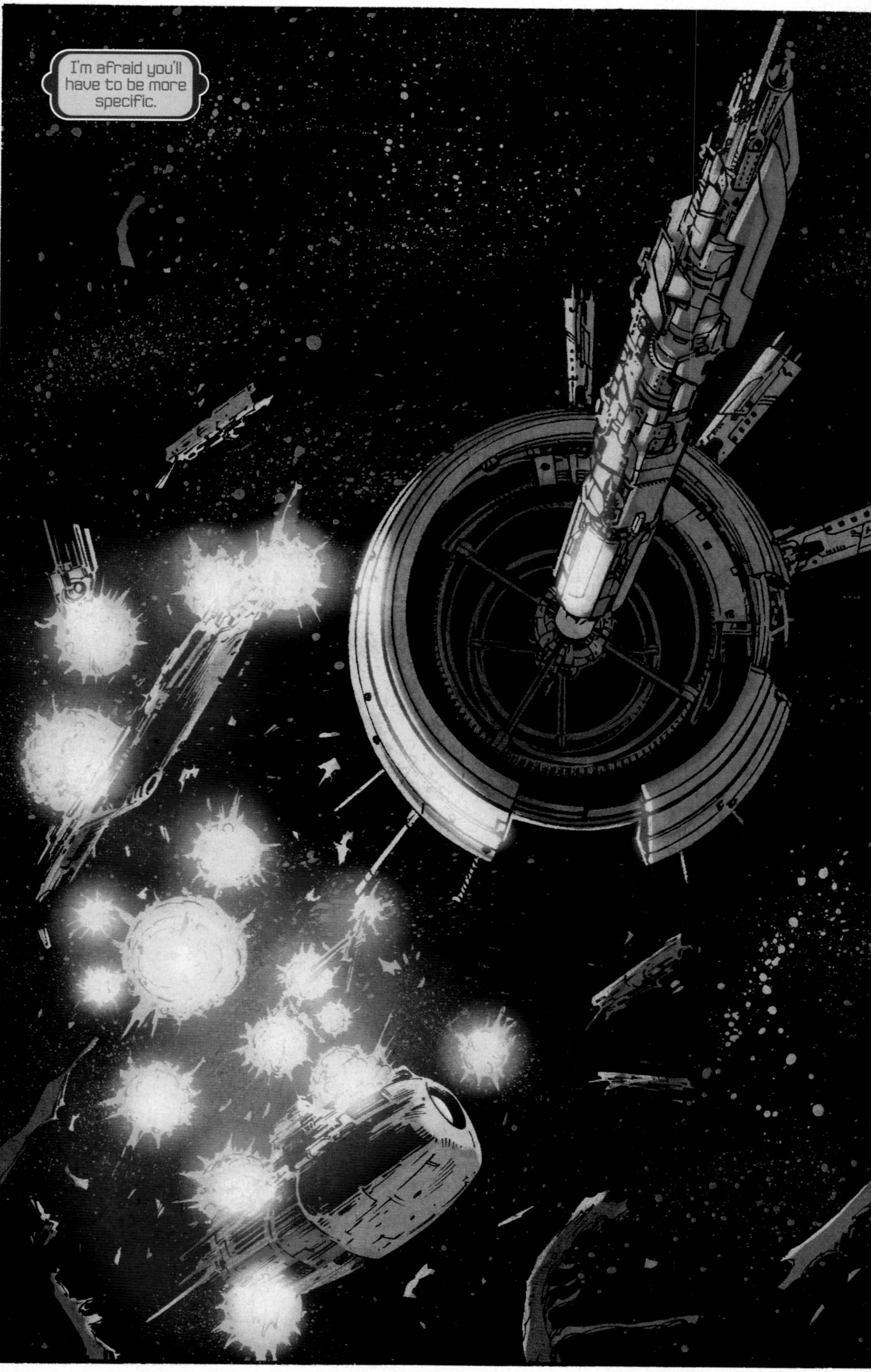
I'm afraid you'll have to be more specific.

STAFF HAD BEEN HERE ON BOARD *THE ORPHEUS* FOR MONTHS, PREPARING, WAITING.

TRANSMISSIONS AND SCANS SHOWED THE ENTROPIC DECAY WAS ACCELERATING QUICKER THAN EVEN OUR WORST EXPECTATIONS.

ATOMS BREAKING AND SPACE FREEZING FROM THE OUTSIDE OF THE UNIVERSE IN.

HEAT DEATH.

BUT HERE THEY'D BE SAFE, RIGHT?

WE COULD PROTECT THEM FROM THE *COLD BLACK.*

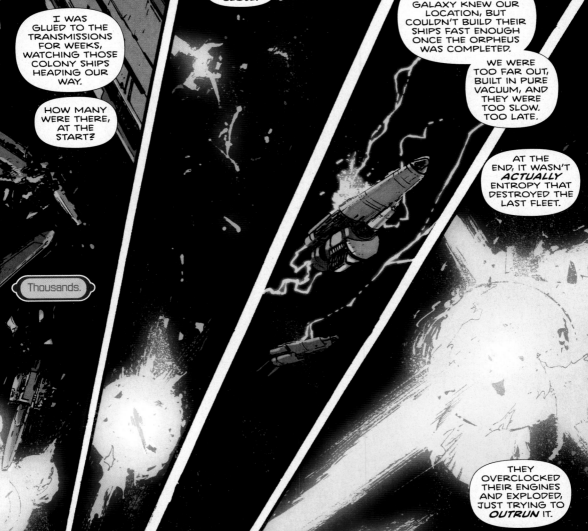

I WAS GLUED TO THE TRANSMISSIONS FOR WEEKS, WATCHING THOSE COLONY SHIPS HEADING OUR WAY.

HOW MANY WERE THERE, AT THE START?

NONE OF THEM EVER EVEN GOT CLOSE.

EVERY HUMAN CIVILIZATION IN THE GALAXY KNEW OUR LOCATION, BUT COULDN'T BUILD THEIR SHIPS FAST ENOUGH ONCE THE ORPHEUS WAS COMPLETED.

WE WERE TOO FAR OUT, BUILT IN PURE VACUUM, AND THEY WERE TOO SLOW. TOO LATE.

AT THE END, IT WASN'T *ACTUALLY* ENTROPY THAT DESTROYED THE LAST FLEET.

Thousands.

THEY OVERCLOCKED THEIR ENGINES AND EXPLODED, JUST TRYING TO *OUTRUN* IT.

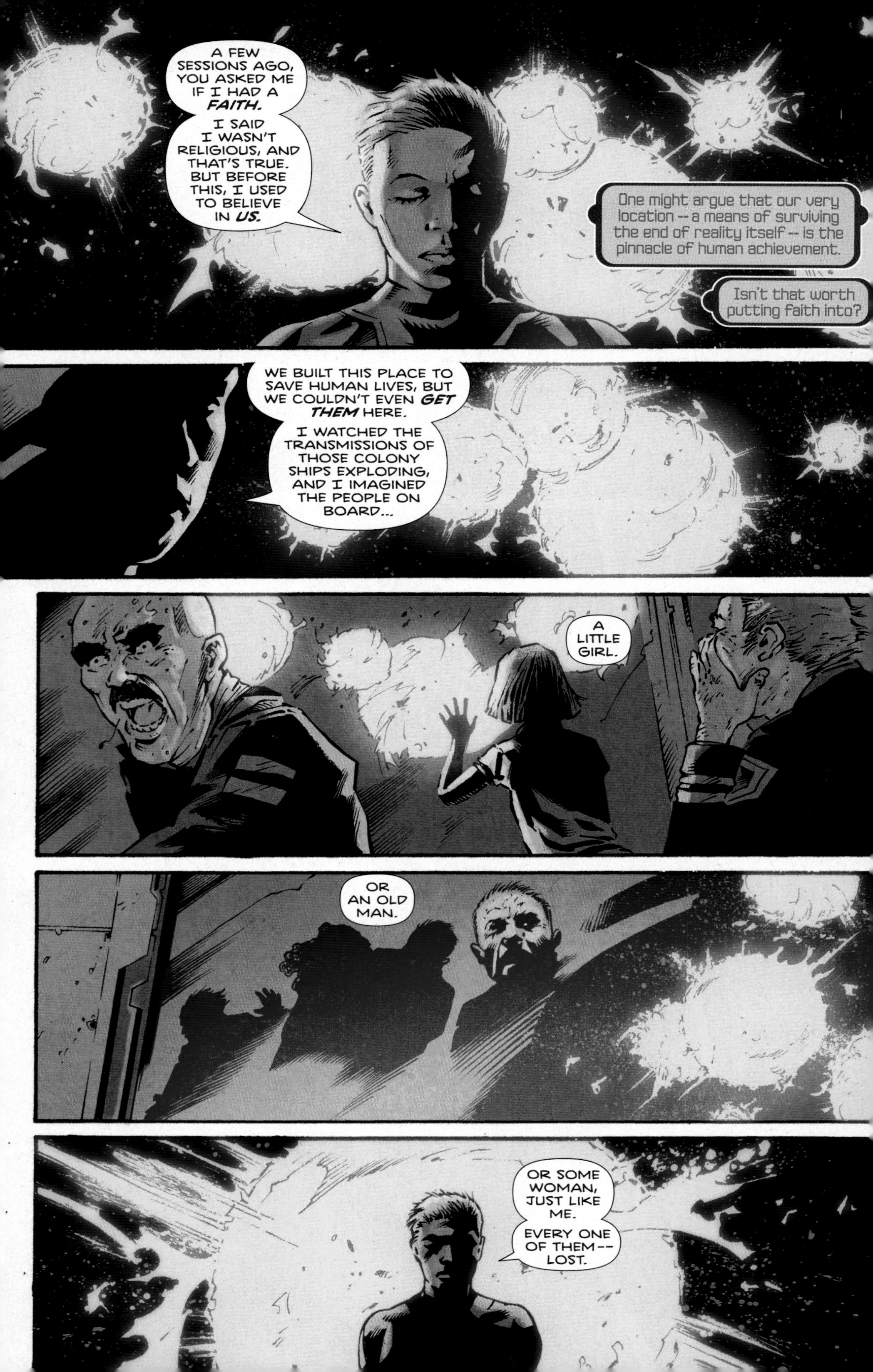
A FEW SESSIONS AGO, YOU ASKED ME IF I HAD A *FAITH.*
I SAID I WASN'T RELIGIOUS, AND THAT'S TRUE. BUT BEFORE THIS, I USED TO BELIEVE IN *US.*
One might argue that our very location -- a means of surviving the end of reality itself -- is the pinnacle of human achievement.
Isn't that worth putting faith into?
WE BUILT THIS PLACE TO SAVE HUMAN LIVES, BUT WE COULDN'T EVEN *GET THEM* HERE.
I WATCHED THE TRANSMISSIONS OF THOSE COLONY SHIPS EXPLODING, AND I IMAGINED THE PEOPLE ON BOARD...
A LITTLE GIRL.
OR AN OLD MAN.
OR SOME WOMAN, JUST LIKE ME.
EVERY ONE OF THEM -- LOST.

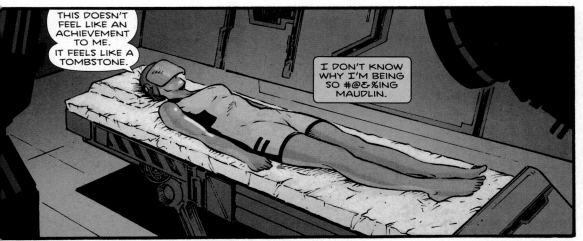

THIS DOESN'T FEEL LIKE AN ACHIEVEMENT TO ME. IT FEELS LIKE A TOMBSTONE.

I DON'T KNOW WHY I'M BEING SO #@&%ING MAUDLIN.

WE'RE FAILURES, NOT SAVIORS.

Begging your pardon, director, but in the two years since you've been in charge of this station's security, you've yet to result in anything I would consider FAILURE.

THANK YOU, SM1TH.

YOU'RE KIND, FOR A *VIRTUAL INTELLIGENCE* WHO'S PROBABLY FOCUSED ON TWENTY OTHER THINGS WHILE WE TALK.

TWENTY-SEVEN. And I've passed this session's report on to Dr. Chalos.

USUALLY YOU DON'T LIKE ME TO CUT THINGS THIS EARLY.

WEEKLY THERAPY IN THE SIMULATION CHAMBER, MANDATORY FOR EVERY STAFF MEMBER ON BOARD.

TWO HOURS A MONTH I HAVE TO FACE A WHOLE UNIVERSE'S WORTH OF IRRATIONAL SURVIVOR'S GUILT.

In this case, it seemed necessary. We have company.

MAYBE THAT'S THE POINT. UNLOAD ON THE AI AND NOT MY SUBORDINATES.

SEBASTIAN.

SORRY FOR INTERRUPTING, DIRECTOR.

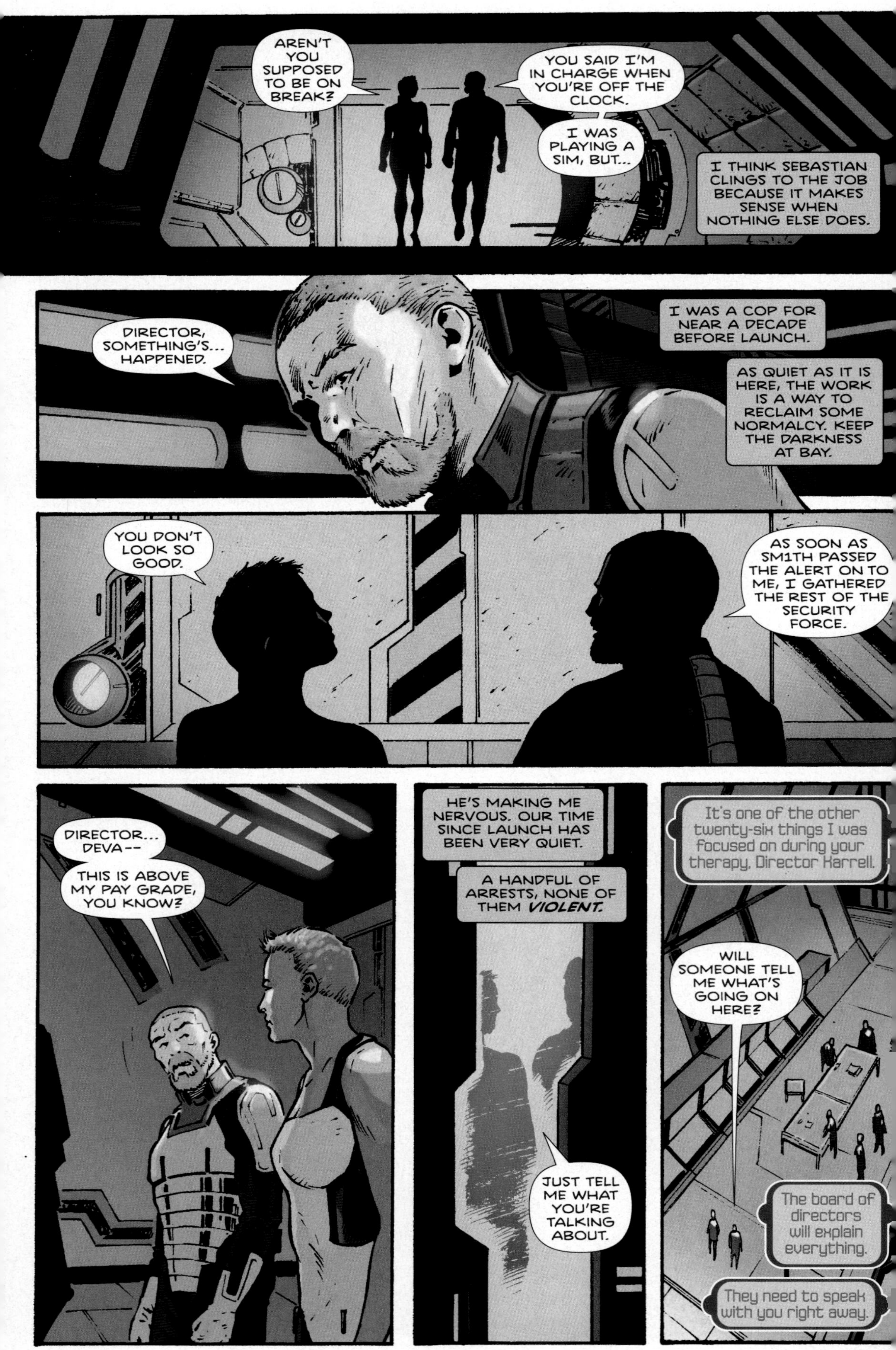
AREN'T YOU SUPPOSED TO BE ON BREAK?
YOU SAID I'M IN CHARGE WHEN YOU'RE OFF THE CLOCK.
I WAS PLAYING A SIM, BUT...
I THINK SEBASTIAN CLINGS TO THE JOB BECAUSE IT MAKES SENSE WHEN NOTHING ELSE DOES.
DIRECTOR, SOMETHING'S... HAPPENED.
I WAS A COP FOR NEAR A DECADE BEFORE LAUNCH.
AS QUIET AS IT IS HERE, THE WORK IS A WAY TO RECLAIM SOME NORMALCY. KEEP THE DARKNESS AT BAY.
YOU DON'T LOOK SO GOOD.
AS SOON AS SM1TH PASSED THE ALERT ON TO ME, I GATHERED THE REST OF THE SECURITY FORCE.
DIRECTOR... DEVA--
THIS IS ABOVE MY PAY GRADE, YOU KNOW?
HE'S MAKING ME NERVOUS. OUR TIME SINCE LAUNCH HAS BEEN VERY QUIET.
A HANDFUL OF ARRESTS, NONE OF THEM *VIOLENT.*
JUST TELL ME WHAT YOU'RE TALKING ABOUT.
It's one of the other twenty-six things I was focused on during your therapy, Director Harrell.
WILL SOMEONE TELL ME WHAT'S GOING ON HERE?
The board of directors will explain everything.
They need to speak with you right away.

THANK YOU, SM1TH. WE CAN TAKE IT FROM HERE.

WHAT'S THIS ABOUT? OUR YEAR-END ASSESSMENT IS TWO WEEKS AWAY --

I HOPE THEY'RE NOT GONNA CHEW US OUT.

THERE'S *DIRECTOR TENANT* AND *DIRECTOR CHALOS,* BUT WHAT ABOUT SCHEIDT?

DIRECTOR TENANT, AH, PERHAPS IT'D BE BEST IF THIS WASN'T DONE IN THE MIDDLE OF A LOCKER ROOM.

IKE IS RIGHT. TAKE A LIFT TO THE COMMAND DECK RIGHT AWAY -- WE CAN DISCUSS THIS BETTER IN PERSON.

WHAT THE HELL IS GOING ON?

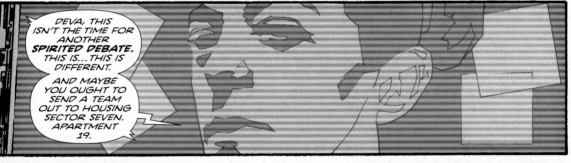

DEVA, THIS ISN'T THE TIME FOR ANOTHER *SPIRITED DEBATE.* THIS IS...THIS IS DIFFERENT.

AND MAYBE YOU OUGHT TO SEND A TEAM OUT TO HOUSING SECTOR SEVEN. APARTMENT 19.

19? THAT'S...

SEBASTIAN, TAKE A SQUAD.

I'LL GRAB A LIFT.

I READ ABOUT A MONUMENT BUILT LONG AGO -- BACK ON EARTH, WHERE WE CAME FROM.

THERE WAS A MAN WHOSE WIFE DIED, AND IN HER HONOR, HE WANTED TO BUILD THE GRANDEST TOMB IN HISTORY.

AND HE DID.

BUT IN THE YEARS IT TOOK TO FINISH THE PERFECT TOMB, THE BODY HAD GONE MISSING. NO ONE COULD FIND IT, AND THE GREAT MAUSOLEUM REMAINED, AN EMPTY WONDER.

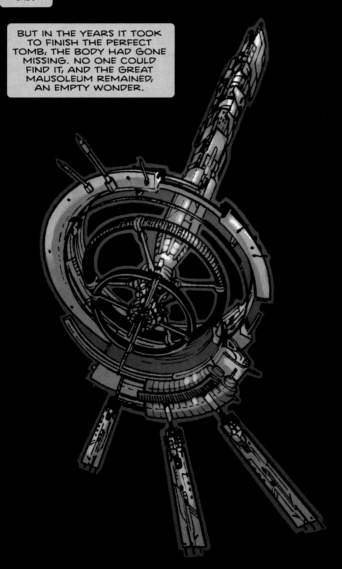

THAT'S WHAT THE ORPHEUS FEELS LIKE -- HUMANITY'S PERFECT TOMB, OUTWITTING THE END OF ALL THINGS, THE ULTIMATE HABITAT...

BUT NO ONE ON BOARD BUT THE PEOPLE WHO *BUILT* IT LEFT TO APPRECIATE THE DAMN THING.

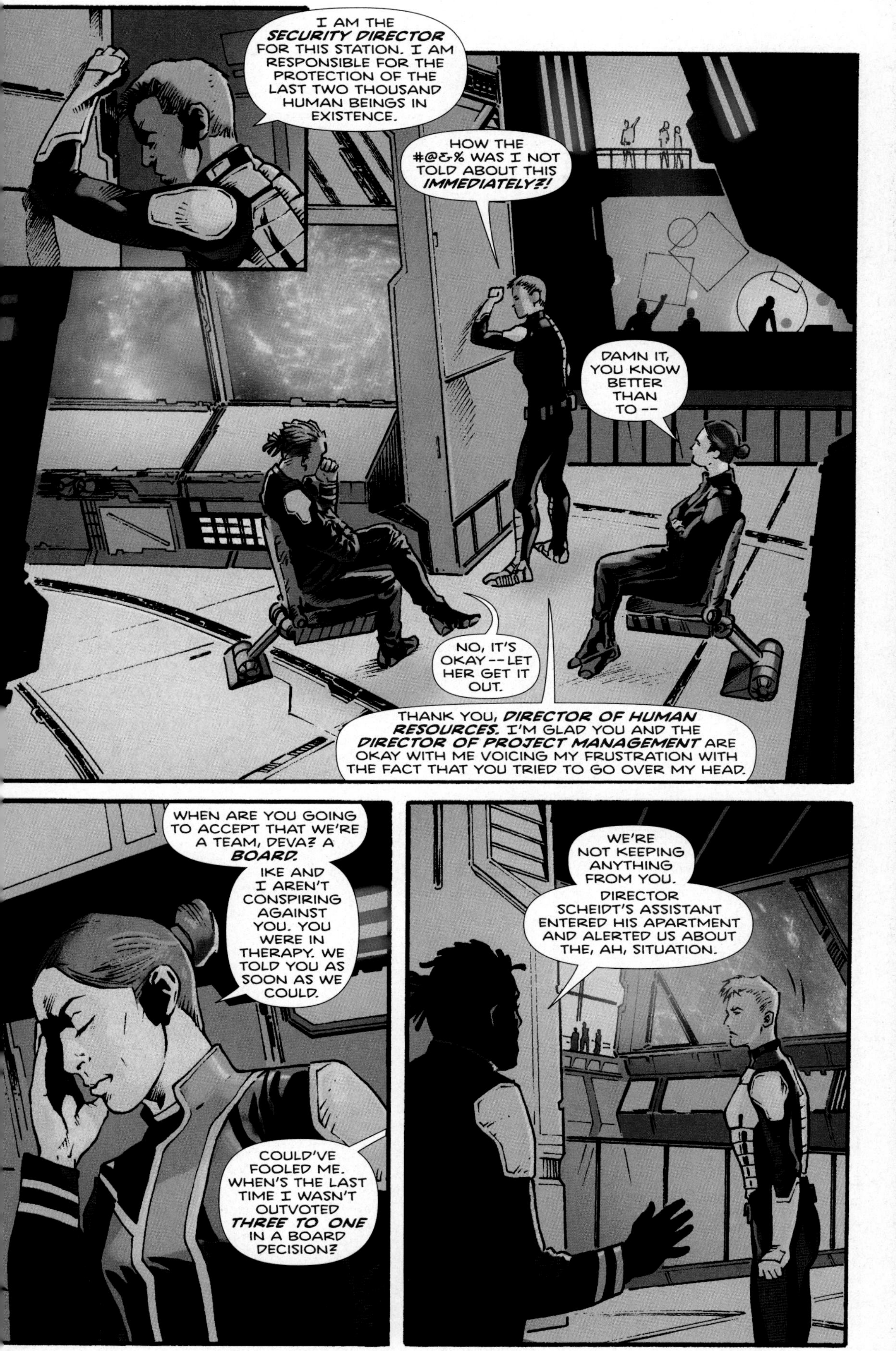
I AM THE SECURITY DIRECTOR FOR THIS STATION. I AM RESPONSIBLE FOR THE PROTECTION OF THE LAST TWO THOUSAND HUMAN BEINGS IN EXISTENCE.
HOW THE #@&% WAS I NOT TOLD ABOUT THIS IMMEDIATELY?!
DAMN IT, YOU KNOW BETTER THAN TO --
NO, IT'S OKAY--LET HER GET IT OUT.
THANK YOU, DIRECTOR OF HUMAN RESOURCES. I'M GLAD YOU AND THE DIRECTOR OF PROJECT MANAGEMENT ARE OKAY WITH ME VOICING MY FRUSTRATION WITH THE FACT THAT YOU TRIED TO GO OVER MY HEAD.
WHEN ARE YOU GOING TO ACCEPT THAT WE'RE A TEAM, DEVA? A BOARD.
IKE AND I AREN'T CONSPIRING AGAINST YOU. YOU WERE IN THERAPY. WE TOLD YOU AS SOON AS WE COULD.
COULD'VE FOOLED ME. WHEN'S THE LAST TIME I WASN'T OUTVOTED THREE TO ONE IN A BOARD DECISION?
WE'RE NOT KEEPING ANYTHING FROM YOU.
DIRECTOR SCHEIDT'S ASSISTANT ENTERED HIS APARTMENT AND ALERTED US ABOUT THE, AH, SITUATION.

YOU MEAN THE SITUATION IN WHICH OUR *TECH DIRECTOR,* ALVIN SCHEIDT--THE CHIEF TECHNOLINGUIST ON THIS STATION, A MAN CAPABLE OF PRACTICALLY REWRITING THE ORPHEUS' CORE CODE--

SPONTANEOUSLY DECIDED TO ABDUCT HIS NEIGHBOR, JALIL EVANSON, AND YOU ALL WAITED HOURS TO ALERT ME AND THE REST OF SECURITY?

IT'S NOT LIKE HE'S GOT ANYWHERE TO RUN. I'M SURE YOUR TEAM HAS--

LET'S SEE.

SEBASTIAN?

IT'S COLD HERE, DIRECTOR. SPOKE TO THE ASSISTANT WHO FOUND THE SCENE--

"DEFINITE SIGNS OF A STRUGGLE.

"SCHEIDT APPEARS TO HAVE CRACKED EVANSON'S DOOR LOCK. MAYBE CAUGHT HIM UNAWARES?"

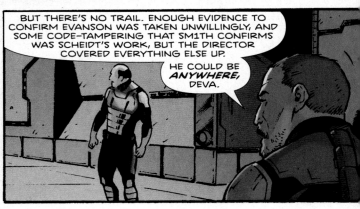

BUT THERE'S NO TRAIL. ENOUGH EVIDENCE TO CONFIRM EVANSON WAS TAKEN UNWILLINGLY, AND SOME CODE-TAMPERING THAT SM1TH CONFIRMS WAS SCHEIDT'S WORK, BUT THE DIRECTOR COVERED EVERYTHING ELSE UP.

HE COULD BE *ANYWHERE,* DEVA.

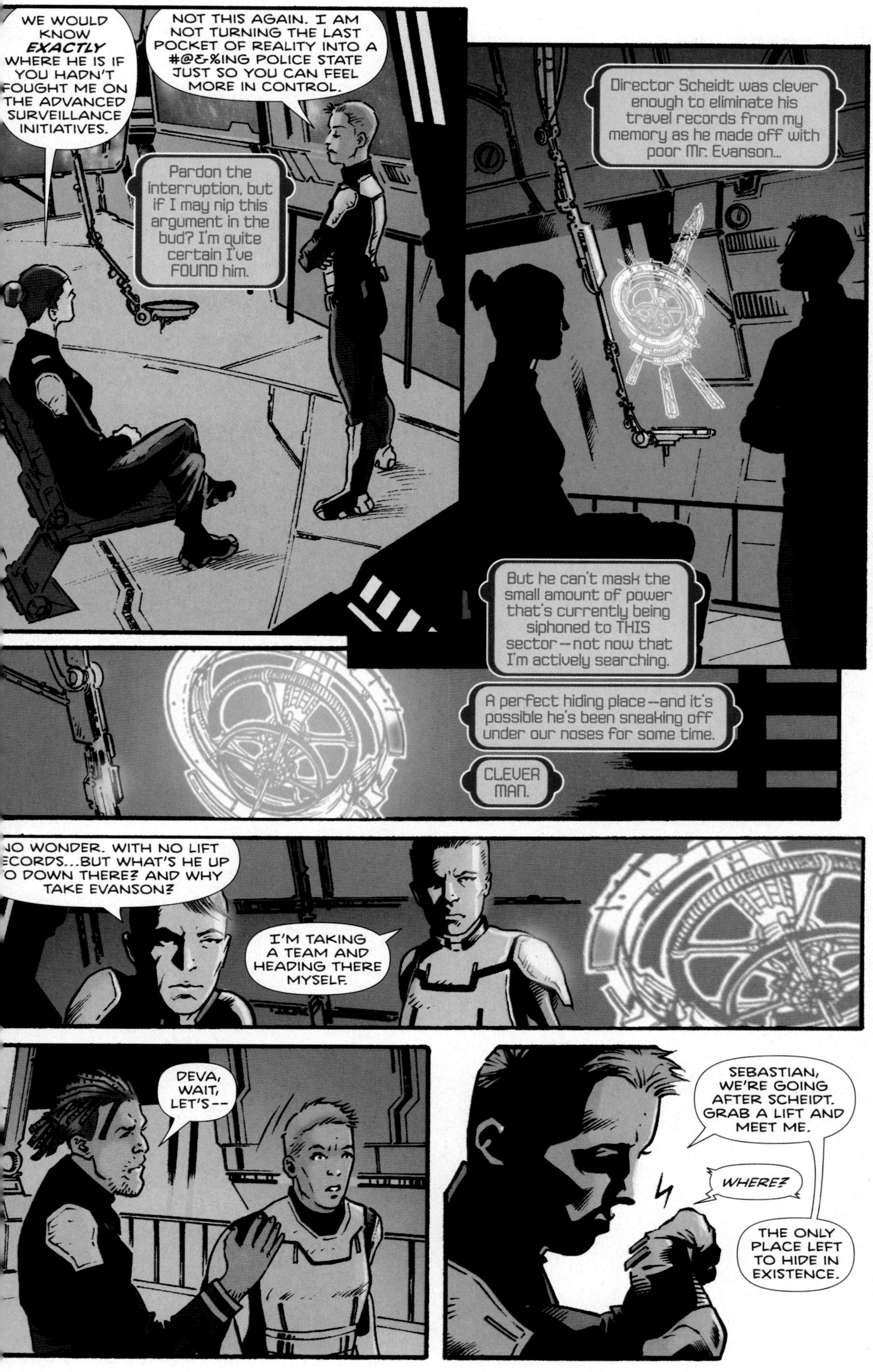
WE WOULD KNOW *EXACTLY* WHERE HE IS IF YOU HADN'T FOUGHT ME ON THE ADVANCED SURVEILLANCE INITIATIVES.
NOT THIS AGAIN. I AM NOT TURNING THE LAST POCKET OF REALITY INTO A #@&%ING POLICE STATE JUST SO YOU CAN FEEL MORE IN CONTROL.
Pardon the interruption, but if I may nip this argument in the bud? I'm quite certain I've FOUND him.
Director Scheidt was clever enough to eliminate his travel records from my memory as he made off with poor Mr. Evanson...
But he can't mask the small amount of power that's currently being siphoned to THIS sector--not now that I'm actively searching.
A perfect hiding place--and it's possible he's been sneaking off under our noses for some time.
CLEVER MAN.
NO WONDER. WITH NO LIFT RECORDS...BUT WHAT'S HE UP TO DOWN THERE? AND WHY TAKE EVANSON?
I'M TAKING A TEAM AND HEADING THERE MYSELF.
DEVA, WAIT, LET'S--
SEBASTIAN, WE'RE GOING AFTER SCHEIDT. GRAB A LIFT AND MEET ME.
WHERE?
THE ONLY PLACE LEFT TO HIDE IN EXISTENCE.

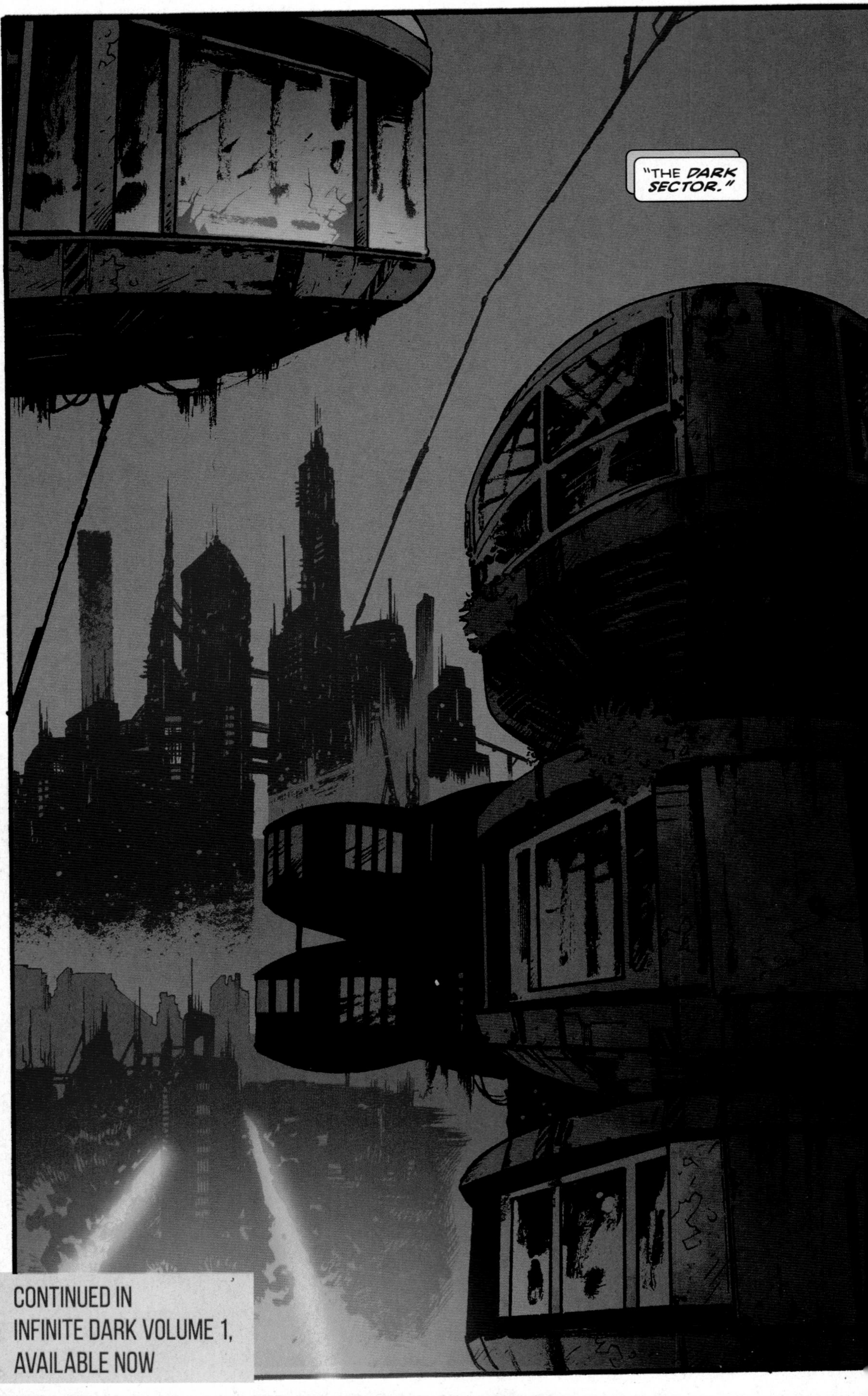
"THE DARK SECTOR."

CONTINUED IN
INFINITE DARK VOLUME 1,
AVAILABLE NOW

The Top Cow essentials checklist:

IXth Generation, Volume 1
(ISBN: 978-1-63215-323-4)

Aphrodite IX: Rebirth, Volume 1
(ISBN: 978-1-60706-828-0)

Blood Stain, Volume 1
(ISBN: 978-1-63215-544-3)

Bonehead, Volume 1
(ISBN: 978-1-5343-0664-6)

Cyber Force: Awakening, Volume 1
(ISBN: 978-1-5343-0980-7)

The Darkness: Origins, Volume 1
(ISBN: 978-1-60706-097-0)

Death Vigil, Volume 1
(ISBN: 978-1-63215-278-7)

Dissonance, Volume 1
(ISBN: 978-1-5343-0742-1)

Eclipse, Volume 1
(ISBN: 978-1-5343-0038-5)

Eden's Fall, Volume 1
(ISBN: 978-1-5343-0065-1)

Genius, Volume 1
(ISBN: 978-1-63215-223-7)

God Complex, Volume 1
(ISBN: 978-1-5343-0657-8)

Magdalena: Reformation
(ISBN: 978-1-5343-0238-9)

Port of Earth, Volume 1
(ISBN: 978-1-5343-0646-2)

Postal, Volume 1
(ISBN: 978-1-63215-342-5)

Romulus, Volume 1
(ISBN: 978-1-5343-0101-6)

Sugar, Volume 1
(ISBN: 978-1-5343-1641-7)

Sunstone, Volume 1
(ISBN: 978-1-63215-212-1)

Swing, Volume 1
(ISBN: 978-1-5343-0516-8)

Symmetry, Volume 1
(ISBN: 978-1-63215-699-0)

The Tithe, Volume 1
(ISBN: 978-1-63215-324-1)

Think Tank, Volume 1
(ISBN: 978-1-60706-660-6)

Warframe, Volume 1
(ISBN: 978-1-5343-0512-0)

Witchblade 2017, Volume 1
(ISBN: 978-1-5343-0685-1)

For more ISBN and ordering information on our latest collections go to:
www.topcow.com
Ask your retailer about our catalogue of collected editions,
digests, and hard covers or check the listings at:
Barnes and Noble, Amazon.com,
and other fine retailers.

To find your nearest comic shop go to:
www.comicshoplocator.com